THE
BLACK
HAND

THE BLACK HAND

H. M. REINHARD

THISTLEQUEEN

PRESS

Cover Art by Nevena Jevtić

Thistlequeen Press

ISBN 979-8-9894291-0-3 (paperback)
ISBN 979-8-9894291-1-0 (hardcover)
ISBN 979-8-9894291-2-7 (ebook)

For a younger Hannah, who dreamed up worlds to replace her own.
Look at what we've created.

N
W
E
S
FYALL MOUNTAINS
ROHLEACH
TAMHAIN
CORAVEN
NERO
SGUDAL DESERT
SOL
RAMAL
PYESAK
MERGUR
ZARAK
SIEREN
EWITHWARK
VINGARD
ISLANDS OF SAMA
ELDUR
HYTHE
RÖKKUR

ONE

Not all heroes are saints. Not all villains are monsters.

Arix knew this. She'd known it from the first time she'd picked a pocket, the first time she'd cut a set of gilded purse strings. It wasn't about being good or being bad. No, nothing in life was that simple.

It was about survival.

Jewels and gold braid dipped from earlobes and cleavage alike as each gem-studded lord and lady paraded past Arix like nymphs on display. Dresses cinched so tight it was a wonder that their occupants hadn't already fainted and had their gold weighted bodies dragged away to some gilded couch. Decadence dripped carelessly over shoulders of gauzy wraps studded with tiny shells and jewels, haphazardly tossed from their shoulders at the door and into Arix's waiting arms. If they only knew to whom they were passing their belongings.

It took every ounce of strength, in every careful placement of her hands, in the dip of her chin, not to laugh at them. Not to grin, wide and toothy, at them. It wasn't their frivolous costumes, their feathered boas and feathered masks, the ridiculous clacking of their shoes; it was the assurance they all had. The confidence that nothing could touch them; no one could take from them what they unrightfully strangled from others. They assumed they were safe.

The corner of Arix's mouth twitched. They were not.

Each guest strolled into the manor house, their bejeweled bosoms and braided vests accompanied with a matching mask, only vaguely doing the job of covering each owner's face as the masks dipped for winks and sips of champagne.

Arix's own full black mask fit snugly to her face, matching the other servers that stood at attention near the walls or hovered with trays ever tinkling with the exchange of empty glasses for full ones. It was easy enough to fit seamlessly into the wait staff at the party. Baron Edvard von Hourst had so graciously hired additional staff for the event, to the great dismay of his housekeeper, and Arix had easily slipped into the streaming line of new faces sheathed in black masks. No one had questioned when she had taken up her position at the door, slipping her hands into rich pockets as she took each needless cloak or wrap and whisked away.

She knew some of them, the pompous peacocks, recognizing the lords and their wives and occasionally spotting their mistresses arriving a few moments later. There was a great amount of pomp to it all: the flowing skirts and the cinched waistcoats and the shimmering veils. All Neroan aristocracy, sipping and sighing and so full of themselves it was a wonder they didn't burst in a glorious display of bowels and beading. Arix would have reveled to see it.

As the last of the guests trickled in, she slipped away from her post at the door and picked up an empty tray. Servants were as invisible as ghosts when going about their work, and as she stepped between the swishing skirts and dangling feathers, snippets of conversation hung greedily in her ear.

The man she was looking for was easy to find. He was the loudest in the room, surrounded by a puddle of guests, and two servants that kept his glass and painted porcelain plate full. Baron Edvard von Hourst was in the middle of retelling a story that Arix had heard too many times already. He'd told it once, the first time she met him, when she'd been disguised as a lady of the night, and again when she'd approached him as a secretary to see if he'd drop any new tidbits to the tale. He hadn't. It seemed the story was almost exactly the same every time he told it, a story he'd memorized by telling over and over again to unsuspecting strangers and close guarded friends.

"So there we are, surrounded by the looming trees in Eldur's forests, and surrounding the measly band, all of them looking rather shocked they'd been surrounded at all. And here before me was the great rabble rousing General Kane, pissing himself now that he was finally facing justice. Bumbling on and on about his cause and his men and begging for his life. Spouting lies like great crocodile tears, and making up all sorts of nonsense about having to do his duty, and protect his daughter, and the like."

The baron's glass sloshed dark purple port over the sides as he clutched a frilly young thing in a swan mask closer to his side. She was practically swallowed up into his bright purple jacket; she, looking very pleased with herself, and he, looking very much like a bright purple cabbage that had been left too long under Rökkur's summer sun.

"Well, when you've been to war and fought for the king as many times as I have," the old cabbage went on. "You see these rebel Carn are truly no better than gutter rats, willing to say anything to save their own skin." As an afterthought, he added "Goddess save them." Before slurping his port and returning to his story.

The swan preened, leaning further into his arm. "So what did you do?"

"About what?"

"The general. With all that blubbering and lies."

"Well I took off his head!" The baron slapped his thigh, jarring Arix slightly as she slipped past them, picking up discarded glasses. The slap hung in the air for a fraction of a moment, before he continued back into the tale.

"Right there in front of all his followers. The great general was no more. Then of course we dispatched the rest of his little band and proceeded back to the palace, where I presented his head to the king himself. The king expressed his deepest regard and favor towards me and awarded me a place in court. I visit on occasion, and it's such a pleasure to sit with the king as equals."

Arix had to bite her tongue to keep from chuckling at the thought.

"The king must have been very grateful if he graced you with his actual presence." The swan continued.

The baron's chest puffed out a bit, and he cocked his head at her, tapping the tip of her nose with a sausage finger.

"Indeed. And of course I would have been satisfied with merely Our Majesty's presence, but he also awarded me with a great many gifts. Nothing the Carn will achieve in all their miserable lifetimes."

There was of course more to the story than that. It was rumored that the 'great many gifts' he spoke of were a small chest of rubies, and Arix had done enough digging to know that there was more truth than fiction to the ruby bit. Of course, no one had seen the king in years, so that part of the story was much more elaborated fiction.

The baron was moving on now, describing in detail exactly what he did with the general's body, but Arix had already moved away, slipping down an unoccupied hallway. As she made her way deeper into the house, fewer paintings hung on the walls, and some corridors hung completely empty and cold, no tapestries to banish spring's cold hands from seeping through the walls.

These things Arix paid no mind to, ignoring the faded rectangles of empty stone and rooms devoid of lavish furnishings. Instead she moved toward the stairwell leading to the tower, noting the lack of guards as she moved up the stairs. Near the top she slowed, balancing her tray and evening her breathing. The guard around the corner watched her as she rounded the last few steps, placing his hand on the pommel of his sword as she neared.

"What are you doing up here?" the guard stepped forward, his grip tightening.

"Goddess! None of that!" Arix laughed, throwing up her hands as she pulled the mask from her face. "Just came to give you a drink. Housekeeper's saying all goes well downstairs. Figured hard working men need a break on a long boring shift."

She batted her eyes at him, holding out the tray. The man didn't move.

"You need to go back downstairs. Now."

Arix pouted, then took the glass from the tray and swigged down the contents. The champagne was diluted with peach water, not that any of the guests downstairs had probably noticed.

Grimacing, she offered the guard a sheepish smile, her hand slipping into the pocket of her skirt. "That was disgusting. I'm sorry that I offered you something so unappetizing."

Before the guard could step forward to offer another warning, Arix was already moving, the metal serving tray gonging in an off-key clank as it bounced over the man's bald head knocking him back into the door behind him.

It wasn't his fault exactly. He had never been trained properly as a guard, and had only taken the job because someone told him once that he had a good sword arm. Which at the time had been true. And to look at her, Arix did seem rather harmless for a girl, and at most, the poor man had suspected her of petty theft and at the very least a wandering imbecile. By the time he realized what was happening, the girl had shoved something into his nose and he was lost to sleep on the floor, a faint shimmer of silver powder on his upper lip.

Quick work of his pockets turned up no key, which wasn't surprising, so Arix pulled her picks from her pocket and opened the door herself. The room was small, disappointingly so, and practically empty. A few small sacks of gold on a shelf in the corner and a small box containing what might be the last of the family jewels. The box contained some nice pieces, including one silver necklace with a blue stone in the center, though upon closer inspection, Arix determined it was a fake. A few gold rings, more gaudy necklaces, three jeweled brooches, one exquisite, and very real, diamond-encrusted ring, and a hair pin shaped like a dagger.

Arix stood in the center of the room, eyes trained on the seams where the walls and floor connected. The room felt much too small, much too cramped to host all the treasures of a baron. As her gaze traveled down the length of the far wall, she noted a gap, with a faint line running down its length, and a worn spot on the wooden floor. It took a few knocks and some pressing, but in a matter of moments, Arix had the panel of wall sliding and slipped into the room beyond.

In the center of the room stood a desk, scattered with papers and ink pots, maps of Nero's various trade routes pinned to the walls. And beside the desk sat a large chest, well made, and glimmering with gold fastenings. Arix wet her lips with her tongue, slowly moving to the chest. It was unlatched. She swung open the lid, stepping sideways slightly should there be some nasty guardian inside.

There was none.

In fact, the chest held only a few things, these of which Arix beheld with a frustrated glare. She turned away from the chest, ruffling through the desk and its bits of parchment. All the papers were stated similarly: Bankruptcy.

Arix groaned as she collapsed into the high backed leather chair, her hand resting under her chin as she stared at the hulking wooden table and all its drawers and scrolls. The masked girl pondered for a moment, her eyes training over each inch of the surface. She thought about ransacking other rooms, looking for anything that might provide monetary value, but something told her she would not accomplish her goal. The baron wasn't a smart man; he had proved it by his display tonight.

Arix kicked the leg of the desk in frustration, the thud of her boot resounding through the wood. And then a clank. Arix stared at the desk, moving to her hands and knees as she crawled beneath it, feeling the edges with her fingers until she found a small metal latch. One good wiggle and a compartment opened, a small leather bound book dropping into her waiting hands. Arix unwound the string that kept the book closed and quickly scanned over the figures, eyes growing wide as a smile spread across her face.

Her plan had been a simple one, but it appeared that fate was offering her a different solution to her problem.

That left only one thing to be done.

Hauling the chest out of the room had been no small task.

It was heavier than it looked, and Arix was deign to admit that the ornate box nearly knocked her over once or twice on the way back to the main hall. Though, instead of taking the path back she had come, Arix made her way to a side staircase and crept into the alcove of an upper balcony that overlooked the revelers below. The balcony was dark, usually reserved for musicians, and by the amounts of dust, hadn't been occupied in a while. The baron probably couldn't afford a full band of musicians anyway. Arix took another trip back downstairs, setting the last of her plan into motion as she gathered up the bag of her nightly collections she had left in the front hall, and grabbed a glass of champagne and an oyster fork. Another server eyed her as she walked past, but Arix just gave the girl a smile and a shrug as if to say, *"You know how rich people are."*

Once back up on the balcony, Arix checked that her mask was securely in place as she carefully maneuvered the chest up onto the wide stone railing between herself and certain death. Below her, the baron was still in the center of the room, exactly where Arix had left him, seemingly telling the same story to a new set of rapt listeners. He now had the swan girl draped in his arm, her mask slid back off her head and hanging by ribbons down her back.

The revelers below were interrupted from their giddy and drunken conversation as tinkling glass rang out for attention. They turned their eyes to their host, but he looked about expectantly, smile frozen on his face. A polite cough had now joined in the call for attention, and after a moment, the mutual gaze of the elite turned toward the masked figure who stood above them, one foot balanced on the lid of an ornate box, champagne flute and fork in her hands.

"Attention, all guests of our illustrious host, Baron Edvard von Hourst. Thank you all for attending this evening, to a truly raucous and exciting event that many of you will be able to tell anecdotally at parties for years to come."

The room stared, some amused at the novelty of it all, the display of a servant making proclamations on a balcony. Others looked too drunk to care too much and continued their conversations, albeit in hushed tones. Suddenly a shattering of glass ricocheted through the room as the champagne flute dropped from the balcony and shattered to the marble floor. The swan girl let out a squeal as guests stepped back from the glass.

"You won't want to miss this ladies, yes you at the oyster cart. For what you are about to hear will both shock and amaze you."

The attention had shifted now into one of annoyance at having their party disturbed, while others gazed up at her with merry drunken faces. A few chuckles pittered through the room, those who released them assuming she was a maid that had gotten drunk off her employer's champagne, and the stupid girl would either fall to her death or spout some interesting gossip.

Arix's eyes twinkled beneath the mask, and though they could not see her face, she smiled brightly. Below her, the baron had called over another server, motioning to her form towering above them.

"Allow me to introduce myself. I am but a common thief, here to relieve you of your belongings." Arix waved an arm toward the baron with a flourish and bowed to her audience. "For which you have our dear baron to thank, as it was he who brought me here tonight."

Those below gaped and a few had the audacity to gasp, which, to Arix, always gave her a warm tingle down her spine. A few guests began inching for the door, while others glanced toward the baron, their demeanor having changed in the past few moments towards their host.

The baron's face was frozen, anger like plow lines creased across his forehead and his cheeks bloomed sort of a crimson plum color. The color of anger indeed, and Arix only smiled at him. The few guards he had gathered to him, turned and left the room, making their way toward the staircase that would bring them closer to her.

"It is he who called me here with his long tales of riches and rubies. How could any upstanding thief such as I ignore such a summons? But before I make my departure, I must share with you a little something I found while rifling through the baron's drawers. The most riveting little book that I would like to share with you all." She held up the small leatherbound notebook and watched as the baron's face shifted from purple to white.

Arix flipped the book open causally, licking her finger to turn the pages as she tsked, a feigned air of shock in her voice. "My, my, my baron! What things you keep in this little book of yours."

She lowered the book slightly and peered out at the now rapt audience, no fear in their faces. She could see it in their eyes, even now they thought themselves safe. What could one lonely thief do against a volley of guards? And besides, to lose a necklace or two was one thing; to miss out on gossip was something else entirely. Secrets, no matter how small, held their own monetary value.

"Shall I read it to you?" Arix grinned.

Someone in the back called out, "Read it!" which was quickly joined with a few laughing others. Arix's grin only broadened. There was nothing quite like the hungry elite.

"Let's see here…" Arix turned and began pacing along the railing, each step carefully placed as she flipped through the book's pages and tsked again. Behind her she could hear footsteps on the stairs.

"It appears the good baron has been doing some fine business, investing quite a nice purse of money into foreign shipments of silk. And look here!" Arix placed a mocking finger on the page as she slid down and read some of the names aloud. "It appears to be your business partners: Lord Vermoin, Lord Pastille Lei, Lady Everial, and oh! A significant sum invested by the Mayor Luxmere. A whopping thirty-two thousand gold!"

The room below was silent and electric with anticipation as Arix looked out, scanning the crowd. "There you are! Mayor Luxmere, that's quite an investment for a man who handles the taxes of others. And here we have two accounts. The public transcript of the ships, having sunk off the coast of Eldur near Nimbosia. Tragic, that. But look! Here it says, there were no ships. No shipment. No shipwreck. How strange…"

Below her, the air sizzled as whispers had already started. Those who found themselves standing near Mayor Luxmere and the other investors, looked on in scandalous glee, their mouths already moving behind their hands. Someone beneath the balcony laughed outright. The mayor himself no longer stared up at Arix but instead glared at the baron, his gaze stone cold and sharp.

"And there's more it seems. Shall I go on?"

Skirts were rustling now, tittering laughter making its way through the room. They were like suckertails that hid in shallow waters, ready to bleed their host dry. A large man in the corner, from Tamhain it looked like, with a prolific white mustache bellowed for her to continue, and so she did.

"It says here that our dear baron has been having an affair with the dear Duchess Oliviae. From the lack of surprise I expect most of you knew that, but it says not only was our dear baron fucking the duchess, but he was blackmailing her dear husband, the Duke of Adamisal, while he did it!"

The crowd was outright gleeful at the news, the Duke and Duchess in question huddled in the corner and trying desperately to squeeze their way through the crowd toward the door. The duchess held a hand over her swollen belly protectively. In contrast, the throng around the baron had diminished further, and the swan girl was nowhere to be seen. Arix glanced to the door behind her, a musician's chair wedged under the latch as the wood trembled against the pounding from beyond.

"And here, look! Another investment gone wrong. This time on a trade route through Zarak. All those casks of wine just vanished! How strange! Earl Stroghen, did you not lose a great deal of money in that venture? It says here your cousins lost everything; the entire house of Volna locked away in some debtor's prison."

The crowd below was reaching a fever point now. The baron had already attempted to escape the room twice, but had been cut off, his desertion thwarted. The friends he had drank with all night were turning on him, their false camaraderie replaced with the steel eye of malice. Summertime sweat and hungry glee hung heavy in the ballroom.

"And why do all these things? Why cheat and steal from you? To pay off his debts. It's all here and more, I'm afraid."

The wood of the doorway behind her splintered, and Arix returned to the center of the banister, resting her boot back again on the lid of the box. Below, someone had grabbed Baron Edvard van Hourst by the scruff of the neck and was dragging him backwards.

Arix's arm rose above the clamor as she called, "And what of the famous chest of rubies?"

Stillness gripped the room as every eye was trained on her, on the boot that weighed the lid of that large ornate box. All that could be heard was the splintering of wood and the half mad ravings of the baron as he struggled from those that gripped him.

"Here is what remains of the baron's wealth."

The box tethered for a moment and then fell as Arix kicked it, hurtling towards the floor where it smashed, four rubies and a few silver coins rolling beneath the skirts and boots of the onlookers. A quick scramble and those few rubies were gone.

"But what are jewels and coins compared to what you all really want?" Arix held up the book high. "Then have it."

And as the baron bellowed a resounding 'No!' the pages fluttered down in a slow shower of parchment, like petals from a blooming tree, drifting slowly down to the hungry occupants below. Up in the balcony, the door finally gave way and the guards burst through, knocking over chairs and music stands alike. But they found nothing. For the banister was empty.

The thief was already gone.

TWO

The stone rooftops, cool from the night air, spanned out across their own wavering horizon as Arix slipped among the shingles and chimneys. Below her, she could hear the clattering of the guards attempting to follow into the early morning dawn. But as she moved further from the manor house and deeper into the city, their clamor faded. Her work was almost done. Almost.

Cutting down from a rooftop, Arix swung down to a balcony and skittered her way back to the ground, twisting and turning as the stones of the city grew dirtier. As she neared an exceptionally ragged part of the city, she slowed further, damp hand rubbing against the material of her shirt until she heard a low whistle and cough.

Croak was waiting for her.

"Evening." She muttered under her breath, grinning at him.

"Find what you were looking for?" Croak's raspy voice inked through the darkness as he materialized from the shadows of the stone alley, his arms folded across his chest. Croak wasn't his name, but it's all anyone had ever called him. There had been some horrible accident from his youth, leaving his skin a strange leathery texture and his voice gravely and cracked.

Arix shook her head. "No, but I think I found something better. The baron won't be bothering anyone else for a long time. That's if they don't string him up tonight."

She reached into the folds of her bag and tossed Croak the cloth sack containing the gold and jewels she had nicked from the baron's guests. He caught it easily enough and inspected the contents.

"The baron's wealth is no more."

"Thank you, Arix."

The girl shrugged off the thanks, tossing her black mask into a heap of garbage with the gesture.

"Sell the jewelry to Rym; do you know him? He'll give you a good price on the jewels and he keeps his mouth shut, so nothing should trace back to you. Give the proceeds to Tabitha and her family. Goddess knows she went through hell and back working for that asshole."

Croak nodded, tucking away the pouch of jingling jewels, then handed Arix a bag of his own. "It's bread and cheese. Good thieves shouldn't starve."

"Thanks, Croak. Keep your head down and go to the tavern right after this. Make sure people see you out and about."

"Will do. Best of luck, Arix. Goddess guide you."

"Goddess guide you. Oh, and Croak? Tell Tabitha the baron won't be bothering anyone else for a long while."

~

Arix took her bread and her cheese to the rooftops, the clay roof tiles at her back as she tore into the food. The sky was turning from its bleary summer darkness into the hazy blur of orange morning. The shingles warmed as the sun dragged itself over the horizon and across the city below. She'd spent the last year in Nero, traveling between its larger cities, and it was almost time to leave. By now, she might be too recognizable, and even with the precaution she'd taken to keep her face hidden behind masks or scarves, there always seemed to be someone on her trail.

With one last look at the city, glowing warm in the sunlight, Arix turned her back and made her way down from the rooftops and out of Coraven. She had enough saved up to purchase a horse, and then she would be out of Nero. Maybe she would leave the western realm and head north to Tamhain for the remainder of the summer. Then perhaps west and into the deserts of Zarak for autumn. Or she could travel only half a day south to the capital, Mergur, the shining jewel of the country. For a moment, her mind flickered to Eldur, traveling the old familiar roads, to once more stand on the great cliffs that overlooked the sea. Arix pushed the thought away. She would not go back to Eldur. There were too many memories there that she wished to forget.

Perhaps she would go to the capital, after all. There were hoards of people there, and she'd be able to easily slip between the pushing crowds and disappear as one of the nameless gutter rats.

As it turned out, purchasing a horse was easier said than done, and Arix skirted the fluttering blue fabric of Coraven's guards twice before giving up entirely on the horse and hitching a ride with an old creaky chicken merchant. She quickly fell asleep under the summer sun in the back of his cart. What would have taken Arix a couple days on horseback, turned out to be much longer in the back of a chicken cart. By the time they had reached the very outskirts of Mergur, the sun was dipping its orange glow back over the horizon after a week on the road.

The bit of food she had shared with the farmer on the road had been enough, but as the cart rattled down the streets of the capitol, the gnawing of hunger along the inside of Arix's ribs reminded her that she no longer had to settle for travel rations. With a nod of thanks to the chicken man, she strode through the streets, eyes trained on the windows she passed. The tavern she stepped into was small, a spattering of locals dipping into food and drink. Arix slipped quietly among them and settled at a table in the back, facing the door.

A small discussion near the bar was quickly turning into an argument, and those who may have otherwise glanced in Arix's direction were much more engrossed in the imminent altercation. A smiling young woman approached the table, wiping wet hands on her clean apron.

"Has it finally cooled down out there? Cook says it's the heat will last the week, but I told him summer's nearly over now. We'll be seeing cooler days, I guarantee."

Arix turned her gaze to the pretty face and smiled back. "Only a bit. Goddess, I'm ready for autumn."

The girl laughed. Her eyes crinkled almost closed as she did so, her round cheeks merry and rosy. "Don't you worry. Crisp air and apple ale is right around the corner. You hungry, love?"

"A bowl of whatever they're eating." Arix motioned to a nearby table, where two men were horking down huge steaming bowls of stew. Between them, fresh bread lay broken and steaming. "It smells heavenly."

"And the bread, aye?"

Arix's grin broadened. "You are a gem."

The girl blushed and bustled away, her skirts deftly swishing between the tables on her way to the kitchen.

The argument at the bar hadn't yet turned into a brawl, although it looked like it may be coming to that. The two men argu-ing might have been brothers, with the same brown mop of curls and crooked noses. While she couldn't hear every piece of their conversation, it was clear they were discussing politics.

"...well it's all over Mergur, now ain't it?"

"Oh, and because you heard it from Joysa, that must mean it's all over the town?"

"It's near been a hundred years, and don't the story go that it's every hundred years?"

"You know, Pappy saw him once."

"That's right horse shit! Pappy aint that old!"

"Aye he did, a wraith of a man, nine feet tall, darkness and death following in his shadow."

Arix tuned them out, glad to see the girl already returning with her food and drink. But instead of setting it down and leaving, the girl stayed, hovering over the table, her voice tumbling into conversation.

"Here ya go! Rabbit stew, made myself, so let me know what you think. Best stew in town. You in town on business or plea-sure?"

Arix blew on the stew, resting her hands around the outside of the wooden bowl. "Just on my way to see some family. You've got a quiet little spot here, it's nice."

The girl smiled, a dimple deepening her right cheek, as she slid into the chair across from Arix. "It's a bit quiet out here on the outskirts of the city, but we find ways to keep busy. Most people travel right by, head straight into Mergur. Most people who come in here are regulars, and every once in a while we'll get somebody interesting passing through." She brushed a stray curl behind her ear and motioned to the stew. "What do you think?"

Arix took a hesitant spoonful, then instantly felt her shoulders relax. The stew was excellent, filling up all the caverns in her empty stomach after a long week spent with chickens. The rabbit was soft, thick and savory with rosemary, and the potatoes were cooked just right. Arix took another bite. "This is amazing."

The girl beamed, then stuck out her hand. "I'm Ingrid."

Arix smiled back and offered her own to the girl. "Bell." The lie slipped between her teeth easily. Taking another bite, she motioned to the two arguing brothers with her spoon. "What are they talking about?"

The girl glanced at the bar and rolled her eyes. "Politics. The king, the country, the Carn. Those two come in here all the time and get into arguments every which way. Mostly about where this country is going. It gets old fast."

"Anything exciting?"

"Bern, that's the younger one, thinks they're bringing back the Black Hand."

The corner of Arix's mouth twitched up. "Ah, the hundred years."

"My mam always said it was a hundred and fifty." Ingrid was leaning her cheek against the palm of her hand, watching Arix through thick lashes.

"And my father told me that years were nothing to a king. If the crown wanted a Black Hand, there would be one."

"With the Carn causing troubles, people think it's about damn time we have a fighting chance. I'm sure you heard about the newest attack on Ewithwark?"

Arix glanced up from her stew, her blood hiccuping in her veins. "I haven't."

"Just happened yesterday. Tried attacking the outskirts of the city, but there were already soldiers in place, and the whole thing got shut down pretty quickly. If we had a Black Hand, he could wipe out the insurrection for good."

Arix took a swig of her ale and leaned back in her chair. "Anything from King Taurus?"

"Not that I know of." Ingrid copied Arix's movements, leaned back in her own chair, her face scrunching together as she looked her over. "No one's seen the king in ages. Not that he's about to come strolling in these parts."

Arix dipped another spoon into her stew. "No, I suppose not."

The hair on the back of her neck prickled slightly,

"Have you heard anything about the rumors? About the king?" Arix glanced over to the bar, where the two men had settled down a bit and were drinking together rather than swinging at each other. The rest of the tavern was quiet, and most people were minding their own business.

"Are the rumors true?" The words were slow. Careful.

Ingrid chewed on the inside of her lip, and her voice lowered to a whisper. "About the king being...locked up?" She peeked a glance at the other patrons, who were busy minding their own business. "I heard the council have him shackled up in the dungeons under the wall. That he's...you know..."

Arix waited patiently as Ingrid squirmed under her stare.

"That he's gone mad." The girl finally squeaked out.

Taurus Galadher, from his first breath, had been destined for greatness. King Taurus grew up sitting at his father's feet, trained by the best swordsmen, the best tutors, the greatest war-heroes. When his father died, he did what he had been groomed for his entire life and took his place on the throne. And as it usually is with new shiny things, the kingdom prospered and all was well. But after a few years, alliances were made and formed and the king took a wife who died in childbirth in their second year of marriage.

As the years passed after her death, King Taurus became less known by his people until one day when he stopped appearing in court altogether. Laws and taxes were issued with his crest, and battles and wars were carried out with the approval of his seal. It was said that while the king still lived, he acted not as a king should, and without an heir, the kingdom would eventually fall to a rival country. Or worse, the Carn.

Arix had heard the rumors herself when passing through Sol a couple months ago. She had sat quietly at the bar gripping her ale as the old innkeeper had spouted to his seven patrons the stories of the mad king.

"Is there any truth in it?" Arix curled her fingers around her mug, feeling the heft of the metal.

Ingrid shrugged. "Couldn't say. But the castle's been swarming with people and new guards for months now. Something big is about to happen."

The two girls watched each other across the table, and after a moment, Ingrid blushed and turned away.

"You have anywhere to stay tonight?"

Arix's eyebrows rose. "Not yet."

"Stay with me." Ingrid's brown eyes sparkled in the tavern light. "I live just next door."

"Do you always invite strangers to stay?"

Ingrid smirked. "Only the pretty ones."

~

Arix drank at her table while Ingrid finished up her work, then the two slipped down the street and up to the third story of a small house next door. Ingrid soon had a fire blazing in the hearth, and the two settled down on the floor in front of it. In no time, the little house warmed and Arix found herself kissing across Ingrid's collarbone and across her chest, untying the bodice and sliding her fingers across the curves of her stomach.

Ingrid moaned, her head falling back against the floor rug as Arix's kisses trailed further across smooth skin, pausing along the curve of her belly and the dimple on her hip. Sliding further as she inched skirt fabric down and slipped between the girl's legs, fingers trailing soft circles as the barmaid panted.

There was no need to rush, no capture to evade, no coins to steal, and so Arix took her time, relishing every wave of pleasure that Ingrid issued forth, back arching against the rug beneath her. She moved achingly slow, sliding her thumb in lazing circles while she curled her fingers and stroked, Ingrid writhing beneath her, begging her to go faster.

It was nice, the electric skin on skin contact, the feeling of gooseflesh and sweet salty taste of Ingrid on her fingertips. Bodies pressed together in front of the fire, slick and soft, until both were exhausted. Arix pulled a quilt from the bed in the corner and wrapped them both in it, Ingrid's hair, knotted and loosed from its braid, splayed across her chest as the girl slept, her cheek over Arix's heart.

In the morning, Arix gathered her things and left, Ingrid offering a bleary farewell before nuzzling back under the blankets. Arix sat in the stairwell to pull on her boots, and then carefully crept down the last few stairs to the door. She stepped out onto the street, the warmth of the sun momentarily blinding her as she froze.

A semi circle of guardsmen stood with their weapons raised at her, trained on her very spot. An old man stood at the center of them, his arms crossed, frazzled gray beard sticking out in all directions. In his left hand he clutched a piece of blue glass. He looked rather pleased with himself.

"I suppose," Arix began, grinning at him. "That it would be rude to go back in now."

"Indeed." The old man replied.

"After I've just said my goodbyes."

"Yes."

They stared at each other, amused grin meeting unabashed optimism.

"Lay your bag on the ground and place your hands out in front of you." He finally said.

"And if I don't?"

Instead of responding, the man lifted a finger and with a snap, a crossbow bolt landed in the ground, not inches from the toe of her boot.

"You could have said please."

Slowly she slid the bag off her shoulder, raising her arms out straight in front of her. Two men from the end of the semi-circle approached, manacles glinting in their hands. But Arix would not look at them, instead, she stared into the frosty blue eyes of the old man. And grinned.

"Watch her!" The old man was shouting, and the guards with the manacles were scrambling, and Arix was already pushing past them and sprinting down the road.

They were hot on her tail, racing after her as she dodged them, laughing all the while. They were bigger, and definitely stronger, but she had agility and the lack of clumsy armor on her side. She turned, skittering into an alley before bounding over a crate and up the brick wall. The rooftops would offer her freedom. Height would be her friend.

And then…

The brick beneath her fingers turned slick, the stones melting like chocolate. She slipped, falling towards the street below. Her body glanced off the crate, slinging her sideways into the muck of the alley floor. She felt her head crack against the ground and she choked at the sky in an attempt to pull air back into her burning lungs.

Motion of the guards blurred against the edges of her vision and she caught the old man saying: "Send word to Lord Bardon that we are on our way. We have her."

Everything in her mind was filled with the one insatiable urge to breathe, but her chest coughed beneath her as she struggled.

The old man leaned over her, blotting out her view of the sky. Grinning from ear to ear as she heard him say: "This will be very entertaining."

And then all was darkness.

# THREE

Her head had cracked open, her brains leaking out down her neck, Arix was sure of it. From the thundering wave of agony that coursed from her temples, it seemed the only logical explanation for the resounding pain. Gingerly, Arix moved her fingers up to feel the back of her head, finding no cut or oozing organs. Every movement was sluggish, her whole body feeling as though it had been crushed beneath a cart. Arix clenched her eyes, fighting the throbbing voice that told her to slip back into unconsciousness.

She was moving, the wooden floor beneath her head rattling and making her bones shake. She could feel the iron around her ankles, heavy and slow. Her fingers moved again as she traced more pain arching down her side and hissed as she reached her ribcage. Bruised for sure, maybe even cracked.

It took all the willpower she had to wrench open an eye and stare in dumb lethargy at the space around her. A bright blue sky hung bright above her, the edge of buildings stretching up towards the heavens. The wheels beneath the wagon were creaking against cobblestones, and the head of a rider could be seen to the left. Pushing herself up with a painful wince, she surveyed her surroundings.

The wagon in which she lay was creaking through the streets of Mergur, following some route through the city. They were making their way out of the outskirts, heading toward the city central.

Arix slowly lay back down against the creaking floor of the wagon, head spinning. They would want her head for this. There was no denying that she was facing her death. She'd spent the last seven years skipping about the country, and the bad business with Baron von Hourst was only the latest in a long list of her criminal endeavors.

Images of death filled her mind, trying to remember what Mergur did to its prisoners. If it was a matter of jurisdiction, she'd prefer her trial to be in the capital. Each state had its own favored medium of death to its prisoners.

Tamhain, the northern state, was known for beheading. Quick and easy, your blood pooling back into the earth from whence you came. Zarak, in the east, performed hangings with fervor. The southern state, Eldur, was the worst. Arix remembered pushing her way through the throngs of people as a child, the air filled with smoke and burning flesh. The screams weren't something anyone could easily forget. And yet, burning prisoners alive was always a crowd pleaser.

Nero, the western state closest to the sea, and her hunting grounds for the last year, was quite well known for their drownings. It was not a death Arix was looking forward to.

In Mergur, your judge would decide your fate: anything from stoning to servitude, starvation to a life chained away in a dungeon.

Perhaps, Arix noted with a wince, it would be better to be drowned and have the whole thing over and done with.

Arix forced herself to think on different things. Maybe she

would get an honest judge. Maybe she could argue her case. After all she'd been masked. How could they prove that she was the one who'd robbed all those people and humiliated the baron? Maybe her sentence would be lenient. Forgiving. Time in the stocks, but with her life intact. A hefty fine that would try to indebt her to the king. She'd get some job in the city, long enough to pay her fine, heal up from whatever lashing they might give her, then head out again, keeping a low profile and maybe finally settling somewhere. It was such a small slim chance, but it was all she had to hold on to.

So Arix grasped it with all her might, forcing her mind to make plans and think of her future. She could work as a bounty hunter, traveling through the four realms, tracking down murderers and bandits, and perhaps the occasional rebel.

The wagon jolted to the left, and Arix's head smashed into its side. Everything ached, and it took all her strength to pull herself into a sitting position and peer at her surroundings. Arix blinked. Where the outreaches of the city had been lined with grime and weathered houses, the center of the city was something else entirely. While most cities of this size would have been dirtier as you headed toward its center, the center streets of Mergur were clean, the white stones worn smooth from the many feet that traversed it. There were all manner of people here, from all corners of the country, their unique clothing giving them away. It was a rainbow of jewels watching the people go by, a bouquet of flowers, each with their own colors and styles and attitudes.

The smells in the air were a mixture of spices and cooking meats, leather and smoke. Each new street brought new colors and scents, as they made their way past the wax district, the heavy smell of melting wax and heady soaps lingered in the air.

Arix's mouth watered as they passed a meat stand, an edla's

crispy brown skin steaming over a spit. She hadn't had roasted lizard in years and her stomach whined at the inside of her ribs at the scent. Mixed together with the smell of cooked meats and fresh cheeses were baked apples with cinnamon, the smell depositing her right back into her childhood, the spice a gateway into her past.

Even though she had visited the capitol before, the sights and smells still took her breath away. She felt like a small child again, watching the flurry of colorful fabrics and varying shades of skin tones meld together in a brilliant rainbow display. Two women laughing caught her eye, and Arix turned her head to watch. The first, a porcelain skinned Eldurian draped in layers of thick pink sweeping skirts and lace that came all the way up to her chin, her chestnut hair braided daintily back from her face and fastened with a thousand pearl-headed pins. The other, a midnight skinned Zarakian, her saffron sheer scarf and lehenga edged in gold stitching and jeweled fringe that gracefully fell around her ankles. The two were as different as could be, both in dress and appearance. As the two lovers embraced, kissing deeply, Arix lowered her gaze at the intimacy of it. As though she were intruding on their moment.

As the wagon turned, the slope of the road shifting, Arix raised her eyes to the wall that loomed before them. At the center of the city was a walled fortress, home to the king and nobility. The court was its own world, separate from the outside city. It contained its own gardens and glades, and while it was set in the busiest and loudest city in the realms, it remained a calm pool surrounded by a constant bubbling economy.

The wagon stopped outside the wall, where she was searched, then led on foot through the gate. Before them a large courtyard opened up, holding a training area for the soldiers who supplied protection for the palace and dignitaries. Another gate across the courtyard started a whole new wall, which served as a second ring in defense. As they moved through the gates and passed the second huge entryway to the castle, Arix took note of the amount of guards, the weapons, the guard towers. A stretch of water lay between the two walls, drawing a full moat around the circumference of the palace and its grounds. Its murky waters could hold anything, and from where she was escorted, Arix could not tell its depths.

As her escorts pushed her further into the hulking grounds, the gates closing with such finality behind them, Arix's heart picked up speed, its erratic rhythm making her throat close up. Her stomach was clenched up in knots, twisting and writhing inside of her. The world was vast, and she was only a small kernel within it, ignorant and slow compared to the world around her.

Everything she had ever known, all the things she had ever done, were so small; her circle of influence like one small ripple in the ocean. Even her greatest achievements meant nothing compared to what she was about to face. Somewhere deep down she had known it all along, and that had been fine. She worked within her circle of self- supplied justice, going where she needed to and making friends and connections along the way. And now what? Her world had just been wrenched farther open than she had ever expected, and turned on its head.

Goddess, she was grateful she hadn't eaten anything this morning or else it'd be trying to crawl back out of her stomach right about now.

The great palace loomed up before them, spired fingers of onyx stone. Terrifying against the bright blue sky, it resembled a great storm cloud that rose up from the earth. The size and beauty was terrifying and breathtaking all at once, leaving even its greatest guests feeling timid and small and unimportant. There was something dark and mysterious about it, unmoving, yet reaching up like a hand towards the sky. Fingers yearning for something just out of reach.

Arix fully expected to be escorted around to a side door, but the old man with his white beard marched her directly through the giant iron doors leading in from the main courtyard.

"She it, then?" A guard muttered to him as they passed.

The old man made no motion that he had heard the man, and instead led the way through the main hall and into a giant room, its vaulted ceilings arching up impossibly high above her. Columns lined the sides, leading up towards a large dias where a throne sat, empty.

Her momentum was stopped with a jerk, as one of the guards pulled against the back of her shirt.

"Stay here." He settled her between himself and another guard as the old man sauntered towards the dias. "Don't talk to anyone, don't cause trouble, and don't move. Do that, and you might not die today."

Arix did as he asked. She kept still, eyes flitting away from the ceiling and down to the occupants of the room. There were others, like her, with guards hovering at their sides in the center of the giant space, all waiting patiently. But as she stared, Arix's stomach dropped further and further into her as she realized that she was the only one standing dripping and dirty. Everyone else shone, polished and pristine, hair arranged neatly, clothes glimmering of expensive fabrics.

A girl, only ten feet from her, wore a deep plum colored dress, sleeves draped all the way to the floor. Her long brown hair was wrapped around her head in intricate braids. As if she realized she was being watched, the girl turned, her gold eyes piercing Arix's gaze.

She quickly glanced away.

Arix wanted to melt into the earth. What in the Goddess's name had she gotten herself into?

Dignitaries and nobility stood along the edges of the room, whispering amongst themselves, swathed in the same fabrics and finery.

It seemed that they had all been waiting on her, for once the old man reached the front of the room, a large boom echoed through the chamber, followed by a second and third. Heads turned toward the dias, and all chatter died.

"Announcing Lord Bardon of the high council."

Oh, fuck.

Arix's eyes darted, searching for an escape. Window? Side door?

As if he read her thoughts, the guard on her left placed a strong hand on her shoulder, and Arix forced herself to calm down.

It was fine. It would all be fine.

There had to be an explanation why she was here. There had to be a reason she was in this room with the most powerful man in the entire country. A royal pardon? An auction?

How her stomach could dip any lower, she did not know, and yet it felt as if it had fallen straight through the floor beneath her feet. Was she about to be sold to the highest bidder? Slavery had been outlawed in Rökkur for decades, but…

Lord Bardon mounted the steps and every head craned to get a better look of the man who sat at the head of the king's council. His brow was furrowed, analyzing those before him, his hands clasped tightly behind his billowing black robes. Briefly his gaze swept past Arix, and she dared herself to keep breathing.

"Welcome to Castle Zma'ai." His voice was loud, yet slightly strained, as if he had a sore throat. "I know many of you are confused at why you have been brought here, taken from your families and homes. The truth has been kept from you because the information we are about to tell you could ruin this nation, and give power to the rebels. We have always been strong, and we will not allow our country to be taken from us by trouble makers and outliers. It has been the order of this council," His arm swept towards the dignitaries lining the walls. "That we move forward to provide the King comfort and counsel during this time. After much deliberation, and great meditation on the part of the King, it has been decided that what is needed at this time is a Black Hand."

The room stilled, and in a moment of pure horror, Arix felt a laugh bubble in her throat. She clapped a hand over her mouth, manacles jangling from her wrists, eyes wide. Goddess have mercy...

Lord Bardon went on, not knowing that below him, a thief in the back was struggling to maintain composure. "This country has not had the need for a Black Hand in over a hundred years. And now, more than ever, one is needed. This decision is not made lightly on behalf of the King or the council. If you understand the severity of this choice, then you know why you've all been brought here. Some of you may already have met Lakai on your journey here, though you may not know that he is the last incantor in the four realms."

He motioned to his left, and Arix followed the motion until her gaze rested on the old man.

Lakai stepped forward and addressed the group. Arix gaped, the terror that had been dragging her down, completely dissipated. It was being replaced by something much worse... incredulous, betraying laughter.

"These are desperate times. Thus they call for desperate measures. The Carn rebels gather in the Fyall Mountains, and countries which used to be our friends have seen our trouble and may soon become our enemies. Our borders risk being invaded while we tear ourselves apart from the inside. Even within each realm, there is unrest and talk of desertion. This cannot take place. Hence we have gathered all of you; perfect candidates for the task-"

Arix snorted. The guard next to her tightened his grip on her shoulder.

"You will all begin training to hold the position of the Black Hand, and compete against one another to win. You will be tested in horsemanship and martial weaponry, strategy and leadership, refinery and espionage, molding you to be the victor. You shall-"

A wheeze echoed in the silence.

Around her, others were turning to look. Arix clamped down on her tongue, blood filling her mouth as she fought against the laugh that squeezed at her insides.

Lakai cleared his throat and went on. "You shall train with some of the greatest minds, and use what you learn to protect this nation. To become heroes-"

The wheezing had turned into an incredibly unattractive snorting sort of hiccup that was bubbling on the edge of outright guffaw. Lakai was staring daggers into Arix, and the guard beside her had such a hard grip on her that it brought tears to her eyes.

But the laugh would not give up.

"To become-"

Arix could hold it back no longer. Her laugh twisted like a tear through the room, scarring the silence. Her eyes watered and tears squelched down the side of her nose. To make matters worse, the more she laughed, the deadlier the silence around her became.

There was a voice in her head begging her to shut up, Goddess save her, she was about to be executed right here and now for her stupidity. After a moment, she composed her laughter, her sides aching.

"I'm sorry." She raised an arm as a vague apology towards the dias. "Please, go on."

Lakai's steel blue eyes cut her though, and the last of the laughter died in her throat.

"And what, might I ask, is so entertaining?"

Arix glanced around her, hoping to find someone, anyone, who might be as confused as she was. As amused by all of this as she was. Instead, annoyed gazes met her own.

"I just..." She glanced back to Lakai and gestured to herself, ragged boots, threadbare cloak and all. "I think you have the wrong person."

"No. You and those around you have been picked because you possess something that others do not."

"Unfortunate timing and a predisposition for bad life decisions?"

He wanted to kill her. She could see it in his eyes, blazing blue waters glaring across the marble expanse between them.

"No. You all have the magick vein."

The smile on her face froze. The whole world around her slowed, the air idling. She didn't have any more magick than a stick might. She wanted to laugh again. To cackle and point a daring finger across the room and tell Lakai what a fool he must be. But the laughter that had been bubbling out only seconds before was replaced by abject horror so deep and yawning that she choked on the air in her own lungs.

"The reason you are here, the reason you all have been chosen for the task, is that you are the last in all the realms. You are the last. The only ones left with magick flowing in your veins."

Goddess above.

FOUR

A moment ago everything had been moving so slowly, and now the words rushed about like a wind. The stupor was drifting away and Arix's mind darted with the information. She had thought the last of the magick users had died off years ago.

"In addition to all of this physical training, you will also be studying to be an Incantor. As you train, you will be tested to prove your worth. To prove yourself worthy of the mantle of the Black Hand."

"What if we don't pass?" She'd already embarrassed herself enough as it was, might as well be the one to ask the burning questions. "What happens if we fail one of these tests?"

"You will either pass, or you will fail. And failure will result in death." Lakai said simply.

Someone near the front tried to run. He broke away from his escort and headed for the door, pushing others out of his way as he scrambled away. His eyes were wide and bloodshot as he rushed past Arix. He barely made it another few feet past her before four guards grabbed him and tackled him to the ground. He screamed and writhed, fighting to free himself, but the palace guards were more than capable of holding him at bay. They dragged him from the room, his protests echoing down the halls long after he had been removed.

So much for that idea.

"Understand this." Lakai's voice boomed in the renewed silence. "You will either become the Black Hand or your life will end. There is no other option. There is too much at stake for the stakes not to be set so high is your lives. Your training begins today."

Lord Bardon stepped back toward the center of the dias. "There will be a series of six tests. Each test will assess your skill in varying areas. You will need to pass them all to become a true Black Hand. To help you learn and hone your skills, each of you will be assigned a trainer and tutor. Your trainers will work to make sure you are physically capable to withstand the trials, and your tutors will work to make sure you are mentally capable. During the trials you will not be allowed to leave the grounds. If anyone attempts to leave," Lord Bardon paused and turned his gaze to Arix. "You will be removed without question. After all, the King only needs one Black Hand."

Arix shifted her weight, rocking to the balls of her feet as she twisted to look at those around her. There was a clear definition of those who would be competing with her and those who were just part of the court and privy to the information Lord Bardon had just told them. Arix counted twenty-four of them, including herself, that stood in the center of the room. So few?

The girl in the plum colored dress was looking at her again, those golden eyes seeing everything and saying nothing. Arix smiled at her, and the girl quickly looked away. How old was she? Fifteen? Younger?

"Your first test begins now."

Arix looked back to the dias. Lakai was grinning at her.

Fuck. What the hell had she gotten herself dragged into?

~

Arix shifted her weight from one foot to the other, her eyes narrowing. She stood in a line of other contestants and felt her confidence returning. This was something she was good at, something she could succeed at. She would show them. She would win their games and prove her worth. And when they trusted her enough to let their guard down, she would run.

Lord Bardon stood before them, Lakai at his side, in a field that lay beyond the castle.

"Welcome to your first test. Choose your weapon and choose your steed. You will be paired up, and your task is this: to unseat your opponent by any means. If you succeed, you have passed the first test. Your rooms and a hot bath will await you."

He didn't have to continue for them to understand. If you failed, you were dead.

"We will start here," Lord Bardon motioned to Arix's right, "and moved down the line. Choose your weapon and your horse, then return to your place."

Behind Lord Bardon a huge table held a variety of weapons. Arix was familiar with most of them, but there were plenty she'd never seen before in her life. She turned, sidling a glance down the line. While the other competitors might have been dressed better, by the looks on many of their faces, they were as unfamiliar with some of the weapons as she was.

Beside her, the girl in purple stood, hands clenched tightly in front of her. She was eyeing the paddock just behind the table, filled with horses, stamping in the warm summer earth. The first of the line walked slowly up to the table, choosing a mace with deadly spikes on the end. The girl in purple was fidgeting now, a strand of her braid having come undone.

"What's your name?"

The girl started, turning those golden eyes on Arix. She seemed to just now notice their proximity.

"I'm sorry…what did you say?"

"Your name," Arix grinned. "I asked your name."

"Oh." The girl managed a small smile, but Arix could tell she wanted to turn back to look at the table.. "I'm Lace."

"Which one are you gonna pick?"

Lace glanced back over her shoulder at the table of weapons. "I…I don't know."

"You ever shoot an arrow?"

Lace shook her head.

"Held a sword?"

Again the girl said nothing, though her face was growing paler.

"What about an ax? Have you ever chopped wood before?"

Lace's brow furrowed. "Well, yes. But I don't know if that's…"

Something was clicking together in Arix's mind. "Have you ever ridden a horse before?"

By the look on her face it was clear she had not. "My family just had mules on our farm, and I've only ridden them a few times. They were for pulling carts."

So the girl was a farmer. Arix glanced down at the dress with long trumpet sleeves. They might have dressed her up like a noble lady who belonged in a castle, but underneath it all, she was as common as Arix was.

"I don't think I can do this. I've never even…" With every word, Lace's breath was quickening and her eyes grew wider by the second.

"Take a breath, Lace." Arix watched the line growing shorter as their turn neared. "Stay calm, and just treat the horse like you would your mule. Pick a weapon that feels familiar to you. An ax or a staff. Take a breath. You'll be fine."

She smiled as she said it, calm nonchalant against Lace's frenzied breathing. But inside, Arix pitied the girl.

Then it was Lace's turn, striding towards the table with hesitant steps. She chose an ax, and then a small tawny mare from the paddock.

Arix moved towards the table, eyeing one of the rapiers at the front. Her father had taught her to hold a sword. But it had been years now. Her gaze roamed towards the left back corner where a shortbow stuck out. Picking it up, she searched for the quiver, which lay on the opposite side of the table, as if they had purposefully been separated.

Arix stepped into the paddock and slowly picked her way through the herd, eyeing feet and occasionally glancing into mouths. All of them were in excellent condition, though it was temperament that caused them to vary so widely. Arix was about to grab the reins of a dappled gray mare when a shrill whinny caught her attention.

He was so dark, his coat almost looked blue, his long mane dancing every time he tossed his head. Arix stepped forward slowly, whispering sweet nothings as she ran her hands down his legs and his back, feeling the pulsing muscles beneath. He was young and strong, the tallest horse she'd ever seen. His ears twitched back, listening, as she continued to talk to him. He pawed at the ground once as she led him away, his prance a surprisingly elegant bounce for a horse as big as he was.

His stood calmly in line beside Arix as the rest of the competitors made their choices. Beside them, Lace was still quivering, but she gripped the ax well, and her horse stood calm at her side.

"Mount up!" Lord Bardon's voice boomed across the field.

It felt silly. Crazy, even, to be standing here all lined up like this. Arix almost laughed again, as she checked the girth on her saddle. She felt like she was playing a game, playing a part, like she had so many times before. If this was what they wanted, she could do it. She'd play their stupid little games for now.

She had to hop a bit to get her foot in the stirrup and haul herself up onto the back of the giant horse. It was the tallest she'd ever felt in the saddle, and her heart skipped a moment to be up so high. He sidestepped, adjusting to the new weight and then calmed as Arix patted his neck, running her fingers through the rough strands of his mane.

"Make a circle with your horses, and when your name is called, you will face off against an opponent. Your goal is this: unseat your opposition. When you have completed your goal, return to the outer ring."

Arix urged her mammoth of a horse into the quickly forming ring. She laid the bow across her lap, strapping the quiver of arrows to the side of the saddle. Lace moved into a spot down a ways, and Arix felt relief settle into her as she watched the golden eyed girl. Even though it was her first time on a horse, she seemed to be doing fine so far.

A hush fell over the ring as they waited. Around her, the competitors were poised, ready to spring into action as soon as their names were called.

"Thomas Blueridge and Revena Kali."

Arix eyes slid across the ring to see the man who had tried to flee earlier. Two guards flanked his horse, crossbows in their hands. It was clear they had no intention on chasing him away if he tried to run again. The girl, Revena, moved into the ring slowly, carefully watching him. Each movement she made was purpose-ful. She kept her posture loose, watching and waiting rather than making the first move. Arix was impressed.

Arix leaned forward in her saddle, watching the girl as she side-stepped the first attack, prancing to the left. She made no move to fight Thomas, cocking her head to the side as she watched him barrel clumsily past her. Thomas whirled around, frustra-tion painted across his face in red. He came at her again, but she dodged it a second time, his mace swinging through the air where she had sat only moments ago.

On and on they went in this manner, Thomas swinging his useless weapon and Revena sliding just out of reach. With each attack he grew angrier, but Arix saw what the girl was doing. Rev-ena Kali was playing a game. She could have easily unseated Tom during his first attack, but she was waiting. Waiting for him to make a mistake so obvious that she wouldn't need to do a thing for him to fail.

But most importantly, Arix realized, Revena was keeping her abilities to herself. The ring was more strategic than just a duel. It allowed each competitor to watch the others, to look for weak-nesses and strengths. And Revena wasn't allowing that.

"Fight me!" Thomas cried out in frustration as his attack missed his target once again.

His face was beet red, and his horse balked beneath him as he tried another hairpin turn. As he yanked on the reins, the horse's head shot up with a snort, promptly clubbing Thomas in the face. In the saddle he teetered for a moment, before losing his balance and landing on the ground, blood pouring from his nose.

Cheers sounded around the ring when he landed, though Arix remained quiet, watching Revena turn slowly back to her place.

"Revena Kali is the victor." Lord Bardon called, his arm raised toward the girl. "Next, Elihu Sadar and Idris Levente."

Arix watched the next couple of rounds, keeping an eye on those she thought did well. It was no surprise that those who had never held weapons before today did poorly, knocked off their horses out of sheer inexperience or bad luck.

"Leopold Baibre and Bellarix Sable."

Her time had come. And she would show them exactly what she could do. No magick necessary.

She glanced around the circle and spotted a boy about her age who held a quarterstaff. Arix watched his eyes skim the circle as well until their eyes met and locked. He smirked at her, and tightened his grip on his staff.

Arix charged him.

She'd thought, at first, that she might try to wait it out, as Revena had done, but after watching a few others do the same, realized that starting out bold would probably be the best way to knock her opponent off balance.

The boy's strategy seemed to simply push her off her horse with his staff, but he was having trouble handling his horse with only one hand. As the two neared each other, Arix swung her horse to the side easily, and hit the boy in the back of the head with her bow. He jerked forward, his horse stopping abruptly, and tumbled to the ground, his staff thrown from his grasp. Arix wheeled back around, shocked that the fight was over so quickly. Clearly the poor boy had no horsemanship skills. She would have been able to avoid that fall at the age of five.

A jovial laugh escaped her as she hopped from the saddle and stuck out a hand. "You alright?"

He took her offered hand and slowly got to his feet. "That was fast. You've got quite a swing."

They shook hands, and it was when he reached down for his

staff that Arix remembered that she had just completed her first test. She had won. And he had lost. A strange pit sat in her stomach.

"I'm sorry."

Leopold turned around and stared at her. He nodded, understanding her meaning, and walked back to his position in the ring as Lord Bardon called out her name.

"Bellarix Sable is the victor. Next, Lace Fornder and Celeste Ayala."

Arix had not even gotten back to her place when a blood curdling scream sounded off to her right. Her ears rang at the sound and she flinched from it, hand dropping to her bow instinctively as she looked. Lace lay crumpled on the ground, two throwing knives embedded in her chest. She hadn't even made it all the way into the circle yet.

Lace's now riderless horse trotted around the circumference of the ring, and as Arix watched it, caught sight of the Ayala girl. Her arm was still upraised after throwing her knife, and a small satisfied smirk played at the corner of her mouth. The blonde lowered her arm slow, and slid off her horse in a graceful dismount.

Everything moved slowly. Like treading water, it felt as though she couldn't get to Lace fast enough. Arix dropped her bow and ran, collapsing to the ground beside the golden eyed girl.

"Goddess, Lace can you hear me? It's going to be ok, I swear." Arix's voice didn't sound like her own, stupidly calm and quiet.

Lace's teeth were red with blood, a look of surprise still on her face. The knives in her chest were buried to the hilt, the front of her plum dress already sopping blood across Arix's own clothes.

"I didn't even see her. I didn't..."

And she was gone.

It had been so fast. Two quick throws and the girl's life was over. Cold white anger traced along the back of Arix's neck as she gazed down at those gorgeous golden eyes, looking for an opponent that had moved too quickly.

"Those are mine."

Her gaze traveled up from the perfectly polished boots to the blonde Celeste standing above her, her arms crossed. The girl looked bored.

Arix stood, forcing her stupid slow feet to move as she backed away from the body. Celeste placed a foot on Lace's neck, and with a solid yank, pulled the two blades from the dead girl's chest. Lace slumped against the ground like a wet rag.

A ghost of Lace's fingers still gripped Arix's forearm, and she had to turn away. She didn't even know the girl. She had to look at anything else but Lace's body. Like moving through tar, Arix turned away, forcing her shoulders back as she walked back to her horse. The numbness was fading, slowly drowned in cold thick fury that roiled through her stomach.

She mounted, keeping her eyes trained on the ring before her as Lord Bardon announced the next competitors. It was all clear now, crystal clear as some deep pool disguising its depths with its clarity.

Arix glanced around at the remaining competitors. The purpose of this test hadn't been to survey their abilities. It had not been to ascertain their skill. But it had been ro remove the lower class. For as she surveyed the winners and the losers, a pattern arose from them all. It was the nobility that were winning. Those who had been raised on the backs of horses, raised with weapons in the hands. It was the peasantry that had lost. Those who had been raised behind a plow and a cauldron.

Arix's jaw clenched as she looked for Lord Bardon and Lakai, standing to the side of the circle, watching with cool gazes at the death they had just brought.

Her knees were squeezing, readying to spur her horse forward. Ready to draw from her quiver. She could end this now, with one well placed arrow, she could end this stupidity. This aimless shedding of blood. With one arrow she could-

"That was good of you."

Arix turned to see the man next to her, a mop of brown hair curling around his ears.

"Out there." He said, motioning to where Lace's body was being dragged away. "No one should die alone."

Arix said nothing, turning back to the circle. The anger in her skull seethed.

"I guess this isn't really the best time, but I'm Michael."

Arix kept her gaze forward as the last two competitors were called, fighting as though nothing had just happened. As if an innocent girl had not just been brutally murdered. Finally she turned back to look at him, swallowing her anger down deep inside her.

She'd spent the last seven years taking from these elite. Taking from them and returning their stolen wealth back to where it belonged. She'd taken up the mantle of a thief because it had been better than do nothing. She had lied and stolen and cheated into pockets and halls and ledgerbooks to even out the scales. She'd righted wrongs. And in those seven years there had always been one consistency. Justice was not a quick road.

She would find her revenge. But it would not be today. For that, she would need to wait.

"I'm Arix."

Michael smiled.

"The victors may return to their rooms." Lord Bardon announced, dismissing them away with a wave. "Tomorrow morning you will begin your training."

Around her, the other competitors were dismounting, handing their reins over to the guards who stood posted around the field. Slowly Arix slid out of the saddle, careful to keep her bruised ribs from jarring.

Instead of handing over her reins like the others, she walked the horse back to the stables herself, her grip tight on the leather straps. Fury ricocheted through her heart.

FIVE

"Where are you from?"

Michael fell into step beside Arix, leading the dappled gray she had almost chosen along beside him.

The sight of the ring was still echoing in Arix's head, but she pushed it away, adopting a smiling demeanor. "All the boring places in the world. Cracks and crevices where you might lose a sock or a key."

She expected him to laugh, but he didn't. Instead, he peered through thick lashes at her, his free hand stuffed into his pocket.

"Did you know her?"

"Who?"

"The girl. In the ring."

Arix looked away. "Not even a little. She just... It happened so fast."

He said nothing to this, and Arix couldn't decide if she found his silence annoying or not. They moved into the barn, leading their horses to two empty stalls near the end. Sweet hay and leather mingled in Arix's nose and it brought her back to a memory she had long forgotten about. Her father's strong hands lifting her higher than she'd ever been in her life, the feeling of coarse horse hare gripped between her fingers. Arix shoved the unwanted memory away.

Michael leaned over the gap in the wall, separating their stalls. "You never said."

Arix sighed as she pulled the bridle off her horse's head. "I never said what?"

"Where you were from."

Arix snorted. "Don't you think that maybe there's a reason I didn't mention it, rich boy?" She turned to look at him, to really look at him.

To her surprise, he had the common decency to blush slightly. "I don't mean to pry."

"I'm from Eldur."

"Where in Eldur?"

"Tiny town on the coast. You wouldn't know it."

"I might. I'm straight out of Vingard. Well, just outside of Vingard."

Even though he was her age, he was soft to look at, smooth and young and untouched. He looked like the kind of person she wouldn't even think twice about stealing from. But by the way he curried out his horse, it seemed he'd done it a million times before.

"What did you do? Before coming here?"

He asked it so nonchalantly, just a casual question, pretending like he wasn't snooping. It made her sizzle on the inside. Who did he think he was?

"I was a thief." She matched his tone; casual and flippant. "You hear about the temple in Sieren that got raided? The statue that was stolen?"

He turned to look at her, eyes wide as dinner plates. "That was you?"

It hadn't been. It wasn't her style to steal from holy places. But he didn't need to know that.

"Yep."

"Wait, I thought the temple was robbed by a group. Ten at least."

Shit. "All lies, I did it all on my lonesome."

His eyebrows went up and he grinned at her. "You must be one scary lady to do that all on your own."

Arix grinned back. "The scariest. You better be careful. Noble boy like you, I might just seduce you and rob you blind."

Michael's cheeks tinged pink again and he turned away to pull off the last of the horse's tack. "I'm sure you could."

His eyes crinkled when he smiled. He smiled too much.

Arix hauled her tack into the hall, placing it on the empty racks. Michael matched her stride, stepping out with her, but stopped when Arix made a move to go back into the stall.

"Are you going to dinner?"

"Do I have to pay for dinner or is it just a perk of having no control of our lives for the next year?"

Again, he surprised her when he did not laugh. Instead, he cocked his head and stared at her. There was something about his gaze that annoyed her.

"What?"

"You're an interesting person."

She swept into a deep curtsy, her knees almost touching the straw covered floor. "I'm honored to have your approval."

This annoyed him, which made Arix smile brightly. She liked annoying him. Payback, she supposed, for asking her stupid questions.

Instead of responding though, he offered her a small smile and turned away leaving Arix staring after him, and wondering what it was exactly that made him so incredibly likable.

~

If she had been allowed, Arix would have slept in the stable with her horse, but two guards had come looking for her and she had been escorted back into the castle as the sky grew red.

While its outsides had been an inky black, the inner walls were of crisp white marble, veins of indigo blue etched deep into their being. Curtains of indigo draped the windows and black and silver tapestries depicting unicorns and fountains and great gushing gardens decorated the walls. Masterful paintings that took Arix's breath away in their detail hung sparsely, as though merely placed there to fill an empty space. Passing an open door, Arix noticed rows of armor lining the wall, jousting lances hung above them on the wall. The expanse of the castle was huge, and seemed somehow impossibly bigger on the inside.

At last, her escorts reached a large oak door, brass knocker and handle attached to the front. The two soldiers took up post on either side of the door, motioning for her to enter.

With every passing moment, with every new step, her lungs had constricted, squeezing the inside of her chest until she could not breathe. She had reprimanded herself during the walk, considering all the other predicaments she had found herself in over the past few years, and was thoroughly annoyed at her own residing fear. When she had broken into Warden Sviengard's private stable and stolen her prize horse, the odds had been greater against her. As long as she kept calm, she could come up with a plan. Though it was never easy, she would always find a way out.

Arix lifted a hand to knock.

"Just go in." The soldier on the right said, his voice annoyed.

"They're waiting on you."

She lifted the latch and pushed through the door, eye widening as her gaze skittered around the room. It was a bedroom, decorated in soft whites and ivory, gold and indigo accenting the furniture. The white stone walls had been inked in stenciled tree branches and fruit. A four poster bed stood against the wall, sheer curtains draped beautifully down to the floor. The bed was covered in clothing from the four realms: blues and purples and greens and creams.

Pouring water emanated from an adjoining doorway off to the right. There was a soft giggle and someone speaking in hushed tones, though the sound of the water muffled the words, and Arix couldn't make out what was said. A maid emerged, curtsied quickly and scooped up the clothing off the bed. Nearing the far left wall, just next to a large writing desk, she stepped through an alcove revealing a hidden door that entered into a small room.

Arix stepped further inside, very aware of what a mess her boots must be making to the lush carpet, and peered into the small room where the maid had gone. The portion of wall expanded inside and was lined with clothing and shoes.

"Excuse me?"

The maid turned to see her and curtsied again. "Miss?"

"Oh, uhh, no. Just Arix." Arix stumbled into a returning curtsy. "Should I take off my boots? I'm going to track mud all over the place."

"If you wish. Miss Charlotte is already drawing your bath."

Arix blinked. "My bath?"

The maid seemed unfazed and continued to hang the beautiful dresses among the others. "These are to be your private rooms, Miss. You shall remain here for your stay in the castle."

Arix felt as though someone had suddenly punched her in the

gut. The maid hung up the last of the clothing and squeezed past back into the main room, Arix following in a daze.

"I'm sorry, but I don't-"

"Miss Charlotte, I've finished with the clothes." The maid cut her off, ignoring her questions.

A woman who looked much more like an ox, entered through the right doorway, her frame towering over Arix. Behind her, Arix spied a giant tub steaming with hot water. A double walled fireplace took up the space between the two rooms, and two more maids were heating water over the fire to pour into the bath.

"Well you're skin and bones, that's for sure." Her voice held a thundering northern accent, and her grayed hair that had once been blonde pulled away from her face in a modest bun. "And filthy too, I'm sure your mother would be ashamed."

Though she had never known her mother, Arix felt a deep resounding gong of guilt, and a blush rose up her neck.

Never had she been in a situation like this. It was all so odd that every new piece of information knocked her more off her guard, leaving Arix feeling exhausted. She had played the part of a lady before, but it had always been just that: a part. Now she was caught completely off guard, unsure of the role she was supposed to play.

"What am I doing here?" Her voice, to her horror, squeaked, and she cleared it awkwardly.

"All the competitors have been given quarters in the castle. This one is yours."

Miss Charlotte said it so easily. As if she'd said it a hundred times, and Arix was just one in a long line of idiots she'd had to explain it to today. She gestured to the tub and Arix gaped.

"The bath is for me?"

"Yes."

"And I'm staying here and not in some dingy dungeon cell?"

"That is correct."

"But I'm not..."

"Young lady, you reek of sweat and blood. You've tracked in enough mud to bury a house under, and I'll not have anyone in this palace, no matter their rank, in such a state."

One of the maids was tipping a bottle over the water, and a slurried mixture of white flowers and green leaves tumbled in. The scent wafted into Arix's nose, the soothing smell of lilies and sage filling the steaming air around her. Like a mother's caress, the smell eased Arix and she relaxed slightly.

"What else is in that water?" she asked, eyeing another bottle that spilled small rocks into the bath.

"Salts. To soothe any aches." While firm, Miss Charlotte's voice had softened, coaxing her forward. She held out a hand. "Let's clean you up, child."

Arix was not one to turn down a bath. Especially a bath that smelled so nice.

She stripped out of her clothes, piling them together in the corner with her muddy boots. Her skin was marred with scars and bruises, and her side was black and blue from her fall this morning. She tried to attempt some semblance of modesty, but Miss Charlotte and the other maids were unfazed, helping her naked body into the tub.

An involuntary sigh escaped her mouth before she could stop it as the hot water enveloped her in its embrace.

"There you go, dear. Just you sit here and soak, let us worry about getting you clean." Miss Charlotte mumbled, soothing.

When was the last time she'd taken a bath? She did not remember. It was so strange, being treated and cared for by someone else. She'd been a nobody her whole life, and now she was being treated like a somebody. It was odd.

She couldn't decide if she liked the feeling or not.

But she was tired, her head filled up and overflowing. This morning when she'd woken, she had not expected her day to play out as it had.

This thought in particular had her doing mental summersaults. Had it only been this morning? It felt like an eternity had passed.

The more Arix thought, the more tired she became. The steaming water was doing its work, and one of the maids had started washing her hair, her fingers raking the dirt from Arix's scalp. At some point, Arix must have fallen asleep, and before she realized it, was being lifted out of the tub by the strong arms of Miss Charlotte and wrapped in a warm fluffy towel.

"You're exhausted. They've saved a bit of supper for you, so you'll eat and then to bed. It's been a long day and I daresay to-morrow will be just as long." Miss Charlotte motioned with her head to the last remaining maid. "This is Wren. She'll be your personal help if you need anything. I'll leave you in her capable hands."

Arix was helped into a nightgown by Wren, the girl from the closet, and sat in front of the large mirror in the corner. The aching in her ribs had eased slightly and her head no longer pounded. While Wren brushed her hair, Arix ate the bowl of soup and bread that had been left for her, eyes half mast. Only when the bowl was empty did she finally look up to see herself in the mirror's reflection. It was not a self that she recognized. When was the last time she had actually looked at herself in the mirror?

Her frame was average, with no special assets to speak of. Her nose was her favorite feature, speckled in enough freckles to make her look young and sweet. Her auburn hair had grown long without her realization, reaching down her spine to her hips. While her father had always called her beautiful, Arix was content with just being simply pretty. It was easier to blend into a crowd when you weren't ravishingly beautiful.

Arix glanced past her own reflection and studied the girl who was combing out her hair. She looked a lot like Lace in the court-yard, with brown hair and soft eyes.

"No one's ever combed my hair before. Thank you."

Wren smiled, setting the comb back on the table. "Ready for bed now?"

The covers were cool and soft, the mattress so soft that Arix for a moment wondered if she was resting on real swans. Wren tucked the mountains of duvets around Arix, sealing her into the bed, snug as a bear ready to hibernate.

"Sleep well, Miss Bellarix. If you need anything, there will be two guards stationed outside your door."

Arix barely heard her, her head already buried deep into the warmth of the blankets. Perhaps it would be worth it to become a monster, as long as she could sleep in a bed as beautiful as this one.

SIX

Arix jolted awake, her fist clenched in the sheets. Someone was banging on her door. It was still dark, though the early gray of morning had begun sifting its way through the panes of glass at the window. She stumbled to the door, eyes bleary, and opened it part ways. Lithe fingers shoved it the rest of the way open, and Arix stumbled back as a man held open the door, a once broken and now very crooked nose taking up most of his face.

"Get dressed, and be quick about it. We've got work to do. If you aren't in the stables in five minutes, I'll have you worn out so badly you won't even want to think about riding."

With a slam of the door, he was gone, leaving Arix' mouth agape and staring after him. It took a second for it all to sink in before Arix turned and climbed back into bed. She pulled the covers up over her head and was drifting off again in seconds.

When she heard when the door opened again, she tucked the blanket further over her head, listening to the steps of boots on the floor. They stopped by her bed, paused, and then left. Satisfied, she went back to sleep.

Ice water, so cold it felt like it broke bones tumbled over her, soaking her and the bed and everything else. Arix threw herself out from the tangle of icy sheets with a howl, tumbling until she crouched on the other side of the bed, hand reaching for a weapon she no longer carried.

"Oh look at that." The man said flatly, discarding the empty bucket on the floor. "You're up."

Arix stared at him through slitted eyes and bared her teeth. The man only glared back.

"If you aren't in the barn in two minutes, I'll be back with slop next time." Then he was gone.

Arix sat in the puddle of water, staring at the closed door.

That fuck had ruined her bed.

Hastened with the clarity that only ice cold water could provide, Arix pushed into the closet and grabbed the first pair of riding pants and shirt she saw. The boots took a second to pull on, lacing stupidly up to above her knee. Outside the door, her two guards stayed just on her heels as she made her way outside and into the bleary morn. As promised, the man was waiting outside the stables, stretching his legs against the side of the building, a bucket of brown slop at his feet.

"Ready? Let's go!"

Without waiting for an answer, he took off, jogging towards the forest. Arix followed after him, doing her best to keep up, the two escorts keeping pace behind her. They ran together for a few minutes before Arix started feeling a slow stitch in her side, becoming ever more prominent as her calves burned beneath her. Her ribs were aching with every jolt of her boot, reminding her that only yesterday morning she had fallen to the stones of the alleyway. She pushed on regardless, doing her best to keep up despite the screaming in her side. By the time they reached the end of the forest, Arix wanted to die. She hadn't run this hard in years, and she could only thank the Goddess that she didn't have anything in her stomach.

Her running companion said nothing when Arix dropped to her knees and dry heaved bile onto the forest floor, though he did stop, jogging in place until she was back on her feet. He went only a little slower then, as Arix struggled to match his pace, her side aching and her mouth feeling drier than ever. When the half-hour long run finally ended back at the stables, Arix nearly threw herself into the horse trough, drinking in the dirty water in great mouthfuls.

"Don't drink that fast or you'll make yourself-"

Arix vomited all over the ground.

"-sick."

Wiping the tears away from her eyes, Arix sat back on her heels and stared up at him. Sweat glistened on his forehead, stupidly large hands resting on his hips.

"We'll be running every morning until you can do it easily. Maybe you'll finally teach your body to build up some endurance."

Arix only stared at him some more, her eyes glazing over.

"I'm Tobias. I'll be training with you every morning until lunch. Since you're so out of shape, a good run in the morning will set you straight. You might as well give yourself another dunking since we'll be moving straight on to horses."

Slowly rising to her feet, Arix stuck out her hand. As much as she hated water dumped on her in the morning, she could respect her trainer's methods. And she liked him, under all that gruff and mustache.

"Arix."

The two shook, and Tobias strode into the stable. Arix still felt weak in the knees but followed him just the same, and saddled up her horse.

"I had wanted to start out in the ring today, but it seems we are too late. Instead we'll be heading out to the field past the forest. It'll give us a bit of privacy and space, and we'll see how well you do on the back of this beast."

Arix glanced past him and saw someone practicing jumps within the fence line, their blonde hair braided back tightly against their head. Celeste Ayala's form was perfect, her posture pristine; an elegant silhouette against the orange sunrise sky. Every stride was perfectly timed, her jumps just as graceful. Cold fury laced through Arix's insides.

"She's all show." Arix turned to see Tobias watching her. "You will be better."

They walked, leading the great monster of a horse between them as they made their way out to the western field.

"Have you come up with a name for him yet?" Tobias peered under the horse's neck to look at Arix.

"Doesn't he already have a name?"

"Not yet. Besides, what if his name was Stumpy? You'd have to change it then. The Black Hand will need a horse with a good name."

"Then you name him."

They strode on in silence, the soft thud of each hoof the only sound between them. The field opened out before them; the same one from yesterday. The table still stood off to the side, empty now of weapons.

"Up you get. I saw you yesterday on him. You work quite well together."

Arix mounted, air whooshing from her as she hoisted herself into the saddle.

"He's so huge, it takes me a minute to get on him." she grunted.

"That's why you need to keep running." Tobias slapped the horse on the shoulder. "Work up those leg muscles so you can keep a handle on 'ole Ganoth here."

Arix chuckled. "Ganoth? The giant from the legend? Is that the best you could come up with?"

"What?" Tobias adjusted her left stirrup, and grinned up at her. "A giant black horse the size of a mountain. Why not name him after the mountain giant who ate a whole village? Seemed perfect to me."

"Ah but he isn't just some oaf, are you boy?" Arix patted his neck and then moved him into a quick trot around Tobias. "Let's show him how graceful you are."

With a squeeze, the horse took off, hooves thundering across the grass, each powerful stride meeting the ground with a trembling force. Tobias squinted into the morning sun as the two raced down the length of the field and back, horse and rider barreling through the grass, spirits united. They did truly look magnificent together, Arix's flaming red hair streaming out behind her, hunkered down so low on the horse's back that their manes tangled into one.

The rest of the morning went by quickly. Arix thighs burned from the morning run, but something about being on the back of a horse made everything about life feel better. Tobias had Arix run through a series of training exercises, acquainting both horse and rider with new techniques. While the big horse was strong and graceful, his size caused a delay, and it seemed he matched Arix in stubbornness. Their movements together were beautiful as long as they were going fast. But when slowed to a trot, the large horse seemed to drag his hooves, lumbering along as if he were a work horse.

"He won't listen to you if you are unsure of yourself." Tobias yelled across the field as the horse continued to slow to a walk in the midst of a trot.

Arix grit her teeth, pushing him back into the faster gait. He listened well enough, but his reactions were slow, as if he hated being told what to do.

"Me too, friend. Me too." Arix whispered into his velvet ears.

By lunch, Arix's stomach was growling so loudly that Tobias was looking at her funny, and her legs ached so badly she could barely walk back to the stable. Tobias leaned his forearms on the stall door and watched as Arix unsaddled the horse and brushed him down.

"You know we have stable hands for that."

"I'm aware." Arix rubbed a curry comb in circles down the black coat, working out the sweat and loose hair. "But I was taught that a good horsewoman takes care of her own mount. It builds a bond."

Tobias tilted his head to the side. "Who taught you that?"

"My father."

"Your father was a smart man."

"What do you think of Osiris?"

"For the horse?" Tobias asked.

"Yes." Arix rubbed the horse's soft muzzle. "God of Death. I think it suits him well. Certainly would suit a Black Hand."

"I still like Ganoth." Tobias chuckled. "But he's your horse. I'll let the stable master know so they can engrave it on his tack."

Arix exited the stall, noticing that Michael's horse next door had the name Luminess engraved in a small metal plaque on the door.

"It seems like a lot of work for a competitor who may not be here next month." she mumbled.

The two walked together in silence back to the castle, their boots crunching into the soft white gravel.

"You must get it out of your head that you won't succeed." Tobias stuck his hands in his pockets. "I could train you perfectly, and your tutor could teach you every bit of history in the world, but if you don't have the fortitude to take yourself all the way to victory, then you'll fall. You will die like a dog and everyone will forget you ever existed. Your name will fade into obscurity like dust. Only you can stand and make your way ever forward. To engrave your legacy into time itself. No one can do that for you."

"That's a bucket of horse shit if I've ever heard it." Arix grinned.

Tobias looked at her. "For now. But you will not always think building a legacy is horse shit, Bellarix Sable. One day, you will care very much for the memory you leave behind."

~

The window was warm against her forehead, a contrast to the cool skin that met it, still chilled from an ice bath. Her room was a good four or five stories off the ground, her window facing the edge of the gardens and the beginnings of the woods. Each tree and plant was cultivated to look perfect, yet also natural, as if the earth grew perfectly rounded and shaped hedges. The land stretched out past the castle, melding with the gardens and fountains, and on the outskirts of what she could see was a great wood. So far and so deep that she could not see the city beyond the wall.

How easy it must be to forget that there are people in the world other than yourself.

Wren entered, teetering a large tray in her hands. "Since you don't know your way around just yet, I thought I'd bring you your lunch today. Dinner you'll have to eat in the hall with the others though, so don't go feeling too pampered."

Savory meat and vegetables filled the tray, with a thick slice of steaming bread. But what caught Arix's eye was the small silver pot at the corner of the tray. In it, the smooth creamy yellow of butter. *Oh, the thought!* She ate slowly, relishing each buttered crumb, and licked her fingers when she was done. Butter wasn't something to be wasted. The food was amazing, the best she'd ever had. The meat dripped juice down her fingers, and the vegetables were slathered in a sweet tangy sauce.

Teacup in hand, she leaned her head back against the window, knees curled up underneath her. Part of her said she could get used to this. And part of her said there was a reason a thief was being treated so well. A reason she was feasting on goose and butter.

Oh, see! Don't you see? See what a life you might have here!

She would not let herself forget. There was a reason she had become who she was. There was a reason she stole and a reason that she belonged hidden in the shadows of the gutter. Not in the pampered room of a lady.

"Your tutor is waiting for you, Miss Bellarix. The guards outside will escort you when you're ready." Wren gathered up the tray, and with a small smile, was gone.

The two guards stationed outside her door were the same two that had been there this morning. Arix tucked her hands behind her back, watching them as their shiny boots tapped away against the marble floor, leading her down the corridor.

"I suppose you two drew the short straw?"

They did not respond.

"Is this your job, then? To escort me to places and make sure I don't try to escape?"

The one on the left quirked an eyebrow. The one on the right just glared.

"Ah, I see. You *did* draw the short straw. Sorry about that. I suppose you'd much rather be guarding some important dignitary or doing rounds along the wall or-"

"Do ye always talk so much?" Said the one on the left. He was short, shorter than she was by a few inches, arms bulging at the seams of his shirt. Peeking out from the collar of his uniform, blue tattoos spiraled up his neck and disappeared into the thick crop of black hair at his scalp. He spoke with a clear Tamhain swagger, his words taking on a hitched lilt.

"I do." Retorted Arix with a grin. "I find it passes the time quite well. Who are you?"

Blue tattoos turned back to look at her, blue eyes gleaming, and matched her grin with his own. "Ulfur."

"And you?" Arix turned to the one on the right. "Since we'll be spending a lot of time together, we might as well get acquaint-ed."

The other man only offered a disgruntled swear under his breath. His dark skin was freckled over with tiny white scars, a mane of locs spilling out from his beret and bound down his back in strips of leather. Instead of a guardsman's sword, he carried a spear with a wicked barb on the end.

"Tha' one is Abbas. Ignore him, he's just grumpy is all." Ulfur hissed the last bit under his breath as if their conversation were a private one.

"Enough. Shall you tell her your mother's name next? Or per-haps the city you grew up in? Do you not know there is a power in naming? And she-" Abbas said this bit with disgust "-need not know everything."

Ulfur and Arix exchanged a wide eyed glance.

"My apologies." Arix took an extra step, quickening her pace, to walk between the two men rather than a step behind them. "I'm Arix, as I'm sure you both know. I like strawberries and knife fights, and I expect to be fully thwarted by the both of you if I should take it in my head to try and escape."

Ulfur chuckled. Abbas said nothing.

They stopped before a large oak door on the first floor, and Abbas and Ulfur took up positions on either side of it.

With a waggle of her eyebrows to Ulfur, Arix raised a hand and pushed open the door.

And promptly had the breath stolen from her lungs.

SEVEN

The door had opened up to a small study, the floor space taken up by a giant desk, neatly organized into stacks of books and a gold tray of parchment. Beside the tray lay a pot of black and gold ink, a black quill laid gracefully beside it. The woman behind the desk made no move to have heard Arix enter, black hair streaked delicately in silver, her lavender eyes downcast to the work in front of her.

But it was neither the woman nor the desk that made Arix's heart lurch in her chest. No, it was instead the floor to ceiling shelves that lined almost every wall, save the one with the window and the one with the massive map of Rökuur.

The door closed behind Arix with a soft thunk, and it was only then that the woman spoke, never looking up from the paper she filled with her elegant script.

"My name is Desirae Penduleux. I'll be tutoring you over the next couple of months." The woman's voice was strong, her accent crisp and indiscernible. "We will be meeting here every afternoon to study. Sit."

Arix did not sit. She stepped to the nearest shelf, hands tucked behind her back, as she studied the titles on the spines of the books, carefully tucked against each other like row after row of perfect teeth. There was mathematics and history and a massive collection of mythological creatures, all gathered to their own shelves and carefully organized alphabetically. Many were old, though kept in miraculously good condition, the gold dipped covers ribboned in the scars and cracks that all loved books must possess.

Her fingers tipped up to gently trace down the spine of *Aurelius' Lore and Beginnings,* feeling the hard leather.

"Don't touch that." Desirae snapped.

Arix jerked her hand away, the tips of her fingers burned by Desirae's words. She turned away from the shelves, her hand firmly behind her back again, and strolled to the large map on the wall. Rökkur was splayed out in beautiful watercolor whorls, every river and road and mountain range carefully etched. Each of the four realms were colored differently, their god-children painted around their edges, breathing their life into the world of men.

At the top, painted lush green was Tamhain, the northernmost realm, and the largest. Tamhain held the Fyall mountain range, and the largest forests in the world. Untamed and unmatched in beauty, Tamhain was watched over by the Goddess Arduinna, Kaoss' first-born.

Below Tamhain, the eastmost realm, was Zarak, where the Fyall mountains swooped downward into desert plains and hot burning sands. Painted yellow, Zarak was watched over by Kaoss' second child, the god Zephyrus, painted with his gaze upturned toward his older sister.

In the south was Eldur, painted red for the god Vulcan, its vast fields and countryside carved with long winding rivers that curved from its rocky cliffs. Vulcan was painted as though he stroked the cliffs, his left hand turned toward the compass at the corner of the map, a moon and sun at the center of the cardinal points.

At the west was Nero, the blue paint covering the Isles of Sama off its coast. Kaoss' last child, the goddess Nereus was painted as though she floated on the back of a massive whale that lay hidden under the waves of Nero's coastline.

At the center of them all, as if the god-children reached for one another, the capital of Mergur lay, joining them all together. Violet paint, outlined in gold ink marked the very center, and Arix imagined a speck of a form underneath that gold, a miniature painting of herself, hidden in the walls of the royal palace of Zma'ai.

An impatient cough resonated behind her and Arix turned to look at her new tutor. Ms. Penduleux had put down her quill, her hands folded in front of her on the desk. Annoyance streaked across her face. She gave the chair in front of her desk a pointed stare.

Arix offered her most winning smile before sliding into the seat.

"Now then, as I've said, I am Desirae Penduleux, your assigned tutor for your short stay. I have no time to teach you the basics however, so most of your lessons will be taught by my assistant. He'll go over the basic letters with you to get you started. I expect you to be able to write all your letters by the end of the week, and have you reading by the end of next."

Arix felt her eyebrows slide up into her hairline. "I'm perfectly able to read, Desirae. And my *letters* are quite good."

Her tutor sniffed. "That's *Ms. Penduleux* to you. Show me."

She slid a heavy book across the desk at Arix, and smirked as the girl struggled to open the gilded cover.

Arix turned to a random page and began to read: "It follows, consequently, that the divine cannot be discussed by itself without reference to pantheonality, as we thus endeavor to do. Pantheonality belongs as necessarily and intrinsically to the divine unity as eternity does to the divine essence. If we do indeed follow the teachings of-"

"That's quite enough." Her tutor sounded annoyed as she slid her quill and paper across the desk. "Now write. I will dictate to you."

Arix knew her script was horrendous, but it was better than nothing. Her tutor dictated a few lines to her, which Arix dutifully scribbled down. After a moment of looking over the writing, Desirae scowled over the top of the paper at her new pupil.

"Well."

"Still plan on shoving me off to your assistant?"

"Indeed not. At least you will not be a total waste of my time."

"What kind of things do they want you to teach us?" Arix leaned back in the overstuffed armchair and crossed her arms over her chest. "History?"

Desirae's mouth tightened, her chin raised.

"Yes, history. But also mathematics and court etiquette and geography. We've determined you can read and write." She glanced down at Arix's script and added, "Barely."

"Yes, yes, I'm aware my script is shit. I've never been proficient at putting words down onto paper."

"No foul language. It's unbecoming." Desirae shuffled a few papers on her desk and set the large tome aside. "The fact that you can read and write will simplify things. While some of your competitors are higher class, there are still a few who came from small farming villages. Knowing you're ahead of the curve will grant you an edge that others do not have."

"It seems everyone has drawn the short straw when it comes

to me." Arix grinned as the woman pursed her lips and leaned back in her own chair. "I bet you would much rather be working with that Celeste girl. She seems to be a favorite around here."

Desirae stood, knuckles white against the table. "Enough. Let us see what holes lie in your education, shall we? Name the first kings of Rökuur."

For the remainder of the afternoon, Arix answered Desirae Penduleux's questions, as her tutor determined how much she knew in each area of study. As it turned out, Arix was well versed in continental geography, since she had spent so much of her life traversing through it. She was decent enough to get by in history, and knew basic mathematics. Though when Desirae pulled out a blackboard and started writing equations that contain letters, Arix's head went fuzzy. In court etiquette she failed miserably, which was no real surprise to either of them. She knew very little about high court or the proper names and titles for everyone who resided there. She knew absolutely nothing about military strategy, which Desirae pronounced was probably for the best, since, as she put it, "It is easier to learn something new than to replace faulty knowledge."

The two went back and forth on History, since Arix knew the stories of folklore and tradition, while her teacher knew dates and facts. It was sort of fun, when it wasn't humiliating. Their little tit-for-tat conversations were entertaining, since with every answer she gave correctly, Arix could see Desirae grow more irritated. But with every answer she did not know, her tutor's lavender eyes would smirk, as if to say *What else did I expect from a common thief?'*

"I'd ask you the difference between an oyster fork and a snail fork, but I'm afraid you wouldn't know the answer to that either, would you?" Desirae batted her lashes innocently, and made her millionth strike on the paper in front of her.

Arix slumped further down in her chair. "Why would I need to know that? Don't you just start on the outside and work your way in when it comes to cutlery and courses?"

Desirae ignored her. "When may you approach a Duke?"

"I'd much rather talk about the Black Hand." Arix dug the pad of her thumb into the soft spot of her right eye socket. The headache forming behind her eyes was reaching a throbbing point that was making her jaw tick.

"How low must you curtsey in the presence of a member of the council?"

"I mean," Arix went on, picking at the stitching on the arm-rest, "If we're competing to become the Black Hand, shouldn't we know more about it?"

"What is the correct way to hold a goblet?"

"...who was the last Black Hand..."

"Who murdered Queen Alana in the year 1049?"

"...what happened to him..."

"According to modern medicine-"

"...why magick died out..."

"-what is the most common use of the engorged dragon slug?"

Arix snorted. "The engorged dragon slug?"

Desirae gave her a steely glare across the expanse between them. "Just because you have questions does not mean I will answer them."

She paused, eyes narrowing slightly before leaning forward and clasping her hands on the desk in front of her. Something seemed to give and she gestured a hand in Arix's direction.

"What do you want to know?"

The corner of Arix's mouth turned upward into a grin. "What exactly is the Black Hand?" She leaned forward, bracing her elbows on her knees. "There are legends of course. A ghost, half dead and half alive, that lived off the blood of his enemies. A wraith imbued with dark magic, trapped in a blood contract and doomed to walk between the worlds forever."

Desirea scoffed, her lavender eyes rolling. "Goddess, commoners will believe in just about anything, won't they?"

"I'll pretend I didn't hear that bit about commoners. So what's real and what's fiction?"

A cool expression revealed nothing of what Desirae really thought as she laid out the facts. "All these stories are ridiculous. They're all based in fear rather than intellect. The Black Hand does have a contract with the king, but it isn't some wild sorcery, it's a legally binding document. It states that the incantor is on loan to the council and serves the king. The role is usually in a protectorate capacity, serving as the king's champion, solving political and military problems on behalf of the country."

"But I thought there weren't any incantors left."

"They're rare, not extinct."

"So that's what the competition is? To pick the next incantor?"

"Yes."

"Seems like a waste, if they're killing off all the K'rvi."

Desirae's mouth tightened. "I beg your pardon?"

"If there are only a few K'rvi left, it seems like a waste to-" Desirae's movement behind the desk caused Arix to pause, as the tutor suddenly stood, her chair screeching as it slid backwards.

"Do not use that term." Her voice was cold, dead.

Arix's eyebrows slid up into an arc. "K'rvi?"

Her tutor's eyes had turned to violet ice, the cold in her voice leaving Arix feeling frostbitten. "That is a slaver's word. A vulgar term used by vulgar men. It is a word of the past, thank the Goddess, but I will not have *my* pupil uttering it with such callous indifference."

Arix blinked, stunned into silence.

Desirae turned to stand behind her chair, pushing it slowly back into its place. "We're done for today. We will meet again tomorrow after lunch in this study. And in the meantime, you will read this."

Her tutor pulled a book from a low shelf and tossed it onto the desk. It landed with a thud that echoed in the small space.

"You will read it and you will educate yourself so that you will not make the same mistake again. Good day."

She turned, standing in front of the window, her back to Arix in a silent, simple command: Leave.

Arix eased the book off the desk, trying to think of a pithy comeback; a joke or something to have the last word. But she found nothing to say, so she turned and left, the small history book tucked under her arm.

Ulfur and Abbas took up positions on either side as she walked back to her room. She stared down at the book in her hands, fingers tracing the rigid blue spine as her eyes rested on the title.

A History of the Slave Trade in Rökkur: How A Country Lost Its Magick.

EIGHT

Arix stuffed another forkful of pigeon pie in her mouth, relishing the taste of the mushrooms and onions mixed in with the bird. She'd had pigeon pie before, but not like this. The crust was so flaky and buttery she wanted to cry. Her next bite was halfway into her mouth when Michael slid into the seat beside her.

"Go away. I'm enjoying my dinner."

Michael laughed, reaching across her plate for the pitcher of wine. "I can see that. Making love to your food out in the open? Scandalous."

She took another bite of pie, making sure to let out a moan while she chewed. Even though his cheeks blushed scarlet, Michael's grin only widened.

"I'm sure the chef appreciates your compliment." He chuckled. "How did your afternoon go with Ms. Penduleux?"

"She's a pompous bitch, but she's smart. So maybe I'll learn a thing or two after all."

Michael laughed again. It was a lovely laugh, light and airy.

"You don't know who she is, do you?"

Arix didn't like this game. She had played it all afternoon

with Desirae, and she was tired of feeling stupid for not knowing things. After all, there was plenty that she knew and they did not.

"Are you going to tell me, or are you going to be an ass and make me guess?"

The smile faded from his face.

"Sorry. Desirae Penduleux is a scholar at the University in Vingard. She studied under all the great masters, Poplov and Shinva and Baste, and she taught some of the most important people in the modern world. You're lucky to have her as your tutor."

"Then she really did draw the short straw with me." Arix said between bites, a smile drawing across her face. "Serves her right."

She reached for another piece of pie, the creak in her stomach having faded after the first slice. Arix glanced around the table, watching the other competitors enjoy their dinner, chatting quietly amongst themselves.

"Have you met any of the others?" Michael asked, noting her interest. "There are some very impressive people here."

"No. Why would I want to know any of them?" Her mind drifted back to the ring. Had that only been yesterday? The image of Lace's blood soaking the ground was seared into her mind.

"I just figured you would want as much strategic advantage as you could get."

Arix glanced over to see him smiling. He gestured down the table, pointing out a couple familiar faces.

"Celeste Ayala I'm sure you remember."

She did remember. She remembered the savage way that Celeste had ripped her knives out of Lace's chest. How her face had remained cold and indifferent.

"How could I forget?"

"Celeste is Lord Ayala's eldest daughter. Nobility. Her grandmother was a priestess in Sieren. She's been trained in every art imaginable. She's a favorite."

"Stuck up little rich kid with a powerful daddy? No wonder."

Michael motioned down the table with his fork, pointing out a few of the others. "I met Helios Nascha this morning at breakfast, and the one next to him is Nikolai Winter. I don't know much about them other than their fathers are connected with the military. And then there's Revena Kali."

Arix followed the line of sight from Michael's fork, watching the girl with the mass of black curly hair, her plate piled with vegetables, no meat in sight.

"She was impressive." Arix said, more to herself than to Michael.

"She is. She grew up in some sort of noble family in Zarak, but left to go out on her own when she was fourteen. I heard her tutor is going to start her on second level Nimbosian since she already knows it so well."

"I didn't even know there were levels to the Nimbosian language. I don't think I've ever heard it spoken."

Michael took a sip of his wine. "You'll hear it more in the capital. A lot of the merchants speak it, for trading purposes. My father speaks a little. He used to do a lot of trading with Nimbosia in the early days."

"Not anymore?" Arix turned to look back at Michael, noticing the pained expression. "Daddy lost some important customers, did he?"

Michael's eyes shifted down and away, focusing on the glass of wine in his hand. "There's been a lot of fear about the Carn's movements. That they're watching the trade routes. We had some interceptions and merchandise was lost. Nimbosia has cut a lot of ties with us. The country is losing money."

A knot formed in Arix's stomach. "I didn't know that."

"Not many do." Michael finally looked at her. "It might be why the king is enacting a Black Hand. The Carn are getting more bold, more unstable. They attacked Ewithwark and burned the city to the ground. A lot of good people died just because the Carn didn't get their way."

Arix casually pushed her plate away, and put on her most winning smile. "There's always someone trying to stir up the pot. I don't plan on ruining a good dinner with all this depressing talk of the Carn."

Michael had not moved, his eyebrows still huddled together, blue eyes clouded with worry.

"Besides," Arix gave him a light punch in the arm. "That witch tutor of mine gave me homework already and I need to get started."

He made a move to say something, but Arix strode away, her hands stuffed into the pockets of her skirt, whistling a tune as she went. She didn't want to hear it. She didn't want to hear any more of the Carn or buildings burning or people dying. She'd had enough of that to last her whole lifetime.

~

After spending an hour flipping through the book, Arix had read enough. The writings of *A History of the Slave Trade in Rökkur* was boring as dirt, turning what should have been an interestingly awful tale into one so filled with dates and facts that it was clear the author had never been entertained in their life.

Most of the facts she already knew: Back when magick had been common, those who possessed magickal blood were one in a hundred. But over the years, magick had begun to die out and the number became one in a thousand, then one in ten thousand. The slave trade had specialized in those with magickal blood, targeting rich and prominent families who would pay a pretty penny for an adopted daughter or son with with magickal blood.

Arix had always heard the term *K'rvi* as a slang for those with magickal blood. She hadn't known that it had originated from the slavers who made their livelihood on the blood of innocents. And she would not be using it again.

Tossing the book into the window seat, Arix climbed into bed, determined to get enough sleep tonight. If today was any indicator, she'd be up before the sun tomorrow, running laps with Tobias.

But instead of falling into sleep like she had expected, Arix spent the next couple hours fitfully rolling in the covers, the sheets tangling her legs and making her feel panicked. She needed air. Fresh air.

Throwing on a blanket and stuffing her feet into her slippers, she eased open her door to find two new guards outside. She nodded to them, padding down the stairs as they followed behind her at a distance. Downstairs, Arix slipped out the side door and stepped into the night air.

The moon was a bright sliver of light in the sky as she picked her way down the white gravel trail into the gardens. The lighting caused long shadows to cloud the path, their strange shapes dancing on the ground. White roses gleamed blue and lavender, the bushes teal and black in the darkness.

Arix ran her hand over the tops of the hedges, fingers skimming across the leaves. Her father had taken her to a garden like this once in Vingard when she was little, and carried her on his shoulders when she got tired. She remembered arches and mazes filled with flowers, their blooms happy under the summer sun. Being in a garden at night was a completely different experience, the heady floral scent filled the air, yet the sight of beauty in darkness turned the place foreboding, as if it had a dark secret that it would keep till the grave.

Turning, she looked back at the castle, the dark towers nearly touching the moon above. What things it had seen. Ever watching as history streamed through it. Kings and queens crowned and killed, death and life as cultures shifted. Its ever present towers looming, a silent observer of Mergur's history.

"She is beautiful at night."

Arix whirled to see a cloaked figure resting on a bench.

The figure raised an arm in her direction. As if trying to soothe a startled horse. "I didn't mean to disturb you. Very few people are usually out in the garden at night."

The voice was low and velvety smooth.

"You didn't disturb me." Arix stepped backwards, eyeing the stranger, and watching the guards that stayed a distance away. "I just needed some fresh air."

The figure leaned back against the bench and Arix hesitantly sat beside him, leaving a bit of space between them on the seat.

"So what are you doing out here in the middle of the night?" Arix pulled her knees up, wrapping the blanket tighter around herself. She should have brought something warmer. The air was already starting to shift away from summer, the nighttime cool enough to need a wrap.

Tipping his head to the side, the figure stared up at the moon, arms crossed over his chest. "I couldn't sleep either. And though I had intended to sit out here alone, I'll admit that I could use the company."

Arix's voice took on a soothing tone as she rested her cheek on her knees to look sideways at him. "Good thing I came along then. I'm a good listener, you know. If you've got something on your mind, I'll be glad to offer an ear."

She had played this part before. The lost, sweet, whimsical woman, ready to lend an ear, lend an arm, lend a helping hand to her bed, all if it meant she could gather the information she wanted.

"No…" He sighed, heavy and slightly hitched. "I will not trouble you. Though if you could not sleep, perhaps there is some burden you wish to bestow on a stranger?"

"No…" Arix matched his tone and his sigh. "As you said, we don't know one another."

"What if I tell you my name?" He asked. "Then we can pretend we're old friends, and unburden ourselves."

Arix laughed before she could stop herself. She could see part of his face when he turned toward her, the slight stubble along his chin, the strong jaw beneath. A smile hidden there as well, shadowed under the hood of his cloak.

"I am Arduinna."

"I am Osiris."

She laughed again. "No you aren't."

"Neither are you Arduinna."

Her smile faded. "You know me?"

The hood tilted as he studied her. "I do."

There was a tug at her insides. That feeling was back, like she was the last to know a joke, the only stupid one in the room. She'd been made to feel inferior all day, and she was sick of it. Her sweet demeanor dropped like a stone.

"You know me, but I don't know you." She stood from the bench, wrapping the blanket tighter around her shoulders, her voice clipped. "Seems like an unfair advantage."

His hand rose in the air and Arix flinched, stepping further away from him. The hand froze in mid-air, then fell limp into his lap.

"I've upset you. I apologize."

He rose slowly, his looming shadow towering over Arix. She took another step back. Goddess, he was tall.

Slowly Osiris bowed, then turned away back toward the path, disappearing into the shadows of the garden.

Arix stood on the crushed gravel, a shiver of cold running down her spine as she clutched the blanket tighter around her. She'd reacted badly. She could have played the game, learned who he was. But the day's exhaustion was getting to her.

She'd chosen the name of the Goddess Arduinna on a whim. She hadn't thought he would know her face, call her out on her deception. And he had named himself Osiris.

Another shiver ran down her spine, but this time, the chill was accompanied with a hot blush that crept up her neck.

He had named himself Osiris, god of death. And as lore told it, Arduinna's lover. It was the name she had given her horse that very morning. A coincidence?

She took her time walking the white stone paths before her cold feet drove her back inside and up to her room. The heavy down comforter folded her into its depths as she curled into a ball, pillow wedged between her cheek and arm. She was finally tired, her head fuzzy and heavy, mind reeling. Too much had happened today. Too much to process. She needed rest.

And so she slept, finally, the moon watching over her as she drifted off. Watched her while she dreamed of the cloaked man with the velvet laugh.

NINE

Tobias did not have to wake her the next morning. When he arrived at the barn, Arix was already waiting for him, her ever present guards like shadows on her heels as they ran through the woods. For some unimaginable reason, her ribs ached more today than they had yesterday, and try as she might, she still had to stop twice to dry heave alongside the path. Yet still, she pressed on, her mouth a thin line against the raging wave of curses in her head.

This morning when she had awoken, she'd stared out the window at the gray dawn, fists clenched at her sides. She had always made her own path, beating one into existence if she needed to. When she was cornered she had always found a way out, always charmed and talked her way to her freedom. And it had worked. For years and years it had worked and she had slipped between the law's fingers like a little minnow, too small to pay much attention to, and too slippery to ever hold on to for long.

Until now.

She'd let her guard down. She'd been caught. She knew the reality of her situation, the reality of the price she would pay for all those years of theft. But it had not come. Instead she was here.

Running at the crack of dawn with a bunch of spoiled rich brats, greased and bribed into this competition to become the Black Hand.

She had arrived here battered and confused. And she was still battered and confused, though for different reasons. But if Arix was anything, it was a survivor. She would keep her head down and she would work her tail off and then…

Then what?

A tightening grip of panic was squeezing her insides, fighting with her will to remain calm, to keep running. But what in the hell was she actually doing here? She would be going up against professionals. People who had trained their entire lives to be here, now. She was a gutter rat, a common thief, and they were the best glistening jewels the country had to offer the king. And yet…here she was.

To be here, she had to have magick in her blood. But there was no way it was possible. People with magickal blood didn't end up on the streets. People with magickal blood were rare, almost extinct, and they were kept safe and secure. She'd lived on the streets most of her life. There was nothing rare about her. Nothing about her to be kept safe and secure.

There was another option that weighed heavy in her mind, pulling her deep into her boots, causing her toes to trip on imaginary roots. What if they had made a mistake? What if Lakai had been wrong and she had no magickal blood in her? How quickly would they slit her throat and pretend she had never existed at all?

Arix chanced a glance behind her at Ulfur and Abbas as they kept pace a few lengths behind her. Abbas watched her with slitted eyes, as if waiting for her to make a run for it. To give him a reason to raise his spear and strike at her.

She tucked her chin into her chest and focused on her breathing. There was a decision to be made. And she knew what she had to do. Now she just needed to wait for the opportunity to do it.

To run. To get out before they could look at her too closely. Before Desirae or Lord Bardon or Lakai could realize that she wasn't special. She had no magickal blood. She was nothing more than a common thief.

~

All day Arix waited, biding her time and watching for a way out. Abbas and Ulfur were always at her heels, following her to meals and down hallways. Only during her lesson and when she was alone in her room did they remain in the hallway.

It wasn't until dinner that Arix saw the opening she had been waiting for. A servant, carrying a tray of food, slipped just as he was passing behind Arix's chair. There was a clang of metal as the tray bounced off the stone floor, and Arix used the distraction to kick a poor competitor across from her in the shin under the table.

It wasn't much. Just a well placed distraction and a bit of con-fusion, but she had done more with less. She slipped a seat over and grabbed up Celeste's blue cloak as she sidestepped the mess and headed for a side door. By the time Abbas and Ulfur would realize they'd lost her, she'd be gone.

The stable was quiet, everyone still eating in the dining hall. There was one stable hand at the far end, though he only glanced up to nod at her before returning to his work. Arix saddled her horse quickly, throwing off the bright blue of Celeste's cloak and depositing it into a nearby water trough.

"Journey planned?"

Arix spun at the sound.

"Anywhere specific?" Michael was leaning against the door to her stall, an apple in hand.

Arix kept her gaze trained to him. "Just out on a ride."

"That was quite a display up there. Nikolai is going to have a bruised shin for a week because of you."

Arix gave him her most sweet smile. "Whatever do you mean?"

He took a bite from his apple and motioned to the saddled horse behind her. "That's a terrible idea you know. They'll hunt you down."

"I'm just going out for a nice ride. Please move."

Michael moved passed her, rubbing Osiris's nose and feeding him the rest of the apple. "Did you forget the gate? With all those guards?"

"I wasn't going to leave through the gate."

"And what about the wall? It goes around the whole castle grounds, you know. You'd have to climb that."

Arix crossed her arms. "I suppose I would."

"Did you forget about the moat? I hear a giant squid lives in there to keep anyone from swimming across."

"That's not funny."

"I'm not joking, Arix." Michael finally turned to look at her, frustration clouding his eyes. "If they catch you, they'll kill you for sure. No hesitations."

Arix cursed under her breath. "What do you want, Michael? We are competitors, after all."

"Can't we be friends instead?" He offered with a smile.

"No."

"Didn't think so. Well fine then," He brushed his hands on the outside of his jacket. "But you should know that I don't see you as competition. I'd much rather see you as a friend."

"You wouldn't be happy to see me go? One less person to compete against?"

"No, I wouldn't. But I believe we're down to fourteen. Including, of course, yourself and I. If you leave, it'll be only thirteen." He paused, head tilting slightly as he stared at her. His eyes twinkled the blue of the summer sky. "I didn't take you for a coward, you know."

Arix shoved him, his shoulder slamming into the wall of the stall.

"Call me a coward again."

Michael grinned.

The two stared at each other for a moment before Arix let him go and stepped back. "I'm not scared. I just shouldn't be here."

Michael shrugged before turning and entering the adjoining stall. Arix watched as he began saddling up his horse.

"What are you doing?"

"Going with you." He responded simply, sliding the bridle over Luminess's head. "We can watch each other's backs."

Arix chuckled, her eyebrows raised. "You're going to escape with me?"

"Why not? Sounds like an adventure."

"They'll kill you if you get caught."

"Us. They'll kill *us*."

Arix pulled herself into the saddle and adjusted her stirrups. "They won't catch me."

Michael moved his horse up alongside her, a satisfied smirk gracing his features. "They already did."

They clopped steadily out of the barn, Michael following her lead as Arix rode out to the open field. Anyone watching might assume the two were just heading out for an evening jaunt. Once they were out of direct sight from the castle, Arix turned toward the wall, picking up pace as they cut through the wood to reach it. Nearing the edge, the two riders slowed, and Arix dismounted, sneaking forward on foot to study the wall.

There were two guards that were walking along its edge, chatting quietly as they paced against the great towering stone. Arix hunkered down behind the foliage and remained hidden as the pair passed and continued on down the wall.

"They'll rotate by again in about twenty minutes." Michael's hushed voice beside her came whispering across her shoulder and Arix turned to stare at him.

"How do you know that?"

He shrugged. "I've been here two weeks already. I've paid attention." When she continued to stare, his mouth slowly twisted into a grin. "You aren't the only one who's thought about running away."

They waited a few more moments, then Arix stepped out slowly, watching the pair fade into the distance.

The wall of stone was smooth with only a few small handholds with which to scale it. A simple criminal wouldn't have the skills to climb it. Fortunately, Arix was pretty good and clamoring up stone walls and across rooftops. Wiggling her toes in her boot, she settled her foot on a cleft and shoved her body upwards, reaching for the handhold just above her head. It was difficult, yes, but Arix kept her eyes above her, searching for holds as she slowly ascended the wall.

Michael was coming up beneath her, much slower. He was slowing her down.

While she climbed, Arix noted globs of black ooze that occasionally dribbled down the stone. Thick oily stuff that had clearly been splashed down the wall. Near the top, she made a mistake of placing her fingers between two stones where the ooze had collected, and her heart slammed into her throat when she lost her grip, catching herself only with her other hand. As she neared the top of the wall, more and more of the stone was splattered with the black oil, and she slowed to barely a crawl.

Beneath her ribs her heart was hammering like a gong, and she glanced down, seeing Michael had yet to reach even half way up the wall. Twenty minutes would be up soon and if he didn't hurry, they'd find him and shoot him off the wall. Didn't matter if he was a noble's child or not, they would shoot to kill all the same.

A part of her felt bad that he would die. He was friendly and optimistic. But he was slow.

Her thighs were quaking and the tips of her fingers were rubbed raw by the time she finally reached the top. Exhaustion wracked her form, but she kept low as she hauled herself up onto the top of the thick stone. She peered over the edge on the other side and her heart collapsed into her stomach.

Michael had been right.

This new side of the wall was so covered in the black sludge that the stones were a solid color of deep ink. Down below her, the ground on the other side was covered in great iron spikes. If she attempted to climb down and slipped, those spikes would be waiting to catch her fall. If by some miracle she made it past the oil and the spikes, there was a moat, the water murky and dark green, stretching between herself and the second wall. The bank on the opposite side of the water was crawling with soldiers, and the stones that made up the second wall were also coated in the black oil.

The exhaustion of climbing mixed well with her frustration and disappointment at the sight. There would be no easy escaping Castle Zma'ai, at least not over the wall. If she had been anyone else, she might have cried, or laid down on the top of the wall and cursed. But she was not anyone else. She would find another way to escape. It was still early days. Another opportunity would present itself and she would go. Maybe leave Rökkur altogether. But she would find a way.

Shoving her emotions aside, Arix climbed back over the edge and made her way back down. Michael noticed her descent and did the same. The two neared the bottom at the same time, throwing themselves back into the woods just in time for the two soldiers to come back into sight, unaware what had just transpired.

The two competitors waited in silence until the men had passed and were out of earshot before Michael turned, his legs splayed out on the ground, breathing so hard his chest rose and fell in great gulps.

"What did you see?" he asked around the mouthfuls of air.

Arix wiped a gob of tar off her boot and onto the grass. "Easy climb on the other side. There's even a ladder built into the stones. And then a straight line to the docks. Simple."

Michael stared at her. "That bad, huh?"

Arix began quick work on her other boot, taking the time to clean off any of the oil, and refused to look at him. She stood, offering Michael her arm. "I just couldn't leave you stranded like a cat stuck in a tree. They'd shoot you for sure."

He allowed her to haul him up to a standing position and grinned. "So you're telling me you had a chance at escape, free and clear, and you came back for me?"

"Let's be clear. I only did it out of sheer pity for the poor little noble boy, Michael Woodhale. I do rather have a big heart you know." Arix kept her face serious, but her eyes betrayed a small smile and she clapped him on the back as they returned to their horses.

"You know I'm not nobility, right?"

Arix shrugged. "Still a snotty rich boy."

"Does this make us friends now, Arix Sable?"

Arix glanced back at him and grinned. "Only if you beat me back to the stable on that old nag of yours." Then she was off, with barely a glance behind her.

When they reached the stables, Arix blamed her loss on Osiris, claiming he was too big and clumsy for his own good. Yet even though he had lost the race, Arix gave him a peck on the nose before leaving him in the stable. Next time, she wouldn't let Michael win.

There would be another chance to leave. She would make sure of it.

TEN

By the end of the second week, Arix had finished her morning run only once without vomiting up bile onto the forest floor. Each day she found new muscles she hadn't known existed, thanks to Tobias and his rigorous training schedule. They continued working on horsemanship skills, and added in basic swordsmanship and footwork. She was rusty, but her long lost lessons in wielding a blade were slowly coming back.

Each day fell into the same pattern, the hours weaving together in a comfortable cycle. In the morning she would run and train with Tobias. Then it was a bath and lunch, either in her room or in the main hall. Lessons with Desirae took up the afternoon, often ending in the two debating over the accuracy of one historic tale or another. Since the mythos of the country's origin varied so widely depending on where you were from, there was no single agreed upon legend, though there were details that overlapped.

The creation story was beautiful and tragic and Arix loved every second of it. The story of the gods were so honest, so true. Their story told both the good, their youthful lives filled with joy and promise, as well as the bad, ruined by pride and selfishness.

Arix felt drawn to the gods and goddesses, but to Kaoss most of all. It was the true story of motherhood, of sacrifice and giving gifts to your children in the hopes that they may better the world. Maybe she loved the story because she had not known her own mother, the nurturing comfort she never had. Or maybe it was just because she loved tragic stories.

There was one part of the story that always drew her attention, and it hovered there still, in the back of her mind, as she stared out the window of an alcove, the textbooks in her arms forgotten. Osiris, the god of death. It had been the very story of creation that she had thought of when she'd named herself after the goddess Arduinna, Kaoss's eldest daughter. And when the stranger had named himself Osiris, Arduinna's lover, she'd been frustrated. She didn't like not knowing who he was.

Since that night, Arix had played over their conversation in her mind, and looked for his shadowed face in the halls of the castle. Two weeks had passed since they had first met there under the thumbnail of the moon, yet she often found herself awake in the middle of the night, daring herself to go for another moonlit walk. She had, once, about a week after her arrival, and had sat on the bench, her curiosity urging in impatient whispers. But he did not come.

She was convinced he was another competitor, hiding his face to keep her from knowing him. Some ruse to find out more about the enemy, as Arix kept mostly to herself, and only occasionally spent study time with Michael. But she didn't see Michael as competition. Sure, he was in the same space as her, working towards the same goal, but only because the two of them had no other choice. Besides, Michael and her only talked about meaningless drivel. Lesson plans and occasionally comparing study notes on the histories of Rökkur.

He had continued to keep his eye on her since their escapade at the wall, pulling up a chair next to her during meals, and attempting small talk whenever passing each other in the stables. Try as she might to ignore him at first, Arix couldn't shake the fact that it felt good to have someone to joke with, even if deep in her gut she knew she should keep her distance. She found herself laughing often while around him, the tension between them dissipating.

"I swear, if I have to hear one more thing about Lord Ashain and his stupid policy regarding Nero's temples, I'm going to throw myself into the moat." Michael proclaimed, making Arix jump. He threw a stack of books at Arix' feet and deposited himself into the same window seat.

"Will you mourn me, Arix? When I've been devoured by monsters over council policy?"

It had become a joke between them ever since their trip to the wall that no one could survive the moat, since it was allegedly filled with giant squid and poplait fish, mouths brimming with barbed teeth.

Glancing over the top of her copy of *Trade Routes: The Isle of Sama Volume IV*, a tome undoubtedly written by a group of stuffy old men, Arix grinned.

"The one about spiritual orgies or how the high priestesses should wear a veil?"

"The orgies." Michael's eyes twinkled. "One day I'm going to Nero to spend a whole week in the Temple of Zeyneba."

Chuckling, Arix tossed her book into the discarded pile on the floor, and picked up one of Michael's history books.

"I'm still waiting for my invitation to come with you, though maybe you'd want some privacy." Arix' eyes went wide in feigned surprised. "I can't possibly imagine what you'd want to do there."

"You got it easy, you know." Michael grumbled, his boot pushing at Arix's knee. He slumped against the window, and Arix couldn't help thinking it made him look like a petulant child. "Desirae is interesting and mysterious, and she doesn't make mathematics sound like the droning of a water wheel."

"Believe me, she's not all that mysterious."

Arix watched as two competitors went by them, noses stuck to the words of their books. Arix leaned forward and motioned for Michael to do the same.

"Have you gotten a chance to meet everyone yet?" She motioned with her head to the two who were now nearing the end of the hall.

"The boy is Nikolai Winter, and of course you already know Revena Kali. I know some of them, but there are a few who keep to themselves. Revena tends to keep to herself, although I have seen her talk with Nik a bit. Poor kid's lovestruck over her and she only talks to him because he's a literary genius. She's been using him as a second tutor, which is devious. Smart, but devious."

"Anyone named Osiris?"

Michael glanced at her. "Like the god of death?"

Arix shrugged. It was a long shot anyways.

"No one named Osiris that I know of. But I haven't had the chance to meet everyone yet, though Master Yano says I should be studying their habits."

Arix punched him in the shoulder and grinned. "Is that why you hang around me? Hoping to learn my secrets, are you?"

"Maybe." Michael crossed his arms and smirked, lowering his voice and mimicking his tutor's Zarakian accent. "Now that I've discovered your deep fear of giant moat squid, I have a good grasp on what it will take to finally beat you."

Arix was trying not to snort, the question about Osiris forgotten.

"If he hears you, you're dead."

"I know, I know." Michael stood, stretching his arms above his head and let out a jaw snapping yawn. "I better get back. Master Yano wants to quiz me on court appeals, and I have to go study up a bit. I'll see you at lunch tomorrow?"

"Alright. Save me a seat though. Tobias got me a slot on the masseuse' schedule for tomorrow after training, so I'll be late to lunch."

Michael grabbed up his books and handed Volume IV back to Arix, waving as he disappeared around the corner.

Sighing, Arix took her book back with her to her room, throwing it into the growing pile of textbooks that had already accumulated for her to read during her evenings. At the beginning, she had devoured the books that Desirae had given her, each word like drops of rain after trudging through a desert. After so long without books to read, it had been nice to take up her evenings and late into the early morning hours reading, sucking dry the information within. But there was only so much a book on historical trade routes could do for a mind that thrived off of a good story.

Arix changed into her nightgown and let Wren braid up her hair before she tucked herself into the large bed, pulling out the mountains of homework Desirae had given her. After a few chapters, Arix's mind was fuzzy, the numbers on the page turning lopsided. With a groan she shoved the books away, collapsing back to stare at the ceiling.

Her mind wandered back to Michael. He was friendly, a stupid grin always plastered on his face. It had been so long since she'd had a true companion, a true friend, that she wasn't sure what that really meant anymore. Would he consider her a friend? A companion? Or just someone to share jokes with? She didn't know. Arix found that it bothered her more than she expected that she couldn't accurately pinpoint who he was to her.

Throwing off the covers, she grabbed a blanket off the edge of the bed, wrapping it around herself as her bare feet tiptoed across the stone and carpeted floor and out of her room. She followed the long hallway down the stairs and into the entrance hall. She needed to think, and thinking was best done outside.

~

The two night guards posted just outside the door nodded to her as she stepped between them, her nightly strolls now a sort of routine. Her pace was slow as she made her way down the path, the gravel digging into her bare feet. Pausing under a rose archway, Arix stared at her feet, too lost in thought to notice another figure.

"Hello, Arduinna."

Arix started. Her eyes drifted through the darkness and landed on the hooded form.

"Osiris." she breathed out, thoughts of Michael dissipating like sugar in water.

"Once again, we're meeting in the moonlight." His voice was as low as Arix remembered, and velvety smooth.

She glanced up, but the moon had gone behind a cloud, the edges of its ring barely shining through.

Osiris took a few steps forward until he was under the same archway. The space was confined now with the two of them under the eaves of the leafy climbing roses.

"It's good to see you again." She breathed.

"I'm surprised you think so. I apologize if I offended you last time."

The back of Arix's throat burned. "It had been a long day."

Osiris picked at a rosebud, about to bloom, and handed it to Arix. "You don't like being left in the dark."

She took the bud, twiddling it between her fingers. "I usually pride myself on knowing everyone else's secrets."

The stranger leaned against the side of the trellis, watching her. Even though she couldn't see his face, a shiver ran down her spine, her skin goosebumping under his gaze.

"You do not know me? Truly?"

"No." Arix tilted her head, searching for his features in the darkness. "Are you going to tell me? What are you hiding under that hood?"

"Does it matter? What if I am an ugly old man with warts and skin so stretched and worn that it looks like leather?"

She snorted, a grin pulling at the corner of her mouth. "I suppose if you were old and ugly then I'd have to ask for the wisdom of your many years."

"And if I am a handsome young stable boy who just might try and sweep you off your feet?"

"Then I suppose I'd have to reprimand you for not feeding Osiris those apples I left out."

The hood tilted to the side.

"And what if I am the old mad king?"

Arix paused, studying him carefully. "Then I suppose I would bow and beg your humble pardon for traipsing across your gardens in the middle of the night."

Osiris chuckled. "I'm sure he wouldn't mind either way. The poor man never leaves his tower."

Arix instinctively glanced over his shoulder at the looming castle behind them, and Osiris turned to look as well.

"Well, if you aren't an old man or a stable boy or the king, then who are you? I'll admit, I've been wondering ever since we first met."

The figure turned back, and Arix could faintly make out the lines of his jaw and nose as he smiled.

"Perhaps I shall remain a mystery. Known only as Osiris. Then none of my truths will come to light, and I may stay ever in your good graces. Wouldn't not knowing be better? I can only disappoint you if you know."

The two stood in silence for a moment, Arix staring hard at the hooded face, trying to trace out any details of what lay underneath.

"Who are you?" She whispered.

"Is Osiris not enough?"

"No." Arix took a breath. "It's not."

Her hand reached up, slowly, her fingers brushing the edge of the fabric of his hood. Osiris reactively grabbed her wrist, stopping her in mid-air. The air stilled around them, his grip loosening after a moment, letting Arix slowly push back the hood, his hand still wrapped around her wrist. Arix let out a breath, suddenly very aware of how close they stood. He was beautiful, with devastating deep blue eyes and a straight strong jaw. Shoulder length dark hair pulled back from his face. He was in his late-thirties, lines already forming around his eyes. He kept his grip on her arm, looser now, his thumb sliding over the soft skin of her inner wrist.

"Disappointed?"

"Not at all."

He smiled, revealing straight white teeth and a dimple in his left cheek. "You still don't know who I am?"

Arix shrugged off the fluttering in her stomach, twisting casually to admire the roses around them. "Contrary to popular belief,

I don't actually know everyone at the castle. I've only been here two weeks."

"And yet, you are disappointed. A little bit. Why is that?"

Her knee was twitching, something that only happened when she was actually nervous. Why was she so damn nervous?

"I've just been trying to guess who you are this whole time, and now that I've seen your face, I still don't know who you are."

"You can keep calling me Osiris if you want. It's a better name than the one I was given."

"But why are you here in the castle? I've never seen you."

His grin turned mischievous. "Or maybe you've seen me but you don't remember. Because I've seen you, Bellarix Sable."

Arix lost the grip on her blanket and it slid to the ground at her feet. Her heart was racing a mile a minute.

"Am I that easy to spot?"

Osiris reached out, hand hovering in mid-air, reaching for a loose tendril that spilled across Arix's cheek. His fingers paused for a moment and then fell to his side as he nodded to her hair. "You're hard to miss."

Arix's breath stopped in her throat. Had he meant to touch her hair? She'd been around bold men before, men who thought they owned her. But while they had made her skin crawl, this touch made her scalp tingle, and shivers run down her back.

Mistaking the shiver for a lack of warmth, Osiris removed his cloak without hesitation and placed it over Arix's shoulders, clasping it over her thundering heart.

"Don't want you freezing to death out here. It would be a shame to lose a competitor to the cold."

Arix managed out a small smile, though her mind raced. Even in the cool dark, Arix could tell that Osiris was dressed well, and his cloak was finely crafted. He held his arm out to her and she took it, resting her palm against the crook of his arm. Beneath the fabric he was strong, muscles shifting as he led her back towards the castle, picking up her fallen blanket.

"I think maybe it's time we get you back to your room. You'll need your rest for the party tomorrow."

Arix glanced up at him, noting the light stubble on his jaw. "What party?"

"Oops." He grinned down at her. "I wasn't supposed to share that just yet. Pretend I didn't say anything."

"I'll do my best." It would have been easy to flirt back, to press herself into his side and pout. She could easily play the part of the preening lady, and pull him back into the gardens. It would certainly be a nice distraction. But something told her that he was not someone you could fool. Not someone you played with.

"Does this mean I'm going to be seeing you around more?" she asked.

They entered through the doors and made their way up the steps toward Arix's room. She was only vaguely aware of the guards that trailed a respectable distance behind them.

"Perhaps. Although we don't run in the same circles. You have your studying, and I have my own matters to attend to."

They neared Arix's door, and she made a motion to remove the cloak from her shoulders. Osiris's hand stopped her.

"Keep it. It suits you."

"Thanks." Her fingers slipped over the fabric, the thick material sliding smoothly beneath her hands.

"You're most welcome."

"Thank you for walking me back to my room. Though I'll admit, it's weird that you know where I live."

He smiled sheepishly, and Arix thought her heart may have melted a bit. He truly was beautiful. "Sorry. I know a lot about this castle. I've lived here for a while."

"And I've only been here two weeks."

"I make it my business to know the people who reside in these walls."

"Very mysterious." Arix breathed.

Osiris reached out, and Arix placed her hand in his as he leaned forward and kissed it. "I must ask a favor of you before I bid you goodnight."

"Yes?"

"When you see me tomorrow, pretend you don't know me. My position here allows me certain freedoms, but strolling through the gardens at night with a beautiful young woman sends the wrong message. Would you do me the honor of keeping this little rendezvous a secret?"

Arix hesitated, the rosy feeling in her stomach fading a little. "Is it because I'm a competitor or because I'm a thief?"

His lips pulled back into a smile. "Your status as a competitor. If you and I are seen alone together, it will compromise your place, and my role as well. Your past has next to nothing to do with your future, Arduinna."

"You might as well just call me Arix now, since you know who I am."

He let out a small, almost wistful sigh. "I suppose I could, couldn't I?"

Slowly he rotated her hand and kissed the palm as well. Arix shuddered slightly, his lips lingering on the spot.

"Goodnight, Arduinna."

"Goodnight, Osiris."

After the door was closed, and after Arix had returned to bed, her heart thudding in her chest, she slipped her fingers across her breasts and down her stomach; her palm still burning from the kiss he had left there. She imagined that her fingers were replaced with his as she slid that hand between her legs, back arching under the touch. Every stroke brought her closer to climax, the cool sheets clinging to her sensitive skin as she thought of his face, imagined the press of his body against hers. The corded muscle of his arms holding her to him as she reached the pinnacle.

Her hair was splayed around her, tangled in sweat and the hungry scent of desire and release as she fell asleep. She dreamed of nothing. Nothing but his breath against her palm.

ELEVEN

Arix squeezed her eyes shut and drew in her breath in short wisps. The corset under her dress was pressing sharply against her ribs, and even though Wren had promised to keep the strings loose, Arix could not help looking sharply over her shoulder at the girl after the ordeal was over.

"This is ridiculous." Arix mumbled, "I can't breathe."

"Of course you can." Wren said matter-of-factly. "And I should have made it tighter still. Now for your hair."

Arix rolled her eyes. Fancy shoes had never offered assistance in a hasty retreat in the pasty, and she doubted they would help her now.

"You seem rather excited, Wren, considering it's only dinner."

Wren spun from the vanity and stared at her. "Only dinner?! It is a banquet celebrating the first harvest of the year! And you'll be meeting all of the important people of the court, and you'll get to stuff yourself on every delicacy that Rökkur has to offer. And dancing! Miss Arix, you haven't truly been to a party until you've been a King's party at Castle Zma'ai."

Arix's heart skipped a beat, and she sat up straight.

"The king will be there?"

"Well, no. But the parties are thrown on his behalf by the council. Really they're just a way to keep the court from being bored." Wren replied, her words muffled by the bouquet of hairpins sticking from between her lips.

Arix slumped back down in her chair.

"I'm not really a fan of parties. It's just a bunch of people preening and giggling and secretly hating each other. I've been to enough to know."

Wren came around to face her and pulled the pins from her mouth. "You won't be stealing from this one. You'll have a chance to make connections, and meet the council. Chef's been preparing all week for this, and I promise you, the swan is to die for."

While Wren tittered over her hair, Arix stared down the stranger in the mirror. She'd been this dressed up before, for cons she had run in the past. She should be used to the feeling of being trussed up, yet a small darkness roiled in her belly. She had always dreamed of being dressed up like a princess, what child hadn't wished for it? But now that she was here, about to go to a party she could actually *enjoy*, she felt strings of guilt tying tighter around her heart, cutting off circulation, cutting off the bliss of being decked in jewels from head to toe. What game was she playing at?

"There. What do you think?" Wren stepped back, biting her lip as she surveyed her work.

Arix smiled at her through the reflection in the glass. "It's beautiful, Wren. Thank you."

Wren offered her a beaming smile in return. "You're beautiful."

Ulfur and Abbas were waiting for her in the hallway, the former offering a low whistle as she slowly spun for them.

"What do you think? Good enough for Castle Zma'ai?"

"Ye be looking fine enough to charm a whole duchy, tha's for sure!" Ulfur pretended to wipe away a tear. "Our little thief is growin' up."

Arix curtsied low and followed after them as the two guards escorted her down to the banquet hall. The hum of guests milling about seemed like a roar from the top of the stairs. Candles lit the deep ceilinged room, and a great chandelier hung like a flying swan above the guests underneath.

Arix was ushered into line with the rest of the competitors, and they were announced one by one as they came down the main staircase and into the hall. Each was brought to a name place at the table, seated by some dignitary, advisor, or men and women of the court. As the seat was pushed in under her, Arix tried to remember everything she had learned recently. Not that she was absolutely perfect at it just yet, as Desirae liked to often point out during their lessons.

The man to her left was a bishop, old and well liked in court for his jovial nature and love for fine wine and music. To her right was Madame Bouchard, the Duchess of Piana, a coastal city in Eldur. Arix made conversation with the latter, commenting on the splendor of the room, and then proceeded to listen while the lady gushed over the lavishness of King Taurus and his generosity in allowing them a visit in court for such a long period of time.

"Did the king himself invite you?" Arix asked curiously.

"Of course not! When we arrived, we were welcomed immediately and ushered to our quarters in the castle," said Madame Bouchard, waving down a servant carrying the wine pitcher. "The king need not invite his favorite cousin to stay."

Arix smiled politely, "When did you arrive at court?"

Madame Bouchard smiled and patted Arix's hand. "Why, as

soon as we heard of the competition, we set out at once. My dear daughter, Ciel, is competing herself you know."

The lady seemed rather proud of herself as she pointed down the table to the chocolate haired beauty. Arix had seen her once or twice before, but didn't know the girl well at all.

"There she is in the violet satin. A position as the Black Hand would be agreeable for her future, and I do believe the court has already taken a liking to her."

Bouchard was right. Ciel laughed daintily as she sipped her wine, lashes batting at the men around her vying for her attention. Arix could not help but think of a siren off the coasts of Nero, luring men to their death by way of her beauty.

"And you, my dear? What position do you hold in court?" Madame asked, a light smile on her face.

"I am competing as well."

The smile faded. "Oh you are." It was not a question. "And where are you from, girl?" Her voice held a slight edge, and the dear lady made no attempt to conceal it.

"Eldur." said Arix, only slightly uncomfortable. She could easily lie and make up some large well to do family name and claim her birthright, and yet she felt that this was a place she did not want to start making things up. "I grew up in Hythe. It's a coastal town off of-."

"I haven't heard of it." Said the lady, cutting her off, her lip raising a bit at the corner. "And your family?"

"My father was a blacksmith." Arix knew this would not receive a nod of approval.

Madame Bouchard sat straighter in her seat and sniffed at Arix, her nose raising a considerable amount as she shifted to her right, further away.

"Peasants should not be allowed the same roles in court that are allowed to the elite." And with that, Madame Bouchard turned away to engage in conversation with someone else.

Arix stared down at her plate, piled high with fruits, mainly peaches. Her anger was seething underneath her skin, and she could feel her ears had gone hot. Why had she told this pompous poodle about her father? She knew Madame Bouchard was right; she didn't belong here or in this fancy dress or even in the castle. Her place was taking from these people, not living among them.

"Don't mind Aphelia," said the voice to her left.

Arix turned as the bishop stole one of her grapes, "She has a chip on her shoulder that is tipping her scales." His smile was genuine, yet the pentagram engraved pendant around his neck made Arix feel self conscious.

"Do you know her well?" She asked as the man picked up his goblet only to discover he'd already drunk its contents.

"From court only, though her reputation spreads far for sticking her bulbous nose into things beyond her business." The old man tapped his nose as he said it. "Pay her word no mind. The great Goddess loves all her children, even those from Hythe." He winked then and stole another grape, motioning to one of the servers with his other hand.

Arix' gaze traveled down the table as the other guests feasted. This was not her scene; making small talk with the royals and the noblemen and pretending she was one of them. Michael caught her eye on the opposite side of the table and a couple chairs down. He was engulfed in a conversation with Revena, the two chatting amiably. While many of the other women were flaunting themselves at men, this girl seemed to be in genuine conversation.

Dinner was as amazing as Wren had said it would be, with dish after dish of delicacies. The courses of soups and creamed fruites, followed by swan and peacock with cranberry jellies. There were asparagus soaked in pork fat, and stewed mushrooms and spinach. Course after course arrived until Arix felt she was going to burst. What were buttered biscuits compared to this?

Bishop Forir kept Arix in good spirits through the meal, pointing out different court members around the table, and sharing tidbits about them that she didn't know.

"...and then of course you've met our lovely Aphelia Bouchard. She is a distant cousin to the king, and therefore takes it upon herself to live here at the castle."

"Does she ever leave?" Arix asked, stuffing more swan in her mouth.

Bishop Forir laughed. "Occasionally. She had a home in northern Eldur, which is managed by her eldest son. Ciel is her firstborn and she wouldn't for a moment think of being anywhere other than here for the competition."

"Does everyone know, then? Why we're here?"

"Yes. Now that the first test is complete, most of the country knows what's happening. Nothing has been announced officially, but secrets are not kept well in the capitol. While you've been here studying, the rest of the world has whispered."

Arix sighed and leaned back in her chair.

"What else can you tell me? I was hoping my tutor would be here this evening and conduct some introductions, but I haven't seen her yet."

"And who is your tutor?"

"Desirae Penduleux."

"Ah yes." The Bishop took another sip of his wine. "The professor. She's quite good, you know. You're lucky to have her."

"Not tonight apparently."

He smiled. "Don't fret. Here, grant an old man the first dance and I'll point out the rest of the court monkeys to you."

Arix took his outstretched hand, and the two exited the dining hall and entered the adjoining ballroom. The marble walls were covered in tapestries, and the ceiling was painted with dancing horses and seraphim, stripped for battle, blades held high. The sounds of strings echoed through the room, and Arix noticed the musicians hidden into an alcove off to the right, near the back of the room.

Joining the other dancers on the floor, Bishop Forir stepped into the circle, surprisingly light-footed for a man so old.

"You dance very well."

Arix smiled. "I've had a little practice, though I still have a long way to go."

"It is a blessing that you pick things up so quickly. There will be a steep learning curve to being able to fit in well at the palace." He spun her away from himself and then back in. "May I offer a word of advice."

"Please do. I could use all the help I can get."

"Pretend you know what you're doing, even if you don't. You looked like a scared deer when you came down those steps, and you lost your cool when talking to Madame Bouchard. You will have to do your best to keep a straight face and your wits about you here. Otherwise you'll be torn apart."

Arix nodded, raising her chin a little and trying to look less nervous.

"That's good. Keep your chin up. Don't let these people look down on you just because you aren't of noble blood. What runs in your veins is stronger."

She could feel her eyes go wide at his comment. Could he tell? Did he know that she was the odd man out? No one could know that she didn't have an ounce of magick in her veins. No one could find out. If they knew, her life would be over.

"You mean…"

"Magickal blood, yes. In time. I have no doubt they'll start teaching you more once you've passed a few more tests. Magick is dangerous, and they don't want it in the wrong hands. For now, let's continue our lessons."

Arix smiled as though a storm wasn't raging in her skull, a stone as heavy as the castle itself deep in her stomach. Instead she listened, trying to calm her fears with every step as the bishop spun her around the room, pointing out various council members, of which there were a total of thirteen.

"Lord Bardon is at the head, of which I'm sure you're already aware. He foresees everything that happens within the castle, and is the only one on the council with direct access to the king. Beneath him is Lord Heseth. He works directly with- that man, do you see him?- the one in the red sash."

Arix nodded.

"Heseth works with that man beside him, General Hawes. Those two know the most about our military than anyone else. Pompous men who like to talk strategy because it's the only thing about them that's remotely interesting."

Arix smiled. "I've heard the names before. There's a problem right now with Tamhain's troops, isn't there? Something about the Warden not wanting to lose her men. Desirea mentioned it in our lessons this week."

"Yes. Warden Aliska has been asked to send more troops to fight the Carn, but a lot of them are stationed in the border mountains-"

"Between us and the country of Koen." Arix finished his sentence. "Yes I know."

"Aliska should be here tonight. It would be smart of you to speak with her if you have the chance."

Arix felt her throat squeeze up.

"I'm not sure I would have anything much to say."

"Oh, don't worry. Just the regular pleasantries and you should be fine."

A brief memory flashed across her mind. She'd met the warden before, though it had been under rather…different circumstances. She'd been dressed as a liveryboy, and Warden Aliska had lost her best horse that day. It had been a good horse.

"And who else?" Arix asked, stumbling past the memory.

The Bishop glanced around him. "The priestess on the left, near the musicians? That is High Priestess Esme Halotus. She holds a seat on the council as representative for the Goddess. Her temple is based in Sieren. She is talking with Quellen Vod, Warden of Nero." He leaned in and whispered. "It is rumored that they are quite...close. To be honest, Vod and the High Priestess have always teetered in their public appearances. He's married, and she doesn't believe in marriage. It causes an interesting dynamic."

The High Priestess was stunning, swathes of sheer white fabric draped together with a gold belt. Her form was just barely visible underneath, and the neckline plunged all the way to her stomach, the curves of her breasts obvious. Scandalous clothing for anyone, much less a Priestess. She was surrounded by men and women alike, though was clearly in conversation with the warden. She laughed, the delicate sound twinkling over the music. The warden himself matched her in looks, his dark skin matching hers almost perfectly, black hair running in long waves down his back. He was dressed in colors of the ocean: swathes of seafoam and teal stitched with silver thread.

"They look exquisite together. She's so beautiful."

"And cunning. I've never met her match charm and quiet perception. She may seem sensuous and blithe in a party setting like this, but she is always aware of her surroundings. Sly as a snake and as beautiful as a dove, that one. She plays both parts exceptionally well."

Arix's gaze shifted down the room, but stopped near the far side, her step faltering. Though the man that had caught her eye faced away from her, she recognized the broad shoulders and long, dark hair. Her heart picked up pace, its thundering sound louder than the music in her ears.

"And...who is that?"

He wore traditional Neroian clothing, an embroidered dark blue tunic and gold pants. His hair was tied up neatly in a half ponytail and a gold stiletto was pierced through it. His calm aura oozed charm and grace and dignity as he chatted casually with a group of court ladies. They fawned around him, batting their eyelashes in time with their fans.

"Ah. How could I ever forget. That is Orion Karcharias. He's from a noble family in northern Nero. His familial holdings and land are an asset to the crown, so he has a seat on the council."

"What's he like?"

"Quite charming. He's rather popular with court ladies. He's very quiet in the council. When I first met him myself, I expected someone spoiled, considering his upbringing. But he's got excellent taste and is quite the conversationalist. He's been very supportive of the council's decisions and doesn't demand much. A very agreeable man."

"Will I be on the council if I become the Black Hand?"

Bishop Forir looked at her then, taking his focus off the rest of the room.

"Miss Sable, if you become the Black Hand, you will be above us all."

All the food in her stomach suddenly dragged at her and Arix felt her feet stop their movements. The bishop pulled her to the side and out of the way of the dancers.

"I didn't know." She breathed out, her voice barely above a whisper. "I didn't know the Black Hand had that much power."

"Steel your emotions, my dear. You're white as a sheet."

Arix pressed the back of her hand to her neck and jaw, willing the heat to cool.

"I knew the Black Hand was powerful, I knew the position was important. But I didn't know how high up it would be. I didn't know I'd be that close to the king."

"They haven't gone over this with you yet? I'm surprised. Have you even begun any magickal training yet?"

Arix shook her head. "I think I need a drink."

She wandered back to her seat, leaving the stunned bishop in the center of the dance floor. She stared into the contents of her goblet, the wine and her vision spinning.

"Easy there, or you'll be light on your feet before the night's halfway over."

Michael took the empty glass from her and placed it back on the table.

"I don't need you telling me how much to drink. I did perfectly fine on my own for twenty-five years." Though she hadn't meant to snap, barbs laced into her words as she dipped her cup back and emptied its contents.

"You're right, you're right!" Michael laughed, heaping himself into a seat beside her. "I was hoping to steal a dance with you before your whole evening gets taken over by men who think you're just a pretty face."

"I just came from there." Arix nodded to the room behind them.

"Would you make an exception?"

She glanced up at him, his eyebrows slightly raised and a grin playing at the corner of his mouth. He looked so good tonight, dressed in green and gold, a tendril of his hair falling across the side of his face. He looked a bit like a cherub. Innocent.

The more she stared at him, the more her barbs and thorns melted away. She smiled and offered out a hand.

Grasping her hand with his, he led her back through the double doors of the ballroom, twisting between the flowing skirts and laughing faces, and throwing them into the dance with ease.

Michael spun her around, and as their palms touched and bowed to one another.

"You do look amazing, by the way."

Arix snorted, glanced up at him, surprised by his grin stretching from ear to ear.

"Don't be ridiculous."

"I'm serious! I've been hoping for a chance to tell you. Who knew a criminal would look so good dancing on my arm? My father would be scandalized."

Arix laughed again, lightly slapping him. "You sound like an idiot."

"Maybe. But I'm not the only one who's noticed how good you look." He glanced to his left, and Arix followed his gaze. More than one gentleman was staring at her as she swept past them.

Arix's nose wrinkled. "They're staring at me like I'm a prize horse."

"A war horse…" Michael mumbled as he pressed his hand to her side to spin her out.

"Don't spin me so hard!" Arix laughed as the two came back together. "I've had enough swan to feed the entire country."

Out of the corner of her eye she spotted a flash of blue, drawing her away from Michael. Osiris danced past her, engaged in conversation with Celeste as he spun her round and round the floor.

Something spiked in Arix, a sharp barb between the ribs.

Michael twisted her back the other way out of Osiris's sight and barely avoided a couple that teetered precariously on the edge of drunk.

Pushing thoughts of Osiris away, Arix focused on the feeling of Michael's arms wrapped around her. It was nice, being held like this, though it didn't elicit the same response she had felt last night. Instead, she focused on the dance, and avoided the embarrassment of stepping on Michael's feet as they made the final turn around the floor.

The song came to an end, and the two bowed to each other, faces flushed pink and laughing. As they parted ways, Arix had all the intention of circling back to her seat for another drink, but instead was asked to dance again.

She'd gone through four more dances with strangers before Arix's sides were heaving and she forced her way through the throng and out of the stuffy ballroom. She'd let herself go and have fun, trying to forget that any day now she'd be found out and executed. There would still be plenty of time to find an escape. To find a way out and slip between the crown's fingers once again.

If she was honest with herself, she was enjoying the party. Enjoying the music and the beautiful dress that swished around her ankles. Her hair looked perfect and her chest looked amazing, thanks to Wren and the corset she'd been wrestled into.She'd been on the sidelines for so long. She'd stayed on the fringe, blending into shadows and picking pockets from anyone stupid enough to pass her. Yet tonight, she picked no pockets, slit no purses. She let her breathing match the music, and danced.

TWELVE

She found Ulfur and Abbas near a wall, stationed with a few other guards, and (as she noted) in perfect view of both the ballroom and her seat at the table.

"You dance so well, lass!" Ulfur took the small plate she handed to him and popped a peach slice into his mouth, juice dripping off his chin. "You look fine out there."

"Thank you!" Arix curtsied for him, grinning from ear to ear. "I thought you gentlemen might appreciate a little food since you've been standing so diligently at your post."

Ulfur beamed. Abbas ignored her.

"You should both come dance. The music is lively and there are plenty of partners. Oh don't look so stuffy, Abbas, I bet you're a terrific dancer." Arix squeezed in between them, leaning against the wall as she took a grape from the plate.

"Aye, he's much more dign'fied than I. Dances a right good jig if he's in the mood." Ulfur's eyes twinkled as he said it, but Arix acted surprised anyways.

"Abbas! You dance?" She let her voice sidle up into a squeak at the end, scoffing. "You'll have to teach us some dances then.

Ulfur and I will be the best of students, I assure you."

"No funny bus'ness."

"Exactly. Yes. No funny business whatsoever."

Abbas continued to ignore them.

"Truth told, I do miss a good jig. I used to dance up quite a storm in the old days, though these dances I'm not f'milliar with."

Arix sprung away from the wall and held out her hands to Ulfur. "I'll teach you!"

The northman's face froze in terror, and he gripped at the plate a bit tighter. "Ehh, not to insult ya, lass, but I canno dance with ya."

"Oh come on, it'll be fun! It's easy, I swear." Arix pulled the plate from his clenched fingers and passed it to Abbas, who, to her surprise, took the plate without complaint.

Ulfur was stiff as a board as Arix pulled him away from the wall, drawing their hands together. The man's ears turned a deep shade of rosy pink as she slid his other hand around her waist and rested her matching arm on his shoulder.

"Now, we're going to make a little loops with our steps, going this way-" Arix prodded him into a step to the left, "-then back this way." and prodded him to the right for two steps.

"Then we twirl."

They did. For his credit, Ulfur was not as clumsy as Arix had expected him to be, and after a few steps, he seemed to have caught on. They danced a lazy circles as Arix giggled, Ulfur's gaze continually glued to his feet, which were almost hidden beneath her swishing skirts. When he did finally look up to her, he was grinning a lopsided toothy grin.

"Well blast it all, I think I just might be learning som'thin! Just got to get the hang of-" Ulfur's gaze flickered away to something behind her, then dropped her hands immediately, his posture snapping to attention as he stepped back from her.

"Beggin' your pardon, my lady."

Arix whirled to find an amused bishop and very unamused Warden Aliska behind them. Arix dropped into a low curtsy, red burning behind her ears.

"Miss Sable," The bishop motioned to the woman beside him. "I'd like you to meet Aliska Sviengard, Warden of Tamhain."

Arix pulled her mouth into a smile and as her stomach hardened. "An honor to make your acquaintance."

The warden did not smile, her features set into an unreadable expression. "Bellarix Sable. You look unfortunately familiar."

Arix's insides tightened.

"I must have one of those faces." Arix said, trying to smile away the bile that was rising in her stomach. "I assure you, I have not had the pleasure of meeting you before this evening."

"I doubt it." Warden Aliska said flatly. "I do not forget those who have stolen from me."

Arix swallowed down the lump in her throat, pushing on. "I'm sure I don't know what you mean."

Warden Aliska Sviengard cocked her head, her gaze icy. "It would do you well to remember not to lie to me again. I tolerate nothing but the most brutal of truths, however difficult they may be for you to admit."

For a moment the two women stared at each other, each locked in, daring the other to look away first. In the end, for all of her willpower, Arix looked away first.

"Hmmm." The warden turned back to the bishop. "You wanted to introduce me to some of the other competitors?"

Arix curtsied again as the two turned, Bishop Forir giving her an apologetic look as he escorted the warden away. She let out a long sigh, deflating back against the wall between Ulfur and Abbas.

"Well that could have gone better."

Both Ulfur and Arix turned, surprised, toward Abbas.

"You both look like edla lizards with your mouths open like that." Abbas said, turning back to face the room.

"I just didn't expect you to say anything to me this evening." Arix mumbled as she leaned back against the wall.

"Just because I do not speak often, does not mean I do not speak at all."

Ulfur and Arix exchanged a glance.

"Well, maybe I should have you both escort me back up. After that complete and utter embarrassment, I think I want to take a long bath and then go to bed."

She was about to turn back toward the staircase when a tinkling of glass caught her attention. Lord Bardon stepped onto a small platform near the musicians, his crystal goblet upraised.

"If I may have your attention, on behalf of the council, a display of feats by the Sieren Entertainment Troupe will begin shortly outside in the gardens. Please make your way outside and enjoy a glass of champagne on your way out."

The excited throng moved out of the ballroom, past the three onlookers and streamed out the front double doors.

Arix looked around for a familiar face amongst the crowd, but saw neither Michael nor the Bishop. Her left shoe was loosening, and with the crowd pushing in around her, Arix tripped. A hand caught her arm, pulling her to the side of the crowd as the ballroom emptied out.

"Thank you, I-" Arix glanced up into steel blue eyes.

"It looked like you might be trampled by that horde. I thought I might try and save you." Orion grinned smoothly.

Arix dropped into a low curtsy, her eyes darting to the ground.

"Oh come now, Arduinna. No need for bows."

Straightening, Arix reactively smoothed at her dress around the waist. "You're on the council. I do believe there is some small need for bowing."

His eyes gleamed as he bowed back to her, fist over his heart. "Orion Karcharias, at your disposal."

"Well at least you aren't a stable hand."

His grin broadened, and Arix noted weathered lines around his eyes when he smiled. He had seen much in his short years. Seen perhaps too much at the table of the council.

"Might I escort you to our entertainment this evening?"

He offered her his arm, and Arix almost thought about refusing it, playing some sort of flirting game with him, pouting or blinking her long lashes at him until she had won some sort of invisible battle. She'd played these games before, when she was pretending to be a courtesan or a noblewoman. The game was all the same, no matter what your station. A woman simped and simpered and cooed until she got exactly what she wanted.

But she had been playing a game then. She had been pretending to be someone she was not. And being around Orion made her want to be herself.

She slid her arm into his, feeling the corded muscles of his arm under the gauzy shirt. They each grabbed a flute of champagne from a server near the door and made their way out into the gardens. Most of the guests had gathered themselves in the middle of the garden, where the paths opened up around a large fountain. Orion led them a different way, skirting around the crowd and near the bench where they had first met.

"You look stunning in this dress." he said, his gaze hovering over the maroon velvet near her shoulder.

As they passed behind a bush, away from the view of the

crowd, Orion's fingers dipped down her arm, just barely skimming the surface of her skin. Arix felt goosebumps travel up her spine and prickling up where he had touched her. Thought pulsed in her mind of the last time they had talked. The last time he had touched her hand, and what she had later done with that hand.

Arix flushed scarlet at the thought.

"I always thought gingers shouldn't wear red." Arix tried focusing on the conversation. "I suppose this dress is the exception to that rule."

"You're less of a ginger you know. Much more of an *auburn*." He said the last bit as though he were a silkman, describing his wares to a particular customer.

"Well, thank you all the same." Arix responded around her laugh, the apples of her cheeks growing warmer despite the night air. "Who did Lord Bardon say was performing?"

"The Sieren Entertainment troupe. Talented acrobats and jugglers, fire breathers and sword swallowers. They travel through the capital at the beginning of every fall."

"I've never seen a sword swallower. That sounds..." she flinched. "...painful."

Orion chuckled, low and deep, his deep gravelly voice filling the space around them. "They've had a lot of training. And not everyone is *cut out* for it apparently." He winked.

Arix rolled her eyes, though she couldn't keep the smile from her face at his joke.

Drums echoed through the garden as the performers stepped out of their hiding places behind bushes and eaves, mingling in with the crowd as they performed their stunts.

Arix watched the troupe with amused entertainment. They were interesting to be sure, but it was more fun to sneak her gaze to the side and watch a childlike awe overtake Orion's face. With each new stunt of burst of flame, his eyes would widen a bit, and his mouth would curve up into a different smile. At one point, during a rather daring escapade involving two women, six knives, and a hoop of flame, he actually gripped her arm. It was just a second, a squeeze and release, but such clear excitement was better than any acrobatic troupe.

When the revelry finally ended, the crowd thoroughly drunk on champagne, the party dispersed, ladies and lords bidding each other good evening. Arix walked in silence as Orion escorted her back to the castle. He was grinning a bit crooked, and it somehow made him even more charming than he already was. Near the doors, Lord Bardon stood, nodding to the guests, a small satisfied smile on his lips. When he saw Arix, on Orion's arm, his smile hardened to a thin line, glancing down at their intertwined arms before turning to look past them.

"Don't mind him." Orion whispered, once they were past, his voice warm by her ear.

"He doesn't like me." Arix muttered back, her grip on his arm tightening. "He's got a good reason not to. After tonight, I don't think I'll be as welcomed by your friends."

Orion laughed, and Arix felt it rumble down his arm and through her own. "*Friends* is a strong word. Aliska is a hardass. I'm sorry she upset you earlier."

Heat crept up Arix's neck as she cringed. "How do you know about that?"

"By tomorrow morning it'll be all anyone will be talking about." Orion's eyes twinkled with mischief as he escorted her up the grand staircase. "The thief who robbed Warden Aliska blind under her own nose. She's much too proud to have told the story herself, but Bishop Forir has quite the waggling tongue, you know."

Arix grit her teeth. "I should never have let him introduce me to her."

"You'd have to meet everyone on the council soon enough. Besides, one bad opinion doesn't ruin an evening, yes?"

"It depends on the opinion. Right now that opinion is that I'm a thief and Warden Aliska would just *love* to see me beheaded."

His left dimple appeared again as Orion's laugh rang out in the stairwell. Reaching out, he smoothed his fingers over her hand, his good mood setting his mouth into a boyish grin. "I'm on the council too, don't forget. Her opinion doesn't matter all that much."

Orion's voice lowered, tucking her arm further into his as he continued ascending the staircase. "I would like to think that perhaps you would be more concerned of my opinion over an uptight woman like Aliska Sviengard."

Of all things, the back of her knees were sweaty, making her feel like a stupid schoolgirl. How was she always such a mess whenever they spoke? He was as calm as a winter pond and she felt as though all her insides were melting.

"I know what I am. I'm an ordinary thief. I've pretended to be a lot of different people in my life, but here, everyone already seems to know who I am."

They had arrived at her door, but Orion did not let go of her arm. He eyed her carefully, and Arix could feel the blush creeping up her neck. What the hell was wrong with her?

"You might be a thief, but being here means you're anything but ordinary. The Goddess and the Crown have both used all kinds of people to achieve greatness. Who knows what you might do here? Who knows what you might achieve?"

He bowed to her, having arrived at her door, and took her hand and kissed it gently.

"Goodnight, Arix."
"Goodnight, Orion."

THIRTEEN

Arix was sure she was going to vomit. Vomit and run and get shot full of arrows and die. She gripped the armrests of her chair, her knuckles whitening and her fingernails pleading for release as she dug them deep into the carved wood.

She'd arrived for her normal lesson with Desirae, but instead, she'd found Lakai sitting behind the great oaken desk, cleared of the usual books and volumes. Instead, a strip of leather had been laid out across the desk's surface, with scattered orbs and shards of crystal laid across it.

"Today," Lakai said, his crystalline voice ringing like a bell in the small space. "Is the beginning of your magickal training."

The edge of her vision was going blurry, and her head was pounding like a mass of thorny vines had been stuffed up her nose and behind her eyes.

This was it.

He would ask her to do some feat. Some magical feat to prove that she had magick in her blood, and when she failed, he would know that she didn't have a drop of magickal blood in her. And then she would die.

Even though he'd been the one to grab her up off the street in the first place, she'd be the one who would get blamed; probably impaled on a stick on the wall for everyone to see what a fraud she was.

"I understand this is all very new for you." Lakai folded his hands across his chest, leaning back into Desirae's chair as he examined her. "It must have come at quite a shock for you when you learned your purpose here. But know that what I aim to teach you will set your life apart from everyone else's."

Arix nodded feebly.

Lakai's eyes narrowed as he noted the clenched fingers and the green pallor of his student. "Do you fear magick?"

Arix managed to shake her head lightly, clearing her throat to continue. Instead it came out as a wheeze and she decided it might be best to leave words to Lakai for now.

He stood, his simple robe spilling around him as he turned to stand in front of the window, hands clasped behind his back.

"I grew up in a family that knew the importance of magickal blood. A family that was waiting for a child to be born who had it spilling though their veins. From the day I was born, I knew what my future would be."

Arix glanced at the door. She could make a run for it. His back was turned, which gave her a few precious seconds to escape. She could feign an illness or let loose the vomit in her belly. Surely she'd be allowed back to the safety of her room if she was violently ill.

"Come here, Arix."

So much for running for the door.

"Well, actually…" Arix began, slowly drawing herself into a standing position. "…I'm not feeling quite well-"

"No amount of bellyaching is going to get you out of this. No matter how scared you are." Lakai's eyes twinkled, as he turned to look at her, their glassy blue gaze laughing. "Come here and see what lies in your veins."

Arix slowly rounded the desk, her stomach clenching into an even tighter knot than it already was in. Sifting through the crystals laid out on the strip of leather, Lakai lifted a flat piece of round clear glass. Motioning, Lakai took Arix' hand and held the glass over her palm. Through it, Arix saw the veins in her hand more clearly, the lines stretching through to her fingertips and back.

"Do you see these lines here?" Lakai pointed at the grooves that made up Arix's worn hands. "See this cross here? And these marks here? These are telltale signs of magickal blood."

Arix stared at the lines that had been on her hands her whole life, never noticing the way they crossed over each other and danced in whorls across her palms.

"These three lines here," Lakai went on, pointing at her ring finger. "Make up a small triangle beneath this finger. Another sign of your magickal blood. Do you see the way your veins follow these lines through your fingers?"

She stared.

"And look now-" Lakai exchanged the magnification glass for a shard of flat purple crystal as big as her hand, holding it against her arm in the same way. "-do you see it?"

There, beneath the purple crystal, she could see a glow. Her entire arm had a wavy aura that crackled and shimmered like diamonds in the sun or lightning in a midnight storm.

She looked up to Master Lakai, then back down at her own palm.

Jerking the piece of glass from him, she moved toward the window, holding up her arm and watching the slice of veins travel from her fingers down her hand, through the thin skin of her wrist, and down her arm. Purple crackles and shimmers sliced up her arm.

"You didn't believe it."

Lakai said it so matter-of-factly that Arix forgot to pretend.

"I thought I was minced meat."

They stood in silence as Arix watched herself through the purple crystal. She was magick. Really and truly. Though it should have relieved her, she found that the ball of anxiety in her chest and the vomit in her belly didn't lessen.

Arix stepped back from Lakai and held the glass in front of her so she could see him through it. The same shimmer and crackle surrounded him as well, the air around him wavering as though in the desert. She lowered the glass, looking at him normally, and the glimmer was no longer visible.

"That's how you knew who I was. Why you caught me? You were looking for the shimmer."

"Yes."

Carefully, Arix set the purple glass down on the desk, a sudden chill rippling down her spine.

"And in the alley? When I tried to climb the wall and fell. That was you, keeping me from escaping."

"Yes."

"Magick?"

"Yes."

She nodded slowly, walking back towards her chair and slumping into it.

"I hunted you for a rather long time, if that makes any difference." Lakai matched her posture and lowered himself back into his own chair. "I had a hard time pinning you down in one place for too long."

When she said nothing, Lakai went on.

"The magick in you isn't quite as strong as some others that I've seen, but you do have potential, if you're willing to put in the work. Becoming an incantor is no easy task."

"I've done just fine without magick my whole life. I'm pretty sure I can handle myself just fine without it."

Lakai studied her with a frown. "You will study. You will learn to use the gifts you have been given. If you do not, you will not do well here, Bellarix."

Arix looked down at her hands, fingertips skimming over the lines on her palms. She had always been ordinary. An ordinary girl with nothing to make her matter to an angry and selfish world. And now she meant something? Just because of a little shimmer? No one else had shown her how to fight, how to wield a bow and arrow, how to lift a sword. She had taught herself in back alleys and with bloodied knuckles. She had done it herself, by her own strength. When the world had spat on her, she had spat back.

Yet, here she was with shimmering veins and new whorls and lines in her palms telling her that her destiny was different. That she was different. She'd had a leg up this whole time and never knew it. And it felt like cheating.

With magick came power. And she knew what power did to people. It warped them and turned them against their fellow men. Power destroyed common decency and turned a good man into a bad one.

She would not let that happen to her.

"I understand, Master Lakai."

"Good. You and I will begin meeting once per week in the afternoons, and go over a few lessons. During the week it is your responsibility to stay up to date with your readings and personal practice. I will test you every time we meet, and I expect you to know every answer. Is that understood?"

"Yes, sir." Arix's face was grave. No more jokes; no more laughter.

"Then we shall begin."

They started with the basics: the history of magick, how magic had been utilized, and the events that led up to magick all but disappearing in Rökkur.

Magick was like any art; it needed to be learned and practiced to be mastered. Though unlike other arts, magick was not available to anyone. Magickal properties were said to lie in the blood, and only someone who contained magickal blood could study to become an incantor, a magick user. At first it seemed that only nobility contained magick, so when someone from the lower class was found to contain the potential for magick, parents had been known to sell off their children into noble families. Often families intermarried in the hopes that magick would remain in their familial line.

In the year 1143, during the reign of King Alakizra, a great enemy had risen up, ready to destroy the then small kingdom of Rökkur. King Alakizra had called forth the first champion of the crown, the first ever Black Hand, an incantor so powerful that he had wiped away the king's enemies and won the war. In celebration of his victory, King Alakizra had built a new city to be the capital of their great, new, and powerful nation. On a small inlet, he built Mergur, the capital and raised up Castle Zma'ai from which to rule.

For many years, incantors and kings had flourished. With the help of magick, Rökkur grew into one of the most powerful countries in the world. And then one day, it all stopped. Incantors became few, magickal blood disappearing to become a rare commodity. The price of magick was raised, and a panic settled over the country.

300 years had passed since the first Black Hand had appeared, and the new king recognized that magick may disappear altogether if he was not careful. The few incantors that remained became employed under the crow for the study and the preservation of magickal knowledge.

Only when the need was greatest, would a Black Hand be tasked to serve the king when swords and poisons were not enough. Only when the need was greatest, would the Black Hand be called to serve.

"Let us discuss magickal components." Lakai had long since prompted Arix to take notes of the lesson, and had finally moved from history into practical teaching.

"Magick is cast via incantations, or commonly called *cants*. Some cants require certain materials or ingredients to be performed. Others require an item that channels the energy needed for the magick to flow. These incantations are broken down into three categories: verbal, kinetic, and natural. Verbal cants are those that require you to speak in order to bring the cast into fruition. Kinetic cants are those that require precise movements of the hands and body. Most often kinetic cants are the hardest to cast, as the movements must be precise, or the cast will not be complete. Natural cants require a natural component, such as herbs or crystals or liquids."

Arix jotted down a few notes as Master Lakai proceeded on, listing different ingredients that would be wise to keep on hand. If the old man noticed her lack of effort, he said nothing.

"Every incantor," he continued. "Usually has a workshop or study where they keep their ingredients in preparation. Many incantations must be prepared in advance, the items gathered for the cant to be completed. A magick user cannot simply throw their hands in the air and expect something to happen. It takes great amounts of work and hours of study."

They worked through the afternoon, and Arix missed dinner in the main hall due to the old man's droning. There was a voice in her head, loud enough that it took extra effort to concentrate on Lakai rather than the voice that whispered to her. She had been caught because of magick. She was here because the king had decided that her life was not her own. That her purpose was to serve here, to train, to study, to become an incantor. And to then become the Black Hand.

If it were not for this thrum in her veins, if it were not for this magick that she had never known she'd possessed, she would be wandering the streets right now - a free woman.

Arix dumped the stack of books that Master Lakai had given her into the corner of her room, eyeing them scornfully from her window seat. She would read them eventually. If anything else, she would need the extra knowledge when going up against another competitor. With a groan, she halfheartedly moved her way through the stack. It was interesting, sure, but it was all ingredients and moon phases, and it was enough to make Arix's head spin. She much preferred her morning workouts with Tobias, and even the morning runs were better than pouring over endless textbooks.

The following week, Master Lakai tested her on her knowledge, which she clumsily struggled through and barely passed. List after list of ingredients muddled themselves in her brain, and seemed to vanish completely when Lakai tested her. Not only were there ingredients to keep track of, but they each had a purpose; each stem, leaf, flower, and where they could be harvested, pieces of useless information rattling around in her skull like hollow stones.

The more she learned, the more complicated magick became. In addition to knowing a cants' necessary components, the incantor would also need to draw a circle on the ground around them, known as a casting circle, and perform the incantation from within it.

Then there was the moon to think of. Depending on the lunar cycle, some cants were stronger than others, and needed to be cast under a certain moon to work properly. For example, a Mastery of Flame incantation would work the strongest under a third quarter moon. If the incantor attempted the same cant under a first quarter moon, the control would be considerably less, or could even backfire.

"A good incantor is always aware of the ether above and around them." Lakai would say, every time Arix had to pause to think of what moon they were currently under.

With every new lesson, Lakai added more to her list of work, adding a series of simple cants, correcting her finger exercises until she had just the right tension. After hours of working on kinetics, her fingers ached, refusing to bend the way she wanted them to. Even curling her fingers around the handle of her afternoon tea made every bone in her hand ache.

It felt like slogging through a bog. With every passing day, the next test grew closer, and yet her days were weighted down with training for magick that did not want to work for her. No matter how hard she forced her fingers into awkward shapes and pushed her tongue to form foreign words, the enchantments would not cast. While she ran every morning with Tobias, sparring with him in the ring, or discussing military strategy with Desirae, those cants cycled through her head, laughing at her.

She had never needed magick before. They would not get the better of her now.

It was three days before her next magick lesson when, casting a light enchantment, Arix succeeded on her incantation. It was small, of course, but there, in the darkness of her room, a jar of glow worms at her side, she produced her first casted light. It hovered before her face, small as a pinhead, but slowly grew to the size of a marble. A small glowing orb, hovering above her cupped hands. Arix laughed and collapsed back onto the floor, exhausted. She held up her hands in the firelight, examining the calluses and scars left there by years of hard work. And what remained of all her hard work with magick? One small glowing orb.

Arix's excitement over her first cant began to turn acrid in her throat.

What would one pinprick of light do against a locked door? Against a heavy Baron's purse? Nothing.

Even with something burning dark and ashy in her throat, Arix tried again with the simple enchantments Lakai had given her: light, watered shape, moved stone, and wind. One cant for each element. When Tobias came to fetch her the next morning, he found her sound asleep on the floor, bowls of water and small stones scattered around her, and scowl etched into her brow.

~

"Again."

Arix took a breath, sweat dripping down her back. Lakai had moved their lesson outside, and they stood in the small field near the forest. He had given her more cants to try, ones that needed more space to be cast. It had been two weeks since she'd made that stupid little pinprick of light, but despite the accomplishment, Lakai had only pushed her harder.

The afternoon air had shifted from the last remnants of summer's heat into the cool beginning crunch of autumn, the trees slowly starting to curl, their leaves starting to brighten goldenrod and crisp vermillion. This was Arix's favorite time of year, when fall breezes twisted through your hair, and all the world began to curl in on itself in preparation for winter.

Arix squared off in the circle she had drawn in the dirt, facing a bale of hay placed fifteen paces away. Bracing herself, and focusing her energy on the bale, she brought her hands up in front of her, circling her middle finger clockwise around her left palm, then pushed the finger down toward the tips.

"Vatra."

She said the word while thrusting her hands forward and focusing all her attention on a middle point near the bottom of the bale. A sliver of smoke rose, then the base of the bale caught fire, slowly catching the rest until the whole thing was aflame.

Arix let out a breath of relief before dropping to the ground, her arms weakly propping her up.

"Thank the gods." She murmured, her gaze at the sky.

"You can do better than that, Bellarix." Lakai barked, his robed arms folded across his chest. "I want more elegance in those kinetic movements. Your fingers need to loosen up. The bale should explode with fire, not kindle. Everyone else has been able to succeed. Get up, let's try again."

Arix glanced to her left where the rest of the class chatted quietly. Curse group lessons. They made her feel so stupid. Arix stood to her feet, biting back a groan. With a wave of his hand, Lakai extinguished the flaming bale, restoring it back to its previous form. The ground around her returned to its original state as well as Arix redrew the circle.

"What if I need to do battle? What if I don't have time to draw a circle? Besides, you don't use a circle. I could shoot ten flaming arrows at it in the time it takes me to draw one fucking circle." Arix reached for her waterskin on the ground and took a drink, the water cool against her throat.

"I don't need a circle. I have a core."

"And what's that?"

"We haven't gotten there just yet, but now is as good a time as any I suppose." Lakai's features remained hard, chiseled lines across his face, and signaled for the other students to approach the circle. Lifting a small amulet out from beneath his robe, he held it out for them to see. The silver material held a green stone in its center, runes marked around the edge.

"This is a core. Many incantors use objects like these to help them cast. Some can be forged as weapons or as an amulet like this one. They assist in the casting, and provide shortcuts, like removing the necessity of a casting circle. Many incantors use cores as a way to cheat their way through magick, often relying on them instead of their own abilities and knowledge. Cores allow an incantor to better channel and focus. They come in handy during battles or situations that require action without hesitation."

Arix watched as he tucked the piece carefully away.

"Will I get one?" she asked, glaring down at the circle in the dirt.

"You don't just get one!" He barked, striding away from her circle. "You have to earn it. Everyone, step back. Bellarix will perform the cant. Again."

There was tittering laughter from the group of competitors, and Arix felt the corner of her eyes crinkle. Michael gave her a reassuring thumbs up and a smile that said *'I believe in you,'* though his pitying look in his eyes said something more like *'Goddess, you're bad at this.'*

Arix squinted at the block of hay, biting back a groan, then performed the cant again, trying to see the bale burst into flames in her mind.

It worked better the second time, the left side of the bale engulfed in hot flames, then quickly overtaking the rest of the hay. The bale reset itself. This time, she couldn't hide her groan of frustration.

"Again."

FOURTEEN

By the end of the day, Arix was exhausted. Her fingers ached, her head ached, and every last ounce of energy had been sapped out of her body. Each movement felt sluggish, dragging her limbs through tar pits even for the simplest of tasks. She knew she was making progress, Lakai had even said as much, grumpy old man that he was. But she still felt she was wasting her time.

Arix stripped out of her sweaty clothes and lowered herself carefully into the bath that Wren had drawn. The hot water melted into her bones, the scent of vanilla, cinnamon, and oranges drifting up to her. Her head fell back against the back edge of the tub, eyes closed. If she wasn't careful, she'd fall asleep like this.

Out of the corner of her eye, she could see the creamy paper of the envelope, now resting in her window seat. It had come after dinner, notifying her and the other competitors that the next test would take place the following morning. With a groan, Arix turned her gaze away and focused instead on the bits of dried orange peel floating on the water's surface.

She'd probably have to use magick to pass the next test, and the thought of the council and Lakai pushing her into using it made a hot anger fill every pore of her being. She preferred to fight with the tools she already had; the ones that came easily to her: knives and arrows and lock picks. Magick was not her strong suit. Magick was a shortcut she did not want to use.

Nevertheless, lists of cants streamed through her mind, slowly compiling the cants she had learned the past couple of weeks. The basics, she had learned early. These were elemental cants, controlling earth, air, fire, and water. Then were spirit based cants, controlling people or animals; protection and weapon cants. The kinetic finger work was harder for those, and the words for the cants themselves were longer and more complex. Pronunciations that made her tongue twist wildly in her mouth and pronounce certain letters with vibrations.

There were two incantations in particular that always got mixed up in her mind. Both had verbal and kinetic components, which were handy since as a castor, you didn't need materials to make them work. One, Lightning Touch, shocked someone of your choice as long as you could touch them. The other, Ice Beam, caused a person to slowly begin to freeze. Both the words and the kinetic motions were similar for these cants, and Arix often found herself mixing the two.

She dunked her head beneath the surface of the water and let out a scream, bubbles flying from her mouth and breaching the surface above her. If she had to hear Lakai tell her one more time that her finger work was sloppy, she'd Ice Beam herself right into the moat. As she slowly came out of the water for air, Arix started empty-eyed at the ceiling. Her brain felt like muddled mint. She had thought magick would be simpler. A snap of the fingers and voila! Magick! But no. Instead it was much more akin to smashing ones foot repeatedly into a cow's ass and expecting leather boots to appear. Not a particularly fun way to spend an afternoon.

After her bath, Arix retreated down the hallway into what had become a familiar pattern. Ulfur and Abbas followed as she made her way up to a terraced roof, then stood guard just outside the door. The roof had been used for a while as a getaway place for couples, at least until the competitors arrived and Arix and Michael began meeting there as a way to get out of the marble stone walls. Now, the roof was slowly being turned into a garden, courtesy of Michael's vegetable skills.

She found him already there, watering the tomatoes, which were struggling to perform under the pressure of the thriving herbs that were already blooming on the roof. That and the fact that Michael was trying to grow them in the wrong season.

"Any new luck?"

Michael turned to look at her, annoyance splashed across his face. "They're being difficult."

"Maybe they're shy."

The sky was almost dark, the last flickers of pink and purple dripping low near the horizon, slowly being overtaken by deep blue.

"That's not how tomatoes work."

Dropping to the blanket that had already been laid out, Arix tucked her arms behind her head and stared at the heavens.

"Any guesses on tomorrow's test?"

Michael returned his watering can to its position and came to join Arix on the blanket.

"Revena thinks it's going to be a written test."

Arix groaned aloud. "Goddess, you'd think the sun might shine out of Revena's ass the way you talk about her."

Michael laughed. "She's nice. I think you'd like her."

The few times that Arix had actually had a conversation with the girl, Revena had been curt and quiet, saying very little, even though Arix had peppered her with questions in hopes it would get the girl talking.

"Yes but she was sweet on Nikolai Winter, and we all know how that turned out."

Unfortunately, for all his brains and education, Nik had drunk too much wine the night of the party, and attempted to storm the gate, shouting about dragons and revolution. Arix never saw him again.

Out of the corner of her eye, she saw Michael wince slightly. He was a good man. Albeit sometimes too good, always trying to see the best in others, but it was what endeared him to her over the last weeks.

"What do you think the test will be?" Michael asked.

Arix adjusted her arms and propped her ankle across her knee. "No idea. Although I'm sure it'll have something to do with magick. Maybe extinguish a burning building. Or save some damsel in distress. Break a magick curse!" Arix grumbled. "I'm sure it'll be something to prove just how *useful* magick can be."

Michael rolled over, propping his head up on his elbow. "But maybe the damsel is a dragon in disguise. And when she's rescued, it's actually a trap."

"Or," Arix countered, mirroring his posture, "She'll be so grateful for saving her, she'll grant us lands and titles and I'm sure she'd be inclined to offer out a kiss or two."

Michael laughed at that.

"I'm sure whatever it is, it'll be easy. The last one was."

"Not for those that didn't make it." Michael picked a piece of loose thread on the blanket. "We started out with twenty-four and we're already down to twelve."

Arix said nothing, thinking to their small number that was about to grow smaller still.

"How can they afford to kill off the losers? Aren't we supposed to be the last magick bloods in the country?"

Michael shrugged. "I doubt we're the last."

"Maybe there's a whole crypt of them."

"All stashed away in some dank dungeon, ready to be brought back in a horde of undead incantors"

The two chuckled and Arix leaned back until she was flush with the ground again.

How would the other competitors do tomorrow? Did they all struggle like she did with magick? From what she had seen in their group lessons, Arix seemed the only one who struggled for magick to obey her.

Celeste was clearly excelling. She had been trained for this her whole life, thanks to her upper class birthright. She'd probably known from infancy that she had magick flooding her veins. In every group class, her bale of hay burst into flames or her bucket of water froze in an instant. But she never overexerted. She never showed off or showed her hand, making it impossible to know if she'd been trained in all this before. In terms of sheer ruthlessness, after what she'd seen at the first test, Celeste would be a tough opponent even without magick.

Revena only stuck out in Arix's mind because Michael clearly admired her. Michael had only really become her friend because he had pushed and pushed to gain her attention, and despite herself, Arix enjoyed his company and optimistic outlook. She'd never even considered becoming friends with anyone else.

"Who knows how many we'll lose this time." Michael muttered. "I have no clue what to expect tomorrow."

Arix smirked. "Worried about Revena?"

"You too, you idiot."

The stars were finally coming out, the last of the orange sunset disappearing into night.

"Don't worry about me, rich boy. I lived a long while on the edge of a knife."

Michael rested his arms above his head. "But that was different. A wrench has been thrown into the game now. The stakes, and the difficulty, have gone up."

"I'm either going to survive, or I won't. There's no point in worrying over something you have no control over."

"But we do have control. We decided whether we live or die."

"Unless it's swimming."

"What?"

Arix jabbed Michael in the side. "If the next test entails swimming, then I suppose you'll have to go on and become the Black Hand without me."

Michael's laugh was warm as he jabbed Arix back, his fingers digging into her ribs. "I can't believe you don't know how to swim. I thought you lived on the coast."

Giggling, Arix moved closer, her head resting on his arm. "Rocky cliffs don't really provide the best atmosphere for a seven year old learning to swim."

"You've never talked about it. Your life before." Michael paused for a moment, his chest rising and falling with his breath. "I mean, I know you were a thief, and I can assume you did it to survive. But you must have come from somewhere. You must have had a family. I heard you say your father was a blacksmith?"

When she made no move to respond, Michael let out an exasperated sigh. "Tell me a story, Arix! You've lived a full life, and I've always done as I was told by my father. I'm dying to know at least something of your adventures."

A moment passed between them, silent. Arix wanted to change the subject, back to when they were laughing and speculating about the future, not reminiscing on the past.

"It's not a happy story."

"I still want to hear it."

Arix took a deep breath, then slowly let it slip back into the night. "My mother died when I was two. Some sickness swept through the town and took her with it when it left. I don't remember her in the slightest. My father raised me and my older brother, Caelum, by himself after she died. You would have loved my father, Michael."

Arix felt that odd ache in her chest, an ache that pushed her to cry tears for them. Yet none came.

"He was a scholar, a true scholar, at heart. When he married my mother, his parents disapproved, and so he moved away to be with her and have a family. He taught himself a trade to get by, as a blacksmith, but he would make money by teaching some of the wealthier townspeople. And he used to play the violin. It was so beautiful. Cael and I would sit on the floor for hours listening to him play. To be honest, he's probably the reason I've gotten even this far in the tests. He taught me mathematics and history, and how to read and write.

"One day the Carn attacked Hythe. It was back when they were just starting to gain a following, popping up in the mountain towns all long the east territories. I guess they wanted to make a statement, but they burned the whole village to the ground. My father tried to stop them, to save as many people as he could. But in the end, they killed him. Right there in front of us. Cael tried to get me out but he was hit by an arrow and then I was all alone. So I ran. As hard and as fast as I could go. Somehow I ended up in Zarak where a family took me in for a while."

She was skipping over things. Leaving them out on purpose. Part of her thought she kept them to herself because they were just too painful. Too private. Her grief to bear alone.

"After that I was on my own. I did what I had to to get by. I found out I was good at sneaking in and around places. I was smart enough to know what I had to say and do to look like I belonged. Things just escalated as I got older. I got better and smarter. I taught myself to be better, to avoid eyes, to slip into the background. I tried to right the scale when I could, I suppose. And then Lakai found me and brought me here. You know the rest."

Arix let out a long breath. She'd refused to think about it; how her life had played out, so different from the life her father had wanted for her. All of his dreams and hopes dashed by simple disease and disgruntled countrymen.

"You really taught yourself?"

"All on my own." Arix felt her chest swell with pride.

She had taught herself to pick a lock, had taught herself how to talk and walk and show off her cleavage in just the right way to get where she wanted to be. In the end, ladies and whores were not all that different. They both fought for the recognition that men bestowed.

"Life is its own lesson, too. If you aren't stealthy enough, they'll chop off your hand for stealing a loaf of bread. The more you steal, the steeper the price. If I wasn't good at what I did, I wouldn't live to see the next sunrise. That's enough motivation all on its own."

And it had been. It still was.

"You know," Arix said, staring up at the constellations, "I used to feel, somewhere deep inside me, that maybe I was special. Maybe I was different from the rest of the people in this country. That somehow my pain set me above the rest. But after all that time spent in the world, traveling through broken and burned up towns, I've realized that my pain doesn't make me special. Pain is just pain. And everyone goes through it in one way or another. Maybe in different ways, but it's still hurt and loss. Everyone's lost someone to the rebels, or to sickness, or hunger. Or just to life."

She felt Michael's fingers touch her arm, a silent message saying *It's going to be alright.'*

It wasn't until he wiped away her tears that Arix realized she was crying.

FIVETEEN

When Arix awoke, the crisp bright weather of autumn had been replaced with a miserable slog of dreary clouds. The sky hung low and brooding, petulant against autumn's bright call.

Breakfast was eaten at the large dining table rather than the competitor's individual rooms. Arix watched the others, paying more attention to who was left. After her conversation with Michael last night, she had realized that she didn't know the other competitors at all. She'd shared five group classes at most, and even then, she'd paid more attention to her magick than she had to the others.

Celeste wore her blonde hair pulled back into an intricate braid, and wore a tunic-like dress with high slits on either side, her leggings showing when she walked. Celeste was most talented on the back of a horse, and from what Arix had seen, was incredibly well versed in a variety of weapons. She chatted lightly with those around her, as if they weren't about to head to their second test.

Some of the other competitors Arix vaguely recognized from the first test, and a few from the party as well, though she still didn't know all their names. Ambrose, the eldest of the competitors, was loud and jovial, his hair graying slightly at his temples. According to Michael, he had danced with almost every lady at the party, and already knew intimate gossip of the majority of the court. His charismatic nature allowed people to speak freely with him, and his charming smile melted all hearts. Apparently women who were mad at their husbands were quicker to spill their secrets while spinning around a dance floor with a charming gentleman. He had danced with her as well, Arix recalled, their steps light as they had skipped across the floor to a merry jig.

Another competitor Arix recognized was Helios, long hair woven in with bits of leather and beads that reached down the length of his spine. When they passed each other in the halls or stables, which was often, Helios always offered Arix a curt nod, which was always promptly returned. Arix liked him. He was courteous to everyone, but made a point not to become too close with any of the others. Wise.

Across the table from Michael sat Revena, her blue-black coiled hair pinned partially back against her head. When she smiled, the room seemed to radiate joy. Everyone who interacted with her seemed to relax, their whole nature melting, rough edges smoothed under those dimples. Arix had seen very little of Revena's personal training, as she didn't practice out in the open like most of the other competitors. She chose instead to practice in a private sparring ring with her trainer. In their group lessons with Lakai, Revena's cants often took an odd turn, as if the magick arced in connected lines before reaching their target. It was almost unsettling, and Arix still couldn't figure out why.

Arix picked at her porridge, spooning another drizzle of honey into the already too-sweet slurry. She was nervous, and she didn't like feeling so unsure in the face of a test. The rest of the table was on edge, and even under Ambrose's jovial conversation, his smiles never reached all the way up to his eyes. The clatter of dishes and silverware was at a minimum as they finished eating and the servants took the mess away.

The attention in the room shifted as High Priestess Esme entered the room, a guard on either side of her. Her hands clasped delicately over the gauzy blue fabric of her dress that flowed around her like water.

"Competitors. Today is your second test in the march towards taking up the position as Black Hand to the King." Her voice was luscious and sensual, her words flowing together like a cant. "Please follow me."

The twelve contestants followed her out through the hall and stepped out into gray filtered light. Muted purple clouds had formed, threatening to pour rain at any second. The High Priestess moved with the grace of a flowing stream as she led them around the side of the castle and past the gardens. Arix stared at what had once been the empty field that she daily trained in. Overnight, a large hedge maze had appeared, its edges curving away from them to form a circle. The hedges reached high above Arix's head, some thirty feet in the air. In the gloomy light the hedge looked almost black, so dark green were the leaves.

"There are six entrances to this maze, you will enter at each opening and make your way through the labyrinth. Those who have not reached the center by the stroke of the noon bell will be eliminated. Lord Bardon awaits you at the center. You will know you have reached it when you see him. But be warned," the High Priestess turned to look at them as they stopped outside of the first entrance to the maze, "there are monsters in this place. You will have to keep your wits about you to move through it. Be smart. Be cunning. Do not think you will win because of your bravery. For monsters are not defeated by fortitude alone."

"You two." The Priestess pointed at two contestants to Arix's left. "You will enter here. Once everyone is ready at their entrance, a bell will ring. When you hear the bell, then enter the maze. May the Goddess have mercy on you."

She turned, leaving the two wide eyed competitors, and made her way around the outer edge of the hedges, leaving two competitors at each entrance. Michael squeezed Arix's arm and whispered "Good luck" as he stepped into position at the second opening.

Arix and another girl were the last to stand in position, the priestess wishing them the Goddess's mercy before she turned back towards the castle.

"I'm Arix."

Her companion barely acknowledged that she'd spoken.

"Tanis."

Her nose bent at a slightly odd angle, a break that had healed crooked. On anyone else it would have been a characteristic of a lopsided face. On Tanis it just made the girl look mean. Arix checked her weapons and small bag of ingredients as she offered the girl a grin.

"Best of luck, Tanis."

Instead of a response, crooked-nose just spat into the dirt, her eyes fixed on the hedge opening. In the distance, the bell sounded, and the two made their way into the maze. The walls were so high, they blocked out even more of the dim light, and Arix blinked to try and adjust her vision. Tanis, a few steps ahead of her, spun, heel dug into the ground as she created her casting circle. Muttering under her breath, Tanis produced a small light which hovered before her as she walked.

The path turned sharply to the left then split off in two directions. Tanis took the left, Arix took the right. She made her way cautiously, peering around the corners before taking them. After only two turns, Arix found herself facing a dead end.

She slowly traced her steps back to where she had begun and took the path to the left. It forked out ahead of her in three different routes. The one to the left turned back in on itself, looking like it ran along the outer edge of the maze. The middle went on for another ten feet before splitting again. The third path was a dead end.

Using her heel, Arix gouged an arrow in the ground pointing down the path to the left, taking it slowly. Her best bet was to keep moving, and try to eliminate as many paths as she could before working her way to the center. As the route continued to branch, Arix continued choosing the leftmost path, watching her corners, and marking her ground with her boot.

As she turned again to the left, Arix pulled up sharply, grabbing onto the branches of the hedge to keep herself from stepping further forward. One of the other competitors stood before her, frozen, staring at a large beehive that was nestled into the leafy wall. Bees were slowly pouring out of it, and the girl was backing up slowly, the bees twisting in the air as if searching for a predator.

"Just back away slowly," Arix whispered. "That's too fast. Slow. Down."

The girl glanced at Arix and nodded, taking a step backwards. Her movements were jerky, and the swarm turned after her. The girl let out a guttural whine and then turned quickly to run. Before Arix could shout warning, the swarm was biting and stinging. With a scream the girl dropped to the ground, trying to cover her head against them. Arix stood frozen, unable to tear herself away as the girl writhed in pain, her arms flailing. Then it was over. Her body went limp, the swarm setting on her form. Seconds inked by but Arix still did not move. Neither did the competitor on the ground.

"She's gone."

Arix glanced up to see Andai, a competitor from Zarak standing behind her. His eyes were flecked with pain, his brow slightly furrowed.

"Keep your wits about you," He continued, still staring down at the girl's swollen body. "Don't forget your magick in here. Don't lose your head."

He glanced over at Arix then, and she swallowed hard and nodded.

He pointed back down the path that disappeared around the corner ahead of them.

"Know where the path goes?"

"No. I think that's where she..." Arix cocked her head at the girl on the ground, "...was coming from."

Andai stepped forward towards the girl and drew his circle, the bees slowly rising back up. With a quick and precise motion Andai cast an ice beam, catching the bees in the air, their little frozen bodies dropping to the ground like pieces of hail. His feet crunched over them as he walked around the body and around the corner, within seconds he returned.

"Dead end."

Arix nodded again.

"Do you know that one?" Andai asked.

"What?"

"Do you know that cant? The ice beam?"

Arix nodded.

"Good. You'll probably need it again. Good luck."

He patted her shoulder as he passed, tucking his head scarf back up to cover his face as continued around a corner and back into the maze.

Arix bent to study the bees. They wouldn't be flying ever again.

She retraced her steps back quickly, her heart pounding in her chest. Keep calm and focus. Breathe. Continued on for a few more minutes, keeping to the left. With the curvature of the hedges, she determined she must be traveling around the outer edge of the labyrinth. Every time she changed her course or took a different path, she marked it, turning back as needed.

A few drops of rain fell, pricking her skin through her long sleeves. The wind was beginning to whistle through the twists and turns, high above her, although Arix was glad to find that most of the hedges kept the wind from gutting through her.

Somewhere from the other side of the maze, a sharp scream sounded and Arix dropped to a crouch, her back against a hedge. Even though it was far away the sound cut through the air like a knife. Her skin crawled beneath her shirt, and the hair on her neck rose.

She crept forward, inch by inch, ready to use her small dagger if she needed to. But what use would the dagger have been if the bees had turned on her? Rounding another corner, Arix found herself at one of the other entrances, now empty. She continued forward, looping around as the path turned towards the center. Relief flooded through her. Finally she was moving towards the center.

Nearing another fork, Arix marked her way as she took another left. The air was becoming tinged with the smell of orange blossoms, and Arix noticed the scent becoming stronger as she followed the solitary path. Rounding a corner, she found the shrubs peppered with orange flowers with bright yellow centers.

She stopped dead in her tracks.

The flowers looked harmless enough, but something in her gut told her not to trust seemingly happy flowers. Drawing a circle and preparing a fire cant, Arix hesitantly burned one of the flowers, watching as it flamed brightly for a moment, shriveled to ash.

Nothing. Taking her time and moving slowly, Arix burned up each flower along the hedge as she moved around the corner. To a dead end.

A groan escaped her throat before she clamped her mouth closed. She'd wasted too much energy traveling down a path that went nowhere, but she wouldn't allow her temper to give away her position.

It was a solid ten minute walk back to the last marking. As she moved, she wished she had thought to bring along a waterskin. Even though the rain had picked up and had started to drizzle heavily, her mouth was parched. A huge drawback of using so much magick was that it took a toll on her physically. Mentally she cursed the orange blossoms for wasting her time.

The humidity of the rain was causing wisps of mist to cover the ground, becoming denser as she moved toward the center. Great. All she needed was another swarm of murderous bees to come at her from within the fog.

Perhaps it was the rain or the exhaustion from using so much magick, but Arix began to feel tired. Her eyelids drooped, and she vigorously rubbed at them to keep them open. Her vision was going fuzzy around the edges, and she soon felt that every step was a weary one. The path was beginning to straighten out, forming a long curved hallway that ran ahead of her. She crept along the curve, her shoulder brushing the wall of green to her left. With every step, her feet crunched against the dirt beneath, dragging little pebbles in their wake.

She noticed that up ahead, a competitor was sitting on the ground, their head leaning on their crossed arms. Arix stopped and watched him for a moment, barely catching the slow rise and fall of his shoulders.

She approached slowly, but he neither looked up at her, nor acknowledged her presence as she gave him a wide berth. Was he-? Arix looked closer. He was asleep.

A tingle ran up her spine.

"Hey, you." She called, kicking a small rock at him.

He didn't move.

She stepped forward slowly until she was close enough to kick the toe of his boot with her own.

Still no response.

Arix reached over and gave him a shove. He fell to the side, his eyes opening slowly and blinking at her. But instead of righting himself, or yelling at her, he tucked his arm over his head and closed his eyes again.

After trying a few more times to wake him with no success, Arix continued on.

Napping? Arix thought, slightly surprised that she found herself disgusted with him. This is my competition? Pathetic.

The path continued to curve towards the middle of the maze, and she stumbled on, feeling heavier and heavier. Her only explanation for her drowsiness, she reasoned, was some sort of cant that made them sleepier the closer they got to the center. Something to deter them from reaching their goal. To keep herself awake, Arix began pinching herself on the arm or face, the pain giving her a slight shock and forcing her eyes back open.

The path split again, but while the left turned back towards the edge, the right path kept moving towards the center. Arix went to the right. It was only a few minutes after she made that turn that she realized she hadn't been marking the ground for some time.

This realization didn't bother her though, as she was sure she was moving towards the middle. She would be at the center short-ly. She was positive.

There was another person up ahead, on their back, dead eyes staring at the sky. Body barely visible through the density of the mist. As Arix passed them she smirked.

Ha, she thought. *They were weak. Not like me.*

There was a scuffle up ahead, like the sound of a skittering mouse across the ground, but louder.

Probably nothing. There's nothing to be afraid of here. Not this close to the center.

Her feet were dragging, and a root caught the tip of her boot, dropping her to one knee. It was comfortable. So comfortable. She had expected the gravel and dirt to be hard, but instead, they felt soft. She smiled. Beautiful magickal dirt. Arix drew a hand across them, feeling their softness. And warmth. The ground was warm, a comfort against the cold falling rain.

Just a moment. I'll just stop for a moment. Catch my breath.

She sat, and the closer to the ground she got, the more com-fortable it was. The ground was as soft as her bed and the rain a soothing blanket. Arix stretched out, hugging the earth as she lay on her stomach. And the earth hugged her back.

She'd never felt so at peace.

So comfortable.

So tired.

SIXTEEN

Arix was in a mental cocoon. Her own private little space of warmth. Nothing else mattered because she didn't matter. She was a speck, floating within the universe, her life within it meaningless.

A voice far away was yelling, but Arix tuned it out. She dipped in and out of space and time. An eternal loop that arced in and out of reality, and she was riding on its back in inconsequential bliss.

A crack of light.

She turned her face away from the crack that had begun to take form in her mental cocoon. It was sharp and painful and she ignored it.

Then pain. Piercing pain under her nails, so violent and intrusive. Arix wanted to pull away but she was too tired.

Whatever it was jabbed again, and for a moment, one brief, beautiful moment, her brain was clearer. A living flower crouched over her, its orange and yellow petals staring down at her, a stick in its hands.

She was being dragged to her feet, but she fought to stay down, to hug the earth and bury herself deeper in her cocoon of ether. There was a slight scent of oranges, and the fuzziness around her formed into solid lines. The living flower pulled her to her feet and began dragging her back the way she had come.

There was an orange bloom of color out of the corner of her own eye, just barely hanging on to her hair as she trudged along behind. The living flower set her down on the ground again, checking the body of the boy Arix had passed earlier.

The flower muttered under her breath and picked Arix back up again.

She could feel the rain again, she realized. When had it begun to pour? Looking down, she noticed her clothes were drenched, as if she'd been thrown into a lake. Her feet were finally taking steps on their own now, and she was leaning less and less on the flower as they went.

But she wasn't a flower.

Arix looked again, forcing her eyes to focus on the form. It was a girl. A girl with raven hair and a bouquet of orange and yellow flowers clamped in her mouth. She had them stuck in her hair, and wore them in a braid around her neck. They passed another turn, before Arix was able to speak.

"What happened?"

The two stopped at a four way intersection of hedges, and Revena removed the flowers from her mouth, breathing hard.

"Some sort of monster. Mist makes you sleepy. It feeds off your energy." She rolled her shoulders, then pointed to the right-most path. "Take that until you reach a hard turn, then just keep following it. When you hit a fork, take the right path. When you get to the pit, wait there. I'll meet you."

She turned to leave, stuffing the stems of the flowers back in her mouth, and heading back into the fog where they had come from.

"Wait!" Arix called, but Revena had already disappeared around a corner into the mist.

Following Revena's instructions, Arix kept to the path, taking a right whenever it split. She felt like she'd walked forever, and knew if she hadn't been paying attention, would feel completely lost. As she made a turn, the ground opened up in front of her into a large pit, five feet deep and about fifteen feet across. She could have easily climbed down and then out the other side, but there was something strange about the dirt at the bottom of the pit, and Arix had no interest in tempting fate. She waited for nearly twenty minutes before Revena reappeared around the corner. She was alone.

"How well do you know the moulder cant?" She asked, removing the flowers from her mouth and dropping them on the ground.

Arix shook her head. "Not at all."

Revena nodded. "Figures. That's ok, I think I can do it again."

The strain was visible on her face as she spoke the cant, the earth at the bottom of the pit boiling and burbling as it slowly filled. About halfway up, lines began to gut through the dirt, and Arix realized that the hole had been filled with razor thin wire. If she had jumped in the pit, she would have been caught in the wire and been cut to ribbons.

A chill skittered down her spine. Thank the Goddess she had waited.

Once the earth had formed a bridge, Revena took the first cautious step, testing the ground as she went. The ground held firm, though with each step, the earth sucked at the bottom of Revena's boots, attempting to pull her down. After she was across, Arix quickly followed.

They walked in silence, following the path as it stretched and turned before them. Only twice did they get turned around in a dead end, but were quickly able to recover their steps. Arix had begun to shake from the cold, and Revena noticed.

"Here." She stopped, casting another cant Arix didn't know. The movements were similar to a fire cant, but the words were different, the phrase longer.

She felt her body grow warmer, and her clothes dried, despite the rain that still pelted them from above. Arix rubbed the warm fabric of her shirt between her fingers.

"How did you do that?"

Revena shrugged. "Just a little bit of magick."

"Is it a new cant?" Arix asked as they continued moving through the maze. "I didn't recognize it or the other one you said. Mould Earth?"

"I just modified the heat cant and turned it into a water re-pellent incantation too." Revena kept her eyes forward, answering Arix's questions in low volume mumbles, ever aware of their sur-roundings as they continued to move through the maze.

"Teach me."

Revena glanced over at her. "It's not like I know what I'm do-ing. I just play with the words until they feel right. Kinetic motions too. There isn't a pattern or system. I just…"

"Guessed?"

The other girl nodded.

Arix shook her head bewildered, a twinge of jealousy biting at her throat. "You're good at this."

"I'm good at magick. There's a difference. I was watching you at the party. You danced so beautifully and chatted with everyone like it was second nature. I hate events like that: rooms filled with people and music and dancing." Revena shuddered. "I despise dancing."

"You were watching me?" Arix was surprised. She didn't think anyone was paying much attention to her. "You know your way around this maze somehow. How did you find me back there?"

"You and I entered from different ends of the maze. I ran across Isadore, she's a competitor from Nero, in the mist, balled up on the ground. She died right there in front of me. I knew that there had to be something about the fog, so I retraced my steps and tried to go a different direction. Every way led to a dead end. So I went back to try and cut through. When I started feeling tired, I turned back again. Tried climbing over one of the hedges. And then I found these." Revena fingered one of the orange and yellow flowers that was still in her hair. "So I used them to get through the mist and try to get people out. I ran into Ambrose and got him out and sent him this direction. I just hope I was right."

Reaching forward, Arix brushed her fingers against the petals of the flower. "May I?"

Revena pulled the stem from her hair and handed it to her.

It was the same flower that Arix had burned up near the beginning of the labyrinth.

"And these helped against the mist?"

Revena nodded.

"How?" Arix examined the petals, the stem, and the center of the flower, but nothing about it stood out except for the bright color. "How did you know they would help?"

Revena stared at her as though she were stupid. "They're Lady Saguaro flowers. They grow in the desert. In Zarak, groups that live deeper in the Sgudal Desert often use them to purify water or air during sandstorms. You've never seen one before?"

Arix only stared at the flowers. They had been a blessing, not a trap. And she'd burned them without knowing what they'd do.

"No. I've never been that deep into the desert before."

"They usually grow on cactuses rather than on a hedge like this," Revena reached out and picked a leaf from the maze wall. "But then again, I'm not really surprised since the whole maze grew up out of nothing overnight."

"Thank you."

"You're welcome."

There were voices up ahead, and the two slowed their pace, more aware of their surroundings.

"I'm hoping that means we're near the center?" Arix whispered.

Revena shrugged and motioned for Arix to flank her while she moved around the next corner. The path curved slightly inward, and straightened out into a long passageway. At the end it opened up into a small circular room where a few people were waiting. Celeste and Michael were two of them.

Arix grinned, lifting a hand in a wave as Michael waved back, a smile on his face.

"Wait!" Revena hissed as Arix moved down the corridor.

Pausing, she stopped to turn back. "What?"

The raven haired girl was still waiting further back, her eyes searching the hallway.

"I think it's an illusion. Just...walk slowly."

Arix kept her hands in front of her as she moved forward, taking painfully slow steps toward the end of the hallway. All at once her hand was stinging, and when she yanked her hand back to her, an angry red line of blood was already streaking down her arm.

"Shit." Arix mumbled, sucking the heel of her hand into her mouth. Revena was at her side now, slowly examining the space in front of them.

"It's not real."

Arix slowly moved her uninjured hand forward inch by inch until her fingers hit something soft. She moved her hand around, feeling until she touched something pliable and stringy. Hair. Quickly she pulled her hand away.

"There's a wall here. And there's something on the other side. A person maybe." she said. Revena nodded.

She moved to the left slightly, and put her hand through again. Her arm was almost up to her elbow when she felt something cold and metallic pierce the tip of her finger. She pulled it back.

"There's a wall on the other side. Lined with spikes, I think."

Revena leaned forward and the tip of her face disappeared into thin air. After a tense few seconds, she withdrew, her mouth drawn into a scowl.

"Follow me."

She pulled Arix with her to the far right hedge and pushed herself as flat as she could against the brush. Arix followed, doing the same, and emerged on the other side of the invisible wall, just barely avoiding a column lined with long, needle-thin metal spikes. She eased around it, stepping where Revena stepped as they weaved around the columns. There were two dead competitors impaled on the spikes, too relieved to think they had found the center of the maze to stop their momentum as they walked directly into their death. Arix looked away, her stomach turning.

The spiked columns were lined like an orchard of trees, Arix realized as she and Revena began weaving their way between and around them. Once past, the space opened up into the small circular center of the maze. At its core was a spiral staircase that led down into the earth. The corridor at the bottom wound down a long hallway with torches burning on either side. Arix and Revena moved slowly, taking their time, watching for signs in the floor, or a brazier tilted the wrong way. Every step was torture. Seeing the doorway at the end of the hall and not being able to run toward it.

When they did finally reach the door, it swung open easily, Lord Bardon waiting for them on the other side, six other competitors with him.

"Well done. You have completed the second test." his voice boomed in the enclosed space.

Glancing around, Arix saw Michael along with Celeste and a few of the others sitting near one of the stone walls. They talked quietly to each other, although most seemed too exhausted to speak. Arix lowered herself to the ground on the other side of Michael. He leaned over, pulling her into a hug. It was strange, feeling his arms around her. But it felt good. Nice.

"You made it through. I'm glad." he said with a small smile before turning to Revena. "And you! Stayed out of too much trouble I hope."

The girl grinned and gave Michael a light punch to the arm. "Just fine and dandy." She nodded toward Arix. "Your friend here almost didn't make it."

Michael whipped his head around to stare at Arix, his brow furrowed. "Are you alright?"

Arix gave him a small smile. "I wouldn't have made it through without Revena." She glancing over at the girl. "She saved my life. More than once."

They sat in silence, curled against each other on the floor of the stone room under the maze until the final bell sounded. Another competitor had joined them, Tanis, though she cradled a broken wrist against herself. No one else had come out of the maze. As they walked back towards the castle, Arix looked at the eight competitors that surrounded her. So few left, and it was only the end of the second test.

She knew the next few months would be hard and slow. And after what had happened in the maze, she needed to train harder. Revena had come to her rescue, and for that reason alone was she still alive. If she wanted to escape with her life, magick might be the only answer. High Priestess Esme's words rang in her ears.

Monsters are not defeated by fortitude alone.

She had to be smart. She had to be cunning. But for now…

Arix glanced sideways at Michael and Revena as they walked beside her. Maybe for now she could just enjoy having a friend or two.

SEVENTEEN

The weather was still dreary and rainy the next morning when Arix woke for her morning run. Tobias looked happy to see her when they met at their usual spot outside the barn, though he said nothing as they jogged off toward the woods. The maze had since vanished again, leaving no trace of the death it had wrought only the day before. Arix stared at the empty field but kept running.

She trained hard that day, putting all of her energy in trying to outsmart Tobias' moves. He was always a little bit faster, and it bothered her how slow her movements felt. As though she was under water. Tobias didn't ask about the maze, and Arix didn't tell him. It hadn't been a test of strength or skill after all, but one of magick, perception, and wisdom. In her mind, she had failed. It didn't matter that she had made it out alive and in one piece. She had only done so because of Revena.

In the afternoon, Desirae pestered her with questions about the test and Arix did her best to satiate her tutor. Desirae had an almost morbid fascination with the puzzles and traps that Arix had run into, and was especially interested in the monster with life sucking mist. After pushing their lesson back even further, Desirae spent an hour speculating about what kind of monster it had been, naming them off like Arix could give her a clue as to who it was. It was the first time that Arix found herself annoyed at her tutor, reading her books quietly while Desirae chattered excitedly to herself.

At long last the sky became tinged with pink, and Arix excused herself to dinner. She sat with Michael, and was glad when Revena shyly asked to join them. They ate in a huddle near the end of the long dining table as the rest of the competitors kept to themselves, engrossed in books or their food.

Michael told them of a small river that had run through his section of the maze, that when touched, pulled you into it, like a sticky tar. Upon reaching a dead end, he had burned his way through a wall and come out on the other side, not ten feet from the center. Arix told him what had happened in the maze as well, and how Revena had used the flowers to get her out. Revena did her best to shrug off the praise, but her ears darkened despite herself and a small shy smile sat at the corner of her mouth.

Andai joined them later during dessert, and the story was told again of how Revena's fast acting and knowledge of the Lady Saguaro flower had saved more than one life. Andai, who was also from the deserts of Zarak had also known the flower, but by the luck of the Goddess, hadn't run into the mist at all.

Apparently, the first to have reached the center was Celeste, followed by Idris, a young boy from Nero, barely out of his teenage years. Then Ambrose, Helios, and Michael. Andai had watched another competitor, Ciel, run right into the spiked columns and had therefore climbed up and over the hedge entirely.

For a moment Arix was reminded of her conversation at the harvest banquet with Ciel's mother. What would they say to her about her daughters death? Would she even be told the details at all?

Arix and Revena had come after Andai, and Tanis last. No one was sure if the other competitors had perished in the traps or if they hadn't made it to the center by the bell.

Andai had a theory about the maze, where it had come from and where it had gone after. There was a good chance, he had said, that it hadn't been made by one incantor. Lakai was strong, but not that strong, after all. But, if there was already a maze with traps in place, a simple teleportation cant would take them straight to it. He thought that the maze had never truly been there at all, but was just an illusion. The maze they stepped into was somewhere else, far away. Thus, it was easy to remove the illusion the following morning. No clean up, no tear down. Just a simple cant.

They sat in silence after that, wondering if anyone had made it out of the maze after the bell. Even if they had, according to Andai's theory, they would be far far from the castle. Maybe even out of the country. With no hope of making it back to their lives before.

~

There was someone waiting for her outside of her bedroom door when she arrived back, her stomach full of lamb stew.

"Good to see you made it through the maze." Orion said, his eyes twinkling, his arms folded across his chest.

"Barely. I got lucky." Arix smiled, leaning against her door. "What are you doing lurking around the competitor's rooms?"

"I wanted to see how you were doing after the test. It seems we lost a few top contenders."

Arix's grin faded slightly and pushed open her door. Orion leaned against the frame, but did not move to step inside.

"Would you like some tea?" she motioned to the armchair by the fire but he shook his head.

"I came here because I wanted to ask if you would accompany me on a stroll through the castle. Zma'ai has a lot to offer, and you've barely seen a third of it. If you would allow me," He bowed low. "I would like to show you some of the more beautiful parts of your home."

Arix's heart twitched at the smile he gave her.

"It's not really my home."

"It will be if you become the Black Hand. Wouldn't you rather know what kind of castle you live in?"

He straightened and smiled. He was too charming for his own good.

"I do have some work to do…" Arix glanced sideways at Ulfur and Abbas who were pretending not to listen in.

Orion noted her glance. "I can assure all parties here that you and I will be most safe from each other."

Twisting his head to peer into the door, Ulfur gave Arix a huge lopsided grin.

"I suppose I could." Arix gave Ulfur a clear *Don't make that face at me, you nosy busybody'* look, to which Ulfur responded with a *When a hot lord asks to take you on a walk, you shouldn't refuse'* look.

"Excellent!" Orion held out his arm to her, eyes twinkling, pretending he hadn't witnessed the exchange. "I promise that you'll love it."

They made their way down the main staircase, then took a hallway that Arix hadn't noticed before. It was a tight fit, probably meant for only one person, but Arix followed his lead as Orion led her through the castle. Somewhere during the walk, Arix found she was holding his hand and her face blushed slightly.

When they emerged from the hallway, a large double door

stood before them, carvings and runes engraved into the dark wood.

"Alright, now you have to close your eyes." Orion said, his hands covering her face.

Arix snorted. "Is this necessary?"

"Yes." He whispered, his breath warm in Arix' ear. A shiver ran down her spine as his voice tickled the hair at her neck. "Reach out and push open the door."

Arix did as she was asked, reaching forward to find the latch and turned it. She felt the air change as she pulled open the door, Orion maneuvering her inside. Her footsteps softened as she stepped from marble to wood. They walked forward, Orion turning her to the left and right as they walked around the room.

"We're here," His voice rumbled softly in her ear. "You can open your eyes now."

His fingers slipped from her face and she opened them.

They stood in the center of a ballroom sized hall with a floor to ceiling ornate window directly opposite the doorway, allowing the dark blue sky to twinkle in, drawing shapes on the floor with its shadows of the great candelabras that were strewn about the room. All about them, bookshelves miles high stretch from the floor to the ceiling. Scattered across the floor were soft armchairs and under the window, a massive cushioned window seat that could have comfortably seated fifteen.

Arix pivoted, her gaze scanning the room and found it hard to breathe. As she stepped further in, her gaze flit about the room, catching anything and everything. Desirae's office was nothing compared to this compendium of knowledge.

She approached a shelf with caution and glanced down the spines, searching for a familiar name.

"What do you think?"

Arix turned back to Orion whom she had forgotten, and blinked. "Where did you find all of these?"

The corner of his mouth turned upwards only slightly, "They more or less found me. I was snooping around one day and found this place. I thought you might enjoy it. Welcome to the king's library."

Arix turned back to the spines and pulled one out.

"Galeos?"

"Poetry." Orion leaned over her shoulder and opened it up to the first poem.

> *In nature's tapestry, good and evil entwine,*
> *Threads of light and shadow, a design divine.*
> *As stars adorn the night, and roses bear their thorns,*
> *Life's dichotomy reveals where wisdom's born.*

"I've never heard of him." Arix said slowly, taking the book from and continuing to read the remainder of the poem in her head.

"Not many have"

Arix looked over her shoulder into his face. "Why not?"

He reached over her shoulder and took the book from her, placing it gently back on the shelf.

"Because it hasn't been written yet." He whispered, his eyes twinkling with the secret.

Arix stared at him as he walked the shelves, hands clasped behind his back.

"What do you mean hasn't been written?"

"Magick."

Arix stepped back to look up, the tops of the shelves disappearing out of reach from the candle's light.

"At least, that's my running theory. Something about this place is enchanted. The books here span through history, bound neither by days or decades. Some of them are near impossible to understand, but here they are, nonetheless. All that has ever been written, and all that ever will be."

Arix's heart beat so quickly in her chest, she felt like it would explode out of her. Her eyes were burning, tears trying to escape. So much knowledge. The sheer amount of it made her knees weak.

"How did you find this? Are we even allowed to be here? It feels sacred. Like we aren't even supposed to know it exists."

Orion sat in one of the armchairs and watched as she read the spines of the books she passed, her arms now clasped tightly behind her back terrified she might disturb something holy.

"Like I said, it more or less found me. When I first came to court, this place was dusty, most of the furniture rotted away. As if it hadn't been touched in years. A place like this deserves to be taken care of. Not left to decay. If King Taurus cared about this place, he wouldn't have left it in such a state." There was a twinge of annoyance in his voice.

"I thought the kings loved magick. All that power in one person's hand. And this?" Arix spun in a circle, motioning to the towers of books around her. "This is the epitome of that! Information and magick, all kept for only one person."

"Be careful, Arix." Orion said, a laugh on his lips. "You're sounding a little treasonous."

"It feels wrong."

Arix turned to look at him, her eyes burning.

"Why did you show me this?"

Orion rose and joined her by the rows of books. His eyes glittered stormy blue in the firelight, pieces of dark hair falling around his face as his eyes roved the spines.

"You seemed like someone who would appreciate it." He said

simply, finally turning to stare at her. "Not everyone understands the magnitude of a place like this."

He said it so plainly, so openly, it made Arix's heart skip. He had found this place in disarray, and had restored it. Why?

Suddenly she found it hard to look at him.

"It was my father who taught me to love books." Arix said, turning away. "He thought it was important for me and my brother to love stories as much as he did."

"You have a brother?"

"Not anymore."

Arix pulled another book down off the shelf, examining the contents; more poetry.

"I'm sorry, Arix."

"Please don't be." Arix turned back to him, wishing she'd said nothing at all. "It was a long time ago. You know, you're the second person I've told. It's strange, but I haven't talked about my family in a very long time."

Her chest hurt. This was why she didn't talk about them or think about them. It was so long ago and yet the details were still so vivid. She did not want to relive it.

"What's your favorite book?" She asked, pulling him away and leaving the past behind as they strolled between the shelves.

Orion led her down past row upon row until it felt like they had walked for an hour. It didn't seem possible that so many shelves could fit inside a real building. Arix had seen the castle from the outside, and there was no possible explanation for it.

No, that wasn't right. Magick was the explanation.

Finally he pulled her into a little alcove where a high back chair sat beside a small side table. He motioned for her to sit, then handed her a heavy volume. *The Divine* by Antheridial Gie, followed by *Lost Unto Self* by Jomil Thonn.

"I don't have as much time to read as I'd like, but the library suggested these to me. I'll admit I struggle with the language at times, though the poetry really is beautiful."

Arix opened the second book to its marked place, her eyes scanning down the page. It was beautiful, yes, but hard to follow. It seemed to tell the story of the devil.

"What do you mean, the library suggested it?" she turned the pages slowly, though with each new line, she found herself more confused.

"We walked a rather long way to get here, yes?"

"Yes."

"And it should take us just as long to get back, yes?"

"I suppose so."

"Come with me."

Leaving the books in the chair, Arix followed Orion as he rounded a bookshelf and disappeared from sight. Rounding the same shelf, Arix stopped short, her eyes wide. They were back in the main entrance. She glanced back and the alcove was gone.

"How?" She breathed, stepping back away from the shelves to the safety of the open floor.

Orion chuckled. "I told you, this place is magick. Sometimes I'll just wander around and see where I end up. The library takes you where you want to go if you focus hard enough, but she's a bit stubborn at times."

Arix's head was swimming.

A snort brought her out of her stupor and she glared at Orion as he fought to hide his smile.

"What?"

"You looked so surprised." He laughed. "Like I'd just dumped a bucket of water over your head."

"You did just show me a magickal library that moves! How am

I supposed to respond?"

He only smiled at her.

The ache in her chest grew.

"Actually, I should probably go. I have a list of spells to study."

Orion's smile faded slightly, but he quickly covered it by offering her his arm.

"Then I shall escort you back to your room, my lady."

Arix took the offered arm with a smile, but glanced back as they passed through the door of the library. It seemed to thrum with energy compared to the simple stone hallway outside. She could have sworn it whispered to her as the heavy oaken door fell into place with a thud.

Come back soon, Bellarix Sable.

EIGHTEEN

It seemed to Arix that she saw Orion everywhere now. He passed her in the halls, happened to be in the barn at the same time, bumping into her outside the council room. There were evenings when Arix fought the urge to join him strolling the gardens at night, her mountain of homework keeping her locked indoors. He was always surprised when he saw her, glancing up, his blue eyes catching the light as he paused in his conversation to smile at her or offer a nod. And every time he smiled, her insides would squirm and her ears would go pink.

It bothered her, the way he made her feel. Restless, like she wasn't working hard enough at her studies or wasn't training as much as she could. Arix's studies, no matter how hard she tried to concentrate, seemed like a stone she was constantly butting into. She was distracted, her mind flitting from one piece of information to the next, never seeming to settle long enough to learn everything. Every step forward was a struggle. Every new cant learned by scraping and clawing at the pages and damning her own self for not learning fast enough.

As the days streamed into each other, Arix found herself

spending more and more time with Michael and Revena. They practiced incantation work together, and Revena taught them how to cantweave different ones together to create something new. They were given new, long, and overflowing lists of new enchantments and charms, and they taught each other; late into the night on the garden roof.

Many of the new cants were only more complex versions of the ones they had already learned. Morph Water became Birth or Destroy water, calling little puddles across the roof at will rather than altering one that was already there. They learned more spirit based cants, such as the ability to charm someone into trusting you, though none of them could get it to last longer than a few seconds.

At first the kinetic movements were stiff, each motion needing longer to cast. But with practice, the incantations became as easy as breathing. Michael, the girls had begun to notice, had a special affinity for earth based cants, and was overjoyed to learn through the Herb Linga cant that his tomatoes were in fact quite healthy and happy, and just a little shy.

Experimentation was the root of learning, and it appeared that learning with friends was much preferable to learning by one's own self.

~

"This is a terrible idea."

"I've triple checked the calculations." Revena was grinning like a fool, stray curls falling over her eyes as she ticked the items off on her fingers. "Waning crescent moon, old crow's feathers, and we've got the words and kinetic motions down perfectly. We'll be fine!"

Arix glanced down, her grip on the feather in question tightening as she stared down at the ground seven stories below them.

"Or we could muck it up and die a terrible death of being splattered across the cobblestones."

"A shame. And here I always thought I'd die of old age." Michael muttered beside her.

He was not peering down, but instead had his eyes screwed shut so tightly that his entire face pinched together. Only Revena looked thrilled at the prospect of throwing herself off the roof.

"No one's going to die!" She repeated. "Besides, only one of us has to get it right. One cant will work on all three of us, so if someone chickens out and forgets to say the word, the others' cants will catch them."

She stepped up onto the ledge at Arix's left, and joined her friends by staring down the side of the castle wall, all the way to the cobblestone path of the garden below.

Michael's voice was small and shaky. "What if we all mess up?"

For a moment, there was silence between them as the reality of what they were about to do settled into their bones, and that primal knot of fear tangled up in their bellies. It tangled with the primal whisper in their minds that told them to *jump*.

"Alright." Arix knew if she didn't say something now, they'd never really do it. "Alright, let's do this."

"Can't hold hands." Revena's voice had become slightly less enthused than it had been a moment ago. "We need our hands for the motion. Don't forget the kinetic motions."

"Or splat." Michael muttered.

"Or splat." Revena and Arix responded in unison.

"On the count of three?"

Arix clutched the feather with all her might, repeating the

word over and over in her head.

"One…"

"Two…"

"Three!"

"Letimo nas troje!" Arix screeched, flicking the tip of the feather off the bottom of her chin as she vaulted herself off the wall and plummeted toward the ground.

Revena was screaming, shrill and piercing in the night air. Arix legs kicked wildly, her eyes as wide as dinner plates. Michael was curled into a ball, eyes still screwed shut, his fists balled around the feather, holding it straight outright as though it were an offering.

And they were *floating*.

Revena was still screaming, but Arix managed to choke out a panicked laugh as the trio floated down towards the ground and landed with a small thump in the grass.

They sat in their little pile, staring at each other until after a moment, Arix shakily pulled herself to her feet, looked her friends dead in the eyes and said:

"Let's do it again!"

~

Not all attempted cants went according to plan of course, and the trio spent a whole day stuck in a loop of a mis-casted Borealis Laughter cant. They were finally discovered when Ulfur stuck his head around the door to see why they'd been laughing for five hours straight, and found the three friends clutching their stomachs in pain while tears rolled out of their eyes, all laughing hysterically in various positions around the roof. They took a break after that, resigning themselves to never perform one cant cast between the three of them at the exact same time.

Revena and Arix also spent a good amount of time together without Michael, working through the combination of cants. Revena tried teaching Arix what she knew about sewing two cants together to make something entirely unique. It required quite a bit of experimentation, but Revena had an affinity for coalescent magick, as they'd begun to call it, and it only made Arix more discouraged. Magick seemed to need some sort of talent to work well, and it became more aware that she did not have it. When Arix tried to quit, Revena would always coax her back in with some new coalescent trick, and Arix found herself enjoying the time spent with Revena.

It was commonplace for the competitors to always carry a small pouch with them, containing essential ingredients that may be necessary in casting. The pouch varied from person to person, as some, like Michael, were more adept in certain types of cants over others. Arix carried chalk, string, feathers, incense, spices, bits of leather and other fabrics, dried herbs and flowers, and copious amounts of salt. When practicing, they went through quite a few materials, and new ingredients had to be scavenged or requested via written form to Lakai. To circumvent this rule, Revena had coalesced a cant that no matter how many ingredients you took from your component pouch, there was always just enough to perform the cant. As long as it was refilled once per week, for seven days the pouch contained exactly what you needed and didn't run empty.

A small bowl was usually needed to contain the ingredients, or for the caster to hold them in their hands. This method didn't work very well, since more complex cants required two hands to be performed. Trying to hold a feather, a pinch of salt, and a holly branch wasn't easy when trying to perform a two handed kinetic cant. It was Michael's idea to distill certain herbs into small jars of oils. That way, whenever a specific herb was needed, the caster only had to use a drop or two of oil rubbed between her hands or dabbed on the wrist to empower the cant.

Arix preferred the distilled jars of oil to the loose jostling of ingredients in a pouch. To avoid the bottles clattering against each other and breaking, Arix sewed fitted loops and pockets into the inside of her satchel. Each bottle had its own space, snuggly fitted to keep them from spilling their contents and ruining the pouch. The tiny rows of bottles clinked together lightly when she walked, and the sound soon became a melodic jingle that comforted her. To silence the tinkling of the glass, she merely had to wrap a bit of cloth within the bag to muffle the sounds.

A week before the next test, Lakai began training them in duels, forcing the competitors to train against each other. One would act as an incantor, having to perform cants from within their casting circle, while the other had to move through a series of barriers to reach a small stone. The goal of the incantor was to keep his opponent from ever reaching the stone, using only magick. The goal of the thief was to avoid the cants, and make their way to steal the stone, without the use of any magick whatsoever.

Those casting would have to learn to find inventive ways to keep their opponent from ever reaching the stone, and the thief would have to be fast enough to avoid any of the cants. Revena was proving herself to be the best incantor and practitioner at spur magick, or magick that was cast instinctively. Before Andai had even gone ten feet, she had him battling within a rainstorm, complete with lightning bolts. During Michael's test, he grew a jungle of weeds and thorns that slowed down his opponent, tangling their feet in the brambles.

Arix had grown fond of mind cants, or incantations that played with what the mind could perceive. First she caused her opponent, Tanis, to be distracted by whispers only she could hear. Then, Terror Image, a cant that produced an image of a terrifying creature. All these Tanis skirted, blocking out the whispers and the picture of an ogre while she continued to move toward the stone. Finally, when she was nearly to the prize, Arix cast a sleeping cant, causing the other girl to fall to the ground, dead asleep.

The more Arix practiced, the better she became, her skill growing little by little. And yet, each new lesson with Lakai only showed her how far she had yet to go. Again and again Lakai disarmed her or hindered her attacks, deflecting her cants with even more powerful ones. She was growing in skill, she knew. Her ability seemed to match Michael's but Revena was just plain better than the rest. She was faster, and could recall ingredients with the same speed as if you had asked her to recite her own name. It was discouraging to feel so clumsy with magick, to feel so behind.

Nevertheless Arix pushed forward. But as the days passed, her frustration grew. She would always prefer her lockpicks and a sword. Those were things she knew she excelled at.

Her morning runs were performed in sleet and rain, her fingers moving to keep herself warm despite the cold. Her training on horseback was done blindfolded, using cants to see through Osiris' eyes rather than her own. Modifying a reader cant, her books read to her while she slept, a constant scratching of script in her ear. On nights when she was sick of her studies, the whispering words of Galeos lulled her to sleep.

Most nights her dreams were good: adventures with Revena and Michael, and late night strolls under the moon with Orion. Then, there were those that plagued her. Strange combinations of flaming hay bales and a pair of giant hands that spelled out kinetic movements in the sky. Dark leafy mazes and flying books, with Orion stepping just out of reach around hedge corners. She called out for him and he was there, but when she turned, gone again, lost in row after row of burning books.

She would wake, out of breath and shaking, pushing her way out of bed to the open window. Summer had finally and truly disappeared, autumn in her full glory. The nights were crisp and cold, the competitors wearing cloaks and scarves when outside. Fires blazed in the hearths, and Arix spent long evenings curled up in front of them with a book in her lap.

The night finally came when the next test was announced. They were to await in their rooms, and at the break of light, venture into the forest to search for burdock root. The last to return with the root and present it to the council would be removed from the competition. Anyone attempting to leave the castle before dawn would be removed without question.

Since they were allowed to use magick to search for the root, Arix compiled a search cant, mapping out locations where it might be. She had narrowed it down to the far west corner when a soft knock interrupted her thoughts. Wren entered, and set down a teacup and saucer at her side.

"What's all this?" She asked, peering over Arix's shoulder at the ingredients that were scattered about the floor.

Arix smiled, taking a sip of her tea. Thistle and two sugars. Perfect.

"Test tomorrow. Say, Wren, how big does burdock grow? I've only seen pictures in my herbology book. Is it about this tall?" Arix held out her hand and hovered it at her shoulder level. "Or bigger?"

Wren took Arix's hand and lowered it a bit. "I'd say about here. Though the plant itself has a couple different stages of growth so it could range anywhere in this area." Wren motioned to the empty space between Arix's hand and the floor. "What do you need burdock for?"

"We'll be searching for burdock root tomorrow. There's a lot of ground to cover in the woods. Last person back with it loses."

"Is that what the map is for?"

"Yes." Arix took another sip of her tea and sighed. "I'm trying to find a way to locate it without needing any of the root to begin with."

"Why not simply talk to the plants when you get out there?"

Arix turned and gave Wren a look. The maid blushed in response.

"I just mean..." She stammered, her ears turning beet red, "I saw Master Woodhale talking to his tomatoes. They appeared to be talking back. I thought maybe he was using a cant."

Uncrossing her legs, Arix collapsed back onto the floor behind her.

"Well yes, there is a cant to talk to plants. And Michael's actually very good at it. But the thing with plants is that they don't have a lot of respect for each other, and tend to mind their own business. I might be able to ask a tree where a burdock plant is, but he probably wouldn't know or care to know. They're quite solitary creatures, plants."

She sounded ridiculous, she knew. And if she had heard herself three months ago, she wouldn't have believed it. To anyone else, she probably sounded like a witch, tittering on about roots and trees talking to each other.

"Oh, I nearly forgot," Wren reached into the pocket of her apron and handed Arix a folded up slip of paper. "This was under the door."

The note was not addressed, and when Arix opened it, found a simple script inside.

Meet me in the south hallway on the third floor at

10:30. I need to show you something.
Make sure you are not followed.

Her curiosity peaked, Arix thanked Wren and turned the note over, examining it. No signature, and the penmanship wasn't one she recognized as Michael's or Revena's. Perhaps Orion? Her heart picked up pace. It had been a while since she'd seen him, and maybe he wanted to wish her good luck before her test. Her tiredness suddenly gone, she glanced at the timepiece on her dresser. She was going to be late.

"Just a meeting with Michael to go over notes for tomorrow," Arix lied, grabbing her cloak off the back of her chair. "Wish me luck for tomorrow, Wren. And pray to the goddess for good weather!"

At the door it took entirely too much bribery to convince Ulfur and Abbas to stay behind, promising that if she wasn't back in ten minutes that they could hang her off the parapets by her toes. Arix made her way through the castle, ducking into doorways as she went, and making sure no one saw her creep up the stairs and onto the third floor.

The hallway was dimly lit, most of the torches snuffed out and cold. A figure waited on the far side of the hallway, hood up. Arix approached, trying to keep a grin off her face.

"Orion? Is that you? Awfully secretive for such a-"

The figure turned as Arix neared, and a white powder filled Arix's vision, her nose and eyes choking. Instantly her vision faltered, and her world began to tip. She reached out for the figure, but it stepped out of her reach as she tumbled to the floor. It was as if someone was yanking her down into the veined marble floor, and she was helpless to stop it. A sharp crack sounded in her ears as her skull made contact. Within seconds, she was consumed by blackness.

NINETEEN

The dreams that haunted her would never stop. Arix had given herself up to them, and they terrorized her mind.

Flames licked at her feet as she walked across a crumbling, burning bridge.

The entire ocean slowly froze as she fought to swim against the waves that slowly crystallized around her.

Huge mountains melted like sand under acid rain, burning her skin.

Yet, she ran. On and on she tore through the dream, trying to stay one step ahead of the horrors that raged behind her.

She tore at her hair and raked her skin, yet she could not wake from the city of sleep.

They hunted her, cutting off her advances, dropping her in great wells, where all she did was fall and fall and fall.

No matter what she did, no matter where she turned, they were there, waiting for her. Great beasts made of molten rock and skeletal bones. Each worse than the last, their mouths opened wide; great caverns filled with teeth.

And when she thought she could go no further, there, waiting on a large throne was a man, looming out from a pit of sand, the chair slowly sinking into the mire.

He was laughing, his crazed eyes opened wide and bloodshot, trickles of blood leaking from his nose and ears. He laughed as though the world depended on it, great bellyfulls of sick raking laughter. He gripped at his throne with shredded and bleeding nails, and he stared at her while he did, his great mouth yawning in front of her.

She ran towards him, away from the monsters, stumbling into the sinking sand, fighting harder with every step.

And she sank.

Deep into the sand, the world spinning around her, she sank into the comfort of a breathless death.

TWENTY

The world was a fuzzy outline, with white flashes of light. Arix squinted away from it. She tried to sit up, but her stomach roiled and she threw her body weight to the side to avoid vomiting on herself. Her stomach ached. Her head ached. Her eyes burned against the light and the shapes that coursed around her. A hand rested behind her neck, and someone's fingers stroked through her hair. Someone was talking in the distance but the sound was garbled, as if she was hearing it under water. The voice rose and fell with emotion and something shattered. A loud bang.

Arix turned her face away from the light, burying into the cool fabric on her cheek. She pulled her knees up to her stomach as she lay on her side, trying to block out all the garbled lights and sounds around her. She wanted to die. A slow slipping death of silence, darkness, and oblivion. There was a ringing in her left ear as the voices slowly cleared, making words into semi-coherent thoughts and sentences.

"-upset. Poor girl-"

"-couldn't finish-"

"-outside waiting-"

Her consciousness slipped away from her; sand disappearing through her fingers. The voices faded again as Arix fell back into the darkness.

~

It was night when she awoke again, the first thing becoming clear in her vision: the roaring orange of the fireplace. Her eyelids were heavy and her gaze traveled around the room to a weight resting on the edge of the bed. The soft rise and fall of breathing as the figure rested their head on their arms. Arix groaned as she tried to roll to the side. Wren sat up, eyes wide, before jumping to assist.

"Oh, Miss Arix! Thank the Goddess. Just take it easy now, there you go. Nice and easy."

The door opened behind her and Miss Charlotte came in carrying a basin of water.

"Thank the Goddess. Miss Charlotte, she's awake."

Arix tried to pull herself into a sitting position, but her elbows buckled underneath her and she collapsed back onto the bed. The hanging gauze above her bed looked like spiderwebs.

Arix quickly looked away.

"Easy there, lass." Miss Charlotte handed the basin to Wren, who scuttled into the bathing room. She held her hand against Arix's forehead. "Still too warm for my liking."

Arix tried to speak, but her mouth was filled with sand, and even her breathing felt like she was fighting tooth and nail to draw it.

"Hush now. No need for words." Miss Charlotte's accented voice was soft and soothing as she placed a cool cloth over Arix' forehead. "I'm sure it's all very confusing right now. Just rest your eyes, and all will be explained later. I'll be right here while you sleep."

Arix felt the tears leaking from her eyes and Miss Charlotte ran her fingers through Arix's red knotted hair. The motherly touch was concerned and loving.

"Sleep now."

She closed her eyes, enjoying the cool rag. Her scalp tingled against the touch. She pulled her knees up, reveling in the feeling. Then she was asleep.

~

Her jaw ached, as if she'd been grinding her teeth in her sleep. It felt like the marrow in her bones had been scraped out, leaving her feeling hollow and empty. Her stomach swayed and she lurched to the side in case she vomited again. But her stomach was empty, and instead she found herself choking on nothing.

A glass was pressed to her lips, and she took a slow shallow drink, letting the water cool her throat.

"There she is."

Michael replaced the glass on the side table, and settled back into his chair that was angled next to her bed. His hands wrapped up hers and squeezed it gently.

"You alive in there, Arix?"

"Barely." She replied weakly, testing out her voice.

"You scared us all to death, you know."

"What..." Her tired tongue stumbled over words. "...happened?"

Michael took a breath, squeezing her hands harder. "What do you remember?"

Arix tried stepping back through her mind, piecing together memories and thoughts. There was a large dark piece where everything faded away that no matter how hard she tried, she couldn't remember.

"I got a note. To meet someone. I thought it was…I..don't…"

Michael grimaced, his mouth forming a taut line. "It's alright, keep going."

"Turned around and there was something in my eyes. Then…I don't remember."

She remembered her head hitting the floor; the feeling of utter loss of balance. A ringing in her ears. Her eyes burning. And then the nightmares.

Arix squeezed her eyes shut, trying to block out the fever dream. The monsters, the sinking sand, the laughing king, the voices. Arix's eyes shot open and she tried to move up to a sitting position. Panic rose in her chest, her legs tangling in the blankets. She could hear, rather than feel her breath rattling around in her lungs.

"The test. Did I miss it? I have to go…"

Michael placed his hands on her shoulder, pushing her back down.

"Easy now! There's nothing to be done. You missed it."

The water she drank plunged in her stomach, and Arix turned and vomited into the waiting bucket. Some splashed onto Michael's boots, but he didn't flinch. He rubbed her back in slow circles as she coughed, wiping her mouth on the towel he offered her.

"I'm sorry." She muttered.

"Don't worry about it, Arix."

"What happened to me?"

"You were poisoned." Michael said simply, drawing his fingers through her hair to pull it away from her face. "The night before the test, you were poisoned. Doctor thinks it was probably Witch's Envy leaf broken down into a powder. You had some in your eyes and nose when Abbas and Ulfur found you."

Arix laid back against the pillows trying to slow her breathing. In, out. In, out.

"Who?"

"Tanis Devina."

Arix gaped at him, her eyes wide. Her mind flickered back to the look Tanis had given her before the maze. Resentment, disgust. Then to all those times she'd bested crooked-nose in group class and duels.

"Why? Why would she do that?"

Michael shrugged, his hands running through his hair.

"I think she was mad that you had help from Revena during the maze. She said something about you not deserving to still be here when others were dead."

Arix felt as though she might be sick again. Everything in her was numb, dizzy circles disorienting her mind.

"So what happens now? Am I…" Arix couldn't' make herself say the words. She hadn't ever intended to be the Black Hand, but she hadn't intended to be dead either.

"Disqualified? No. Someone had to lose in this game. When Ulfur and Abbas found you stashed in a closet somewhere on the third floor, the council was furious. They questioned everyone and searched everyone's rooms. Tanis was found guilty and they took her away. I don't know what happened to her. Technically you're still here by default."

The pounding in her head had resurfaced, digging holes into the back of her eye sockets. Arix pressed two fists against them, wishing the aching would subside.

"You've been feverish for five days now. Doctor didn't know

if you'd wake up. Revena was here a bit ago, but she had to go back to training so I said I'd sit with you for a bit in case you woke up."

Michael placed a hand on her forehead. "Fever's broken at least. Nasty stuff, that Witch's Envy."

He was smiling, but Arix could see the wave of relief that sat behind his eyes. He'd been worried about her. Arix managed a weak smile.

"You know me. Nothing takes down Bellarix Sable before her time."

The conversation, however short it had been, had already drained Arix of her strength. She fought to keep her eyes open, and Michael finally left her to sleep. The dreams, at least this time, were void.

~

It was dark again when Arix woke, the room only lit by the fire in the hearth. A form sat facing it in one of the armchairs, long legs crossed in front of him.

"Orion."

He turned as she spoke, rising slowly from his seat and approaching the bed. Each step was painfully slow, like he was afraid that any sudden movements would break her. He sat on the edge of the bed, hands fidgeting in his lap.

"Orion." Arix said again, watching his face. "What are you doing here?"

The lines were hard, his eyes cold.

"Your maid's getting more water. I told her I'd stay to make sure you were still breathing."

Arix sighed, working the air through her lungs slowly.

"I am. I guess you know what happened?"

His chin dipped slightly.

"Tell me. I think Michael was trying to spare me the details. As if I couldn't handle it."

He wouldn't look at her, his eyes still trained on his hands. When he spoke it sounded rehearsed, like he'd said it again and again already. Maybe even written it down.

"Tanis Devina, a competitor from Tamhain, lured you into the third floor corridor. Whereupon she poisoned you with a potent powdered form of Witch's Envy. You passed out and your body was hidden to avoid detection. Your guards, after noting you were missing, went in search of you and found you. You were brought immediately before a doctor who deduced you had been poisoned, and Lord Bardon issued a search of every room currently occupied in the castle. Residue was found in Tanis's room, and she was brought to the council for questioning. She was found guilty and sentenced to death for treachery. Orders were carried out immediately. The following morning, the test was conducted, but because of your predicament, your role was defaulted. You won't have to retake the test, so don't worry. I spoke with Lord Bardon."

"Where was it?" Arix asked, her eyes fighting to remain open.

Orion cocked his head, finally looking at her, confusion on his face. "Where was what?"

"The burdock root. Where was it in the forest?"

"In the westmost part of the woods."

Arix smiled, the corners of her mouth teetering up into a sloppy grin. "I knew it."

Orion let out a relieved laugh. Yet the hard lines of worry still sat around his eyes.

"I thought..." He swallowed, and began again. "We all thought you would die."

There was unshaved stubble along his jaw.

"Worried about me?" She was so tired, her mind wavering and melting back into the holds of sleep. She raised her fingers to graze the stubble on his cheek, though her arm felt heavier than a stone statue. Orion clutched at her hand, holding it to his face. He said nothing, but the look in his eyes said enough.

Arix felt herself slipping away then, sleep calling to her like a lullaby.

"Stay with me." She whispered.

Sleep dragged her away before she heard his response.

TWENTY-ONE

While Arix recovered, her lessons still continued. Lakai visited her in her room, and they worked specifically on verbal cants, repeating them over and over until they were perfect. Everywhere else in the castle, the court was bustling in preparation for Samhain. The celebration thanking the Goddess for the harvest, and preparing for the coming of the winter months.

Samhain was dark and mysterious, a time of year when the veil between the earthly and the divine became thin. Long ago, before magick had nearly vanished from existence, faeries would often be seen on Samhain, the light of the bonfires glinting off their wings. Yet even after the last faeries had disappeared from the realms, the traditions of leaving out offerings for them prevailed. Dishes of milk were set in window frames, pieces of bread and cheese left near the doors. Even the animals knew not to bother these offerings, and every year, the food was left untouched, a symbol to the faeries that they were missed.

The halls of the castle were decorated with wreaths of apples and acorns, gourds and fat orange candles. A large table was set up in the center hall, overflowing with baskets of foods, prepared as an offering for the Goddess Arduinna. A great willow wood man was constructed in the courtyard, to be set ablaze at midnight. It was tradition that the court would gather and throw in letters to their past selves, burning them up to symbolize changes they sought within themselves.

After much prodding and begging, it was determined that Arix would be allowed out of bed for the celebration, only with the stipulation that she would return if she felt too tired. Though it had been two and a half weeks since her poisoning, and though Arix felt much more like herself, the doctor still wanted her to rest as much as possible.

"I want you top notch." He had said. "Ready for what awaits you in the next test."

Another tradition of the court was to wear masks made of wood and bone to the bonfire, hiding their faces should any restless spirits desire to take someone of importance away. With the masks, you were hidden from the otherworld. Hidden from the dead. Arix shaped her mask from a deer's skull, great horns curling up and away from her head. She wore a black dress that clung around her in swathes of sheer fabric, sleeves falling open to the floor. With Michael on one side with his copper fox mask, and Revena on the other with her dragon made of wood, the three entered into the courtyard on the deep black night of Samhain.

There was a feeling in the air at Samhain. Something dark and distant. Growing up, Arix had always thought that this night was filled with the residual energy of magick; the final clinging force left in the world. But now that she knew what magick felt like, knew the tingling of it coursing through her veins as she cast, she realized it was different. There was a thrumming of power, like a heartbeat under the ground, that connected to all of them. It made her feel small and insignificant. A speck within the cosmos, within the vast black velvet of the night sky. It filled her with wonder and with questions she didn't know how to voice. It was bigger than the magick thrumming through her. It was deeper, older.

Masked musicians played music around the fire-lit night, performing old forgotten songs of the gods and goddesses, of death and life and the space in between. The fiddler wove in and out between the guests, his melancholy strings filled with sorrow, yet holding the promise of a secret no one knew existed. Some joined in, singing and dancing around the fire, their masks hiding their identity from those around them.

It was a night of sensual fluid motion. Bodies swaying to the music, to the moon, to the fire. Arix found herself being pulled in, her arms above her head as she swayed to the sound of the strings. And then she was dancing with him, the fiddler, and he swung her round and round, promising a night filled with darkness and intrigue. Her head spun, heady with the atmosphere of the night. She was drunk on the air of Samhian, drunk on the macabre celebration of the circle of life into death.

In the height of the dance, the willow man was lit, the moon shining over it all in the blanket of the sky. They danced on, deep into the early morning, when finally, as the sky turned gray, and mist began to ease in around them, they turned back to the castle, lulled into bed as the sun rose.

Despite all the dancing and frivolity, Arix could not sleep. Instead she sat at her window, flung wide, and watched as the sun snuck over the horizon and cast light over the last embers of the willow man. It was quiet throughout the castle, and there was some different kind of magick in that, being awake when the world was asleep. It made Arix feel like she could fly.

"What damsel there, watching alight through panes of time, and lost am I in her beauty fair."

Below her, the fiddler called up, stretching his bow across the strings as he played for her the last song of Samhain. Deep and old and so beautiful that it took Arix's breath away. She laughed, reaching her fingers out and playing with the sunlight that danced between them.

"I bid thee fair morn, dear lady heart. For the day is dawning, calling me back toward the dark."

He bowed to her, deep and low, and Arix bowed back, nestling her head on her arms as she watched him dance away, still playing his fiddle as he went.

~

During breakfast a week later, Wren brought Arix the summons. Written on the thick glossy parchment of the council, all the competitors were summoned for a meeting. When she arrived, Michael and Revena were as confused as she was. It was still another week before the fourth test. The competitors stood together, waiting for the last of the council to arrive. When the final members were seated, Lord Bardon called them to order, and stood at the head of the table.

"You have been asked here today, a week before the next test, because we face a threat that has not been present in our country for generations. But now, one of our sacred temples in Sieren has been struck, and we must act swiftly if we are to eliminate this threat. What we are about to ask of you will be voluntary. None will be forced to participate." Lord Bardon shifted his weight, his mouth set in a hard line. "During Samhain, a darkness arose from the water and entered the Temple of Nereus. Thirty of the priestesses and priests have been slaughtered by what we believe is a *paramour.*"

Arix felt a chill down her spine, the weight of his words grounding her to the spot. She could feel the tension of those around her, Michael standing straighter, his fists clenched.

"You are the only practicing incantors in the country, and your king asks that you go to eradicate this monster. Those who wish to stay and train for the upcoming test will not be forced to go to Nero. Yet, without confrontation, more in the city will die. But understand the gravity of what we ask you. If you go, there is a fair chance you will not return."

It was silent in the room for a few earth shattering seconds before a voice spoke up from Arix's left. Celeste stepped forward and dropped to one knee, her fist crossed over her heart.

"I serve the King. I will gladly go and rid Nero of this paramour in service of his majesty, King Taurus."

A prick of frustration pulsed in Arix's left temple. All the girl needed to say was yes. There wasn't any need for a grand speech.

A motion to her left caught her eye as Revena stepped forward too, her fist over her heart as well.

"So will I." The raven haired girl said, though her voice audibly shook.

Arix felt Michael also moving to stand with them, and not to be called a coward, Arix stepped with him, her hand over her heart. Fine thing it would be if she was the only one who stayed behind.

Slowly, the rest of the competitors around her also stepped forward their hands over their hearts. Some did it to keep from being left out, the disgrace of being left behind was too much.

Arix walked back to her room alone. They would leave the next morning, departing for Nero out of the Mergur's capital harbor. Since Sieren was along the Neroan coastline, it would be faster to travel by boat than by horseback.

Beside her, Ulfur and Abbas kept pace, though she could tell from the way Ulfur heald his head that they not only knew what she would be facing, but were against it. The frustration in her temple grew.

Goddess, why had she stepped forward? She didn't want to be a coward. She didn't want them to see her backing down from a fight. She'd survived this long, but if she was being honest with herself, the only reason she had was because of Revena and Michael.

Truth be told, she was scared. Wealthy barons were one thing. But a paramour? A paramour was something else entirely.

"Arix."

"Mmm?" Arix kept her gaze forward, not offering Ulfur the courtesy of looking at him.

"You cannot do this."

"Is that so?"

Ulfur's voice turned to an impatient growl, and he grabbed her arm, spinning her to a stop. "You'll die, Arix."

Arix jerked away from his grip. "You don't know that."

"Don't be stupid, lass. You've heard of what a paramour does. They'll be no coming back from this." Ulfur gave Abbas a side glance, frustration evident on his face. "She'll gut you. Navel to nethers, there won't be pieces of you to even bring back."

"You should not speak of things you don't know, Ulfur Tuk."

Arix and Ulfur both turned, surprised, as Abbas spoke.

"She will not gut you, child." Abbas' voice was level. Curt. "But she will drain you of your life."

"What do you know of paramours, Abbas?" Arix watched the lines of his face grow taut and the steel of his eyes harden to pinpricks.

"It is pride and stupidity that made you agree to fight her. And if you are not prepared to face her, you will die without a chance."

"Tell me."

Abbas watched her a moment before offering a small nod. "She will draw you in with her silver tongue. She will speak words that cloud your ears, and she will wait until you are close enough to be trapped by her power. She does not carve or slice, but she seduces. The paramour will not even have to touch you to kill you. Alone with her, she is almost harmless. But it is your allies that will become your enemies. She will twist your minds to one another, and will use carnal relations to drain your bodies of your life."

He sighed, gaze shifting up and down the hallway to make sure they were still alone. As he spoke, he did not meet Arix's gaze, speaking to the space between them instead.

"You will have no control of your body, trapped in your mind as she uses her power against you. It will be brutal and you will hate your own body for turning itself against you. And when you are spent, there will be nothing left of you but a husk."

An acrid taste filled Arix's mouth and her throat grew dry as she swallowed hard. Abbas was right. This was a mistake. This was all some stupid mistake. They would be walking into a massacre.

"There won't be a way to fight her?"

A humorless laugh emptied into the space as Abbas finally looked at her. "Your magick, maybe. But there is a reason that not many know the true power of a paramour. Few live to tell the tale."

The floor was sinking out of her, and Arix could feel her composure sifting away like sand.

"I need to go to my room." Arix turned and ran.

She could hear them behind her, trying to keep pace as they followed her back up the stairs and to her room. Goddess, what had she agreed to?

In her room, she splashed cold water over her cheeks and neck, staring into her reflection in the basin of water. She knew, what, maybe twenty cants? Thirty? Who did she think she was, volunteering for death? For as far back as she could remember, she'd known she was a survivor. And she'd survived this long because she had known when it was time to cut ties and run. Maybe now was that time.

Arix slid to the cool floor, resting her head on her knees.

Ulfur and Abbas would not follow her to Nero. She'd have the chance to get away, to finally escape the clutches of the crown. She'd spend the rest of her life running, but she had a bit of magick now, and wasn't it worth the chance to live?

A life on the run was better than no life at all.

Her mind flickered to Michael and Revena. They would move on. They would forget her.

They'll be dead.

The thought hit her like an anvil. If she disappeared, leaving them to fight the paramour on their own, they might die. And her cowardice would hang over her head forever. She would never be free of the guilt.

Never.

Her thoughts jumbled and tossed in her mind, leaving her exhausted. There were two paths in front of her now, and neither was one she wanted to choose. Was it better to live as a coward on the run, or die a foolish hero?

There was a side of her that wanted to run. To stop lying to herself, to stop playing the game and to run instead. But...

Things had changed. She could admit that to herself. She wasn't the same person. The past couple of months had proven that. She'd made friends in Revena and Michaela and she wasn't sure she could abandon them. Not now.

With a groan Arix pulled herself up from the floor, and flung herself into bed. A headache was working up the back of her neck, and her vision was going wavy at the edges. She needed sleep. She needed a minute for her thoughts to quiet, to make a decision.

Though she tried to sleep, she was met by fitful dreams that kept throwing her back awake, and leaving her in cold and hot sweats throughout the night. Finally she moved to the window, resting her head against the glass as she watched the sun slowly turn the sky from black to blue to lavender. And when the first reach of the sun's rays tipped over the edge of the trees and spilled across the world, Arix watched, still torn. Still afraid. But she had made a decision.

She was packing her trunk after breakfast when a soft knock came at the door. Instead of Revena or Michael, as she had expected, Orion stood in the doorway, hands stuck deep in his pockets. His face was grave, chin high.

"I thought I should say goodbye before you left."

Arix motioned for him to enter as she returned to her trunk, closing its lid firmly and tightening the straps.

"You worried about me?" She said it with a grin, trying to offer the illusion that she was fine. Brave, even. Deep inside her, her stomach was still queasy. She'd barely made it a few bites into breakfast before she'd run to the bathroom and thrown it all back up.

"Maybe. How are you?"

"Don't worry about me." Arix threw him a wink. "I've gone up against much more vicious predators."

"Oh? And prey tell, who they might be?"

"I'm sure you've met Warden Aliska? And after surviving a few months of tutoring with Lakai, I'm sure I can take on anything."

"Promise me you'll be careful."

She glanced back up and saw how hardened his gaze had become. He looked so different from his usual lightheartedness.

"Don't think I can handle it?"

"I'm serious, Arix."

Her smile faded and the ache in her stomach only deepened.

Orion sighed, pushing the hair around his face back. Neat. Put together. Was it to hide the fact that he was falling apart inside? Like how she was at the thought of leaving him?

"You don't have to go, you know. This trip isn't mandatory."

Arix felt her grip on the trunk's leather straps tighten.

"I know."

"Then stay."

His voice displayed no emotion, as Arix glanced back up to look at him. The calm veneer and causal stance made his remarks sound offhanded. As though he didn't actually care whether she stayed or went. But the words were strained, as though it cost him something to say them.

"No." Her jaw tightened.

When he spoke he sounded angry. "Why? Are you going to prove yourself? That's what the tests are for. There's no need to go running off just to prove something to your vanity."

Her stomach tightened. "My vanity? You think I *want* to go off and die just to prove a point?"

"Then stay!" He stepped into the room, pulling her toward him as he rested his hands on her shoulders.

She jerked away from him, stepping back. "You can say that so easily! You already have a seat on the council! You already have everything you want! They gave us no choice yesterday! Celeste was just the first to realize it."

"You do have a choice." He said. "You can choose to stay and train and survive."

"And be taken seriously by who? Even if some of the others came back, I would have no one's respect, especially my own."

"Then it is vanity." He scoffed, rubbing the stubble along his jaw as he turned away from her to pace the room. "They won't have an opinion of you if they're dead by the hand of a monster."

Arix's eyes flashed and her jaw set as she fought to control the edge in her voice. "It isn't up to you. It's a choice I'm making, and I'll go whether you like it or not."

"It has nothing to do with what I like, Arix." Orion sighed, eyebrows furrowed. "I'm not controlling you, I'm just trying get you to think reasonably instead of letting your emotions drive your decisions."

"You think this is an emotional choice?!"

"You *need* to survive. You have to think about how your present will affect your future."

"So now I'm vain, emotional, and stupid?" She spat.

Goddess, why was he making this harder? Couldn't he see that if she stayed, she'd be no better off than if she left? Who would trust her if she took the easy way out and let others do her fighting for her? She'd seen too easily how those of the upper class left the hard work to those they considered beneath them. She would not be like that. She would not let her friends fight and die while she sat around practicing magickal cants in the safety of the Castle Zma'ai.

"That's not what I said, Arix." He sounded frustrated. Tired.

"It's what you meant." Her chest was heaving, anger coursing through her veins.

It was something that she had tried to forget. In the garden at night, sneaking around the library, it had nagged at her and she had pushed it away. But now things felt clearer. Cemented in her now that she had made her decision.

He was like the rest of the aristocracy. And she would always be a common thief.

"Just go." She said, turning back to her trunk. "I have a boat to catch."

He said nothing, and Arix refused to look at him as he straightened. In her periphery she saw him bow, then leave the room, the door remaining open behind him. Like a gaping mouth, laughing at her. Arix marched to the door, slamming it with a bang. The glass bottles of vervain and thyme and other ingredients on her dresser clattered with the force of the door, tinkling in the silence of the room.

She sighed. What good had that done?

Arix rested her hands on the lid of her trunk, head hanging. How had that gone so wrong? She was scared. And that fear was eating away at her insides. She'd lashed out at the first person to point out the easy road; the road she wanted to take. Goddess, it would be so easy, wouldn't it? To just stay here? And she wanted to. So badly that her chest ached.

She lifted her head slowly, staring at the packed trunk before her, decided. There had been times to cut the ties that had bound her, to flee and to save herself. There had been times to take a stand, to set the scales right.

So she would go with her friends, with the other competitors, and she would set the scales right once more. She would kill the paramour. And when all was said and done, she would slip away. She would run.

And she would never see Orion again.

TWENTY-TWO

People gathered along the streets, watching as the competitors proceeded through the capital, venturing through the city towards the harbor. By now it had become common knowledge that a monster was raging in Nero. The townspeople who watched them pass praised the Goddess in their hearts, joyous that the crown was sending its best to slay the beast. Arix rode tall on Osiris, eyes forward as the competitors picked through the crowds. They were flanked by guards on all sides, crossbows at the ready should anyone try and run. To others it may seem as though the soldiers were there to keep them safe. But Arix knew their real purpose.

She had been right. None of them really had a choice in going. Orion was a fool not to have seen that.

The ship in the harbor was small and fast, and as they settled in, Arix could already feel the gentle bobbing of the boat upon the waves of the calm harbor. The smell of the salt water brought back memories of her home so long ago on the cliffs, the salted wind teasing through her hair as she overlooked the deep green blue of the water below. She had never been on a boat before, and looked forward to the feel of the ocean whispering through her hair again.

To her dismay, Arix quickly learned that while she might have enjoyed the sea breeze upon her face, her body despised the constant rocking of the waves as the ship cut through the water. Her stomach roiled, and she spent most of her first day with her head over the side, depositing the contents of her stomach down the side of the beautiful redwood ship. Michael laughed at her while Revena coaxed her down into the hull of the ship, where the rise and fall of the horizon was no longer visible. To distract her, Revena told Arix stories of growing up in the desert, of the cavernous rock cities under the mountains of sand. She told stories of her family too, her community that she had been raised in. Revena had grown up with one father and three mothers, each with their own style of parenting over the fourteen siblings.

"I spent a bit of time in Zarak when I was little. The family I lived with were polyamorous, too." Arix said, a cold compress covering her eyes. "There was a lot of mutual respect between them. I liked that."

"A lot of people think of it as a competition. But I think it helps share the burden of life to have multiple parents. You can't expect every single second of your marriage to be a good one, and when things get difficult, you have two extra people standing beside you to raise you up. My mothers love each other like they love my father. There is a shared understanding between them. I think it has made them all better people."

Arix lifted the cloth off her eyes to look at Revena. "I've always wondered, are they… You know. Do they share a bed?"

"Yes?" Revena's brow was furrowed in innocent confusion. "They always have."

"No, I mean.." Arix groaned, pressing the cool rag back to her flushing face. "Do they ever get jealous? In the bedroom? With so many people?"

Revena's cheeks tinged purple. "I don't think that's really a problem for them."

"But how does that even work? Do they take turns, or?" Arix pushed on, trying to ignore how red they both were turning.

"They...um...they share a room. All four of them. They aren't just married to my father but to each other as well, so...it's a bit of a-" Revena searched for the word. "Collaborative effort?"

Arix pulled up a corner of the cloth to look at Revena, reading between the lines as her own cheeks flamed. "Is that something you would want to be a part of? When you have a family?"

Even though Revena's cheeks still flamed, she grinned. "If the right people come along, yes. I like the idea of being surrounded by the people I love who love each other."

"Me too." Arix grinned

Popping his head into the room, Michael grinned at them. "What's all this? Giggling and laughing and telling stories? I thought you were sick as a dog?"

Right on cue the ship rolled again, and Arix promptly vomited into her awaiting bucket.

"Ah." Michael said, wrinkling his nose and withdrawing his head from the doorframe. "I'll leave you to it then."

~

The next three days passed slowly for Arix, who spent most of her time below deck. By the time she finally had felt stable enough to return above deck, they were nearly to Sieren. The coast stretched out along the starboard bow, the glittering water dancing in tiny waves. There were boats set out in the harbor to meet them, keeping others away from the city.

The entire city of Sieren had been placed under quarantine until the situation had been dealt with. No trade in or out until the paramour had been killed. The streets were empty, save a few people who darted between the buildings, their heads down.

Sieren was a completely different city than Mergur. The cobblestones were interwoven with blue turquoise stones that created patterns and waves through the streets. The buildings were more open, with great patios set into the roofs for basking in the afternoon sun. Towering columns of white stone made up the entrance of some of the larger buildings, tiers and scrolls carved to create the feeling of an eternal wave that swept through the city.

It was easily one of the most beautiful cities Arix had ever visited. She'd spent a good amount of the spring in Sieren and hopping between it and the surrounding coastal towns. The people and the foods had been unlike she'd ever tasted in Eldur, and there was a different kind of openness that she had loved. A vibrancy that filled her up.

While normally the streets would have been full of fruit stands and dancers, instead it was empty, and eerily quiet. There was a sea breeze shifting through the alleys of the city, echoing in the empty streets. The competitors and their escorts made their way in silent pairs. It felt wrong to break the silence, the fear and mourning of those lost still hanging in the air.

Arix adjusted her belt, the pouch of ingredients hanging from it. On her other hip she wore a shortsword, as did the other competitors. Gifts from Warden Uellen Vod, that the competitors could protect themselves with and hopefully slay the paramour. All the training she had done with Tobias had paid off, and she felt better with its weight hanging at her side.

They approached the temple slowly, and stood at the bottom of the great white steps that led up to it. Pillars surrounded the outer walls of the temple, with a large open space for casual worshipers to commune with the Goddess. There was an inner piece of the temple as well, that traveled underground where a high priestess communed directly with the Goddess Nereus.

They had formulated a plan as a group, though Arix wasn't sure if it was a good one. With too many different accounts of a paramour's appearance, Arix and the others were unsure what to expect.

They ascended the steps to the temple. Near the top lay a woman, a priestess, her body shriveled and small, her bones jutting against her skin. She looked like an old woman, her skin weathered and brown. Her hair was white, its ends brittle and dry against her soft gauzy dress. The group moved around her, and Arix saw Michael draw his sword from its sheath. A few others, Andai and Helios, did the same.

Celeste had taken the front, leading them as they moved into the antechamber. The air was filled with the smell of flowers, of peony and magnolia, and scattered throughout the space were vases filled with blooming florals. The floor was littered with pillows and small couches, the bodies of the dead and withered strewn out upon them. The air smelled of sex and death, of sweat and passion and the slight stink of decay.

Beside her, Michael muttered a prayer under his breath, and Arix heard several of the others echo it. The violation of the smells, of the bodies up against bright and colorful cushions felt so jarringly *wrong*, that Arix pressed the heel of her hand into her stomach to fight the panic. The flowers did their part to cover the smell, though it remained, lingering in Arix's nose as they moved into the main lobby.

There they found more of the same. Bodies strewn in various states of undress. As they moved further in, Arix felt Revena's presence at her back. Glancing back she offered a tight lipped nod. Revena's mouth was drawn in a taut line, her gaze forward, refusing to look at the dead. There was fear, true fear emanating from her, the reality of death sinking deeper into them all. Abbas's words hung heavy in Arix's mind. She warned Michael and Revena during their voyage, and Michael had spread the word among them. Whether they believed her or not, they were walking into the monster's pit together.

A clatter up ahead echoed through the stone, and Arix froze, her grip tightening on the hilt of her sword. Celeste paused, then continued on, curving around the pillars and couches toward the second doorway that led into the inner court. As they neared, Arix's heart thundered in her chest and her cheeks turned pink at the sight.

Writhing bodies folded themselves together on the floor, stretched out in a wild orgy. They moved in one motion, limbs stretched out, grasping at pillows and nails clawing against marble. Sounds of sexual ecstasy rang in her ears, moans of pleasure from the participants sang off the pillars and stone walls. They paid no notice to the group of nine that slowly entered their midst, with weapons drawn and cants prepared.

At the center of the room stood an altar, a form laid out upon it, eyes rolled back and teeth bared. She was not as Arix had expected her.

Paramours were known as seducers. Arix had expected to see someone beautiful, someone alluring and lythe. What they found was quite the opposite.

Her skin was a sickly green, thick and weathered. Her hair hung long and stringy like seaweed around her in brown clumps, tangled up in the bodies that surrounded her. Her nails were long and grey, thick and cracked along the ends. It was hard not to stare at her body, flesh pulled taut across her ribs and hip bones, her breasts small.

Arix lowered herself to the ground and crept forward, hiding herself behind the writhing bodies around her. Her companions were doing the same.

"Yes…" The paramour breathed out, her silky voice carrying throughout the room. "Yes. Come closer, children."

Arix froze at the sound, realizing the paramour was speaking to them, not merely lost in pleasure. She watched as the monster stood from the altar, shrugging off the humans that tried to pull her back down.

"I see you, little ones." Her voice was like a song. So smooth and beautiful. The voice didn't match her form, its lilting tone coming from the body of a sickly hag.

"Did you come to play with me?" She continued, stepping down slowly from the altar and circling around the right side of the room.

Andai stood from his place behind a large vase, and cast an ice beam. She dodged it easily, her body moving faster than it was possible. She had movement and grace like a cat, simply stepping out of the way of the ice. She was on him in a moment, and Arix braced herself to hear the sound of his neck snapping, but instead she kissed him, and with a single finger pushed him backwards onto the cushioned floor. Three priestess there grabbed him, pulling him towards them, removing his clothing with blinding speed. He didn't hesitate, didn't fight, but joined in, almost disappearing into the mindless sexual horde.

"Come now, children. Give in to your pleasure. It's so much more fun!" The paramour cooed.

Arix slowly traced a circle around her body in chalk, moving slowly to avoid detection, and began muttering the words for

Predator's Mark. The paramour' head snapped to look at Arix and she grinned. Each of her teeth came to a sharp point in her mouth.

"Little bird, I see you over there," She began picking her way around the room again, toward Arix. "Little incantor, casting your cants and waving your hands. Do you think you came to defeat me? With your weak little magick? This man," she pointed at a large muscled man at her feet, "was the town's captain of the guard. A real warrior. He thought he could kill me, or defeat me. But instead, look at him!"

The man in question was tangled together with a priest, his eyes vacant and empty, his hair slowly turning white.

"Wrapped in carnal pleasures until the end of his days. Which I suppose will be rather soon now."

Arix continued the cant, the movements careful and deliberate, until it was complete.

"Now!" Arix called.

Around her, the other competitors fired their incantations. Revena called up flames that tore into the paramour, the scream turning guttural, as she was pelted with magick. She turned and ran, using the other occupants of the temple as shields. But wherever she moved, Arix's cant held tight, and she couldn't hide.

The Predator's Mark was a cant of tracking. It caused a light trail to follow the prey, and channeled a bullseye mark over the target. While the cant wasn't perfect, especially during the current moon phase, it would do a little to guide the other attacks, pulling them in like a magnet, and keep the paramour from hiding. The only downside to casting the cant was that Arix had to remain in concentration or the cant would fizzle away.

Michael and Ambrose circled around the opposite side of the altar, trying to force the paramour back into a corner. From where

Arix knelt, she could see them readying their weapons, preparing their onslaught of cants, drawing their circles.

Then they stopped. Their bodies went slack. Their weapons dropped to the ground at their feet. For a few horrible seconds they stood, unmoving, and then slowly, they began undoing their clothes, working to undo the buttons until their clothing puddled at their feet.

Arix watched, horrified, unable to force her lungs to scream or cry out as Michael climbed up onto the altar with the rest, disappearing into the sea of bodies. She lost sight of him for a moment, but then a glimpse of brown hair and thrusting force made her look away as bile rose in her throat. She had to hold the cant. It wasn't really him. He wasn't in control of himself. She had to remember that.

Arix glanced to her right as Idris and Revena had begun casting together, creating a rain of acid that pelted down upon the paramour. With their joined force, the rain increased its ferocity, and a scream echoed through the chamber. Celeste was on the other side of the room, fighting away the bodies on the ground that clawed at her, trying to pull her down to them on the floor. Her blade shimmered purple as she pushed them away, scrambling backward over a couch and towards the pillars that lined each wall.

Arix felt a presence beside her as Helios pressed up against the back of the couch to her left. His eyes were determined, and there was a hard set to the lines of his mouth.

"We need to corner her and still keep our distance. She's controlling them somehow with her power. She's drawing power from the ritual."

Arix forced herself not to look at the altar. At Michael.

"We have to get these people out of here. I think if they're within a certain range of her, she can control them. Force them into...this. If we can somehow get them out of her circle of influence, maybe it will weaken her somehow. Take away her source of power." Arix was breathing hard from the focus of the cant, sweat beading on her forehead, but she knew it was helping. It was working. "I'll hold position here, get Celeste and work on taking people out of the temple."

He nodded. "I'll try some mind healing cants and see if we can get them back to normal."

Helios turned and cut his way across the room, hauling up Andai as he went. He shouted to Celeste something that Arix couldn't make out, and the blonde nodded. She grappled a young priestess, hooking her arms and dragging her toward the entrance.

The acid rain had stopped, and Idris and Revena had changed tactics, they kept to the outer edges of the room but continued to attack. Revena was casting large blasts that hurled massive energy towards the paramour, temporarily pinning her against a pillar. Despite the onslaught, the monster was moving towards Revena slowly, pushing through the energy as she took one step after the other. The nails on her feet had grown, each toe ending in a large jagged claw that dug into the marble and held her there.

Out of the corner of her eye, Arix saw a hand reach out. She jerked back and away, the dead eyed glare of two priests staring at her as they swiped at her again, trying to draw her to them. Without thinking she stepped out of her chalked circle, and the moment of panic broke her concentration. She felt the cant immediately dissipate, and Revena stumbled. The energy blasts slowed, their power lessening. Revena glanced toward Arix, a small trickle of blood coming from her right nostril. Arix grimaced, backing up towards the corner of the room.

"Back up!" When the girl didn't move, Arix yelled again. "Revena! Back away from her! Don't get too close!"

Reven lept backwards as if she'd been stung, hurling herself away from the paramour as she tumbled to safety. Arix reached for her, pulling her back behind a pillar.

"We need to get closer to her. These cants aren't doing enough." Revena was wheezing, her breath coming in whistles. She wiped the blood from her nose on her sleeve. "I have a cant that might work but I'll need some ingredients."

"Here." Arix unclipped the pouch from her side, and handed it to her. "Take this. I'm going back out to help Idris. Do what you can. Celeste and Helios are trying to get everyone out. We think she's siphoning off power from the…"

Arix was cut off as she heard a yell. Moving around the pillar to see, Idris was trying to fight off a naked Michael and a few others that had climbed down off of the altar.

"Go!" Revena yelled, already having dumped some of the contents of the vials and oils onto the ground, her nimble fingers picking through the glass bottles.

The paramour was running, but her stride had slowed, which Arix thanked the Goddess for. She moved toward the altar, her stringy hair falling over her snarled face.

Idris yanked his arm in one final pull, and staggered back toward the pillars. Arix caught him as he dropped to one knee, his breathing ragged. Her mind was running, screaming, as she filtered through the cants she had worked so desperately hard to memorize. There was one she hoped would be enough.

"Idris, I'm going to need your help!" She said, already working her hands into the right motions and curls. Idris saw what she was doing and dropped to his knees, chalk already in hand. Once the circle was drawn, he stepped into it and followed suit, their kinetic motions synching up and adding an extra power to the already powerful cant. Arix muttered the words, enunciating and trying to speak as clearly as she could while the paramour continued to move toward them.

With a blast, the cant fell into place, and a shockwave spiraled out toward the monster. Arix could see the power slicing through the space between them, like a ripple of heat. The paramour was thrown, her body twisting in the air as she flew backward, her spine cracking on the pillar with a sound that made Arix's ears sing. The monster lay there, her hands clawing at the ground as thick purple blood oozed from her mouth. She groaned and slowly rolled onto her stomach, her arms bent underneath her.

A headache was pulsing at the base or Arix's skull, but she shoved it away.

"Again?" Idris asked beside her, panting.

Arix clenched her teeth. "Again."

The second energy wave hit the monster so hard, the pillar behind her cracked as her skull thudded back against the marble.

There was a moment then, like a breath, when everything stopped around them. The bodies froze, the priests and priestesses glancing around them. A sob broke the air as a girl threw herself off the altar, her legs shaking as she tried to make her way toward the door. Then as quick as it had stopped, it began again. The girl's eyes went blank, and she turned to calmly walk back to the altar. She climbed the steps with aching slowness, and lowered herself back into the throng.

It had only been a moment. One moment of hope, of broken concentration, but it had been enough. Arix smiled, sweat dripping down her spine. The paramour was weakening.

"Again!"

The cants left Arix feeling drained, and her mind grew hazy around the edges. Her body was exhausted, her nerves frazzled and slowly coming undone. Her eyes darted back and forth about the room, and she spied Celeste near the door, removing another priestess. The priestess's head lolled to the side, her skin withered and her hair white.

"Again!"

And so they charged up the cant again, the energy crackling in the room. And again. And again. As soon as she felt the energy leave her fingers, Arix began recharging. Sweat flowed freely down her back, and the corners of her vision were turning a dark red. She slumped to her knees beside Idris as he hunched over, coughing blood on the marble beside them. Yet still, she kept her focus on the paramour before her, torn apart more and more with every cast of the cant. All around her people were fighting, forcing themselves away from each other as the monster's hold on their minds weakened.

There was movement behind the pillar, a shimmer.

A ripple, tearing through the air as Revena's shortsword pierced through the side of the monster's neck, protruding from the other side. There was a spray of blood, the dark purple liquid spraying as a fine mist and then a steady stream as the paramour hunched over, a wicked snarl carved into her face as her long nails scratched at the weapon that would be her undoing. Arix couldn't tear her eyes away as the paramour's arms slowly fell to her sides, her head lolling back against the pillar, eyes wide.

The relief was instant. It was over.

Thank the Goddess.

Sobs filled the air as the people around them became aware of their surroundings, rushing to cover themselves, violently flinging themselves away from each other. Off the altar, and down the steps of the dias.

It took all the energy she had to pull herself from the floor and approach the altar. Michael's eyes were glazed, empty, as he stared past Arix. His arms wrapped about himself protectively as he sat down on the steps. Pulling her cape off, she wrapped it around his shoulders. He pulled it closed in front of him, his knees drawn up.

He looked like a scared child.

"It's going to be ok." Arix said, reaching out to wipe a strand of hair from his eyes. He flinched from her, an animalistic fear behind those dead eyes as he skittered away.

Arix raised her hands in front of her, her heart breaking in her chest. "It's ok. I'm not going to hurt you. You're safe now, Michael. You're free of her. She's dead."

"She's dead?"

Arix nodded, tears spilling out of the corners of her eyes as she watched him. "Dead. She can't hurt you any more."

Michael hugged his knees tighter to his chest and stared past her at nothing.

TWENTY-THREE

In the classic Nero fashion, the city held a banquet for the king's heroes, ferocious and skilled enough to conquer the great paramour. The monster's body was strung up near the shoreline, in an attempt to ward off any other monsters who might think of entering their city. The competitors were given rooms in the Warden's house, and Arix took her time bathing and dressing in the traditional Neroian clothing that had been laid out for her. The relief inside her made her knees weak, and yet, her heart thrummed in her chest.

She felt light. She felt strong. Her eyes were bloodshot from the heavy magick casting and her lungs still hurt to take a full breath, but for the first time, she actually felt powerful. She had been part of something great. She had been a part of giving people their lives back after that monster had torn their minds from them. Their very wills had been stripped of them, and Arix had played a role in returning that to them.

And how many of her friends had died? None. All her fears and Abbas's warnings felt like petty cautionary tales now. They had won!

The party took place on a pavilion overlooking the water. Massive feasting tables were set, overflowing with food. Music lit up the air, and there was dancing and laughing all around them. The air itself was aflame with relief, as if the very stones under her feet were trying to sweep away the pain and the sorrow and replace it with food and drink and merriment.

Arix strolled from the warden's mansion through the streets toward the pavilion, smiling as people streamed by her. A girl, barely thirteen, grabbed up Arix's hand and together they skipped through the streets as the girl sang a song at the top of her lungs. People around them clapped and cheered, and Arix couldn't keep the grin off her face. More women came up to them, linking their arms together, entwining their strides as more voices joined the victory song. Arix felt as though she was floating as they made their way to the pavilion, crowded together among the torches and braziers.

Warden Uellen Vod stood with his arms upraised over their table as the crowd hushed.

"Yesterday a terror haunted this city. A terror so great, we could do nothing in the face of it." His voice rose and fell with passion, as he gestured out over the city around them. "A monster so deceitful and wicked, that it took advantage of our holiest of places and desecrated that place with its filth. Yesterday there was no hope. No end to the paramour. But today!" He paused as scattered clapping and cheers came from the crowd around him. "Today, the king's champions came and they stared down that horror without fear. They stood up for what was just. They stood up to the monster. And they defeated her!"

With every word, his voice grew louder and stronger, and with it the voices around him rose until the entire city was cheering and weeping and laughing and praising the Goddess for the king and his monster-killing warriors.

"Tonight!" The crowd settled a bit as he went on, holding his hands out over them. "We honor them, and we honor our great King Taurus, who in his infinite wisdom sent them here to us. Tonight we celebrate these heroes. Heroes to this city, this realm, this country!"

Warden Vod motioned for the competitors to stand, and Arix's heart trembled as she stared out over the sea of faces that looked back at her with hope and gratitude, tears shining in their eyes. Her lungs swelled, and Arix held her head high as the crowd cheered again, a roaring cry from thousands of voices.

What was this feeling? Pride? Accomplishment? Arix couldn't name it. But it filled her up more than any feast ever had. She'd helped people before, yes. She'd stolen from the rich and given to the poor, and yet this feeling that was swelling within her was more powerful that anything she'd ever felt before. Her eyes misted with tears and she felt a shiver travel from the backs of her knees up to her scalp. Never had she felt more alive. She would never tire of this ecstasy that filled her deep and wide. She wanted to throw her head back and dance and sing and drink and live.

All her life she had strived for this feeling. Of accomplishment, of victory. All her work as a thief had been to push against the pressing injustice, to right the scales in her own way, and here she had done it! She had been waiting for this moment forever, and here it was: coming to her in a way she had never expected.

And it felt good. It made her feel alive.

With a jolt, Arix realized she no longer wanted to run. She no longer wanted to go back to hiding in shadows with little power and little influence. Instead she wanted *this*. She was strong and powerful, and she could be even more so if she became the Black Hand. This was her chance to do great things. For the people. For the country. As the Black Hand, she would have control over the council. She could make changes that would save lives. It would be this feeling, this victory, every single day. This was her chance to rise.

The music swelled again, and Arix found herself being spun around the dancing floor by men and women as they laughed together. She drank and she ate and she danced some more. The world flew by in a smeared painting of color and fabrics, the tinkling of earrings and goblets. Her fingers brushed with another, and she turned to find Revena dancing and laughing beside her. Together they spun on the floor, clinging to each other and laughing. When the song finally dipped to an end, Arix pulled Revena away before they could be drawn back into the next round.

"I need to catch my breath!" Arix yelled over the din, pulling them away to a quieter table near the corner. There, Michael sat, his eyes skimming over the dancing crowd, yet remaining on its outer circle.

Arix collapsed onto the couch beside him, with Revena doing the same. They panted for a moment, drinking in the view. A man approached, asking Revena to dance with him, and with an apologetic glance and a swirl of indigo skirts, she was up again. Resting back on her elbows, Arix watched Michael. His eyes were still dull, as if a fog had drifted into his mind, and he let it overtake him. His back was rigid, as he stared at their revelry.

"Come dance, Michael." Arix said softly. "The battle is over."

He gave no sign that he had heard her at all, the only motion being his fingers that never stopped fiddling with his ring. It was one his mother had given to him before he had left for the capital.

"Michael?"

When she placed a hand on his shoulder, he jerked away from her, jumping to his feet and backing away. There were bags under his eyes that Arix hadn't noticed before in the shadowed light of the party. His face was pale and exhausted. It made Arix's stomach grow tight to see him like this.

"I'm fine, Arix." His voice was dull. Empty. And she didn't believe him for a moment. But there was dancing and wine and Michael had already been through a lot. She understood if it was too much for him right now.

"Go." He repeated, his shoulder slumping slightly. "I'm fine."

Grabbing a glass of wine off a nearby table, Arix swirled the liquid.

"I'll stay if that's ok with you." She took a sip and then glanced over as Michael slowly lowered himself back to the seat beside her. "You went through a lot today, Michael. You don't have to do any of this if you don't want to. We can leave and go back to the house?"

She watches his face for a response, but the dull glaze remained.

"Please talk to me." Her voice came out as a hoarse whisper. "Please."

"I don't want to talk right now. I don't have words to say. And I don't want to be alone, but I sure as hell don't want to be here." A laugh escaped his lips, but there was no humor in it. "I don't know what to do."

Arix placed the cup back down on the table and crossed her legs beneath her. They sat in silence as the rainbow of colors danced out before them. The night had shifted around them as families had headed home with children asleep in their arms. A new sort of crowd was emerging. Hungry and earnest. The music changed too, sensual and pulsing. The atmosphere shifted, and the raw joy was replaced by pure sexual release. Revena swayed in time to the music, her arms lifted gracefully over her head, her face open to the sky. Someone was kissing down her neck, hand roaming freely across her bodice.

Arix felt a pull toward them; pulled toward the abandon. Her body was aching to be touched, and a flicker of a memory flitted through her mind. Orion so close, yet always just out of reach. She shook off the thought, focusing her gaze back on Michael. His eyes were fixed on Revena, but there was no lust or worry or jealousy there. He looked at her then, and his eyes were dark.

"I can't be here."

Arix hurried to stand and held out a hand to him which he didn't take. Instead he put his hands in his pockets and turned toward the street. Arix followed at his side, as the music faded away behind them. Their soft shoes made little sound on the cobblestones and Michael made his way toward the docks overlooking the water. At the edge, he sat down, his legs hanging over the side as he rested his elbows on his thighs. Arix lowered herself down beside him.

"We should talk about it." Arix tucked a piece of hair behind her ear and watched his face for any sign of a response.

Michael let out a breath that came as a huff. "I don't want to, Arix."

"I think you should. What happened today was bad, Michael. Talking about it could help. After what happened, you aren't ok. I can see that." Arix moved to place a hand on Michael's knee but he flinched away from her. She slowly lowered her hand back to her own lap. "I don't know how to help you."

Michael rubbed a hand through his hair, and leaned back until he was staring up at the sky.

"I don't know how to help myself."

"You have to know how much I care about you."

His fingers reached out hesitant to touch her hair, tucking a piece back into her braid. "And I about you." He removed his hand and dropped it back to the dock.

The water lapped gently against the post underneath them, the sound rhythmic and soothing.

"I thought we were going to die, Arix."

His voice was quiet, scared.

"I was sure of it. I could see, you know. After she took control of me. I could see everything. I could feel everything. But I was stuck, screaming in my own head, trying to break free. And I couldn't. My hands moved without my permission, my body-"

He was shaking, his whole body trembling. Tears slid freely down his face, tracing wet lines down his jaw.

"I had no control. No way to stop what was being done to me, what I was doing. How my own body was reacting. I wanted to stop, I swear I did. I tried so hard to break free of her."

He was sobbing now, his words coming out in angry gasps.

Arix's heart was breaking with him. Every tear was matched with her own as she tried to pull him into her. To comfort him. But he jerked away, violently drawing his body away from her. His eyes weren't empty any more. Anger filled them, anger and pain and heartbreak.

"Stop touching me!" His voice cracked as he shouted at her, his hands in his hair again. "Stop thinking that you can somehow make this better! That you can put your arms around me and by somehow make it all okay. It's not okay! It will never be okay! I'm trying so hard to pretend like what happened doesn't bother me. After all, I'm a man, right? Shouldn't I have enjoyed it?"

The tears continued to stream down his cheeks, and Arix choked back her own sob. She felt helpless. She knew there was nothing that she could do to fix him. Nothing that could repair the violation the paramour had done to him. To his soul.

"Goddess, and all I want to do now is carve off my own skin because I can still feel their hands all over me. I can feel their mouths and their limbs and I just want it to stop. Please just make it stop." He crouched down, his body shaking as his arms hugged his knees to his chest.

The sound of the water mixed together with Michael's sobs, and Arix simply sat and watched, wishing she knew some piece of magick that could relieve the pain. Some piece of history or information that she could erase the horror that he had endured. Yet though she searched her memory, she could think of no secret elixir, no magickal words, no legend that would ease his pain or ease her guilt. And so, she sat with silent tears, watching over him, in the only act she could do. Heart aching for her broken friend.

"I'm so sorry, Michael. I'm so sorry."

TWENTY-FOUR

The sky was turning pink. Delicate clouds floated amongst the expanse, lit up orange from the oncoming sun. Arix slowly untangled herself from her position at the dock, and walked the road back to the Warden's house. The early gray of dawn slowly seeping through the city, a pale lavender hue covering Sieren like a veil.

She had stayed with Michael all night and watched him while he slept, curled up on the other side of the dock. If she could wish anything on him now, she wished that sleep would at the least be a comfort; a respite from the pain. A few early shopkeepers nodded to her as they began the process of setting out their wares for a morning market that had been absent for a week.

Revena wasn't in her room at the house, which Arix didn't find surprising. Even after what they'd all seen, they would deal with it in their own way. The house itself was peaceful and quiet, with the soft shuffling of servants preparing for the coming day. Arix stopped by the kitchen and picked up a mug of hot tea, sipping it slowly as she stood in a corner of the wide room, watching the cook and her assistants begin preparations for the meal.

She was tired, her head cloudy after the night on the dock.

The aching in her heart for Michael was mingled with something else. It gnawed at her, and she found her mind wandering to memories she thought she had forgotten. Images of her father working, sweat glistening off his arms. Running through the rain with Caelum, splashing through puddles that gathered near their house. Faint and distant images of a woman with a kind face. The ache grew.

Arix left the kitchen, making her way back through the house, grabbing Michael's cloak from his room. She made her way back toward the dock, and found him where she had left him, though he was now awake and watching as the water around them began reflecting the pinks and oranges of the sky. She gently placed his cloak by his side and sat down, tucking her legs beneath her.

"I know nothing I say can fix what happened." She said softly, her voice catching in her throat. "But I want you to know that I will always be here. If you need to talk or to just sit in silence."

Michael didn't respond, but wrapped his cloak around his shoulders and stood. Without a word, he turned from her and walked back up the road to the house.

Arix didn't follow. She felt numb; alone. Her insides felt as though someone had hollowed her out and filled her with ash. She had always thought she was best alone. Best on her own, removed from people who might get hurt. Who might hurt her. It was easier. She'd lived that way for so long, doing her best to keep everyone at an arm's distance. But then her life had changed. She'd met Michael and Revena and they had wormed their way into her heart. But what was the use of having friends if she couldn't do anything to help them when they were hurting. She felt useless and small. Unimportant.

She was cold, but not from the cold sea breeze that lifted off of the ocean and whispered its way through her hair. That ache continued to gnaw at her heart, and she realized with a start that she was homesick. But homesick for what? Her home had been gone for years. Her family taken away. There was nothing left. No one left. Just her. She felt more alone now than she had in years. She ached for comfort. For fingers tracing down her spine, smoothing her hair. She missed her father and his soft voice and she missed her old home, nestled into those cliffs by the sea. She missed the woman she couldn't remember, so fiercely that her grief and sorrow yawned out inside her.

And she cried.

Silent aching tears slid freely down her face, her breathing labored as she watched the waves lap at the dock beneath her. She was tired of being alone, she was tired of feeling small.

"Lass?"

Arix turned to see an old man watching her. He held a broken and moldy net in his hands, his boots old and worn, the hat on his head bleached gray from the salt and sun. His face was deeply wrinkled, with the skin nearly hanging off his bones.

"You alright there?"

"The sunrise," Arix said, wiping her tears away and attempting a smile. "It's beautiful."

The man's fluffy white eyebrows rose and a knowing look filled his tired eyes. "You're one of the incantors from the capital, aren't you?"

Arix nodded.

The old man nodded, then slowly sat beside her, carefully easing himself down onto the dock with a groan. He stared out at the horizon with her, watching as birds dove into the water.

"You know, I used to fight for the king. Back before King Taurus. I fought for his father. You see things sometimes in war. Things that shake you. Things that break you."

Arix turned to watch him. Arix knew that look. It was the same look she'd seen in Michael's eyes. Hollow, empty.

"It's not an easy job, being the savior. You sacrifice things you didn't think were important at the time. So much time lost. So many moments wasted."

"Someone has to do it." Arix pushed herself to smile. "Might as well-"

"Stop it!"

Arix blinked at the withered old man's ferocity.

"Let yourself feel, girl. Don't play it off to be nothing." He lowered his voice and folded his hands in his lap, looking down at the cracked fingernails. "It isn't nothing."

After a long moment he finally looked at her, taking one of her hands between his own. "You've done a great thing for the people of this realm. A great thing for the people of this country. And yes, for the king as well. But with all great things come something terrible. With everything gained, there is something lost. Take a moment to think about what you have lost. What your friends have lost. For there is a cost to all things, especially great things. You must cherish what you have every day. For you never know when you may lose it."

The old man patted her hand and stood, gripping her shoulder for support, Arix rushed to steady him, his gnarled hand still clutching her shoulder.

"Safe travels, girl. And think on what I said."

Arix watched him go, his slow shuffle taking him back up the docks towards the market that was now beginning to bustle.

What had she lost in this mad game? If anything she had only gained. She'd gained magick and friends and purpose. Before coming to the capital, she'd scrounged her way through life, keeping low, never making friends for fear that they could be used against her. She took pride in being able to pick a lock and charm her way into a rich man's house. But there was only so much she could do. Only so much a small time thief could achieve with limited resources. She had had no ambition. No drive to be someone better. And even then, she had only proven herself mediocre at best. The memory of the brick wall sliding out beneath her, the fall to the alleyway made her scowl.

If anything, she had grown. She had become stronger. She was a better horsewoman, a stronger fighter; faster, skilled. And now she was armed with something few in the world had: magick.

If she had truly lost anything, it was the naive dreams of a little girl who only wanted to be a hero. Somehow, despite everything, she had the potential to break through the invisible barrier that had always towered before her. She had the chance to scale the wall and achieve great things. She could take a stand, she could actually help people.

Help people like Michael.

She saw his face in her mind; the cold stare of something so deep and dark, and so far from ever returning to normal. If she had been stronger, maybe faster, she could have stopped the paramour. She could have kept the monster at bay and Michael wouldn't have been through that terror.

A shiver crawled up her spine. Arix could only imagine how alien the feeling must have been. She raised a hand and watched the water in the spaces between her fingers.

To have no control of your movements, of your own body. Trapped inside yourself.

Arix's arm dropped, and she turned from the dock toward the road that led to the house.

She would never allow it. Never allow someone to control her like that. And she would never allow it to happen to anyone else.

She would work hard, and she would fight. She would do everything in her power to become a better incantor. And she would fight against the monsters, both real and human, to keep people safe.

~

There was a crowd gathered outside the house; well wishers with armfulls of flowers. But instead of smiles, lines marked their faces, as all turned to stare at Warden Vod's dwelling. A knot formed in the pit of her stomach, the hair on the back of her neck stood. Arix picked up pace as she walked, pushing past the crowd and into the building. In the entryway stood a few of the competitors, their faces grim.

"What's happened?" Arix asked, grabbing the first person she saw.

Ambrose turned, his eyes lined red. His hands were shaking, even though they were balled into fists at his sides.

No, no, no.

The words repeated in her head over and over as she scanned the room looking for him. He wasn't there.

"They found him in his room. I-"

She was already gone, racing up the stairs, heart slamming in her chest. It couldn't be. She wouldn't allow it.

In the hall a smaller crowd was gathered, carrying a stretcher, a form hidden under a sheet. Arix scanned the faces around her.

Not here.

Her eyes slid to the form. It couldn't be him. Not after everything, not after all of it.

"Arix."

A hand was on her shoulder pulling her around. Revena's eyes were hollow as she pulled Arix to the side to let the stretcher pass. She watched as the stretcher descended the stairs, unable to look away.

"Who?"

Revena squeezed her shoulder.

"Andai."

The relief was immediate. She breathed out slowly, willing her heart to beat again. It wasn't Michael.

But Andai. Guilt settled heavy in her bones.

"What happened?"

"They found him this morning. He cut his own throat. Arix, where were you? I was worried sick."

"At the dock. I was with...where is-"

"Arix!"

His voice sounded like music. Like a harp and the ocean and laughter. Goddess, she loved his voice. Arix turned to see him standing there at the end of the hall, his hair tousled, his bag thrown over his shoulder. He looked, to her, like he had all those days ago at the first test.

"Michael."

He let them hug him, arms wrapped around each other and squeezing tightly. All the pain from the night before, all the things Michael had said to her, faded away. Without words, she knew what he felt. What they all felt. They were glad to have made it this far alive. Together.

"I didn't know who it was, I was so afraid..." Arix murmured into Michael's shoulder, her throat aching as she struggled to say all the things she wanted to.

She felt his grip tighten as he pulled her closer.

"I'm right here." He said. "I'm right here."

TWENTY-FIVE

They stayed together that night on the ship, wrapped up on one bunk, pretending that the horrors of the last two days hadn't occurred. Michael's eyes were hollow, and he took longer to answer questions, as though he were somewhere else entirely, bobbing away from them on an impossibly vast ocean. He would not talk about the paramour, and so Arix and Revena did not press him. As Revena recounted her stories from the party, Michael listened and smiled and said nothing. Arix snuck them bottles of wine and the three drank and told stories and laughed until the horrors faded a little.

Eventually the talk slowed and Revena fell asleep, tucked between Michael and Arix, a strand of hair over her face wavering with each of her slumbered breath. On the other side of the bunk, Michael lay staring up at the ceiling of the cabin, eyes glassy from the wine and perhaps something else as well. There was a freckle at the corner of his left eye that Arix had never noticed before, and a small scar along his hairline.

"I won't disappear, you know." Michael turned his head to look at her, his voice soft. "You don't have to watch me fall asleep."

"Maybe I just like looking at your face."

The corner of his mouth twitched into a small smile.

"I really am ruggedly handsome, aren't I?"

Arix matched his smile with her own.

"It's true. I can't look away, you have me under your cant." As soon as she said it she wished she could scoop her words back into her mouth and swallow them away. Michael's smile faltered slightly, and he shifted uncomfortably.

"I'm sorry, I shouldn't have-"

"No, it's fine." Michael whispered, waving away her apology. "You didn't mean anything by it."

"I'm sorry." She whispered again.

Michael looked at her, his eyes still empty, but they softened. A moment passed between them in the tight bunk deep in the hull of the ship.

"Thank you for being here." He reached his hand across Revena, his fingers faintly brushing Arix's. "Thank you for staying with me last night. I don't know what I would have done if I'd been alone."

Arix's skin tingled as their fingers entwined. She ran her thumb over the pad of his hand.

"You're welcome."

Suddenly the room was too hot, and Arix felt the stuffiness of the small enclosed space.

"Want to take a walk?" She tipped her chin towards the door, motioning to the upper deck.

Michael nodded, and they made their way up the stairs and onto the flat surface of the main deck. The night was peppered with stars, the deep dark sky looming indigo above them. The moon was just a sliver, barely visible, yet its gleam brightened each cresting wave of glittering peaks. The boat was quiet save for the sound of wind cutting through the sails, the creaking of the ship beneath them as they sliced through the water. The wood of the railing was cool beneath them as the two leaned over the edge of the ship. The cool air of Nero was slowly shifting into a biting winter wind as they sailed back toward the capital.

"Tell me something. Something I don't know about you." Michael said softly.

Arix laughed, smiling through the darkness at him.

"What do you want to know?"

"Anything. Something no one knows about you."

A million things came to mind. There were so many that she had never revealed to another person. Never shared her experiences or her thoughts. There was so much of it now, the fear of opening up that floodgate yawned in front of her. Her mind froze, flitting back and forth through her memories. Something small. Insignificant. Yet there was an urge to tell him something important. Something deep and personal. After all that had happened, all they had shared and witnessed, Michael deserved vulnerability from her.

"After my family died, I was alone for a long time. I lived with a family in Zarak for a while, but then I wandered. In and out of cities and towns, trying to teach myself to be a better thief. I apprenticed for a locksmith for a while and he taught me the trade. He was a gruff man, but he was kind to me. He let me sleep in his shop at night and brought me food from his own table. His wife hated me but he ignored her. One day one of her rings went missing and she blamed me for stealing it. She said I had turned on them. Used what I had learned to break into their home and take what wasn't mine. He defended me, stood up for me. So his wife demanded that my things be searched to find the ring."

"Did they find it?"

"No." Arix wrapped her arms around herself and pressed into the railing, the wood digging into her arms. "I'd already sold it.."

Michael looked at her. "You took it?"

Arix nodded.

"I was stupid. Too afraid of a good thing. I wanted to have a backup plan in case his kindness ever took a turn. I left the next day. I couldn't stand the shame of living under their roof knowing I'd stolen from them. I tried to buy back the ring later, but it was gone. I never stopped feeling guilty for that. It was then I decided I wouldn't steal from good people. Only those who had more than they needed. More than they deserved. I just wanted to reset the scales a little."

Michael nudged Arix with his shoulder, resting his arms on the railing beside her. "You're a good person, Arix."

"Your turn. Tell me something no one knows."

"I'm an open book. I don't keep secrets."

Arix glared. "Liar. No one truly has no secrets." She pinched his arm. "Come on now, what dark secret do you keep hidden deep in your past? Tell me or I'll throw you overboard!"

He laughed, and it sounded so real. So genuine. The pain was gone, at least for a moment, and she reveled in the sound of his laugh rippling through the air.

"I swear, Arix! I don't have any deep secret past. I'm a very honest person."

Arix snorted which caused them both to laugh again.

"All right, then answer me this: Who was your first love? And you better answer truthfully."

"Her name was Violencia Artempi." Michael smiled. "I was seven, and she was my mother's companion. She was the most beautiful woman I had ever seen."

"An older woman! How scandalous." Arix rested her chin on

her palm.

"Indeed! She had the most amazing golden hair, and she always braided up in these loops around her head. I remember staring at her through the keyhole of my mother's parlor. They would sit for hours talking and drinking tea and I wished so desperately to sit with them."

"Did you ever tell her of your affection?" Arix asked, grinning. "I'm sure she would have been absolutely smitten!"

Michael stretched his arms above his head, flexing casually. "I was quite the catch, even at seven. I could carry a full water bucket all by myself you know."

"What a stallion."

Chuckling, he lowered his arms and leaned forward, resting them on the railing.

"I had planned on revealing the extent of my affections, but father caught me snooping around one day, after which I was banished to my room to study. Of course there others who I tried sweeping off their feet."

"Is that so?"

"Mmm. When I was ten I told my father I intended to marry our cook, Jocque, because I wanted a husband who could make the best strawberry scones in the world. Then when I was thirteen a sweet little filly named Tawny."

Arix scrunched up her nose at him. "Tawny? And how rude to call a girl a filly!"

"She was a filly! The most gorgeous little horse I'd ever seen. She was a gift for my birthday."

Arix smacked at his arm, giggling. "You rich twat! Of course you'd fall in love with an actual horse."

"She brought me the least amount of emotional pain, but the most bruises I've ever gotten in one week. I swear I fell out of the saddle more times than I can count!"

Arix doubled over, grasping at the stitch in her side as she tried to reign in her laughter.

"And I'm sure you loved the whole thing!"

"It's true." Michael grinned.

"And what about now? What lovely someone is waiting for you back home, eyelashes batting in anticipation? Whom hath stolen thy dear heart?" Arix placed a hand over her heart and batted her eyes at him, bending backwards against the railing in a feigned swoon.

Michael turned, leaning back on the railing as he watched her. "No one back home, I assure you."

"No one back home? But surely, your heart is set on someone? Someone here perhaps?" Arix's eyes widened, reaching forward and pulling him in as if she were telling a secret, her voice hushed. "Is it Revena?"

He laughed, giving her a light shove. "I'm serious, Arix! There's no one here or at home. I'm sure my father has made arrangements for some petite little frilly thing, but I much prefer to be on my own."

"It certainly is easier that way," Arix leaned back on the railing, balancing her chin in her hands.

"Maybe. But I guess, the people I've loved have always been someone I've admired. It's never been sexual for me. I thought maybe as I got older, but it's just never…" His sentence hung in the air unfinished.

"You know," Arix chose her words carefully, watching him as she spoke. "I think, of all the people I've met, you're the only one who knows who he is. The only one who knows what he believes. Most people don't know who they are. They don't know what they want to do or who they'll love, and instead of just being themselves, they pretend. It's what I've always done. It serves me right if I end up alone. I push people away until there's no one left."

Michael wrapped an arm around her and pulled her into him. "Don't say that, Arix. You haven't pushed me away. Revena too, she loves you. We both do." He reached out to pinch her cheek with a smile. "Besides, once you've become the Black Hand, you'll have princes tripping over themselves left and right to ask for your hand in marriage."

Arix snorted. "Very funny. If anybody will have princes tripping over them, it's Revena."

"Rubbish. Besides, I think Revena isn't interested in men."

"That clears up so many questions."

"I can assure you, Arix, that as long as you are willing to let people into that heavily guarded heart of yours, you will never be alone.."

There was a tickling feeling in the pit of her stomach. It sat, like a heavy stone, to remind her of something she didn't want to remember. Didn't want to think about. Yet it persisted. She pushed it away, but the flash of Orion's blue eyes waited in the shadows of her mind, and no matter how hard she tried, she could not be rid of them.

"I'm too brash, Michael. I say things before I think. I say things I don't mean."

"You have a good heart, Arix. The right one will see past all your mess and love you for who you are. Not the difficult, hard headed, pompous, entitled-"

"Alright, get to your point." she grumbled, shoving a finger into his side.

Michael winced, then smiled. "And they'll see you. All your rough edges. And they'll love you for it."

She linked her arm through his and stared out over the water. It felt good to have him here. Without the need or push for romance. But having him just stand beside her as a friend, a best friend, was wonderful. And Arix was content.

For another half an hour they stayed that way, leaning over the railing and watching the waves crest beneath the moon. When they couldn't hold their eyes open any longer, they returned to the cabin and curled up on either side of Revena's deeply sleeping form. Michael's breathing quickly fell into the easy rhythm of sleep, though Arix's mind would not let her fall into dreams.

Those eyes remained in her mind. Burning into her soul, she was all too conscious of the cloak she still wore, Orion's cloak, that he had given her so long ago in the garden. So dominating was his presence in her mind, it lurked, waiting silently as she tried desperately to push it away. To think of anything but him.

She would see him soon. Be in the same room again, and it filled her with a sense of anticipation. A sense of fear. She had been terrible to him. Pushed him away from her. With a start, Arix wondered if she'd pushed him away on purpose. She had, after all, intended to run away during this trip to Nero. Perhaps her own fear, for the feelings she had for him, had caused those terrible words to slip from her lips.

When Michael had talked about someone who would love her, someone who would see her sharp edges and see past her faults, her mind had wandered to Orion. To what he thought of her. After everything.

Arix's fingers grazed down the hem of Orion's cloak. The fabric smooth and warm in her touch. She knew what she wanted. She knew *who* she wanted. But did he want her as desperately as she wanted him?

TWENTY-SIX

Arix watched from the bow as they approached the harbor. There was a parade in the streets, with banners and colored flags. People cheered as the gangplank was settled and the competitors made their way down to the dock. The whole country now knew who they were. One of these faces would be the next Black Hand to the king. And it made the crowds cheer all the harder.

Revena waved at them from Arix's side, though Arix found it hard to cheer back. To wave at them all. Her mind was still elsewhere. Her eyes raked over the gathered guards, searching out Orion's face. But he wasn't there.

Of course not. It made more sense for him to be waiting at the castle with the rest of the council.

It was strange to be the center of attention. As they rode through the streets, people thronged around them, throwing flowers. Arix had already tucked a few into her braid that hung over her shoulder. She had stuck to the shadows for so long, and now reveled in the light. She had always secretly wanted to hear her name chanted among a crowd. It gave her a sense of power she'd never thought she would have.

With all the eyes on her, she felt self conscious of her clothing, and especially her cloak. Orion's cloak. While there were no markings on it that would point back to him, wearing it in front of everyone made her feel nervous. Brazen.

Glancing over, she watched Michael smile and wave as they made their final turn towards Castle Zma'ai. The last couple of days on the ship had been good for him. His smile had slowly returned, and his eyes had regained their normal mischievous gleam. He spent less time alone, and as best Arix could tell, was slowly making his recovery after what had happened with the paramour. Yet there were times when his eyes would darken, his mood would turn, and he disappeared below deck for hours. He still refused to talk of the experience, and Arix didn't know how best to breach it. He had bared his soul that first night, and she wasn't sure if it would be wise to revisit those feelings.

The last of the crowds disappeared as they entered through the castle gates, though their sounds could still be heard as they made their way through the courtyard. Lord Bardon met them at the front steps of the palace, and they followed him back to the council room.

Arix's heart stumbled over itself as she caught sight of Orion, his casual glance skipping right past her. She forced herself to look away, her eyes trained on High Priestess Halotus who stood with her hands upraised.

"Blessed be! How overjoyed we are at your return to the capital after vanquishing the monster that took so many lives. This council, and this realm, thank you."

To Arix's surprise, each member of the council bowed, and the High Priestess curtsied low, her hand over her heart. It felt strange, the acknowledgment from the council. She felt undeserving, unworthy of their praise. She herself had only been one small part of the whole to take down the succubus. In fact, it had been Revena who had held the finishing blow. Arix glanced over at her friend. Revena's face was serene, humble.

She would make an excellent Black Hand.

The thought rippled through Arix's mind, and a creeping feeling of unworthiness filled her. Incompetence. Revena was brave, strong, and a far better incantor than she. She had the confidence and the grace to be an amazing benefit to the country and to the king. She had the potential to do great things.

For a brief second, Arix's thoughts slipped.

They slipped into a place she had not considered. A place so dark and deep and black that it stole away her breath and sucked the air from the room.

Arix would lose them.

These dear friends that had become more important to her than she would have ever conceived, would be yanked from her grasp. Either she would lose, and they would continue on in the competition without her, or they would fall behind as she stepped on to becoming the Black Hand.

Of course, this truth had always been there, but she had never before thought it. Never before let it remind her that this was all still a *competition*, and they were her *competitors*.

Would their camaraderie turn? Would the bond of their friendship slip into the snarl of the fight? Was it all just make believe?

Arix didn't know. And she didn't want to.

If it came to it, in the end, to make a decision between herself and her friend, would she push them aside and rise to victory? Or would she step aside, and let someone like Revena become the victor?

Arix glanced sideways at her friend, so serene and humble in light of the council's favor. The thought rose in her again, swiftly and without malice: Revena would be an excellent Black Hand.

"As a reward for your sacrifice, for your victory of the monster, the next test has been rescheduled. You will be allowed an additional two weeks to train and prepare." The priestess folded her hands before her and spoke. "May this extra time of training aid you in your coming victory."

The competitors bowed, their fists over their hearts before exiting the councilroom. Arix turned with the rest of them, forcing her gaze to her feet. An arm slid into the crook of her elbow, and she glanced over as Revena fell into step with her, unaware of the thoughts reeling through Arix's mind.

"I think after facing a paramour, anything else they have to throw at us will be easy." She tossed her hair behind her shoulder and grinned.

"I guess we'll find out."

Revena stopped, and pulled Arix away from the group. Her forehead wrinkled as she turned to face her friend. "You alright? You've been off all morning."

Arix managed a small smile. "Just tired. Looking forward to sleeping in my own bed again."

"I thought you liked it when we all pinched in together on one bunk?" Michael said, approaching their little huddle. "Although I understand why you'd need a break. Revena snores awfully loud… Ow!"

Revena smiled to herself, lowering the fist that had just connected with Michael's upper arm.

"Serves you right. I thought you were a gentleman."

"Your snoring could drive anyone to madness."

"Rude."

Arix tucked her hands into the pockets of her skirt. "Enough, you two. I'm just tired from the trip, and I'm ready for things to get back to some semblance of normal." She bobbed her head in the direction of her room. "I'm going to try and take a nap before meeting Desirae. I'll catch you both at dinner?"

The two nodded, and Arix gave a small wave before heading down the hall to her room. She let out a long sigh as she walked, her boots echoing on the stone. But instead of heading down her hall, she turned and doubled back towards the council's meeting chamber. She perched herself into a nearby windowsill, hugging her knees to her chest, and waited.

She needed to talk to Orion. To apologize for how she had last spoken. Those fighting words still rung in her mind, and the look in his eyes as he had left her room. If she had died during the fight, those would have been their last words to each other. She needed to right some of the wrongs she'd created. To fix what was broken. If Revena really did become the Black Hand and surpassed her, Arix wanted her memory to be a sweet one, rather than filled with bitterness and hate-filled words.

Pride had always been a problem for her, no matter where she went or how hard she tried to fight it. Her tongue always got the better of her, and more often than not, caused the kind of damage that wasn't easily repaired. Even at a young age, she was quick to strike, with pinpointed accuracy at the place that could crumble her opponent.

Perhaps that was how she saw the world: herself versus everyone else. After all the years of self-reliance, was it any surprise that she was this way? She'd been alone for so long, with no one to protect her. She'd had to do it herself. No wonder she was so good at driving wedges between herself and others.

The doors opened, and there he was, his hair swept back into its usual half ponytail, his gait casual as he strode from the room, chatting with Lord Bardon. Arix stood, waiting for their conversation to end. If Orion noticed her presence, he didn't let on, and his expression remained the same. He shook hands with Lord Bardon, then turned his back to Arix and strolled away.

She slowly lowered herself back to a seat at the window, wondering if she should go after him. If he hadn't seen her at all, then he didn't know she was waiting for him. Waiting to mend things between them.

But what if he had?

She wasn't that difficult to read. He would have known she was there to talk to him. But he made no outward recognition of her presence at all, so perhaps he was ignoring her on purpose. Like she had ignored him in the councilroom.

With a snap, Arix rose to her feet and followed after him, keeping a safe distance as he strolled through the castle. He stopped at a large door at the end of a corridor, slipping through it, the door closing with a groan behind him.

This was a part of the castle she had never visited, somewhere near the back of the grounds. She crept forward, waiting to see if he would emerge. After a few moments, she took a breath and pushed through the doors slowly, flattening herself against the other side. What awaited her caused her breath to hitch in her throat.

The room opened up to reveal a small domed cathedral. The walls were interspersed with tall beautiful stained glass windows, large portraits covering the walls in between. They told the story that Arix was already familiar with, the creation of the world and man and magick. On the ceiling a large painting depicted the Goddess Kaoss and her four children surrounding her, bursting from the dark cosmos. Each child faced a different corner of the cathedral, their powers painted into the colors that made up the glass and the murals. The rest of the room was empty, the floors covered in carpets and furs. The cathedral itself was formed in a dome, the circular room almost spiraling into the center.

Arix tore her gaze away from the ceiling and inched sideways behind a pillar. Orion was standing in the middle of the room before a raised dais, where a large marble altar stood, speckled with carvings of white stars. Never in her life had she ever seen something so beautiful.

"Since you've followed me all this way, Arduinna, you might as well come out and say hello."

Arix slowly slid out from behind the pillar, her hands dug fiercely in her pockets.

"How did you know it was me?"

Her voice bounced and echoed in the cavernous space.

"You smell like those bottles of herbs you always carry around. It follows you, you know."

Arix swallowed, her throat growing tight as she finger the pouch that hung at her waist.

"I wanted to talk to you." She said.

He slowly turned to face her, his stance casual. His head cocked to the side as he stared at her, saying nothing. Her stomach twinged. He wasn't making this easy.

"Before I left, I said some things I didn't mean. Hurtful things. I wanted to apologize."

He still did not move, waiting for her to continue.

Arix fought the urge to ball up her fists and run. Instead she stepped forward slowly until she had joined him in the center of the room.

"I was being difficult and pig-headed, and I wanted to apologize for the way I spoke to you."

Yawning silence stretched the air thin between them and Arix's mind whirled as she wished he would say something, anything.

"Do you know why I wanted you to stay, Arix?" Orion finally asked quietly.

"You thought I would die."

"Yes. And that thought was ripping me apart." He reached forward, taking a half step towards her, the distance between them shrinking. Reaching out, he caught a piece of her red tendril in his hand.

"I am not used to caring so much, Arix." He twisted her hair through his fingers, touching only the strands of her hair. "But I do. I care too much." His voice lowered, gravely and rough. "And then when we heard of the paramour, and the council decided to send the competitors, my heart froze. I barely slept at all while you were away, not knowing what would happen."

He did something then that Arix was not expecting. He leaned forward and kissed the red tendril of hair, slow and deliberate, his lips and breath hot and shaking near her ear. As if he was forcing himself not to do more.

"So forgive me," he mumbled into her hair. "Forgive me for trying to force you to make a decision that was for selfish reasons. I wanted you to stay because I was afraid of the prospect of losing you."

Every vein in her body hummed, and Arix felt like she was floating.

"But why me?" It came out as a whisper.

"Because you, Bellarix Sable, intrigue me. You fight me and you argue, and you aren't afraid to speak your mind. You're so incredibly strong. And there's something about that that makes me want to spend every waking moment around you."

Her heart was thundering, the blood pumping through her veins like hot oil. Orion reached out a hesitant finger, tracing down the length of her jaw toward her ear, then down her neck, yet never touching her skin. Hovering barely over the freckled surface.

"I was watching you long before we met in the garden that first night. I watched you in the arena on that first day, picking that big stubborn horse." His fingers were gliding back up to her hair, taking and twisting another piece between his fingers. "Watching you in the hallways, muttering cants to yourself as you paced these hallways, hands and fingers never still. The way you looked at the ball, dressed all in red. If only you could have seen the way they looked at you."

Every word he said was lighting under her skin. No one had ever spoken to her like this. No one had ever said these kinds of things before. Sure, there were always brawny young idiots, trying to get her attention at a bar, or charm her into their beds, but no one had ever bared themselves like this before. It was blunt. Raw.

And Arix soaked it up.

"You are talented, Arix. And it astounds me that you don't seem to see or understand it."

Arix let out a breathy laugh. "You're wrong."

Orion raised his eyebrows at that.

"And what exactly happened with the paramour? Hmm? You fought it off; you killed it."

"I didn't kill anything." Arix felt her stomach sink as she thought back to the spray of blood as Revena's sword went through the monster's neck. "It was Revena in the end. She deserves to be the Black Hand. You saw her this morning. She accepted victory with humility and grace. All I could think about coming off the boat was how much I loved hearing the crowds cheer."

Orion said nothing.

Arix pulled away from him, rubbing her hands over her face as she took a deep breath. "I don't deserve to still be here."

"You're alive, aren't you? And you've come away unscathed from that monster's touch? You came away from Sieren victorious. That means you deserve it."

Arix felt his hand on her arm, sliding up toward her shoulder to cup her face. She looked up at him, eyes boring into her soul.

"You're a survivor, Arix. And this country needs someone to look to to help them survive what's coming. The people don't need humility. They need strength."

Orion leaned forward and kissed her forehead, his mouth trailing soft paths down her face and along her jaw. All those goosebumps and desires rising to the surface. His fingers traced through her hair, leaving tingles in their wake, the smooth tips of his fingers digging into her scalp. He broke away then, a hair's distance from her lips.

Arix waited, her heart running laps in her chest as Orion pulled her close with his other hand. He crushed her against himself, folding her into an embrace.

"I wonder what we could do together. What we could achieve."

She felt alive. Her skin tingled from his touch, her mouth craving the feel of his lips against hers. All thoughts fell away until all that was left was him.

"May I kiss you, Bellarix Sable?" He whispered, his breath warm on her lips.

"Yes."

He kissed her then, tracing lines down her back with his fingers, playing with her hair. She pressed into him, wanting to be closer, to feel more. It felt so good to be wanted; to be held.

How was it that in Orion's arms he held power over her? Some fantastical mystery to life and all it contained. She never wanted to be anywhere else. Every moment needed to count, every thought and breath held captive for moments like this.

And it was moments like this that she wanted to give in to him so blindly, that it scared her.

The kiss slowly grew, soft and gentle turning heavy and aching. He mumbled nonsensical words into her mouth, her hair, her neck. Sharply drawn breath passing between them as Arix's own hands traveled up his back, beneath his jacket, eager to touch bare skin. Her blood was on fire in her veins, possessing her with a sharp drive to be closer. There were too many layers between them, preventing the crackling sensation of skin against skin.

Nothing was said, nothing really, but mutters and whispers and escaped moans twisting through Arix's lips like a cool breeze seeping through your skin on a hot summer night. Her mind swam, coherent thoughts melting under the heat of Orion's touch, his hands on her arms as he pushed her back against the altar. The stone was a shocking cold against the fire between them, and the abruptness of it almost broke their kiss. Almost.

He stopped suddenly, taking a drastic step backwards, hands clenched at his sides.

"If you want me to stop, now is the time to tell me, Arix." His voice was so deep it didn't sound like his own, gravely and filled with lust. Yet he kept his gaze on her, waiting until she gave her permission.

"Please…" She couldn't get the words out, her cheeks red. "Don't stop."

He stepped forward again suddenly, catching her back up in his arms again.

Her fingers wouldn't work, her hands having forgotten how to unclasp and untie the clothing she wore. But Orion brushed her bumbling fingers to the side and undid the clasps, untied the ties, moving with purpose and so slowly that Arix wanted to scream. A groan of frustration escaped her mouth, and she bit her tongue to keep it from happening again. She wanted him so badly that her whole body was aching, but she shoved down that drive, forcing her mind to relax. To enjoy the sensation. She felt as if she was fighting herself.

He stopped then, taking a step back to admire his handiwork, his gaze raking down her body; blue eyes smoldering.

Arix clenched and unclenched her hands at her sides, fighting the urge to cover herself. The last time she had been naked with someone else, it had been months ago in the dark of a tavern apartment with a barmaid she could hardly remember the name of. Here the light was filtering through the stained glass windows, marking the floor in whorls of color. The moment stilled, the seconds stretching as the world stopped around them. Orion gazed at her like she was one of those beautiful windows, expertly crafted, finely shaped.

Then the moment was over, the world finally catching up with them. Orion's arms were around her waist, hoisting her up onto the cold marble of the altar, laying her down. She felt utterly out of control, completely under his thumb, laid out naked while he was still fully clothed.

With the ice cold marble clashing against the heat that thrummed between them, gooseflesh rose along the back of her knees and the outsides of her thighs. An involuntary shiver ran down her back and she squirmed against it. She was acting like a skittish doe, flinching at every new touch.

She tried to focus on the ceiling above her, but a trail of hot breath tripped across her sternum and down her stomach and her spine arced again against her will.

Everything she had ever experienced up to now had been rushed, frenzied. Stashed away in the darkness of a hayloft, or a drunken tryst in a single bed above a sleazy bar. Even the good times, wrapped in silken sheets, pretending to be a loose-lipped duchess… All of that was absolutely nothing compared to what Orion made her feel.

Laid out on this altar, Orion hovering above her, mouth and hands roving and delving and making her mind go numb, she felt like a sacrifice to the Goddess. Her whole being laid out bare and naked under the painted ceiling. Kaoss looking down, her hands spread wide as Arix gripped the edge of the stone altar, her nails digging into the marble. She felt purer than she ever had, worthy of something greater. Yet at the same time she felt small, one small piece in a greater puzzle, her body being molded to a higher calling. She could feel the magick stirring in her veins, rousing her and awakening her. That rush that told her she could do anything, be anything she wanted.

Her body shuddered, her nerves climbing the mountain toward ecstasy. One of Orion's hands braced against her hip, his thumb trailing circles on the soft skin under her navel.

And who was she to even deserve this? Deserve feeling chosen, special, powerful? But here she was, being pleasured under the watchful eyes of the Goddess and her children. It was the most spiritual connection she had ever felt, as she peaked the mountain and threw herself off the pinnacle. Falling fast, feeling as though she would never reach the bottom; never go back to normal. She heard her own breath, the gasp as it echoed through the room, and all her mind could think of was how strange her own voice sounded, bouncing back to her.

Slowly, in masterfully crooked steps, the room around her came back into focus. The marble at her back, the painted sky, and Orion, leaning over her, his weight rested on the hand pinned beside her. Smiling tenderly as he drank her in.

"How do you feel?"

Arix's voice cracked, trying to get out the words, so she merely shook her head and let her eyes drift closed. A rumble of laughter hovered over her as Orion placed a kiss to her lips. Salty. Sweet.

"Breathe, darling."

Blindly she tried to sit up, reaching for the buttons of his pants. Carefully he pushed her back down, pulling her hands away.

"Not today." He whispered, kissing the hollow behind her ear. "This was about you, not me."

Arix drifted on clouds, and slipped slowly toward sleep. It might have been a minute or it might have been a year, she did not know. The bite of the cold marble at her back was drawing her back to her senses, back to herself.

She felt worshiped. True and utter devotion, and her need satisfied. Orion made the whole experience about her, bringing her pleasure while his own needs remained unsatiated. What was it about him that made her feel powerful? That made her thrum with electricity? So often she felt small and insignificant, but Orion made her feel like she actually held her destiny in her hands.

She felt as though she held divine power in her hands.

She felt limitless.

TWENTY-SEVEN

The following two weeks flew by quickly. Every day Arix trained in the morning with Tobias and studied in the afternoon with Desirae. Her evenings were spent with Michael and Revena, talking and laughing over supper and occasionally training cantwork with them on the roof. The weather was growing colder, and a light dusting of snow had settled over the ground. It was incredibly odd seeing the dark stones of the castle surrounded by glittering white. The ground looked peaceful, serene. And yet as every day brought them closer to the next test, Arix worried.

Many nights were spent in the garden, walking the dead shrubbery with Orion. Though she tried to return the favor he had shown her in the domed cathedral, Orion would not let her pleasure him, and instead would draw her mouth to his and kiss her gently.

"Come away with me, lover. Into the dark folds of night." he would say, before guiding her deeper into the shadowed gardens, kissing her softly under the light of the wintery moon.

He was different, Arix realized. Keeping a small space between them, holding her with gentle hands as if she might break.

He was worried, and the closer they got to the day of the test, the less he spoke, his jovial smiling nature replaced with somber contemplation. He began withdrawing himself from her, and Arix found herself filling more of their conversations with meaning-less chatter.

When Arix asked him what was wrong, he would not say and instead grew quiet enough to make Arix worry. No matter how hard she pressed, he refused to tell her, and changed the subject to other things. Councilwork took up more of his time, and Arix wondered if he was avoiding her on purpose. She told herself that he was busy, that he could not spend every evening with her talking about nothing. But in her heart she was afraid. Afraid he was already tired of her. Afraid that all his fancy words were only for show.

The night before the fourth test, Arix decided not to meet him in the garden as usual, but to instead spend her night with Revena and Michael. She shoved thoughts of Orion aside, and with the help of a few smuggled bottles of wine from the cellar, soon banished him from her mind altogether.

"What do you think the test will be?" Michael asked, hay stuck in his hair as the three friends huddled in the warm barn.

It was cold enough now that winter loomed her cold mantle, and their usual spot on the roof was too cold for their regular meetings. So they'd met instead in the stables, curled up in the hay of Osiris's stall. The large black horse ignored them, and dozed quietly, while the three friends burrowed into the fresh hay in the corner.

"Fishing! Who can catch the giant moat squid on their line first." Revena chirped, her cheeks rosy from the alcohol.

"I would have preferred a hint instead of an extra two weeks of lessons." Michael grumbled as he took an extra long swig from the bottle before passing it on to Arix.

"If we had a hint then we'd be better prepared. Isn't that the point though? To be unprepared? Caught by surprise?" She said, taking the drink from him.

The bottle made its way back to Revena, who stuffed a cork in the top and leaned back against the hay.

"What if it really is fighting the squid?" Michael tucked the blanket in around the three of them, an arm propped behind his head. "I'd definitely win since I'm the best versed in giant exotic creatures."

Revena and Arix each slapped his arm simultaneously.

"Ow. I'm right, you know."

"You know," Arix slurred, kicking off her snow soaked boots. "There are only seven of us left. Statistically, one of us is going to die tomorrow."

Michael groaned, picking up the bottle and shoving it at her. "Drink more until you aren't as pessimistic."

Arix sat up and angled her body to face her friends. "I'm serious. There's a good chance at least one person will die tomorrow. And we're getting closer to the end of this thing. We should think about what that means. For all of us."

"You worry too much." Revena smiled, her hand extended for the bottle that still sat in Arix's lap. "Let's not talk about who might die, but instead let's talk about who might win. What will you do if you become Black Hand, Arix? I don't think I've ever asked you."

Arix let out a disgruntled sigh and snuggled down further into the hay, resting her head on Michael's shoulder. He had lost weight in the last two weeks, and hollowed circles always seemed to shadow his eyes. As much as she wanted to press him, to ask, she held back. Made sure he knew she was always there to listen, but gave him the space he needed.

Michael had responded in small smiles and silence. However much Arix might have wished that he talk to her, he chose not to.

"I'd want to make things better for the lower class. The wardens have good intentions, but a lot of the nobility in smaller, less populated parts of the country have free reign over the people under them. I don't think that's fair."

"You want to do away with the nobility?"

"No, I just don't want the nobility to misuse their power."

"Sounds like it would take a lot of time and effort only for the same bad people to be in power."

"Oh? And what about you, Revena...here give me that." -Revena dutifully handed back the bottle-"What would you do then if you became the Black Hand?"

"If? Don't you mean when?" The girl tossed her hair over her shoulder with a grin. "The first thing I'll do is take care of the rebels. The Black Hand has access to so much power and strength. I'd wipe out the Carn, clear them out for good. Or give them the Isle of Sama. Then they can burn down their own damn villages."

Arix took another drink. In truth, getting rid of the rebels would be the first thing she would do as well. She would gladly watch them all burn.

Michael patted Arix's head with a patronly tap. "And since no one asked me, you'll both be glad to know that I don't want to be Black Hand. To be honest, I'm surprised I've made it this far."

"Don't say that. You'd be amazing. Probably much better than us."

"Better believe it!" Arix chuckled into his shoulder. "You're the most patient of the bunch. You'd probably surprise yourself and they'd crown you king on the spot!"

All of them straightened, glancing about to see if they'd been heard, but the stable was empty save for the snowstorm that was beginning outside.

Arix lowered her voice. "But you didn't hear that from me."

Revena giggled. "Careful there, Rix, or you'll get thrown in the dungeon for conspiracy."

"Rix?"

"You don't like it?"

"You shortened the already short version of my name."

"I like it! Gives you a mysterious tone."

"Just what I was going for, thanks."

The three passed the bottle around again as Arix thought of what would await them in the morning. Speculation wouldn't do them any good. There was no way to guess what might be awaiting them.

Michael finally broke the silence with a loud belch. "We've never talked about the king, you know. Here he is in a tower right above our heads, and in the past -what?- four months, we've never seen a glimpse of him once?"

Revena and Arix stared at him.

"Well, isn't it odd?"

"I guess? It sounds like you have a theory."

He stood, teetering for a moment as he fought for balance, then began pacing the small stall. "What if he's dead? What if all of this time the council has just been looking for someone to take over until they find an heir."

Arix let out a snuff. "There's plenty of heirs. There'd be cousins and distant uncles coming out of the woodwork if the king was really dead. Too many people want to rule Rökkur."

"I don't." Revena twiddled with a piece of hay. "I'd hate being a ruler of something so big. As the Black Hand, there'd be power and control, yes, but to be king would be an impossibly large burden."

Rolling sideways, Arix glanced up at Revena from her burrowed place in the straw. "What do you think happened to the king, Rev?"

"Rev?"

"Sounds as bad as Rix, doesn't it?"

Revena giggled as she picked a piece of dried grass from Arix's hair. "I think that the king is researching. Something old. Dark and forbidden, maybe. Old, deep magick to unite the kingdom. Something that will bring everlasting peace. And if he's disturbed or bothered with the mundane tasks of kinghood then the whole world will topple and burn."

"Delightful."

Michael plopped himself back into the straw beside the two girls. "I'm bored. Arix tell us a story of one of your adventures. Something from your days as an outlaw. I need something to take my wobbly mind off tomorrow."

"Oh yes!" Revena sat bolt upright and turned with shining eyes toward Arix. "Something clever!"

"Something daring!" Michael cut in.

Arix laughed. "I have too many stories, I wouldn't know where to begin!"

Revena stuck out her tongue. "Lies. You're proud of running free for so long. So tell us your favorite daring escape."

A million stories dance across Arix's mind, weaving back on each other. They were all stupid luck, things she'd gotten away with just because she'd thought ahead.

"Have I told you the story of the Thief and the Butcher?"

Michael and Revena leaned in, eyes twinkling. Whether from the drink or from the prospect of a good story, Arix couldn't tell.

She straightened, her accent changing as she slipped into the story. "Well, as you know, the fair thief" -she gestured to herself in a sweeping motion- "had long since been chased by Nero's guards. And yet, though they pursued her across the far reaches of the north, she always managed to escape their clutches."

"Except when they finally caught her in an alley…" Michael cut in.

Revena and Arix shushed him and he clamped a hand over his mouth to suppress his laughter.

"One day while riding through the woods, the fair and crafty thief came upon a humble butcher, pulling his wagon of stock to the market. Falling into conversation with him, the thief offered to buy his meat and his horse and wagon. The butcher, knowing that good money may not be guaranteed at the market, took up this odd stranger's offer and sold her his supply." Arix continued.

"The thief, now in disguise as a humble butcher, took her stock to the local market and set up her new merchandise. 'A copper!' she called. 'A copper for a pound!' And all those near her came and bought her wares. The butchers around her grumbled, for they could not match her low prices. The starving people of the village were grateful for the humble butcher, selling meat at such low prices they could afford to feed their families."

"Did you really buy all that meat just to feed the village?" Michael asked, cutting into the story. "How the hell did you have all that money?"

Arix shrugged. "I was a good thief. And the butchers had all raised their prices and none of the lower class villagers could afford it. It seemed the quickest way to get starving people cheap meat."

"Please continue, oh great storyteller." Revena said, motioning for her to continue.

"At the end of the day, the butchers of the market talked

amongst themselves and determined that this new butcher must be of some great land and holding that she could sell her meat for so cheaply. So they offered her to drink with them that night, hoping to find out more of the new stranger. The thief, still dressed as the humble butcher, took them up on their offer and bought round after round of drinks until the fellow butchers could no longer be angry at her.

The fair thief, having done what she had intended, prepared to hasten away back to the woods. But lo! The soldiers of the north entered the tavern, having already heard of a new wealthy butcher. 'Oh butcher,' they cried. 'Have you no more meat to sell to the Warden's men?' The thief, seeing before her an opportunity, said 'I have many heads of cattle to sell, if only you have the coin.' The Warden's men offered her 300 gold for 200 head of cattle, to which the thief agreed, and rode off with them through the wood. After a good deal of riding, she had thoroughly turned around the Warden's men, for they were now lost deep within the forest. Suddenly a great herd of elk came riding by, and away the thief flew with them, disappearing into the wood, the Warden's money in tow, laughing while she went. And that is the tale of the Thief and the Butcher."

Revena and Michael applauded grandly as Arix rose to her feet and took a staggering bow before collapsing back into the hay in a fit of giggles.

"Brava!" Revena continued to clap, a grin stretched across her face. "A truly wondrous story."

Arix grinned. "Thank you. Though that's just the story I tell in bars on late drinking nights. The real truth is a little different."

"Well?" Revena prodded, eyebrows high in anticipation.

"For starters, it wasn't all of the Warden's men, just one of them stupid enough to follow me into the woods. And he was so drunk at the time, he could barely stay on his horse. So it wasn't really a fair fight."

"I'm sure he appreciates your other version, to preserve his dignity of course." Michael chuckled, emptying off the last of the bottle.

"To Arix!" Revena called, raising the empty bottle high into the air. "The cleverest thief in all Rökkur!"

An undignified snort made its way from Arix's nose which sent them all spiraling down into a deep dish of drunken laughter. They laughed until their sides were splitting; until they had forgotten why they were laughing, forgotten about the raging snow storm that blew outside, and forgotten about the alcohol that muddled their thoughts. But deep down, underneath it all, none of them forgot what was coming. None forgot what loomed for them on tomorrow's horizon.

TWENTY-EIGHT

The satchel at her side hung heavy as Arix readjusted the strap for the fourth time. She wanted it tight against her so that it wouldn't sway, but not so tight that her movement was constricted. Her bow was strung at her back along with a few small hunting daggers strapped to her thigh. The competitors were gathered outside a great door deep inside Castle Zma'ai. Michael stood to her left and Revena to her right as they awaited their looming fate.

Long gone was the laughter from the night before, resolve chiseled into their faces. Any trace of fear had been stuffed down beneath the mask of duty and honor to king, country, and self.

That morning, Lord Bardon had given them their task:

"Deep in the catacombs of this castle, a golden chest is hidden. Your goal is to retrieve the box and present it to the council." Lord Bardon shifted as he turned to look at each of them. "That is all. You are dismissed."

Arix had glanced at Revena as they exited the council room and her friend had only given a brief shake of her head as response. There had to be more to the test than simple retrieval. With every step they took, a heavy weight the size of a boulder settled into Arix's stomach. She hadn't known the castle even went this deep into the ground. There was something down here. Something waiting.

The hulking metal door before them opened with a low gravely scraping noise, and the competitors made their way one at a time into the dark antechamber. It was a small corridor, lit by only two torches, that stretched toward a set of steps that went down again and into the darkness. They had already come what felt like miles below the castle, past the dungeons, past the crypts, past all the hidden tunnels deep into the true bowels of the castle. Yet they were to go down further still.

They moved forward slowly as a group, hands hovering at their sides, or slowly drawing their weapons. The group was silent as they crept into the darkness, engulfing them like a smoke cloud. Someone muttered a few words and very faintly, a small orb appeared ahead of them, glowing with dim, orange light. Continuing down, down, down, into the depths they stepped, as the hall gave way to a hulking metal door, bolted closed. It took three of them to slide the bolts back and open the door. Eerily it opened without a sound, though they strained against the weight of it.

Arix felt herself being swallowed into the belly of the great cold beast of the castle.

Stepping forward in the dim light, they were able to make out a landing where the stairs finally stopped at trenches built into the floor where pools of dark liquid flowed. The landing split and two sets of stairs diverged, each reaching into a different direction. Idris reached forward and tentatively touched the liquid, sniffing it before quickly wiping it away on his trousers.

"It's some sort of tar." He mouthed.

Ahead of them, the landing overlooked a deep pit of darkness. With the little bit of light, there was no way of telling what lay below them, or what awaited them on the stairs that stretched down and away from them on either side.

Motioning to her companions, Arix moved toward the left staircase, moving cautiously forward as she formed her own small ball of light that hovered ahead of her. The rest of the group followed as they made their way down.

An echoing crunch broke the silence, and Arix froze, cringing, as she looked down to her own feet. Something had broken under her boot. A strange sheet of white, slightly curved, thin and jaggedly broken into tiny pieces. The stairway ahead of them was scattered with more of the white pieces, glowing eerily bone-white in the orange light.

They continued on, skirting around the broken pieces, as a floor came into view. The stone floor shone, ginting back fractals of light that bounced from it. Next to her, Michael bent and retrieved a piece. A solid gold coin, the king's sigil stamped into one side. The floor was littered with them.

Another trough at the bottom of the stairs went off into the darkness, and in one quick motion, Arix spoke the word for ignition and light burst forth in front of them, igniting the tar, traveling down the line, and snaking in and out of view as the world around them appeared into the light.

A hiss of annoyance came from the back of the group as Celeste and a few of the others ducked back against the staircase, taking shelter in the darkened shadows of the stone banister.

"Idiot." Arix heard Celeste mutter.

The room slowly filled with flickering firelight, revealing a cavernous room lined with pillars. For a moment, it reminded Arix of the temple, with its mirrored pillars and high ceilings. But the light of the fire cast dancing shadows upon what lay scattered about the massive room. Piles of treasures, jewels and gold. Great treasured works of art and beautiful sculptures. Overflowing chests of weapons and luxurious fabrics. Some of the piles reached so high that Arix couldn't see over them, like mountains disappearing into a distant fog. The trenches of fire marked the outer edges of the enormous room.

Despite the surprise of the fire, the air in the room did not stir. The only sound was the soft thrum of flames, and the blood pulsing through Arix's ears. Maybe they had been wrong. Perhaps this test was nothing more than recovery of a golden chest.

Arix took a breath, filling her lungs with oxygen until they tingled then slowly let it out before creeping forward. She moved slowly toward the center, weaving in and out of piles of treasure. All of it was in pristine condition, as if it was regularly cleaned. This was not an abandoned place. It was well kept, well taken care of.

As she moved, she took careful care not to touch anything, stepping over spilled gems and coins. Somewhere behind her, there was a tinkling of metal, as part of the pile she had just rounded spilled down across the path. Revena stood frozen as the coins toppled down around her feet, filling the room with their echo.

A second passed. Then five. Still nothing moved within the room. The pounding of blood in her ears was so loud that Arix wanted to stuff her hands over them until it stopped. Instead she forced herself to turn back to the path, more slowly this time, and moved forward. Every footstep of the companions behind her set Arix's nerves on edge. She felt as though she were balancing on the edge of a knife, teetering on the brink of losing all her nerve and turning back. But there was no turning back. Not now.

"Arix."

She turned to find only Michael and Revena following her

now. The rest were gone.

"We should follow this to the back of the room, maybe there's a door." Revena said, her voice barely above a whisper.

Arix nodded but said nothing as she turned back to the path before her.

There was something nagging at the back of her mind, a tugging at her, light but persistent. Something that was just out of reach. Just out of her grasp. Her mind was whirling to connect the dots, even as the adrenaline pumped wildly through her veins.

There was another rustle to her left, on the other side of a pile of crates, another tinkling of coins being toppled underfoot. The rest of the group must be circling around the outside.

Yet her heart had not slowed its pounding.

The three moved forward, picking between the piles until they came to face a pile so large that it blocked the path ahead of them. They would either have to turn back, or climb over it.

"Arix?"

She held up a hand to quiet Revena, thinking. They would have to turn around. Take a different path. It was like being in the maze all over again. Lost in a sea of things unknown.

She turned, motioning for them to go back, with Michael leading the way this time, turning further towards the right side of the room, until he reached the pillars. There were more of the white jagged sheets here on the ground, closer together now; less scattered. Arix bent, peering at them to get a closer look. Reaching out, she ran a finger along the jagged edge.

The thread in the back of her mind pulled taut.

Her hand shook, her knuckles buckling white as she quickly stood, fist clenched against the shivers that ran down her spine in waves.

"Goddess."

Revena was bent over it as well, and picked up a curved piece of the bone white material. She looked up slowly, her eyes wide with realization.

"It's...."

"What?" Michael asked, concern flashing across his features in the firelight.

"Eggshells."

Behind them a screech split open the air, and a white hot light lit up the stones of the ceiling as fire curled and arched over the piles of gold and treasure.

Arix felt her stomach drop, and her knees shook so violently, she thought she might be sick. Her mouth filled with the taste of ash as a blood curdling scream echoed through the room, the sound engraving itself into every ear that heard it. Some of them had never heard that sound before. Never heard the sound of suffering, of pure pain, a true cry of anguish. Others, like Arix, knew that sound well. Had witnessed too many executions in El-dur, who utilized fire to punish those sentenced to death. It was the scream of someone burning alive.

In all her years of life, Arix had never felt so much unbridled fear. Never had she experienced this kind of terror, so strong that her whole body shook, that every cell in her mind screamed to run or to give up and die right there. She could feel her own bones *--how weak they were!--* under her paper thin skin. Humans were not built to protect themselves. This was why the Goddess had given them keen minds. But what was the use of a powerful mind against a fire breathing beast? Against a...

Her body roiled under the thought, the smell of burning fleshing filling her nostrils. She vomited, her knees quaking as she leaned against the wall for support. Michael's hand gripped her upper arm, pulling her away, back towards the staircase at the front of the room. His eyes were wide, Revena rooted to the ground beside him. Her face as white as the giant eggshells beneath their feet.

"We have to move, Arix. We can't stay here." Michael urged, his voice hissing through his teeth. "Move, Arix. Move!"

So they did, running at full pace back between the rows of the treasure hoard, their minds racing faster than their legs.

Everything they had thought was wrong. Everything they had planned for was nothing compared to what they were up against. Never in her life had she thought that those giant fire-breathing monsters still lived in Rökkur, much less the world. Though she hadn't even seen it, the sound of that roar prompted some ancient voice that told her to run. To go as far as she could and never come back. To abandon everything, including her friends, and save herself.

But she couldn't.

Arix jerked her arm from Michael's grasp, forcing her racing mind to stop, to think. They had magick. They were here to prove their worth. What did she have that could be used against that kind of monster? She forced her mind to turn from blind fear to cold calculation, running through the list of cants in her head, the weapons she had on her. And what was around them? What could they use? Arix glanced back in the direction of the fire, still hidden behind mountains of gold.

They needed to know what they were up against.

"I'm going back."

She didn't wait for a reply, swinging her satchel and digging through the ingredients. In seconds her stealth cant was in place and she was running back towards the fire. As she ran she mouthed the words over and over, enhancing the cant, weaving it stronger. If it failed, there wouldn't be any return.

Her heart thundered violently with every step, bile rising again in her throat, the deep recesses of her mind screaming at her to run. Pleading with her to turn back. To escape while she had the breath in her to do so.

The last pillar was approaching, and she held her breath as she slowed and glanced around the corner.

Scarlet hide, overlaid with scales thicker than Arix's arm. Deadly black talons as long as swords, sharpened to deadly points. Thick leathery wings, hooked at the top with a spiked claw. Each leg pulled taut with thick, rippling muscle, the elongated neck stretched outward, reaching, and mouth open wide. And those three slitted eyes, filled with hatred and greed and want.

One of the last great dragons of the world.

And it lived beneath them, all this time, in the deep holds of the castle, a secret that no one knew, hidden away. What else did this castle hold? What else lay beneath the shadows and folds of the kingdom, guarded by the King and his advisors?

The great red dragon loomed over a pool of gold coins, hollowed by her body, worn smooth. A nest where she could sleep and wait, feasting her greedy eyes on the splayed wealth. She feasted on her horde, and when she needed food, feasted on the young she bore from her own body. Her great red form stretched thirty feet up, towering over them, her wings unfurled behind her. Along her back, great spikes rose up, sharp and angry, trailing down her spine, and bending with every swipe of her tail. The tip of it was so close to her, that Arix could have reached out and touched the end of the last spike, gleaming like glass in the heat of the fire.

And then she saw it.

The great beast hovered over a golden chest, encrusted with red jewels.

Their goal.

Arix's eyes slid across the far side of the room to see Celeste finalize her Predator's Mark cant, and Helios right beside her, blasting up the faint glowing image of a shield. Behind them Idris was kneeling on the floor, a circle drawn in chalk around him as he hastily worked on setting up his next cant.

That meant...

Arix swallowed at the sour bile that tickled her nose as she spied the charred remains of a body on the ground in front of them. It had to be Ambrose. He was nothing more than melted mass of hair and bone now, still burning under the heat of the fire that took his life.

Idris finished his preparation, shouting at his companions. Celeste and Helios each took off running in different directions, and the cant took hold. There was a slight silver flash and then nothing. Yet Celeste continued to run, notching an arrow and letting it fly at the joint where the great flexed wing connected to the body. In the air the arrow turned from ordinary wood to a glowing green streak as it hit its target, bursting into a stream of acid. Though the arrow didn't penetrate the hide, the spray of green clung to the red scales and tissue of the dragon's wing joint.

Reflexively, the dragon turned towards Celeste, stretching out the attacked wing and knocking her back. Her body flew backwards, her arm bent at the wrong angle as she landed in a heap near the wall.

Meanwhile, Helios still moved, his fingers outstretched as a ray of frost erupted from him. Streaking toward the heart of the dragon, a flicker of hope gripped at Arix's heart. Maybe. Just maybe.

But that hope quickly faded as the frost that could have knocked a human out cold, melted in the air before even reaching the dragon's hide. Something like a deep gravelly chuckle erupted from the dragon, and she screamed at the ceiling so high above them. She was laughing. What were they to her, with measly cants and skin as thin as paper? What were they to a dragon?

"Goddess."

Revena was beside her now, cloaked in her own cant of concealment, with Michael right behind her, wrapped in transparent mist.

"What do we do?" Arix mumbled, watching as Helios and Celeste regrouped, throwing up their shield.

"We have to be smart. Like them. We need to work together." Revena was already making her way back around the pillar, rifling through her pouch. She removed a small tin. Smearing the creamy contents on her lips, she turned the corner of the pillar again, and pointed at Idris. His head shot up, staring at them, as Revena mumbled the words: "We're going to attempt to draw her attention here. Try and get to the chest. They'll be no killing her. The best we can do is distract her and slow her down. We have to all work together if we're going to survive."

He nodded slightly and finished casting his cant. Another pulsing aura, and his cant was in place. A faint purple shimmer coated the dragon like an oil slick. Cursed.

The great dragon swiped her tail, and Arix threw herself backwards to avoid the spiked glass barb that whipped to and fro.

"Get her attention, get her to turn around. It's a small space, so it might take her some time to turn those tree trunk legs around." Revena had backed up from the pillar, and begun preparing for another cant, handing Arix the tin of salve. "I have an idea, but it will take some time. Tell Idris that he and Helios should cast Shaded Weapon and wait for my signal. We'll distract her here, so they can attack."

"I can try the Entangle cant." Michael mumbled, already rolling up his sleeves and pressing his palms to the earth, his chalk circle drawn with a swipe of his hand. "Maybe keep her held in place once she turns towards us."

"Good." Revena said. "But not until she's moved away from the chest. No good entangling her over our prize." She grinned, but Arix could see the fear that loomed behind her eyes. She was as terrified as the rest of them.

"If Celeste and I use a duplicate cant and modify it to ourselves, we could get her to attack the copies instead of us."

"Do it."

Arix smeared the sticky salve on her lips, and leaned back around the corner, sending the message. Idris nodded again.

"Let's go."

The two girls shared a look, and Revena clasped Arix's arm. It was strange how someone Arix had only known for a short while had become like a sister to her. They shared a bond, woven through trials and pain. Through terror.

They both opened their mouths together and screamed as loud as they could, Arix throwing up a copy of herself that mirrored her own movements. The two stepped out from around the pillar, and Arix swung her shortsword, connecting with the tip of the dragon's tail. It felt as though she'd hit stone. Her arm jarred, the blade vibrating from the hit.

Swinging her head around the dragon turned, arcing her body as she twisted to face Arix and the clone. An arm reached out, swiping, and Arix ducked, feeling lighter on her feet. Faster. She swung her sword again, aiming for a leg, and ran. Her feet barely skimmed the ground and she took off, faster than she'd ever run before. Her copy stayed behind, running directly at the dragon, as Arix ducked to the side and out of reach. That great claw came out again, swiping at the copy, as it ducked again, barely out of reach.

A great frustrated roar filled the air, and Arix clasped her hands over her ears to block out the noise. Adrenaline pumped through her veins as she ran towards the opposite side of the room, dodging the great spiked tail. As she neared the opposite end, Celeste ran past her, toward the dragon, screaming her own war cry. A phantom arm brushing right through Arix's torso as she passed.

The real Celeste was waiting on the other side of the pillar with Helios and Idris, clutching her broken arm to her chest.

"Fleetfoot?" Celeste asked, her eyes trained over Arix's shoulder as her copy danced beneath the dragon's feet.

"I think so. Must have been Michael."

Those blue eyes shifted for a moment to hers, those perfectly shaped eyebrows going up.

A crack sounded behind them, and Arix turned to watch as thick thorny vines broke through the piles of gold coins and jewels, snaking around the legs of the great beast. For one terrible moment, Arix thought they would snap under the dragon's strength, but by Kaoss' mercy, they held fast, the dragon's front two legs tangled up in the brush. Though the thorns didn't pierce the dragon hide, they held onto each other, and no matter how she squirmed and pulled, they remained.

"Let's go!" Idris rasped, wispy black smoke curling from his hands to form a blade. Beside him, Helios formed a similar weapon made of black smoke, elongating into a spear of shadow. They rushed forward, dodging around the dangerous tail, slashing at the dragon's hindquarters with their blades. The great head whipped around, eyes turned to slits. Another roar.

The temperature of the room rose, and Arix watched in horror as the air around the dragon's mouth rippled with heat. The great maw opened and a pillar of flame flared out, aimed at her tormentors. Idris was already moving away, dodging, anticipating the strike. But Helios… He saw the flame too late, turning to duck and roll. His skin blistered, turning red, and then white, as the heat of the flame passed over him. It didn't even have to touch him. He was screaming, scrambling, his eyes bleeding. Boils and blisters were already forming across his face, his hair singed clean off his scalp.

Arix turned away.

Beside her, she heard, rather than saw, Celeste drop to her knees, a sob clawing from her throat.

The screaming continued for too long, as the residual heat ate away at Helios's body. Arix squeezed her eyes closed, trying to blot the sound from her mind. Forcing herself to look, she glanced over her shoulder to see him stumble into someone's arms, then disappear around the pillar.

Grabbing Celeste, Arix hauled the girl up, gripping her shoulders.

"Do you have an obsidian blade?"

Celeste blinked, then glanced down to her hip. There, sheathed along with five other material blades, the black stone hilt gleamed in the firelight.

Arix wrenched it from her hip, carving a crude star into the soft pad of her palm, below her thumb. Celeste, understanding, tore through her satchel, and removed a small vial filled with crushed white moonstone. They worked quickly, trading materials, as Celeste carved her own jagged star into her hand by gripping the hilt of the knife in her teeth, then stooped to draw their casting circle. Arix clasped a handful of the crushed stone in the opposite palm.

Arix was ready before Celeste, her mouth already forming

the words to complete her cant. A shaft of light, white and cold, punched from the ceiling, forming a great column of light. Caught in the center of the shaft of light, the dragon let out a scream.

A pop sounded in Arix's left ear and she fought against the pain. A second shaft beside her own sprang to life as Celeste's good hand rose beside her, chanting the same cant. Arix felt a small smile curl at the corner of her mouth as she watched the dragon writhe in pain, fighting to free herself from the entanglement and the burning light.

On the other side of the room, Revena emerged, her hands upraised as well, palms drenched in blue powder. She was screaming words, but they were lost in the chaos that consumed the room.

All at once, things stopped. The dragon froze, then swung her head back and forth, letting out another scream. The air around her body turned wavy again and a great stream of fire burned from her mouth...in the wrong direction.

Revena was grinning and running, Michael directly behind her, casting a shield up around them as they ran right past the dragon. She made no move to stop them, the continuous stream of fire still spewing out of her mouth in the direction Revena had been standing earlier. Arix reached out her hand, and Michale clasped it as they approached, the two grinning like fools.

"She's blind. Can't see worth a damn." Revena's face was split ear to ear in a grin, though her skin had the red glow of someone who had spent too much time outside on a hot summer's day. "This is our chance. Helios and Idris will distract her and we'll run for the chest. Michael? Keep that shield up. We'll need it. Ready? Go!"

They ran then, the four of them, straight for the chest, dodging the swinging tail as it swished back and forth. The dragon was waving her head now, trying to span as much space as she could with her fire. Still facing the wrong direction.

The chest was twenty feet from them now.

Ten feet.

Arix slid to a stop, her boots slipping on the coins underfoot as she grabbed at one of the handles on the side of the ornate chest. It was surprisingly light, and she and Michael were able to carry it, hoisting the box between them as they turned back and made a mad dash towards the staircase.

Her heart was thudding in her chest, her breath coming in great heaves and rasps, and deep down, somewhere past her heart, there was joy. She felt exhilarated. Once again that feeling of victory swelled inside her. Greater than when she had faced the succubus, deeper somehow. She could taste it. She could taste the frustration of the dragon, angry and hot as they ran. They had victory in their grasp while she twisted and writhed under the pillars of Starshine.

She glanced back, seeing Idris and Helios turning, running, grins on their faces as they saw the chest being carried away. Someone had cast a healing spell over Helios, and even though his skin was blistered red, he was well enough to painfully hobble towards the front of the room. Victory was written on their faces, and Arix's heart swelled.

Then it was gone.

A great claw came out, broken from the viney hold, swiping through the air. The talon curled, it's sharp angry arc hissing like a sword through the air.

What had been Helios only moments before was turned to pulp in the air. Blood and bits sprayed like rain over the treasure.

Idris disappeared behind a pile of crates overflowing with crimson fabric, and the dragon broke free of her thorny prison.

She half flew, half crawled over the jewels stretched out before her, a rake of fire arcing over the gold, melting it into mountains of molten metal.

There was nothing to say, nothing to think as they ran.

String after string of curses poured out of Michael's mouth as they tripped over piles of coins, weaving through the paths of treasure.

The stairs were in sight. But there were so many of them, and the dragon was so close behind. Arix could feel the back of her neck blistering. Her chest was aching, burning as she forced air into her lungs, pumping her legs to propel her forward, forcing them to go faster than they already were. Someone had cast fleet-foot on them all, and they were running like deer; scared, wide eyed gazelle running from the wild fire that raged behind them.

Arix bounded up the steps two at a time, sweat pouring down her back, her shirt and bag clinging to her skin. Michael was ahead of her now, Revena racing along beside her, head down, mumbling under her breath. Keeping them quick; keeping them alive. Arix tried to think of something, anything that might help, but only one thought raced through her mind.

RUN.

They were up the stairs now, and those great claws were ripping up the stairs behind them, tearing apart the stone landing with those sword-like claws. And Idris was there, holding the door open, his eyes wide as he stared at them, the chest, and the dragon right behind them.

Then everything moved in slow motion.

With aching slowness, Arix watched as Celeste passed through the doorframe, turning and pulling Michael through with the chest. The force of the pull yanked it from Arix's grasp and she stumbled.

She saw her own hands reaching forward, ready to brace herself against the stone floor.

Then another hand, reaching out and yanking her forward through the door.

Someone was screaming.

Maybe it was herself. She didn't know.

Waves of heat. So hot she felt as if she would die.

Turning, and falling to the floor on the opposite side of the door. The coolness of the stone soothing the blisters that coated every inch of her skin. The door closed as Idris and Michael strained against the weight of it.

And dear Goddess, the fire. A curtain of flame, hot white and angry red. And a form, blistered and burned through, crumbling to the ground on the other side. The black hair already burning to ash. The door closing with finality.

Her scream echoing through the door.

And Arix was screaming too, banging against the great iron bar, her fists turning bloody as Michael pulled her back away from the door as the iron bolts fell into place, locking Revena's already burned body in. Locking Arix out.

She wailed, the haunting sound echoing through the halls, her nails cracking and bleeding as she tried digging into the stone as they dragged her away, screaming and crying for her dead friend.

Her dead sister.

TWENTY-NINE

Each step she had taken back up from the bowels of the castle, she had howled like a banshee, dragged back up by Michael, his face set as tears streamed down his blistered face. She screamed at him, cursed him, begged him to take her back to save Revena. Yet while she pleaded, deep in the recesses of her soul, she knew that Revena was gone.

When they had reached the top of the stairs, Arix had batted his hands away, reaching for the chest. The prize they had been sent to retrieve, without regard for the safety of those who had completed the task. She flung it down before the council, spilling the contents all over the floor, sweat pouring down her back and tears rolling down her face. So great was her anger, she hardly noticed the simple trinkets of rings and brooches that spilled out over the marble.

She had cursed the council too, and when the guards dragged her back to her room and locked her in, she tore at her skin and clothes and wailed on the stone before her fireplace until the tears and the pain and the anger faded to an exhausted haze.

Gentle hands had guided her to the bath, where Arix sat

numbly in the cool water. She did not feel the hands that washed the ash from her skin and hair. She did not smell the soothing scent of aloe that misted up from the warmed room. She did not taste the bone broth that was spooned into her mouth before being tucked into bed. Her burns were tended to, a cool salve wrapped over with gauze.

She saw none of it. Felt none of it.

Instead, she only felt the great hole in her chest yawning wider and wider, ready to swallow her whole.

THIRTY

Arix spent the next few days in her room, refusing her training and her lessons. She denied entry to all, including Michael, who stood outside her door with soft words. There were only two people she really wanted to talk to, and one of them was dead. Yet though she waited, Orion never appeared.

She would have refused food as well, were it not for Charlotte's stern voice on the other side of the locked door. She had not seen Wren since the night of Revena's death, when the girl had taken care of her amidst her grief. After that it had been only Miss Charlotte watching over her with that stern northern glare. Arix was too tired to disobey.

The cold of winter was seeping into the castle, inking in through the cracks of the stone. Though she didn't light a fire, the smell of ash would not leave Arix's nostrils, and the thought of lighting a flame to warm the room made her lungs constrict to the point where she felt lightheaded and dizzy and gasped for air.

On the fifth morning, she had had enough. The emptiness that was filling her up was only made worse by the long hours of sitting in front of the window watching the world glisten snow-white. She had to do something, get her mind off the pain in her chest, and the hole in her soul.

So before the gray sun rose, she was at the stable, where Tobias was waiting. She had ignored Ulfur and Abbas' glances, and ignored them still. Their kind words and well meaning looks meant nothing. Changed nothing. They ran in silence through the snow, their breath puffing out before them in the still morning air. Lanterns had been placed along their route, and the path had been cleared of new snow, piled to either side of their track.

It felt good to fill her lungs with the freezing air, pricks of cold so harsh it felt as though her lungs were bleeding. She held tight to that pain; reveled in it. Better to feel the physical pain than the emotional pain.

As she ran, Arix felt a change shift within her. A darkness that formed in her belly, hard as stone and cold as ice. A determination that brought her back to the fear she had pushed away so long ago. She had already lost too many people. She had opened herself to them, her heart soft and pliable, laid out on a platter. That trust, that selfish hope, had allowed her to open herself up to Michael and Revena… She would not be so foolish again.

The future was too unclear. Too many obstacles and variables that could take people she loved from her again. She had allowed herself to hope that maybe this time things would turn out differently.

She had been stupid to think so.

She had done this to herself. A little voice inside her had warned never to make friends with them. These people who surrounded her, lighting her life with joy and laughter. She hadn't listened. She had been stupid enough to think that this time would be different, that these people would be different. That she would be strong enough to protect them. After all, she was stronger now, she was trained. She had magick!

But it hadn't been enough. It would never be enough. There would always be someone stronger, someone more ruthless. Someone better prepared than she was.

It made her feel weak. And she fucking hated it.

So on the snowy path through the woods, early on that winter's morn, she wrapped herself in a shell, placing her broken heart back into her body. She walled it up with stone and iron, and wrapped it tightly in a cocoon of glass.

When she arrived back at her room, a message was waiting from Lakai, beckoning her to his tower. He was sitting at his desk, cluttered with papers and books. A fire roared in the hearth, but Arix forced herself to look away from it as she sat in one of his armchairs across from his desk, furthest from the flames.

When he finally looked up from his work, there were new lines around his eyes, and his skin looked paler. His clothes were rumpled as if he had slept in them, perhaps at his desk. He watched her, his hands clasped in his lap, the silence growing as thin as the air around them.

"So." he stated.

"So." Arix responded.

He took a deep breath and rubbed his brow.

"I know that the passing of Revena comes at a great personal blow to you, Arix. The two of you were close."

Arix said nothing.

"You should know that she and I were quite close as well," Lakai went on. "And her death is difficult for me too. She had excellent potential and a great aptitude for coalescent magick. She was a wonderful person."

"If you brought me here to talk about Revena, I'd rather not."

Arix kept her gaze cool, void of emotion, ignoring the startled look on Lakai's face.

"I just thought you might need to talk to someone about-"

"She was a fellow competitor. An occasional ally. Besides, we all have to die someday."

The words felt like a betrayal. A pathetic lie to hide the truth. Lakai could see right through her words, and she knew it. But there was nothing else to say.

"I see."

"Is that all?" Arix stood, moving towards the door.

"No." Lakai stepped into a small alcove beneath the window, and Arix saw that it was the chest from the dragon's lair. Her heart faltered in her chest.

"I also wanted to give you this."

Lakai waited, hand outstretched towards the box, beckoning her. Arix approached it slowly and crouched down in front of it, her fingers gliding across the smooth lid.

"Part of your reward for the last trial. Each of the contestants were allowed to pick something from the chest. You should pick something for yourself."

Arix stood quickly.

"I don't want a single bauble from that thing."

"Arix."

His voice was filled with sadness, leaking out into the air around them, tumbling through her lungs. Arix sighed.

Lifting the lid, she stared down at its contents, less than before when she had strewn them across the floor before the council. They shone up at her, the snowy light from outside dancing across gems that filled the box. She ran her fingers through, feeling the cold metal glide across her fingertips, the sound clinking in the silence of the tower.

"What do they do?"

"They are called cores. To enhance your magickal power, to boost your cants. They will eliminate the need for a casting circle, and I think you'll find yourself faster when saying the words needed. Listen to them. These aren't just baubles in a box, Arix. Too much magick flows through them for that."

Arix listened, but she heard nothing. The box of sparkling accessories sat, no more alive than any of the jewelry piled in her closet.

"I hear nothing."

Lakai sighed. "Give them time, Arix. Magick is a fickle thing. For some it comes easily. For others it takes more time. More effort."

"More effort." Arix snorted. "You mean more natural born talent. Like the kind Revena had."

Silence.

"You know I'm right."

Lakai eased himself into a chair beside her and sighed. "Yes, Arix. Like Revena had. She was the most talented caster we've had, or will have, in a long long time."

"She should be here. And I should be dead. Roasted alive and scattered to ash."

"Sometimes things happen that we cannot explain, Arix. Things that feel wrong, feel impossible. But the reality remains."

Arix shook her head slowly, disgusted.

"What is the point of magick if you can't do anything to protect the people who actually matter?" She glanced up, locking eyes with Lakai. "She would have become the Black Hand. She would have been good and ruled beside the king fairly."

"Yes, I believe she would have."

Arix felt as though her heart were too heavy for her chest,

pulling her down into the cold dead earth. She leaned heavily against the wall, her bag tinkling lightly as it hit the stone alcove beside her. Wave after wave of sorrow crashed through her, filling her up. Drowning her in hopeless heartache. She had not felt like this since watching the flames destroy her childhood home. And again, flames had taken something she loved. Someone she loved.

And Arix was left behind once more, to pick up the pieces, sort through the jumble in her head, trying to make sense of the pain and the feeling of hopelessness. Was there nothing she could have done?

The rage, the hatred at herself was so strong she could taste it. Like iron filled blood in her mouth, her lungs, her brain. Her hands were burning, the pain shooting up her arm and down her spine.

"Arix."

She jerked back to reality and slowly pulled her hand from the box and unfurled her fingers. In her palm lay a small amulet, a golden orange stone inlaid in black metal. The edges had cut into her hand, and the amulet was smeared with her own blood.

"Pain speaks, Arix. You've chosen well."

Though the room glowed softly in white snowy light, the gem in her hand remained shadowed, the cuts of the stone only drawing the eye deeper into its dark recesses.

Arix slowly lifted the chain until the amulet hung before her.

"So what will it do?"

"Every piece will perform differently for its master. Wear it always, fuse with it. Cast a circle and spend some time meditating. It will reveal its power to you in time. It will become an extension of yourself, Arix. It will become more than just a tool to you"

She glanced at him. His eyes softened.

"Let it help you heal, Arix. Let it help you mend your broken heart. Revena would want it to be so."

"Maybe I don't want to heal."

Instead of putting it on, Arix slipped it into her pocket, and wiped her bloody hand on her jacket. When she finally looked back up at Lakai, his eyes were shadowed again. Pained.

"Thanks." she mumbled, exiting the room.

"I'll see you soon, Arix."

~

The snow had stopped and the sun had come out. Though the sun's rays glinted like diamonds off the snow, the wind still bit cold against Arix's nose as she crunched down the path toward the main gate. She needed to get out of the castle grounds. At least for a little bit, to erase the hope that Revena may come swooping around a corner at any moment. She needed normalcy. Or as much as she could find as a Black Hand competitor anyway.

Ulfur and Abbas stayed behind her, giving her space. Thank the goddess for that.

No one stopped her as she passed through the first gate, the posted guards minding their own business with nary a glance of surprise as she passed. Odd. It was at the second gate that her path was barred by four nonchalant guards who looked only mildly annoyed at her presence.

"What's your business?"

Arix readjusted her satchel. "Yule shopping. Lord Bardon informed us we were allowed into Mergur."

The men blocking her path didn't move.

"Those your escorts?" He glanced to Ulfur and Abbas.

When Arix made no move to reply, the guard looked back towards her. "Just make sure you stay close to them, understood?"

With a brief nod, the three were allowed to pass through, making their way down the road and into the city.

The city was busy as usual, the air filled with bubbling voices, haggling prices or calling out their wares. As they passed, shopkeepers watched her, and Arix wished her escorts had the mind to back up a little and stick to the shadows.

She wasn't quite sure what she had come looking for, but there was something festive in the air as shoppers and shopkeepers alike prepared for the coming celebration. Garlands of pine and evergreen hung everywhere, decorating the outside windows and the edges of carts. Oranges stuffed with cloves hung for sale, filling the air with the sweet smell of citrus and spice. On every other corner it seemed there were burning fires that the townspeople gathered around, sipping cider and hot wine, chatting over their purchases or upcoming events to celebrate the winter solstice.

Arix moved through the crowd quickly, darting around stalls before she cut through an alley onto a side street. If she was going to enjoy Mergur, she might as well do so without her two shadows. With a smile, she turned back to circle towards the main square. Ahead of her a mother and daughter were singing an old Yuletide, and a small semicircle had stopped around the pair to listen.

"Can I tempt you with a hot drink, my lady?"

It took a moment for Arix to realize the shopkeeper was speaking to her. She'd never been called a lady in her life, though she supposed she looked like one, wrapped up in a fine dress and a cloak with the palace seal.

Arix stepped forward under the overhang of the small cart and smiled at the happy rotund little man. "What have you got?"

"Peppered chocolate, my lady. Best in the city!" He grinned wide, the gap between his front teeth sticking out like a woodchuck.

Arix inhaled the scent, pushing back her hood. Warmth and vanilla and a spicy kick, complemented by the dark aroma of cocoa. "It smells devine. But it appears I didn't bring any money with me today."

"What? A pretty thing like you out shopping without any coin?" The man waggled his eyebrows and winked. "Just window shopping then today, eh?"

Perhaps it was his smile, his jovial face, surrounded by holly and evergreen; a pinprick of happiness that poked at the darkness in her heart. Perhaps it was the smell of the chocolate and the peppered chilis. Whatever it might have been, it reminded her of Revena. Revena would have remembered to bring money, or at least something to barter with. Revena would have linked arms with her and caroled through the snow, commenting on how wonderful snowflakes were after growing up surrounded by sandy desert.

In an instant, Arix's smile was gone and her hood placed back up to shield her face.

"I'm sorry, I have to go."

She turned, knocking into a couple that was strolling behind her.

"Wait, my lady, please!" The shopkeep was already ladling the hot chocolate into a mug and came around the side of the cart. He held the mug out expectantly, a smile on his face.

"I told you I don't have money."

"It would be my honor," the man said, pressing the warm mug into her icy hands. "To serve one of the king's incantors."

Arix stared down into the swirling liquid and felt her throat close up. Everything in her ached.

"Thank you." she choked out.

The shopkeeper smiled and turned back to his cart as if nothing were amis, calling out to the passersby for peppered chocolate

"There you are."

The words from behind her temporarily pulled Arix away from her pinpricking tears. Abbas had caught up to her, Ulfur right behind him.

"Please don't wander off." Abbas's deep voice caused a few around them to turn and stare.

Ulfur ignored him, eyeing the chocolate in her mug. "Everything alright?"

"Peachy." Arix pushed past him, doing her best to ignore his worried stare. "Just wanted some chocolate. What are you, my dead mother?"

That shut him up. Ulfur's chin dipped in a gentle shake as he stepped back.

Arix continued through the crowds, doing her best to ignore them. Her insides ached, guilt tracing lines up her throat, but she pushed the feeling away. She didn't care if she'd hurt his feelings. She didn't care if she hurt anyone at all.

She peered through windows and sampled food from the vendors, and wherever she stepped, eyes watched her. Some tipped their hats, wishing her well. Others averted their gaze and scurried from her. After an hour, she was worn. The crowds were making her lungs constrict, and though she was out in the cold winter air, sweat pooled at the back of her neck.

Turning back towards the castle, Arix made her way back through the gates, nodding to the guards as she passed. She stood for a moment, once inside the first gate. She didn't want to go back to her room. She couldn't stand to be back in those stone halls again, knowing that beneath her feet, Revena's body lay in a pile of ash.

"Ulfur."

He jumped slightly, stepping forward as she beckoned him.

"There's a training ring here, right?"

Ulfur nodded. "Aye."

"I heard competitors can come train with the guards here, right?"

Ulfur and Abbas exchanged a look. "Aye."

"Show me."

Her two shadows led her down a length of the wall, past the barracks, and into a large training area set with wooden and cloth dummies, an archery area with targets, and a corded off square for wrestling. Ulfur began explaining their training schedule, but Arix's eyes were locked on two people who were sparring on the mat covered floor.

One was a man, stripped down to the waist, armed with two fighting knives. Sweat poured off of him, the dark muscles in his back rippling as he and his partner seemed to dance with each other in combat. But it was his partner that Arix watched, following the fluid motion, like water being guided through the air.

The girl was lithe and loose, twisting and turning, her white blonde braid whipping around her as she dodged every strike. Her hands were chalked with shield sigils, a pouch hanging from her waist. As the sigils wore down, she would fend off the knives with one hand, reaching for more chalk with the other. Her arm was already healed, and looked as if it had never been broken at all.

"Does she train here often?" Arix asked, cutting off Ulfur in the midst of his explanation.

"Celeste? Aye. She's a bit o' a favorite down here. That's her trainer, Arnav Doshi. Sometimes she trains with him, sometimes she trains with whos'ever off duty."

They watched as with an upward flick of her wrist, Celeste knocked one of the knives out of Arnav's hand, sending it skittering across the floor. It came to a spinning stop at the toe of Arix's boot. Down to only one weapon, Celeste made quick work of the second knife, and soon had it sliding across the floor in the other direction. Arix expected the fight to be over, but Arnav kept going, using his bare fists to drive pummeling blows at his pupil, breaking down her defenses. A hit here, a blow there, blood trickling from a cut above her eye, and yet Celeste remained focused, undaunted. Finally, in one good blow, Celeste struck him across the mouth with her shield, knocking his jaw at an odd angle. A deafening crack echoed through the room, and he dropped to the floor, clutching his face. Celeste let out a triumphant whoop, and dropped her shields to help him up. They spoke for a moment, talking through the fight as the man rubbed at his jaw, then parted, Arnav slapping Celeste on the back before limping away.

Without turning, Celeste called out, "Did you come to watch, Bellarix, or did you come to spar?"

"I didn't know you were here." Arix called back. She stooped to pick up the knife and then approached Celeste, tossing the weapon to her. The girl caught it with ease.

"I come here quite a bit. But I've never seen you here before. Afraid of a little real competition?"

"You're so full of shit, Celeste."

"Maybe. But you didn't answer my question. Are you here to watch or to train?"

THIRTY-ONE

Easing back and forth between her feet, Arix circled slowly, keeping an even distance between her and Celeste. She had discarded her cloak and boots by the wall, and had peeled off her socks as well. The two were fighting with daggers and verbal cants only, a bag of chalk their only ingredients swaying at their belts.

While she kept her gait even and her stance relaxed, Arix could tell that Celeste was well prepared for a fight like this. She was agile, shifting her feet beneath her nimbly with purpose. Celeste grinned, waiting for Arix to make the first move.

"What are you waiting for? I thought you were good at this."

Arix could sense the magic laced into the words, pulling at her to attack, to make a move on a bad count or a bad foot. She'd used the cant once before, and her mind worked to register the incantation, pulling her back from making a mistake. She kept her mouth slightly slack, ignoring the taunts, ready to let the words of her cants slip between her parted lips.

"Starting out dirty, are we?" Arix lunged on the last word, whispering as she went, smearing the floor with clumsy chalk circles, attempting to mark Celeste with a predator's mark.

"And sloppy, it seems." Celeste retorted.

The cant bounced off of Celeste's shield and Arix cursed to herself. She hadn't even noticed when Celeste had put it up. Or had she never taken it down? Her eyes skimmed the ground, looking for a casting circle other than her own, but found none. Where was Celeste hiding them?

A few soldiers had entered the room and had joined Abbas and Ulfur to form a small semicircle around the pair as Arix threw cant after cant at Celeste. Each one bounced off as if she hadn't thrown them at all. The soldiers began cheering every time Celeste spun away, and the blonde girl's smile only widened at the sound of the audience.

"Goddess, you're slow."

Arix grit her teeth and said nothing, dodging a knife swipe. Celeste was teasing her, not even using her magick, only carefully aimed jabs to keep Arix slightly off balance.

"What have you been doing this whole time? Stuffing your face with cakes while the rest of us do the hard work?"

There was a tick in her jaw and it took every ounce of Arix's strength to relax her mouth, letting the word slip between her lips as she cast and lunged again. Celeste parried, spinning out of reach as another cant seemed to slip off of her like water off the back of a swan.

Suddenly Arix felt her back leg catch and barely ducked out of the way in time to miss Celeste's next jab, low, and aimed for her side. Hard to block, hard to dodge. A mess of thorny vines had appeared in the ground beneath her and Arix fell sideways, jerking at her foot to free it from the vines. But she had no time. Celeste was on her in a flash, driving her knife down at her head.

Arix felt a wave of panic flood her veins as she threw up her hands to stop the attack. The two knives collided, both girls grimacing with the effort.

"Look at you. You're pathetic. You think you'll become the Black Hand?"

Something about the words, about the attack, had done something more than the cant she knew should. Arix felt paralyzed behind her eyes, as though her brain was tripping over itself. She couldn't remember the name of a simple cant, much less what words that were needed to create enough force to push Celeste off.

"You're just a small time thief who is going to die under my knife."

Arix felt fear. True fear at being trapped beneath an incantor, grinning down at her, knowing she'd already failed. In that moment the match was done, and Arix threw her hands up to protect her face, flinching away from her opponent's blade. She felt the hot slice of Celeste's knife caress her cheek as it went by, driving into the ground where her head had been only moments before.

Celeste shoved herself back up and stalked away laughing.

Arix felt sick. So sick she thought she might vomit right there on the mat. But she held it in, vowing to herself that she would rather choke and die on her own sick than to let it spew over the floor in defeat. After a moment the cloudiness faded, and Arix found enough strength to pull herself up and slowly stand. The weariness in her mind disappeared instantly as she watched Celeste from the other side of the room. The blonde was still laughing.

"Uh-oh. Seems you're bleeding. Can't handle the pressure of fighting with a real incantor?"

The humiliation flickered and was suddenly replaced by anger. Vengeance. Celeste must have cheated. Somehow she must have broken the rules. Done something to Arix's mind to keep her from thinking clearly.

"Oh ho ho! She's angry now, gentlemen! What are you going to do about it, little thief?"

Arix stood, fists clenched at her sides. The anger filled her up, hot and vile.

"You know, if you'd been faster, you could have kept Revena from burning."

With a roar, Arix gathered the moisture in the room and hurled a great ball of ice at Celeste's back. When she ducked out of the way with ease, Arix yelled again, throwing ball after ball of ice, then fire at her. Each throw curved around Celeste, passing as she walked forward calmly, dodging as though they were nothing.

Her vision clouded, and Arix could feel the strain the magick was putting on her body as the screaming turned to sobs and then finally nothing. She collapsed down to the ground, throwing up what little breakfast she had that morning.

Mortification, humiliation, disappointment, resentment.

They coursed through her, wave after wave. Churning up her stomach more until there was so much emotion bubbling inside of her, that Arix felt like a wild animal, frothing and foaming at the mouth. The ground blurred under her splayed fingers, spiraling. Her depth perception wavered and Arix doubled over as she vomited again.

And then as quickly as it had started, it was over. The waves of red hot emotion were replaced with nothingness, and her breathing returned to normal, dialing down the anger and the hatred in one fell swoop. All that remained was embarrassment and self loathing.

"Pathetic."

Arix blinked as she looked up at Celeste who had finally stopped to stand in front of her.

"Goddess, you're a disappointment." Celeste spat as she

turned away.

Arix wiped at her mouth with her sleeve. "Fuck you. What did you do to me?"

Celeste spun back around to face her. "I didn't do anything you shouldn't have already seen coming. It was pathetic. Your emotions leach off of you in waves. One amplified cant and I could read you like a book. Tweak the dials in your head as much as I wanted."

Arix raked through her mind trying to think of the cant. There were plenty that could calm and soothe, but none that she knew that could turn your opponent to a ball of rage.

"Are you...who taught you that cant?"

Celeste snorted. "No one *taught* me, you pathetic idiot."

"Enough. Stop calling me pathetic."

"But that's what you are!" Celeste stalked over and picked up Arix's cloak, digging her fingers into the pockets. "You have all this power at your fingertips and all you do is waste it. What in hell is wrong with you?"

Finally finding what she had been looking for, Celeste pulled out the amber amulet, the black chain dangling from her fingers.

"I bet you don't even know what this thing is, do you? I bet you think it's just some pretty jewelry that makes you feel like a princess? Your first mistake was not wearing it every second of every day. And if even that's escaped your understanding, then you're hopeless. I can't believe you've lived this long."

She threw the necklace down and it skittered across the floor to a stop in front of Arix, the chain sliding into the pool of vomit.

"And what did you think would happen? With Revena? The skies would open up and you and your little posse would be the Black Hand together? Or that somehow you'd all make it out this mess alive and unscathed? Free as birds to live your lives in your happy little throuple? If that's what you thought, you're a child. This isn't a game. These people, you and I? Only one of us comes out alive. If you thought there was a way around that, then you're naive. Stupid. You deserved to die slowly in the maze or be burned alive by a dragon. At least Revena had some natural talent. Talent that would have proved her to be a worthy opponent in the end. But no. Instead she pushed you out of the way and sacrificed her life instead. What an absolute and utter waste."

Arix could feel her shoulders shaking as she took in every word that spewed from Celeste's lips. She was right. Arix was weak. Revena had been the strong one.

"You wouldn't survive ten seconds as the Black Hand. Second to the king needs to be ruthless. Powerful. Selfish. Being nice and making friends won't get you anywhere in this competition. You think that because you've made it out on the streets means you'll make it as something in these walls? Think again. I've been training for this my whole life. And I'll be the one in the end, standing by the throne of the king."

Arix stared straight ahead, willing Celeste to burst into flame or die of poison. Just so she wouldn't have to hear her words. She just wanted it all to end.

"A Black Hand has to be hard. Make decisions that are hard. Leave behind the people they know and love and die to themselves to protect the king. For the good of the country and for the good of the crown. And you? You're just an embarrassment. To your family, to yourself. To Revena's decent name."

With that Celeste stalked out, pushing her way through the crowd. After a while all but Abbas and Ulfur retreated, leaving Arix alone to clean up her mess.

Somewhere deep inside her, a little girl was weeping, crying over the loss of life. The loss of self. But on the outside, Arix remained clear eyed, pupils tight pinpricks. Everything Celeste had said had been right. Every word hitting her core, the center of her being every time.

Arix was weak. She was nothing. Hollow and lacking talent. She was a mediocre fighter at best, but as an incantor? She lacked the natural ability, the mind to see how cants wove in and out of each other. That was where Revena had excelled. And Michael was the same way. His affinity for earth magick far outweighed anything that Arix was even partially good at. In terms of the remaining four competitors, Arix was the worst incantor among them. She had only survived this far out of sheer luck.

She could give up. She could walk out the gates and never come back. If they killed her for desertion, so what? She could walk away from it all, forget the pain. Forget the things she'd learned.

The amulet before her glinted, twinkling in a light source that didn't exist. Arix reached out and slid it toward her, cradling it in her sweating palm.

Somewhere a tiny voice whispered from within her.

Or you could fight.

~

The hallway was empty. Quiet. Her footsteps echoed as she made her way down the corridor, lit torches guiding her way as she took the stairs two at a time, up the tower and into the darkness. She laid a heavy knock on the door, waiting as she heard the rustling and shuffling from within. She expected him to be bleary eyed from sleep, but when Lakai opened the door, he was fully dressed, his eyes worn red around the edges.

"Arix?"

"I need your help."

"It's ghastly late."

Arix peered around him, pointedly staring at the desk that was cluttered with books and half burned candles.

"It appears you aren't sleeping either."

Lakai let out a sigh and opened the door wider. Arix stepped in and began pacing. The old incantor let her, returning to his desk and sitting down. Once he had settled, Arix stopped and turned to him.

"I need your help."

"So you said." Lakai replied, folding his hands in front of him. "What can I help you with that simply cannot wait until your lesson tomorrow?"

"It's not enough. Only one lesson every other day. I need more training. Guidance."

"If you expect special treatment simply because we shared Revena as a mutual friend does not mean-"

Arix cut him off. "With all due respect. I don't want you as a teacher."

Lakai remained silent, waiting for her to continue. Arix moved to sit in one of the chairs near the fire, resting her elbows on her knees while she gazed into the crackling flames.

"I wonder if it would be possible to have access to Revena's belongings."

"Her things are to be returned to her family." Lakai's voice was clipped. Annoyed.

"And her books?" Arix pressed on, ignoring his look. "Her notes on magick and her ingredients? What happens to them? I highly doubt her family would receive them."

"No, they would not."

"Then where do they go?"

Lakai sighed, then answered very slowly and deliberately. "I suppose they would be added to the library of magickal resources. I'm sure you know she kept extremely documented journals."

"And I want them."

Lakai let out an unfriendly huff of a laugh. "You have no claim to them, Arix."

"She was my friend."

"Maybe. But we can't let important notes like hers simply disappear into the night with another competitor."

Arix slammed her fist on her knees and stood up quickly, the chair skidding back with a screech. Behind his desk, Lakai started, standing as well.

"I will have them." Arix declared, her fists clenched at her sides in a silent challenge. "I will, Lakai. She was my friend and she was so much more adept at magick than I was. I could have learned from her, but I didn't."

Her voice hitched a moment, and Arix took a slow breath to calm down. She spoke again, slower and quieter this time.

"I don't know if I was jealous of her talent, or so self centered that I didn't think I needed help from her. But I do. Someone reminded me today that if I want to win this competition, if I want to actually make it through to the end in one piece and not just barely hanging on by luck, I need to work harder. Push myself further. Go to the very edge of what I'm capable of and throw myself off into the darkness. I owe it to her. To Revena."

At those final words, Lakai sagged, and sat back down into his worn leather chair. His hair looked snow-white, the crinkles and lines on his face more pronounced in the flickering firelight. He was old, Arix realized. Old enough to have seen generations of magick users and incantors disappear slowly from the earth. It wasn't fair. But it had happened. And he had seen it all.

"Please, Lakai. I have to do this. For myself. For her." Arix paused, then whispered more to herself than to him. "And for all the others."

Despite her whisper, Lakai heard her, the words echoing with finality in the quiet tower room.

He stood, and moved to his bookshelf where a small stack of notebooks and journals were separated and pushed away from the rest. Beside them was a small case. Lakai rested a hand on the shelf and turned to face her.

"You may have them for the night. After breakfast, I expect to find them back in their place."

Arix nodded, stepping forward to scoop the items into her arms. The box was surprisingly heavy, and she balanced it atop the stacked notebooks. She offered Lakai a nod and left, taking the stairs two at a time back to her room.

THIRTY-TWO

Gray winter light leaked in through the window and slowly banished the darkness of the room. The fire had burned down, only glowing embers remaining to fight away the cold. Arix's fingers were numb, her back aching, and her wrists were cramped from writing. She was surrounded by dripping wax, held suspended from their candlesticks, replaced many times over throughout the long night.

But it was done.

Every word, every sketch in the margins, every scorched page, had been transposed from Revena's perfect fluid handwriting into Arix's scratchy scrawl. Her own journals, which had remained sparse since the beginning, were now overflowing with the notes Revena had left. At first, she had copied the words carefully, wanting to take care over Revena's thoughts, with the reverence they deserved. But as the hours passed, her writing changed from slow and deliberate to frantic, soaking in as much as she could with the little time she had.

Arix had not yet touched the box, which had been placed on her bed. She eyed it now with bleary eyes and an aching head, the transcription of Revena's notes now complete. Crawling onto the bed, she tucked her legs beneath her and drew the box forward, carefully opening the lid. Inside were odds and ends, letters and jewelry. A silver ring lay on top; two serpents twisted and entangled with one another to form the band, their mouths open, with a small dark blue teardrop jewel nestling between their fangs. Arix had never seen Revena wear it. In fact she had never seen Revena wear any jewelry.

Underneath the ring were letters from her family, specifically her three mothers, writing of their daily lives to their youngest daughter. Arix's heart squeezed in her chest, as she scanned through the lives of strangers. They had written her. And by the looks of things, Revena had written to them as well. There was one mention of Michael, asking how Revena's friends were; if they were doing better in their training. Numerous mentions of Arix. The letters seemed to imply that Revena had written much about her to her family.

The papers crinkled in her grasp as Arix took in the words. Revena had loved her. She'd kept it to herself, never breathing a word, and yet here, her mothers asked if she had spoken yet of her affection, cautioning her to remain composed. To keep her feelings hidden. Apparently Revena had obeyed.

Arix had never even guessed. Memories flashed across her mind's eyes, memories of the three of them snuggled into a single bunk on the ship, Revena linking her arm with Arix, all the times the three of them piled into Revena's room, falling asleep in various positions. Revena had always chosen the closest seat to her, always laid her head on Arix's shoulder. If only Arix had been aware of others outside herself.

She pushed the letters aside, filtering through some small vials and tiny jars no bigger around than her thumb. She moved them aside as well, noting the blue powders, and vial of cat's whiskers. At the bottom of the box, something moved, glinted. Arix froze, watching the tiny eyes shift back and forth. Very carefully she pulled out the last remaining odds and ends and stared down at the magick nestled at the bottom of the chest.

A small pool of water shimmered, the bottoms of tiny lily pads floated upon the surface, and flitting slowly beneath them, a fish swam lazily through the stems and the flowers. Long and white, flecked with orange blotches, the fish watched her as it moved carefully in a loop before twisting back on itself and continuing the pattern in the opposite direction.

An illusion, Arix realized. The fish wasn't real; neither were the lily pads or even the water. She touched the mirror on the bottom of the box, watching as the fish turned and came closer. As he neared, he grew in size, approaching this strange thing at the bottom of his little pond. This strange face watching him from a small square of mirror that had come to rest long ago in the depths of his home.

Some piece of beautiful magick, most likely something Revena had created herself, a mirrored window, watching her little friend swim about in his warm home, while she herself studied far away in the wintery capitol.

Arix traced her finger along the edge of the mirror, watching the fish follow it, his mouth gaping open and closed as if trying to capture the tip of her finger in his mouth.

Carefully she replaced each item back into the box, laying the serpent ring on the top as she had found it. Her heart ached with every item, as she closed the last of Revena's things in and replaced the lid. The last of what remained of her friend.

When Lakai returned to his tower after breakfast, the journals, notes, and box were once again on his shelf, stacked neatly in their proper place.

~

A new blanket of snow was falling outside, and the wind was picking it up in great gusts, pushing the flakes back and forth so they fell in great whirling dances before finally coming to rest on the ground. Armed with a blanket and a steaming mug of wassail, Arix dragged a chair to sit in front of the great window in the king's library, and studied Revena's notes, while making more of her own.

At first it took some time to translate Revena's shorthand, and somewhere on page four, she had a horrible sinking feeling that she had transcribed it wrong. The feeling was short lived however, when the terms were later described in a paragraph about mixing magical components to create something new altogether.

The more she read, the more Arix realized how behind she truly was in her study of magick. Revena had made connections about certain cants; why some were easier to master, while others seemed just out of reach. She wrote about magickal focuses, and how to hone magick to become more concentrated. It seemed that Revena had taken the basics she had learned through Lakai, and expounded them into something more.

Not only that, but she'd come up with a way to imbue items with magick, like she had with the mirror in the bottom of the pond. Small cants, but she had been working on a way to imbue arrows with a Predator's Mark cant that would seek out the target of the arrow's shooter. But it was complicated magick, as the cant had to somehow be connected to the shooter. Only the incantor who enchanted the arrows would be able to use them. According to Revena's notes, she had tried out the cant on hay bale targets, and while the cant worked on single targets, when faced with multiple or moving targets, the arrow veered, striking something else. After nearly injuring her instructor, Revena had put her bow aside until she was sure the cant wouldn't cause the death of an unintended victim.

Revena's notes also spoke of ways to get around a casting circle, and the creation of wands as a focus for cants that required longer to cast. For example, the cant 'Ice Beam' allowed the caster to create a beam of ice to attack an enemy, but could only be performed under a waxing gibbous moon. If the cant was performed under a different phase of the moon, the cant itself and the damage it caused would be considerably weaker. When cast under a waning crescent, the opposite moon phase, the caster might as well have asked for a light dusting of snow, for all it was worth. But with the use of a wand, the phase of the moon could be removed from the equation, with the power drawn from the wand itself rather than the power of the moon.

But a wand was a tricky thing too. They were rare, and while shops that may have once built and designed wands for the incantors of old, Revena had no idea where to find one now.

Arix leaned back in her chair, dropping the book to the floor in frustration. There was so much information that she didn't know. But how? She'd had lessons the same as Revena, and yet she knew nothing about wands or their history. Arix had never even heard of wands, much less having shops where people could have them custom made. It was information from another time, somewhere locked back in their history when magick and incantors were as common as bakers and ironsmiths.

"What's wrong, Arduinna?" A gentle hand caressed the lines on her forehead, sliding down to cup her cheek. "There are lines on your face that could carve out the ice in a pond."

Arix looked up at Orion. Her blood turned icy in her veins and she jerked away from his touch. "You."

"Yes, me." He responded, withdrawing his hand. He leaned against the window, his arms crossed over his chest as he studied her.

"Good to know I'm finally worth talking to." She spat, pulling Revena's notes up to hide her face.

"I was trying to give you space."

Arix said nothing, studying the scrawl in front of her and seeing none of it.

Orion sighed. He sounded frustrated. "Please, Arix."

"You know," Arix said, jerking the book down to stare at him. "I've been thinking about our last couple of chats before I went to face the dragon. You were so distant, so aloof, and I couldn't quite figure out why."

Orion merely stared at her, waiting for her to continue, no admission in his expression.

"And finally, it dawned on me. You were distancing yourself in case I died. In case I got burned alive and scorched into ash. Preparing yourself for the inevitable."

"Arix…"

"Were you relieved when you found out I'd lived? Or were you disappointed that you'd have to deal with me for a little longer than planned?"

"You're right." He said simply.

Arix blinked.

"You're right about me distancing myself from you. This test was so unpredictable, none of us knew who would come back out alive. I was afraid I'd give you a hint or warn you somehow. That my feelings for you would cloud my judgment as part of the council."

"So you shut me out."

"Yes."

Arix took a deep breath. It made sense. Of course it made sense. He had a job to do and so did she. Her emotions, her feelings, were clouding her judgment again. Something she had vowed to let go of. Her attachment to people only brought hurt and misery. How could she fault Orion for doing the one thing she was doing herself.

"I wish you'd told me that." She finally said.

"I didn't know how it would affect you."

Combing a hand through her messy hair, Arix finally stopped glaring and offered Orion a look of sympathy.

"You knew I was difficult before you kissed me."

Orion smiled. "It's true. And yet I kissed you anyway. Difficult and stubborn that you are."

Leaning down he gave her a slow kiss on her forehead, then glanced down at the book. "So what are you working on?"

Arix stared down at the writings in her lap as her mind shifted back to the problem at hand. The problem that would hinder her from winning. "Spending my time realizing how far behind everyone I am."

Orion nodded slowly, the pad of his thumb gliding over her palm. "What can I do?"

"Nothing really." She sighed. "I'm just worried. I don't know as much magick as I should. There are histories lost to me. Everyone else seems to know, but I'm still in the dark."

"Give it time. There will always be things you don't know. Worrying won't help you learn faster." Orion said, his voice matter-of-fact.

Arix felt a twinge of frustration as she pushed him away and stood up, walking closer to the window. "But I need to worry.

How can I become a Black Hand who knows so little?"

Orion slowly rose as he watched her pace the room. "Have you looked here? The king's library is bound to contain at least something you don't know." He said it with a slight smile.

When Arix said nothing, his smile faded and approached her, his arms sliding around her waist and pulling her body to himself.

"Arduinna," he whispered, using her old nickname. "You are strong and resilient. You are smart and capable and think on your feet. If you're worried about something, only you can make the necessary change to fix it."

He kissed her gently, and she felt him harden against the small of her back. Then he withdrew, squeezing her shoulder as he stepped back.

"I'll leave you to your studies. But if you'll grant me the honor, I'd like to take a snowy stroll with you through the garden tonight. I'll see you then?"

Arix nodded, watching him leave through the library's wooden doors. Orion had distracted her, her thought process fizzled out and disappeared under his aura. It was what drew her to him; the feeling that in his company all her worries faded slightly.

But he had been right. She had the ability, the necessary information, she just needed to stop sulking, and learn.

Arix fiddled with the pendant in her pocket, the pad of her thumb running over the cool stone and metal. Pulling it out, she held it towards the filtered light from the window, watching the shards of light passing through and playing follow the leader on the floor.

Up till now she had continued to ignore the necklace, but kept it close to her regardless. What would Revena have achieved if she'd had access to this library while she had still remained breathing? With a jerk, Arix pushed away from the window and strode into the stacks of books, fingers trailing along the spines until she found what she was looking for. She pulled down a dusty old book on Magickal Cores and another entitled 'Magickal Laws and Their Subsequent Values'. Both looked boring and scholarly. Revena would have approved.

THIRTY-THREE

Arix sat cross-legged in the center of her casting circle, the edges pronounced with black salt, a combination of ash and salt to create a component that further enhanced the magick of a cant. It took time to make, as the ashes to create black salt need be from the burned herbs of past incantations, and was the last of her supply.

The amulet sat on the floor in front of her, the amber colored gem seeming to watch her as she stared down at it.

"I call Earth to bind my cant, Air by clarity unto me grant, bright as Fire it shall implant, deep as tide of Water chant. Count the elements four-fold, in the fifth the cant shall hold."

From the prepared bowl of crushed pearl and angelica root, Arix pressed her thumb into the powder, then marked a sigil into the palm of her opposite hand. After a deep breath she picked up the chain and spoke the final element of the cant.

"Utverditi."

Her palm glowed slightly as she reached out and touched the amulet.

That first contact was like opening the door of a stuffy house.

Instantly she felt the temperature of the room shift, her mind opening to understand the amulet and what it could do. Encased in swathes of powers and rules, a tiny voice spoke, calling her further in. The room around her faded to total darkness as her mind stepped forward into the void.

A great sigh filled her, full of relief and cool satisfaction.

"At last."

Deep silence yawned between them. Arix knew the voice, but could not place its origin.

"Who are you?" Arix asked the darkness.

"I am potential. I am growth. I am power. I am you."

The voice held a silent power, intimate, yet unfamiliar.

"And what can you teach me?"

"I can only teach what you herenow possess. I can only bring you the satisfaction of what you already know."

A wave of frustration built in her, but Arix swallowed it down. "You speak in riddles."

The voice let out a great sigh again, each word drawn and stretched. Each syllable pronounced. *"I can no more teach you magick than can the fire you command nor the plants that you grow."*

"Are you a guide? Someone that can teach me more about myself?"

"I like this," the voice said wistfully. *"A guide. Yes, I suppose I am one that will lead you through the shambles of what you know; sweeping away the needless accoutrements of both creation and destruction."*

"What do you mean by creation and destruction? I just want to be better at magick."

"Is that not what all magick is? The creation and destruction of properties? Of elements? When you cast a great beam of frost, are you not creating it from the very air? Twisting it to be what you desire? And then destroying it upon its completion of your request?"

"What about-"

"I do not wish to argue semantics." The voice snapped, the soft relaxed tone disappearing into one of annoyed frustration. *"I chose you for your will, your fire, your potential. I did not pick you for your sass and pridefulness."*

"You chose me?" Arix did her best not to roll her eyes. "I seem to recall it going a little differently than that. As far as I know, you could have been locked up in that dragon horde for hundreds upon hundreds of years."

"Yes, I chose you. I chose you before time itself began. Before your birth and after your death. You were selected before your first breath. Picked far after your skin has decayed into the earth and your bones have been ground to dust."

"And yet, I'm the one who pulled you from the chest."

The voice snorted. *"You may believe that, if it gives you peace."*

Her annoyance grew, and Arix resisted the urge to pull out of the cant and throw the pendant out the window. The voice chuckled.

"What's so funny?"

"You think that you hide your emotions well, yet forget who I am. Not some entity far removed and lofty. I annoy you because I am you. I am the part of you that remains locked away, the part of you that is inhibited by your human emotions, your human skin, your human mind."

"I'm getting tired of your riddles. Maybe I'll give you a riddle and see how you like it."

The voice said nothing, but sighed so deeply, that Arix immediately felt a flow of guilt, though why it came, she could not determine.

"Then I suppose I shall speak plainly. Simply, for your small mind to comprehend. And indeed you are small." The voice became angry, clipped. *"Small and weak, with a weak mind. You wish not to expand what*

you know, to raise yourself to higher bounds, to bring yourself from the slough and mire of your status."

Arix opened her mouth to defend herself, but the voice cut her off.

"You see yourself as a savior. One who did good on behalf of others, carving out a place for yourself among the little people of this great empire. And even here, when you have been given great opportunity and position, you continue to see yourself as small, impacting a small circle. A small world. If you are to truly become who you are meant to be, you must expand yourself, your mind, your being, into something lofty and great."

"But that's not me!" Arix shouted, her arms upraised to the voice. "I'm not some great lofty person. I'm not well read and well versed. I'm just a thief!"

"If you continue to believe that, then you will never rise higher. Your greatest limitation is your own self."

"So what do I do? I've gotten myself into this mess, how do I get out?"

"Kill yourself." The voice scoffed. *"Your body will become fodder for the earth, and then perhaps you will be useful."*

An overwhelming silence filled that empty cavern in Arix's chest. Filled her with dread and despair. To be here one moment and gone the next, your consciousness seeping into the cosmos to join the gods?

"No."

"Why not? Wouldn't that be better? No more fighting to pretend you are something that everyone knows you are not?"

"No."

The voice cursed her. *"Stubborn whelp! Die! Let the world be rid of you! Throw yourself into a simple abyss where you may be at rest with your dead friends and family, and where the world will easily forget you. You have no use in the land of the living."*

"I will not."

"Then you are a fool."

"Maybe I am. But I'll not be bullied into death by the likes of you. I have too much that still needs to be accomplished before my death."

Silence.

"Then you have overcome the greatest trial you will face in your lifetime. Yourself." The voice was quiet again. Calm. She sounded proud; relieved even. *"I am at your command, Mistress. Utilize me to reach your lofty goals. You will find yourself better equipped with me in your possession. Think no more of the moon in her cycles, or your circles cast in chalk. Instead take your power from me. Let me be your supply."*

Slowly the darkness faded, and the room around her came back into focus. Arix blinked down at the amulet in her hand. Slowly she raised it over her head, laying it around her neck. The medallion rested between her breasts, nestled under the folds of her tunic, hidden from sight. It was surprisingly light, lighter than when she held it in her hand. The only reminder of its presence being the cold metal of the chain that lay gently on her skin.

THIRTY-FOUR

The next few days were a bustle of activity in Castle Zma'ai as the servants changed the candles in the chandelier white to green, and draped great boughs of evergreen and bouquets of red berries throughout the hall. The large staircase that circled the main hall was wound in holly and pine cones, and the whole castle smelled of deep, dark spice and citrus. In the center of the ballroom, a monsterous evergreen had been placed, strung up with glass balls, tiny carved woodland creatures, bells, and small white candles that when lit, made the enormous tree appear to be draped in stars.

A great banquet was to be held on Yule's Eve, lasting late into the night and celebrating the return of the light after the longest night of the year. It would be a celebration of rebirth and new beginnings.

Arix had always loved Yuletide. The holiday felt comforting and cozy, wrapped up in blankets and furs, sipping wassail from a steaming mug and watching the snow fall. While once she would have adored the chance to wander the halls of the castle, breathing in the holiday smells, she instead spent the days leading up to it reading and practicing. She borrowed more books from Lakai, who gave her them without question. Even when Michael knocked at her door, tempting her with snowball fights and walks through the wintery wonderland, Arix shooed him off with a wave and barely a glance up from her books.

She was determined, rejuvenated, driven by insatiable fear. It was the same fear that all have deep within them, spurred on by the small voice that rings with tiny truths: *I will never be good enough.*

While she had suspected it before, she was sure of it now.

The night before the Yule banquet, Arix was halfway through her second study of a book on cores and their uses for incantors. Ever since she'd spoken with her amulet, it had whispered at her. Little things that she often couldn't discern from her own thoughts. It was like part of her mind had woken up, and when it spoke, she listened. It was never new information, always a reminder of something she already had learned, already knew. At first it had been unsettling, like an itch she couldn't scratch. But the more she heard it, the more it just sounded like herself. And she began to accept its words as her own.

A soft knock on her door made Arix jump. She listened as the knock came again, a little louder this time. Annoyance made worse by the late hour and lack of sleep skittered across her brow. Her headache, which had been ever growing ever since Wren had helped her slip into her nightgown, was becoming an incessant pounding in her temples. It didn't help that bags were beginning to form under Arix's eyes. Throwing off the blankets, her bare feet padding across the cold floor, she poked her head out the door, and was met by a bundled fluff of bear and beaver skins.

"Here." Michael's voice was still recognizable through the layers, as he tossed half of the fur at her. "You're going to need these."

Arix frowned, stepping back to let Michael into her room. He sauntered in, covered from head to toe in pelts and cloaks. He smelled of mothballs, and Arix wondered how long they had been hiding in the back of closets before Michael retrieved them.

"What are you doing?" Arix asked, her arms overflowing.

"Wrong question." Michael smiled as he sat at the end of her bed. "The better question is what are *we* doing?"

"Alright," Arix felt a small smile tweak the corner of her mouth. "What are *we* doing?"

"You'll see."

Arix gave him a look that could have frozen water.

"What? Before we go, you need to get into as many warm clothes as you can. I brought the furs to help."

"Well turn around then." Arix motioned to the opposite wall, which he obliged as she pulled back on her thick woolen stockings and pants. "Am I going to need boots?"

"We'll be doing a little walking, yes. Make sure you're going to be warm enough."

"So when will you be telling me where in the Goddess's name we're going?"

"You'll have to wait and see." When Arix began to protest, he said "And don't think you can smooth talk your way into me telling you. This is a secret I won't give up early."

Arix swallowed her complaint as she pulled on her heavy snow boots. Michael's determination was clear, and he seemed excited enough that she knew she couldn't ruin whatever adventure he had planned.

"Alright, I'm ready."

Michael turned around as she pulled on her hat, and he stared at her for a moment as if analyzing her. She did a little twirl for him, showing off the many layers. "Satisfied?"

"Yes. Now let's go."

She followed him out into the hallway and found it empty of her normal nightly guard. The two snuck down the corridor and the main staircase until they were exiting through a side door. Arix stopped in her tracks as they stepped out into the snow. The moon had shifted into a waxing crescent and a light snow was drifting down upon a new blanket of perfect white landscape. There was a horse-drawn sleigh waiting in the courtyard, piled high with more blankets. Michael climbed up into it, burrowing down inside like a fox, and took the reins.

"Coming?"

Arix grinned, her annoyance and headache gone, and bounded into the sleigh after him. With a quick snap of the reins, the two were off. The wind tonight was calm and the sky was so clear they didn't need the lantern that swung from the front hitch of the sleigh. They slid smoothly across the ice crystals, making new paths for themselves as the horse's breath puffed clouds of warmth into the frigid air. They coasted along, following the path that Arix took every morning on her run, disappearing into the wooded grove.

"Thirsty?" asked Michael after a few moments.

Arix mumbled a yes through the blankets, and Michael handed her the reins before withdrawing a large flask and taking a swig. He then passed it to her as she handed him back the reins. The mulled mead spilled down her throat and warmed her up in the cold night air. Arix let out a sigh and closed her eyes, savoring the flavor.

"Sounds like you needed that more than me." Michael said, giving her a sideways glance. Though he smiled jovially, there was worry behind his eyes.

"It's been a long couple of weeks." Arix avoided his eye contact, adjusting the blanket around her. "Actually, it's been rather a long couple of months."

Arix wished she could think of something to say that would lighten the mood, but could not. Their sadness was as biting as the winter wind.

"I miss her."

"Me too, Arix."

Michael adjusted the reins to his right hand and put the other arm around Arix's shoulder, pulling her to him. His presence was comforting and she realized how much she had missed him as well, since she had burrowed herself away in her books and her grief. She had left him behind in a way, forcing herself to distance the emotional space between them.

"Have you thought about what will happen? At the end of all this?"

Michael shifted uncomfortably. "I don't want to talk about this now, Arix."

"We have to." She pushed away from him, turning to stare. "There is only one ending to this story, Michael. There isn't going to be some miraculous escape. You or I or both of us will die. There isn't any way of getting around that."

"I know." He said, his eyes trained on the path ahead of them, brow furrowed. After a moment he glanced at her, eyes trying to convey just how much he wanted to change their circumstances. "I know. I haven't forgotten why we're here. But I am trying to make the best of the situation we've been given. I'm trying to live in the moment, and be here, now, with you."

He slowed the horse to a stop, then turned, taking Arix's mittened hands within his own.

"There are only four of us left. Any day could be my last with you, and I want to cherish every second I have. That's why I wanted to bring you out tonight. To spend time with you. You've been so locked away recently, hiding off in your room or Goddess knows where else, and you're locking me out too."

When Arix tried to protest, Michael raised a hand to silence her.

"Please let me finish. I know Revena's death was difficult for you. I think, in a way, it's made us both realize the gravity of our future. But while that has seemingly put you into a frenzy of fear and panic, it's given me peace instead. And knowledge that no matter what our destinies may be, our time together is short. So short, Arix." He pulled her to him, crushing her in an embrace, his breath tickling her ear. It was not a lover's embrace, but one of deep friendship, filled with sadness and so much hope.

And it only made her feel emptier than she already was.

Arix pulled away gently, and cupped his face with a sad smile.

"Then let's enjoy this moment. Let's enjoy the last ones we may have left."

Michael smiled back and pulled her close to him. Arix buried her head in his shoulder and he held her quietly, under that crescent moon and falling snow. While their unknown future gave Michael peace, it filled Arix with dread. It filled her up till she thought she might burst, or die from a broken heart. It leaked out of her in slow invisible tears that seemed to evaporate from her eyelashes before they could fall.

With a quick command, the horses were moving again, and Michael steered them off the path and into a small clearing of evergreens.

"Come," Michael said, pulling Arix up and out of the stopped sleigh and into the snow. "I want to show you something.

They walked through the snowdrifts, as deep as their knees in places, weaving between the trees until Michael stopped at a small sapling, no higher than him.

"I thought that for this year, our first and last Yule together, that we should have our own tree. In memory of Revena's life, and the celebration of the season. Let it be a piece of joy for us during these long nights. I thought we could set it up on our spot on the roof, and decorate it. Just a couple small decorations and-"

He was cut off as Arix flung herself at him, knocking him backwards as she hugged him. He laughed as he fell, holding her tight as they went down in a flurry of snow.

"I love it." She whispered, hugging him as tightly as she could. "I love it so much."

They laid together in the snowbank, holding each other close, as the cold sifted through to their skin. The snow cocooned around them, like their very own little cave of white and moonlight, and they stayed until they could stand the cold no more and Michael tucked her back under the blankets of the sleigh. He cut the tree down himself, and attached it with a bit of rope to the back of the sleigh before setting back towards the castle, dragging it along behind them.

It took some work and a bit of magick to carry it up all the stairs to the roof, but once it was set up, and a fire was blazing in the brazier, they agreed that the work had been worth it. Michael had swiped a few of the decorations from the large tree in the front hall and within minutes, their small tree was decorated in ribbons and glass balls.

While the despair remained, Arix pushed it deep down inside of her. It was worth it to see Michael so satisfied with his work. And as he had said in the woods, she tried to enjoy the moment.

By the time Arix made it back to her room and crawled under the piles of blankets on her bed, it was closer to morning than night. But no matter how exhausted she felt, she found that she could not sleep. Guilt and disappointment rattled around her skull, like rocks falling down an endless cavern, echoing as they tumbled into each other restlessly, and long into the night.

~

The sense of foreboding did not leave her, even into the far reaches of the Yule celebration the following night. Surrounded by the court and council to the king, Arix could not ignore the fact that there were only three competitors other than herself left. It felt more like paranoia, the expectation of what was to come rather than the actual turmoil itself that kindled her uneasiness.

Despite the sinking feeling in the pit of her stomach, Arix smiled and choked down the wine that was poured into her cup. When a toast was given over dinner in the competitor's honor, she stood and bowed with the others, the velvet of her green dress draping off her shoulders and low on her back. She danced until her feet throbbed, and joined in when the hall rang with choruses of yuletide carols. She laughed as Bishop Forir told stories of years gone by and how the world had changed yet traditions had remained the same. And when dawn finally approached to whisk away the night, and Orion stole her away to kiss her under the mistletoe, just when her fears were finally tired enough to submit to the joy of the season, the messenger arrived.

The ballroom stilled, the music stopped, and the soldier, his face terse and solemn told them all the news.

The Carn rebels had taken the underground city of Pyesak, Zarak's second largest city, and one of the great economic footholds of the realm. They had taken it, and were holding the magistrate and the warden's family ransom until their demands were met.

Their price? The king's severed head on a platter.

THIRTY-FIVE

Arix's legs were asleep, and there was a cramp in her shoulder so painful that she clamped her hand beneath her teeth to keep from crying out. As the cramp lessened, she breathed a slow, careful sigh of relief.

Soon, she whispered to herself. *Soon we'll be out.*

With every creaking motion, Arix listened. The ground moved steadily beneath her, groaning as the wood strained under the weight. They would be nearing their destination soon.

Voices. Something rattled to her right. A louder sound of creaking wood as a barrel to her left was opened.

More words. Then silence.

Arix let out another slow breath. A few more impatient minutes passed before the ground beneath her creaked to a halt. There was movement above her followed by the blinding light of a torch as a hand came into view. She took it, pulling herself up and out of the empty wooden barrel and dropping down the red clay street beneath, drawing her bow.

Idris was already out of his own barrel, stretching his cramped muscles. Michael was next, as Celeste all but leapt out of her wooden box.

"Goddess, I think I'm going to be sick." The blonde girl muttered as she doubled over with her hands braced on her knees. "I hate the smell of uncooked fish."

"If the smell were really that bad, you would have emptied the delicate contents of your stomach already." Arix whispered to her, a trickle of satisfaction running through her at the sight of Celeste so unsettled. The other girl glared over at her as she straightened.

"This is your fault, you know. It was your idea to sneak into the city in barrels."

"I didn't hear you speak up during the meeting when I suggested it." Arix huffed. "Is it my fault that you got shy in front of all those generals?"

Celeste took a half step forward, her hand falling to the throwing knife at her side. "I said nothing at the time because we needed a plan and yours wasn't half bad."

"Then what's your problem?" Arix took a step forward to meet the other girl, her own hand grasping tighter on her bow.

"Enough you two." Michael whispered at them.

The two women relaxed slightly, hands falling to their sides.

"Besides," he said with a grin. "Neither of you had to be in the pickle barrel. I'll never get this smell out of my hair."

Arix chuckled, leaning in closer for a whiff. "Mmm. Pickled herring. Lovely."

"The Carn will probably smell us coming before they see us." Celeste muttered as she checked the pouches at her side. "Are we doing this, or not?"

Arix turned back to their guide as he hurriedly moved the now empty wagon further into the alley. Kofi was a merchant who had snuck them into Pyesak in the back of his wagon, an inside man for Warden Los Ke. Kofi was a short man with a black goatee, the swathes of his robes billowing around him in neutral creams. His eyes shifted around them as he spoke in a hushed voice.

"We'll take the back route up to the magistrate's estate, and enter through the servant's quarters." He said, re-adjusting the brimless cap on his head. "This way."

Carefully the four competitors followed their escort as he wove behind houses and through back alleys as they made their way deeper into the city.

After the messenger had brought the news of Pyesak's hostages, the council had met immediately, discussing the action that must be taken against the Carn. They'd attacked small cities before, outlying towns along the coast of Eldur. But never had they attacked such a largely populated place. Not only attacked, but held hostages. Normally the Carn killed mercilessly. This was a different twist in their pattern.

Mergur had been quiet as the four incantors rode through it, on their way toward the eastern road. A spattering of onlookers had gathered, but most remained in their homes, celebrating the season and shutting out the horror.

The ride itself to Pyesak was a relatively quick one, but with the additional soldiers, supplies, and escorts, the trip turned from a couple day's ride to nearly two weeks.

Those two weeks had been torture for Arix. She had wanted to spur on past them all, past their little band of military men on foot, and hurry towards the city. Better yet, she would have liked to turn around and go back to the castle. Either were better than plodding along, mulling over the potential disaster that awaited them.

She had known she would face the Carn eventually; she must have known. It was naive to think she could have gone on with her existence and the rebels would have disappeared into a puff of smoke. But it had been so easy to fill herself up with her studies and with her friends and Orion, pushing away the very reason she was in the capitol to begin with.

Entering the city had been easy enough with the help of Kofi and his merchant barrels. Even though the rebels had taken hostages in the warden's estate at the highest point of the city, the rest of the townspeople had been left alone to go about their normal routines of shopping and trading. It bothered Arix that the city had not been closed off or inhibited entrance in any way. The Carn had never been this sloppy before.

As they snuck through the city, Arix marveled at the beauty of Pyesak. The entire city was built deep under the mountains of sand above, over a surging underground river and into the red stone caverns. At first, the city had been built as a small shelter during sandstorms, a place for traveling nomads to camp. But after many years the city had grown in size and had become the second largest in Zarak. And it truly was a marvel. The streets and buildings were hewn from the red rock, towering up in domes and parapets, archways overhanging the streets in steppes that lead up to different towering parts of the city. Intricately carved lanterns hung on every corner, casting warm yellow light upon the city below.

The sloping streets and stairways led the competitors ever upwards until they arrived at a back door to the warden's estate house. They moved cautiously, carefully looking for signs of the Carn. So far, they had seen none.

A pit had begun to form in Arix's stomach as they made their way through a gate and into the great house. It was silent, the regular scurry of servants gone completely from the empty hallways and sitting rooms filled with pillows and lounging couches. There were signs of a struggle as they moved deeper into the residence, a smashed vase in the hall, a metal tray of food and drinks strewn across the floor.

Slipping along a servant passageway, Kofi scuttled ahead of them, peering around a doorway at a four way intersection of hallways. Idris placed a hand on his shoulder, motioning for the man to move to the back of the group, letting the four incantors lead. He nodded curtly and pointed toward a staircase that led downward.

"This stairway," Kofi whispered. "Leads around to the main room. I've been informed by a servant girl that the family is being kept there. Once you've gone down, it's the third door on the left."

Idris nodded before motioning the other three to follow him down the stairs. Arix strung an arrow into her bow as Celeste drew a second throwing dagger. Beside her Michael held a small shield and his shortsword at the ready. Kofi trailed a few steps behind them as they leveled out and moved toward the third door. Carefully Idris laid a hand on the latch and motioned that it was unlocked.

The door opened into a small room, another closed door on the opposite wall. Casks of wine and shelves of dusty bottles lined the walls, the floor littered with stacked wooden crates. The room smelled musty and there was a faint aroma of rotten eggs. Arix reached out a hand, grabbing Michael's arm as she stopped dead in her tracks.

"Something's wrong." she whispered.

No sooner had the words left her mouth that the sound of shattering glass filled the room and something stung at her neck. Instinctively Arix threw up Rampart of the Faithful, shielding herself and Michael. Celeste was already throwing up her own shield, but damage had already been done.

Arix neck felt like it was on fire, and she clawed at it with a scream. In front of her, Idris was on the floor writhing in agony at the liquid that pooled around him. The pungent smell of rotting eggs filled Arix's nose so violently she jerked her head back, scrambling to get out of the room as she clutched her neck. She turned in time to see Kofi slam the door closed and heard as he clicked the lock into place.

Two men ran, bolting from behind the crates where they had been hiding, racing for the door on the opposite side of the room. As one wrenched it open, the other threw a second vial, the clear liquid arcing over them. The liquid sizzled as it came in contact with the shields, but ran down to the floor leaving them unharmed.

"Acid!" Celeste called, her eyes drawn to slits. "Don't use any fire in here!"

With a slam of the door, the two men were gone.

Michael moved forward and checked Idris's body. His skin was puckered and swollen, and he had finally stopped writhing on the floor. Arix was already sprinting across the room after the men, healing her neck as she went. She felt Celeste at her side as she flung open the door and bolted up the set of stairs. Clattering feet and the sound of broken objects rang ahead of them as the two men dashed out of sight.

Michael was calling her name, but Arix only saw white hot anger at the edge of her vision. She didn't need Michael to tell her what she already knew. Idris was dead.

Up ahead the sound of a door slammed, and Arix rounded the corner to find an ornately carved door. With a solid kick, the door flung open and Celeste and Arix rushed into the room. Ahead of them the two men had joined two more, armed with more bottles of the acid. The man on the far left raised his arm, ready to throw the vial.

"Chekai!" Arix called, sweeping out her arm.

The four men stopped, their eyes wide, frozen in place as the cant took hold of their limbs.

On the floor, tied to pillars and furniture, the wide eyed family of the warden sat, gags in their mouths. One woman started to sob, her shoulders rising and falling as tears streamed down her face. Celeste worked her way around the room, relieving the rebels of their weapons as Arix began untying the hostages. They stared at her in shock, eyes still wide and terrified as she spoke softly to them, undoing their gags and cutting the rope that bound them. Michael finally entered the room, and seeing the situation, wordlessly began helping.

There were fourteen hostages, mostly women and children. Their soiled garments told the story well. They had been tied here for days.

As Arix at last reached the sobbing woman, she fought to release herself from the gag, holding Arix's arm in a vice-like grip. She tried to make out words, but her sobs broke them into pieces that Arix could not understand.

"It's alright, we've been sent by the council. We're here to save you." Arix assured her, trying to speak calmly.

"No, no, no…" The woman kept repeating, shaking her head. Arix could see each red vein in the whites of her eyes. "You don't-no, no! You don't understand!"

Arix muttered a few words under her breath, and instant calm overtook the woman. Her breathing steadied and her grip relaxed slightly.

"It's a trap."

Arix's blood turned to ice in her veins.

"The rebels built some sort of trap to kill you if you came for us." The woman continued, her eyes still wide. "Please, oh please dear Goddess, hurry!"

Arix glanced up and caught Michael's look. In a flash, Arix crossed the room to the four men, her hands going around one of their necks. She dropped the magick and his limbs swung wildly, trying to push her off him.

"What trap is she talking about?"

The man only fought harder, and Arix struggled for a moment to keep her hands on him. A swinging arm came into view, connecting with the man's stomach. He doubled over as Celeste withdrew her fist.

"Answer her fucking question." Celeste growled.

At first, Arix thought the man was choking, wheezing on the breath that had been knocked from him. It only took a moment to realize that he was laughing. Celeste punched him again. He coughed and his knees buckled. Arix went down with him, pinning him back against the floor as she sat on his chest.

"I swear to the Goddess, I will kill you right now and have no regrets." Arix spat out, clutching the man's neck. His laughter quickly turned into gasps.

"Arix…" Michael's voice sounded off to her right but Arix hardly heard him. Every squeeze had the man squirming, and his eyes were beginning to roll back. Then a snap as his neck broke under the pressure.

Someone grabbed her by the shoulder and jerked her backwards, her grip loosening on the rebel.

Michael was gripping her shoulder, eyes wide as he stared at the dead man.

Arix stood, cold venomous hatred in her veins as she moved to the next frozen man. With a wave of her hand, his body relaxed, moving on its own as he scuttled back from her.

"Tell me, or you'll end up worse than your friend." Arix said, keeping her voice as even as she could.

He clamped his mouth closed, but he was shifting his weight, no smile on his face. He was afraid of her.

Good. He should be.

Slowly Arix drew an arrow to her bowstring, raising it and aiming at the man's head. "Tell me now."

A flicker. Arix almost missed it. But there it was, a small flick of his gaze as the man glanced to something behind her. Arix turned to look. A couch, a table, a box.

"Over there?" Arix asked, nodding her head to that corner of the room.

The man's face shifted again. Worry streaked his brow.

"Michael. Go look at that box. Carefully."

Impossibly long moments passed as Michael slowly approached the box. Arix heard him crouch, watched the eyes of the rebel as they went wide.

Then heard Michael mutter in a low voice. "Shit."

Arix turned. In front of Michael, a glowing box sat, runes carved into the top.

"What the hell is that?" She turned back to face the rebel, drawing the bow back and taking aim.

The rebel started sputtering, his arms raised before him in defense. "It's too late now! You can't stop it!"

Arix was already moving, racing to Michael and dropping down beside him on the floor. Celeste had already taken her place, tackling the rebel to the floor, hitting him again and again as he screeched.

"What is it, Michael?"

Worry creased his brow as he examined the box, his face barely an inch away from its glowing blue surface. Runes and words in a foreign tongue were etched around the outside, gears and sliding pins making up the lock on its front.

"I've never seen anything like this." He muttered. "But I can guess."

"How bad?"

Michael just shook his head.

"Is this…" Arix reached a finger forward, pointing at a large symbol on the top of the box. She recognized it vaguely, though there were additional whorls added to the design she knew. Michael snatched her wrist away before she could touch the box.

"Don't touch it."

"Is that the symbol for Frennyrth?" Arix could not take her eyes off the symbol, heavy dread dragging down every fiber of her being.

"Yes. Modified somehow. To make it more powerful."

"How much time do we have?"

The box was already glowing brighter than it had been a moment ago and was slowly starting to vibrate. Michael shook his head. "Not long."

Arix sat back on her heels, eyes wide.

"Can we throw it out a window or something?" Celeste called, mid punch.

Michael looked up at her. "No."

"How big, Michael?" Arix grabbed his arm, forcing him to look at her. "How much damage?"

His eyes were hollow. Despondent and empty. Arix's heart ached looking at him. It reminded her of how he had been after the paramour. Like there was no hope left.

"The whole city. When this box explodes, Pyesak will most likely cave in and collapse."

It had all been a trap. Luring them into the city only to bring it down on their heads. The rebels had never intended to bargain.

Their intention was always to kill. And because of them, coming here and walking right into the trap, everyone in the city would perish.

Arix stared at Michael, his eyes flickering across the surface of the box, mental calculations swimming around in his head. Then his eyes went wide. Horror rippled across his features as he slowly turned to stare at Arix.

"What? Michael, what is it?"

"This…" He was whispering and Arix leaned forward to catch his words. "This was made by an incantor."

"So?"

"None of us made it. And Lakai certainly didn't. So that means…"

Arix's own eyes went wide as she realized what Michael was saying. What it meant. The Carn had an incantor.

"Then what the hell are we waiting for?" Celeste hovered over them, blood dripping from her knife. "Stop wasting time being miserable and turn it off."

Michael's jaw set as he jerked up his sleeves and angled his head to look at different sides of the box, talking as he went. The horror in his eyes lessened as he focused on the problem at hand.

"The Heart of Frennyrth is the base for this box. That cant is the ticking bomb. But the whole thing has been modified to have more of an impact. Extension, radius, maximum damage; these symbols here amplify all of that. But this one, I don't know what it is." Michael pointed to a small symbol on the side of the box, so small, Arix had not seen it at first.

"It's a flower of some kind. Lilies? Maybe borages?"

Arix stared at the flower, something in the back of her mind instantly trying to get her attention. Every time she reached for it, it slipped away from her, just out of grasp.

"If we knew all the elements powering the spell, I could cast something to invert it. But, I don't know all of these symbols. Casting the wrong thing could set it off early."

There was something about the shape of the petals, the center pistil of the flower that tugged and tugged at something in her brain.

"Can you use a spell to identify it?" Celeste asked, crouching beside him to examine the marking.

Michael was shaking his head, the heels of his hands pressing into his temples as if that would make him think clearly. "Not a rune like this. If it's a borage then it could be a time bubble. Millions of years would pass in a matter of a second, everything collapsing together by the passing of time."

"Can you stop it?

"Yes, but if I'm wrong it will set the whole thing off early." Michael muttered, though his hands hovered in front of him as if he was already preparing the cant in his head. The box in front of him was rattling against the floor now, violently banging against the tile.

Why couldn't she remember? It was there, so close, just on the periphery of her vision, glowing a vibrant orange.

Then it clicked.

Arix reached out, grabbing Michael's wrist to stop him before he killed them all.

"Lady Siguaro. It's a Lady Siguaro flower. They're used to purify air. Could it have altered to spread the explosion by feeding off the oxygen in the air?"

Michael stared at her. "Maybe. Are you sure that's what it is?"

She nodded, her eyes never leaving the symbol of the flower. She had never been more sure of anything in her life.

"I'm positive."

"If it's feeding on oxygen, all I have to do is…" Michael jerked open his bag, removing a small vial of crushed coal. He dumped the contents into his palm, rubbed his hands together and traced a mark into the dark powder.

"Everyone back up!"

Arix and Celeste jerked away from the box as the glowing grew until Arix had to squint against the brightness.

Then it was gone.

The blue light disappeared altogether and the box finally stood still.

The three competitors let out a slow breath and Michael collapsed back to lay on the floor.

"How did you know it was a Lady Siguaro?" He asked, peering back to stare at Arix.

A moment passed before she could finally look at him. "It's how Revena saved my life. In the maze? It was the day we became friends."

THIRTY-SIX

Despite the words and tears of gratitude expressed by the Warden's family, the three incantors chose not to stay any longer in the underground city. Something about almost being buried under mountains of sand made them feel unnerved at the prospect of staying in Pyesak overnight. Instead, they left, making the trek back to where the council leaders had gathered, camped around Zarak's capital, Ramal. They had towed the three rebels behind their horses, much to Arix's disdain. She had wanted to kill them right there in the Warden's house, but Michael had stopped her. It was not her place, after all, to determine their fate. None of them were the Black Hand yet.

Their arrival at the camp was met with whoops and hollers, and messengers running out to meet them before they had arrived at the city gates. The Carn rebels were taken away and Arix, Michael, and Celeste were rushed to General Hawes' tent for their report. There, the three incantors shared the details of how they had snuck into Pyesak, lost Idris, and diffused the box that would have killed them all.

When morning came, Arix was glad of it. She wanted to get

out of the desert, back to the castle in Mergur. Even the cactus juice served with her breakfast did nothing for her disposition.

Michael stepped into her room in the middle of her meal, his mouth set in a grim line.

"What's happened?" Arix asked, setting down her glass.

Michael took a seat on the edge of her small palette, pulling his legs up underneath him.

"There's a meeting in an hour." Michael responded. "The council will be discussing what is to be done."

"Just the council?"

"We," Michael said with a cheerless smile, "will not be attending. Warden Los Ke has arranged for us three to visit the hot springs. A thank you for saving his family from the Carn."

Arix stared at him. "The Carn have just tried to demolish an entire city, killing us in the process, and we're supposed to go relax in a hot bath?"

"Arix-"

"We're the ones who saved the city. We're the incantors. We deserve a seat in that meeting!"

"There's more, Arix." Michael's eyes met with hers, worry mixed with the deep green of his irises. "I've been thinking about that box. It was a combination of some of the technology we knew the rebels had, mixed together with magick. Powerful magick. They wouldn't have been able to create without the help and knowledge of an incantor. An incantor stronger than us. Much, much stronger."

"Goddess." she muttered.

"If we're being honest, we got very lucky diffusing that bomb. Without your knowledge, we'd all be dead. I'm guessing the council will be meeting to discuss next steps. How to retaliate. How to fight off a threat that's become this strong."

"So what will happen now?"

"I don't know." Michael said simply. He looked so tired. Arix wondered how much sleep he had gotten the night before.

Silence hung over them as Arix stared down at her hands. Red clay was embedded under her nails, making her hands look dirty. She felt Michael staring at her, but she kept her eyes down, focusing on digging out those tiny grains. "There's three of us now, Michael. Just three. It seems so strange that only a few months ago there were so many of us I didn't even bother to learn their names."

She let out a small laugh, the corners of her mouth turning up, even though there was no joy there. "The end is so close I can taste it. But there are still so many barriers in the way. Too many loose ends that need tying before that final test can take place. And all I keep thinking about is how much I wish Celeste were dead already."

Michael said nothing.

With a groan, Arix threw herself sideways and buried her face in her pillow, her knees curling up to her chest.

"You don't have to like it, but it's the truth nonetheless." She muttered.

Finally their eyes connected, and Michael crawled up the length of the bed to lay beside Arix, his arm bent under his head as he stared up at the ceiling of her small guest room. He looked as if he were about to say something, then stopped himself.

"What?

"You've become angry, Arix." He finally said with a sigh. "Angrier than when I first met you. Wilder, somehow. Fiercer. But not in the same way I admired your fierceness before. You've become bitter. Has all this loss curdled you on the inside?"

"Maybe." Arix muttered, her face buried into the crook of

her arm. "I don't know. Maybe I've always been this angry, and it's only now coming to the surface."

"I worry about you."

The emptiness in her heart yawned wide.

"I know."

~

Arix traced the edge of the patterned towel she had been given, and followed her escort through the cool hallways into an underground chamber deep beneath the Warden's home in Ramal. Walls of dark orange clay lined the passageway and opened up into an underground spring, the blue of the water casting flickering shadows across the ceiling. She nodded to the woman, who bowed and took her leave. Stripping out of her clothes, Arix sank into the bumbling water, the heat seeping across her bare skin through to her bones. She dunked her head under the water and held it there for as long as she could. Only when her lungs were screaming for air did she slowly rise above the surface, just in time to see Celeste's form slip into the pool beside her.

The girl looked tired.

Arix resigned herself to letting her body soak up the minerals, and let her mind drift away from the sandy battles and back to when things were simpler. When was the last time she had relaxed in a natural pool? Years and years it seemed, though in actuality, had it only been a year ago that she had slipped into a mountain hot spring in Tamhain, the snow falling around her in soft flakes? She'd just robbed the Warden, her prize horse tied along with two pack horses laden down with treasure and gold. Only a few months later she'd been at the baron's home in Coraven. It was then that her life had flipped, throwing her into this chaotic journey; a fine bloody mess.

Yet, even in the disaster of it all, she'd learned more in the past few months than she ever would have on her own, stealing from the rich and corrupt. She had real power now, true power. And she was doing more good as a random competitor than she ever had done as a simple thief.

She remembered back to that first day, the castle rising up out of the earth in front of her like a hand reaching for the sky. Moments and memories of her life flitted through her head , reminding her that the path to this place had been long. Filled with fear and worry. Filled with hiding and stealing and lying. There had been good times, before it all. Moments of laughter and drunken songs sung in happy taverns. Moments where she had relished all the shadowed work, sneaking around and unlocking doors in the night.

But then everything had stopped working like a carefully wound timepiece, falling into disarray after she had stolen from the baron. And yes, her little circle had widened. Had gone from being alone to having voices not her own in her head. She had gained a mentor in both Lakai and Desirae, and had gained friends in Revena and Michael. But Revena was dead, and her relationship with Lakai had deteriorated after that death. Even her conversations with Desirae had become nothing more than meaningless drivel. And for what? She felt more alone than ever. Facing a future either dead, or without her last friend in the world. Michael. She didn't want to think about him. If she did, she knew it would lead to a broken heart. So she pushed it aside, focusing instead on something else.

She'd killed a man. It hadn't even hit her at the time. Bothered her at all. In the estate, with their time running out, she crushed his throat so easily. It had been the first time she'd actually killed someone. She had almost expected it to weigh on her. But it didn't. Not even a little.

Was it because of the malice she held onto so tightly? The anger that she targeted at the rebels? Or maybe Michael had been right. Maybe she was just bitter.

Even their group now was smaller. They'd gone from twenty-five to three. She hadn't really mourned Idris. Hadn't really mourned any of the others either, apart from Lace in the beginning. But even then, it was more about mourning the loss of an innocent life than about losing someone she cared about. Idris she had known. Trusted, in a way, to watch her back. Over and over he had proved to be a brave fighter, a powerful incantor. An ally, if not a friend.

Arix opened her eyes to see Celeste watching her. The tension across the pool was thick as the reality of their situation sank into Arix's bones.

The blonde smiled, her straight white teeth looking more like fangs in the blue light. Arix smiled back. They had been allies the day before, fighting a common enemy. But no longer.

Today, they were rivals again.

THIRTY-SEVEN

"May the Goddess grant you a safe journey." Warden Los Ke stood before the incantors, fist over his heart and bowed to them.

It was time to return to Castle Zma'ai. The three incantors turned, making their way out of the meeting room at the Wardens house. Celeste stormed away before anything could be said between them, but what would Arix have said anyway? She felt the girl's frustration mirrored in herself. It had been decided and there was nothing that could change it now. They were giving up. At least that was how it seemed to her. Instead of going back into the desert to hunt down the Carn, General Hawes was taking them, and the three rebels they had captured, back to Mergur. Lord Bardon wanted them back at the castle for the final two tests and the last bit of training that awaited them. The rebels would be tried and found guilty and strung up along the wall as a witness to all who thought they might disagree with the King and the council.

And what then?

The Carn would be left to their own devices and only grow stronger with each passing day. It was madness. And Arix and Michael and Celeste would sit at the castle, listening to their teachers drone on and on about the economics and the histories of the na-tion, when history was being made right outside their front door.

Arix took a deep breath, calming the anger that was welling up inside her. Soon enough the race would be won and she would have the authority to do something about the rebels. Until then, there were still two more tests to complete. Two more lengths to run, and things would be different.

"Anything you need to pack?" Arix asked with a grin.

Michael eyed her warily. "I thought you'd be too upset to be smiling."

Her grin faded slightly, determination setting across her fore-head in hard lines. "I'm not happy that we're leaving. But there are other things to focus on now. The rebels will be dealt with eventu-ally." She linked arms with Michael and pulled him away to where the horses were being saddled. "I'm ready to go home."

"Home? A little optimistic, don't you think?"

"It's the closest thing I have to a home right now, so yes. Home. Isn't there a saying? Home is where you kick your boots off? Where there's hot stew and cold ale and comfort waiting for you?"

"I think you mean 'Home is where a maid brings you hot chocolate for breakfast on a tray.' You seem to be confusing royal means with a sense of belonging."

Arix laughed. "Maybe. But don't you feel like you belong there? With those great gleaming marble walls and long corridors? I used to think I'd feel most comfortable with just a tent and patch of woods. But I suppose that was the best I expected as a vigilante."

"Sometimes I forget that was your life before. Before coming to the Capitol, home was vineyards and the smells of wine and ciders and fireflies on a summer's eve. It's strange to think that I will never see that again." Michael's voice dropped at the end, trailing off into silence.

Arix pulled him to a stop, anger bubbling.

"Don't you dare. Don't you dare say that. It sounds like you've given up already."

He studied her face, the fierceness in it, and his features relaxed into a smile. "I won't give up. I promise."

"Good. Because I don't know what I would do if you did."

The small smile turned into something else as his facial expression turned blank. "You'd be the Black Hand."

General Hawes was pulling himself into the saddle when they arrived at the edge of city, their horses already saddled and waiting for them. Arix shoved her boot into the stirrup and hoisted herself up, resting back into a comfortable position on Osiris' back. There was a whistle near the front, and they moved out. The troops they had brought with them to Zarak marched steadily behind them, the rebel prisoners packed into a wagon in the middle, with General Hawes and Lord Heseth leading the line. Arix and Michael rode together, directly in front of the wagons, listening to the chatter of the guards as they moved away from Ramal.

The journey back to the Capital was much as it had been when they had left for Zarak the day after Yule. The landscape shifted around them as they moved, the sand disappearing into brown-gray grass as they moved out of the heat and back into winter. It was strange to have only just been sweltering under the sun, to now crave its warmth as the ground became covered in ice and snow. A land of gray and icy slush.

They were in the dead part of winter now, when the bright festivities of Yule were fading away and quickly being replaced by ice and slush and dreary cold. It was the worst part of the year in Arix's mind. The air always felt wet with smog and mist, and it clung to them, seeping through their clothes and making Arix shiver and shake from it. When she could stand it no longer, she cast warming heat over herself, sighing at the relief of it.

"Arix, we should talk about what happened in Pyesak." Michael murmured as they rode through the outskirts of a frozen Mergur.

"I'm fine. I don't need to talk." Arix replied, teeth clenched in frustration. He'd been trying to have this conversation for the past fifteen minutes and she was sick of it. "It's done, and talking about it won't change that."

Michael rode quietly beside her, but she could feel his pull. Staring at her, willing her to open up.

"Michael. It isn't important. He was a Carn."

"It is important." He said quietly. "He might have been a Carn, but he was still a person. Misguided and wrong and a terrible person, but a person all the same."

"Are you done?"

Michael flinched at the anger in her tone, sadness creeping over his face.

Arix raised an arm, gesturing to the wagon ahead of them that held the three rebels. "Those men are murderers, Michael. They would have killed thousands if the Carn had set off that bomb in Pyesak. And they've killed thousands of more before that. All for the sake of trying to prove that they won't be governed by the king." Arix hissed, gripping her reins tighter as she shifted her horse closer to him. Something dark was boiling in her belly and Arix embraced the feeling, letting it eat her up from the inside.

"They murdered my family, Michael. They deserve worse than death." She spat out the words and turned, urging her horse ahead.

For the rest of the day she did not speak to Michael, nor did he try to explain himself or bring up the subject again. Instead, they rode in silence through Mergur and up the road to cross the bridge into the castle grounds.

When he knocked on her door that night, she ignored it, pulling the covers up over her head and stuffing her face into her pillow. Guilt seeped through her bones, but she shoved it away, bolting her thoughts from it. She refused to allow it to spread; to acknowledge the fact that Michael was, and always would be, a better person than she was.

She knew it was selfish. She knew that her anger towards Michael was unfounded. He lived by a code, all unto himself. A code that pushed him to be better. To strive for loftier goals. He was all the virtues that Arix had been taught to be as a child. He was all good. But how could someone all good survive in a world that constantly proved it was all evil?

Arix didn't know. The more she thought on it, the more it bothered her. She couldn't quite pinpoint why, but somewhere inside uneasiness lurked, hidden deep behind her ribs. Was it that she knew she would never be as good as Michael? Or was it that someone as good as him would never survive being a Black Hand? That perhaps Michael would never have the strength to do what needed to be done.

The thought hollowed her.

~

"Finished already?"

Arix glanced away from the gray morning light that seeped through the window and gave a tentative smile to Desirae who had just entered.

"Finished." She motioned to the stack of books at her feet and grinned at her tutor. "It's been nice having nothing to do but read."

Desirae moved behind her desk and sat down into her chair, placing a sheet of paper before her. "Even so, I'm surprised you went through that stack so quickly." She watched Arix, her head casually resting in her hand.

"What?"

Desirae shook her head and waved off Arix's look. "Nothing. I'm just surprised by how far you've come. You fly through books on history and lore, you've read almost every book on fighting I've given you. It's impressive. If I'm honest, I never expected it from you. You have surprised me, and I do not surprise easily. You will make an excellent Black Hand."

Arix smiled, though there was no joy in it. All she could think about was how unprepared she felt. Maybe that was why she read so many of the books her tutor offered her.

"Something is bothering you. It will hinder your progress if you don't get it off your chest." Desirae's voice was perturbed, almost annoyed at having to ask Arix the question at all.

Was there something bothering her? Besides the looming test she knew would be coming any day? Besides the knowledge that at some point soon, she would be separated from her friend? Or was it something else?

Arix sighed, leaning her head back against the wood paneling. "Lots on my mind. I've been trying to put them in order."

"You've been back from Zarak for over a week. I ran into Michael yesterday and he asked about you. Have you two been talking?"

Arix said nothing, letting her silence speak for her instead.

"I see." Desirae unstacked and then replaced the books on her desk in a different order. "It's none of my business of course, but you should talk to him. You need to be in the right mindset for the next test."

Arix sighed, pushing herself away from the window seat. She would. Later. "I'm going to take a walk."

~

Arix trudged through the sludge and ice, the bottom of her cloak dragging behind her. If only she'd had the sense to switch to her shorter one. Wren would work herself into a tizzy over the slush, and she would never hear the end of it.

The garden around her was bare, the rose stems frozen solid, the leaves and bushes tinged in frost. Someone had made an attempt to clear away the sludge from the path, but pools of it remained mixed with the gray gravel. The large fountain in the center of the garden splashed no water, and the surface glittered with thin patches of ice.

As she approached it from the north, a cloaked man approached it from the south, seemingly also enjoying the frozen grounds.

Arix's heart skipped a moment, hoping to see Orion's face as the man lifted his hood. Instead she was met with the smile of a man she had not seen since Yule.

"Bishop Forir! What are you doing out here braving the winter wind?" Arix hastened toward him, clasping his arm when he motioned towards her.

"Same as you, I'm sure." He smiled, the lines by his crystal blue eyes crinkling. They stuck out, brilliant and bright amongst the gray world that surrounded them. "Just hoping the cold will clear away some of the cobwebs that linger. Tell me my dear, how have you been? It's been quite a while since we had a chance to speak last."

She linked her arm through his as they continued round the

outside of the large circular fountain.

"Quite changed, I hope. Do I look different?" Arix turned, her arms thrown wide as she grinned, walking backwards. "Do I still look like that scared little doe that you met in the ballroom?"

Bishop Forir laughed, and it was deep and lovely. "No indeed! You seem to be right in your element. General Hawes has spoken non-stop of that stunt you pulled in Pyesak. It was good work. Lord Bardon is pleased, not that he'd ever say so. That man likes to keep much to himself."

Arix restrung her arm through his as they crunched along, her jovial mood shifting slightly. "It wasn't all good. They sent us home. I feel useless here. Reading the same books over and over, knowing that we could be in the desert right now cutting down the Carn forces."

Her voice rose in frustration, the ends of her words snapping as sharply as the cold air. She huffed, her breath coming out in steamy puffs before her. Bishop Forir watched her, and she smiled sheepishly when she noticed.

"Sorry. The council has their reasons, I know. I just liked being able to do something. Everything that happens here, it feels as though it's happening around me, like a great surging stream and I'm just a little leaf floating around in it. Unable to cause change, or to choose where the river pulls me. I like being able to have a say in what's happening to me."

The Bishop was nodding slowly, and it spurred her to continue.

"Everything that's happened here, over these last months, makes me realize more than ever that I have no say in my own destiny. Now, as a cog in the machine as a competitor, and I'm sure later, as the Black Hand, I'll have to do exactly as I'm told. In Pyesak, it felt like the old days. No one stared over my shoulder.

We made decisions that saved people. Fighting the rebels was like that again. Except now, I'm stronger than ever; more powerful than I've ever been."

They stopped walking, pausing at the opening in the hedge that led back towards the castle. Arix tugged her arm free and wrapped her cloak tighter around herself, suddenly cold. Shivers traveled down her spine, her toes curling in her boots.

"And what role does fate play? If it's truly my fate to become the Black Hand, so be it. But in the end, I truly don't know if I've come this far because I've worked for it, or because of luck and destiny."

"You say that as though they are the same. That luck is woven together with destiny; that they conspire and plan together." Bishop Forir moved past her, through the opening in the hedge, and Arix followed, trailing half a step behind. "But if destiny is the river, pulling a young leaf like you along, then luck is the current. Pushing and shoving you away from rocks or hungry fish."

"Your analogy is falling apart." Arix laughed.

Smiling, the Bishop tucked his hands into the deep pockets of his robe. "Where does the river travel? What chooses its path? The current is only a byproduct of the river, not the same thing. The river flows down a mountain because it is the only place left for it to go. The river carves its path down over rocks and under logs. The current is only formed after the river knows its path. Such is destiny and luck. Destiny will take you, rushing with it, down the mountain, depositing you into the sea. It does not care how it gets you there, or in what shape you find yourself in when you arrive. Only that destiny takes you where you need to go. Now luck, on the other hand, serves her own purpose. She weaves and pulls at the right moments, swerving around rocks to protect you or dragging you under when you need a good dunking. Destiny is the conclusion. Luck is your companion along the way."

THIRTY-EIGHT

The envelope was smooth, creamy paper, with her name in italicized script on the front. Arix glanced up at Wren as the maid held it out to her.

"From the council."

Arix stared at the envelope for a moment, the creamy paper ready and waiting to attack her. Then she snatched it gingerly and pulled out the card.

"Well?" Wren asked, trepidation filling her voice. She clutched her silver tray with white knuckles.

Skimming through the words, Arix took a deep breath.

"Announcement of the next test. We've each been given an objective, and are to meet Lord Heseth at the bottom of the Lancer Staircase." Arix glanced up at Wren from her window-seat. "Where is the Lancer Staircase?"

Wren was white as a sheet. "It's on the far side of the castle. It leads down into a portion of the castle that's under the wall."

"What's down there, Wren?"

The girl shook her head as she mumbled, "The dungeons."

Arix huffed, and Wren's eyes widened at her mistress' flippancy. "Is that all? It's a test. They aren't going to toss us in cells and leave us to rot."

"But you don't know!" Wren's voice squeaked, and Arix cringed at the sound. "You don't know what could be awaiting you. The last time you went deep under the castle you came back depressed for weeks!"

As soon as she had said it, she clapped a hand over her mouth then curtsied as she stepped backwards towards the door. "I'm sorry, Miss Arix. I'll go."

"Wren, wait."

The girl stopped.

"I need you to show me where that staircase is." Arix held up the envelope with a grim smile. "The test starts now."

~

The stairway was cold. Much colder than the rest of the castle, and Arix clutched her cloak around her shoulders tighter. Torchlight lit her way, yet the darkness grew like a cloud around her. There were groanings, the whole building above her settling, shifting, thousands of feet above her. A brief moment of trepidation engulfed her, and flickers of a horror story her father had told her when she was young skittered across her mind.

Then without warning, she was at the bottom of the stairs, Michael and Celeste waiting for her in the dimness.

They waited for a few minutes in silence together, as steps resounded in the distance. Appearing from a left hallway, Lord Heseth emerged, his goatee trimmed around to shape his pointed chin.

"Follow me."

He led them down a hallway and further into the bowels of

the castle, passing great iron gates leading down and away to darkness. They emerged above another staircase, and went down until they turned at a small landing. The only sound was their boots on the stone stairs as they turned and descended even further into the earth. At last they arrived in a small antechamber, with three iron doors set into the walls.

Arix blinked in the dim light, surprised to see quite a few more members of the council waiting for them. Lord Bardon, General Hawes, Warden Los Ke, Lord Iman Holding, and Orion. He stood with the others, his eyes forward, ignoring their presence as they stepped into the torchlight.

"We have arrived at your next test." Lord Heseth said, turning to them. He motioned to the three doors that lay behind him. "Choose a door. Behind each is a rebel, captured from your mission in Pyesak. You have already been given your objectives. When you have extracted all the relevant information, exit the room and relay it to the council. The last to gain the knowledge requested will lose. Only two of you will continue onward from this test today."

Before Arix could think to respond, Celeste was already stepping forward, grasping the handle for the first door and pulling it open. Her insides became heavy as Arix glanced sideways at Michael. He was grim, his face blank of emotion. The weight grew inside her. Only two would remain.

Arix stepped forward to the center door, her hand resting on the handle. She pushed her worry aside. Celeste was vicious, yes. But Michael was kind. He'd sooner sweet talk the information out of someone than rip it out like Celeste would. So what was her strategy?

Arix yanked open the door, letting it slam soundly behind her as she entered into the small room. In the center a man sat in a chair, his wrists bound in front of him, a hood hanging over his head. He shook slightly, and the room smelled of sweat and fear. Before him sat another chair, empty. Arix yanked the hood from his head and he stared up at her, jaw set as they glared across the space.

Deep within her, rage was seething, screaming for her to give the man what he deserved. He was Carn. And the Carn had killed her family, killed everything she held dear. Set her on the path she was on today.

"Name." Arix barked.

The man said nothing, his lips pushing together in a stubborn thin line.

"If you tell me what I want to know, I'll make this easy." Arix kept her voice low, deadly. Slowly she removed a small knife from her hip and twisted it slowly. The torchlight from the wall glinted across the blade making it sparkle. The implication was clear.

Still the man did not respond.

Arix stepped forward, crouching in front of him. She moved the tip of her dagger up his leg and across his stomach, finally coming to rest at his sternum. He held perfectly still as she did so, a terrified stillness, as if waiting for the knife to gouge into him.

"I don't really need your name. I don't care. But I'm here to ask you questions, and you are here to answer. If you don't, I will make you. Do you understand?"

Deep within her chest her heart pounded against her ribs, anger boiling at her insides. He was a murderer. If she didn't have a job to do, she would have slit his throat right then and there.

"You..." Arix began, digging in slightly so the sharp point penetrated his clothing. "...are making me impatient. And I don't like being made to wait."

The knife dug further into his chest and he flinched away

from her, leaning as far back as he could in the chair.

"Micah." He finally said, and his voice cracked with the words.

"Good." Her tension on the dagger released slightly, and he relaxed a little. "Do you know who I am?"

Micah nodded slowly.

"That's good. You know what I'm capable of. Answer my questions honestly, and you and I will have no trouble."

He only stared at her, glancing down at the knife briefly.

"How many of you are there?"

Micah remained silent.

"Where is your camp?"

He said nothing, lips pressing together.

"What is your incantor's name?"

His eyes widened at that and Arix sneered.

"Yes, we know about your incantor. Do they have a name?"

Still nothing.

She was running out of time. Every second he refused to answer her questions was another second that Celeste moved toward victory. Arix braced a hand on his shoulder and moved the blade up to rest at his throat.

Arix breathed out slowly, trying to calm the nerves and her pounding heart, letting her breath hiss through her clenched teeth. "Micah, Micah, Micah. You already know what incantors are capable of. You know of the kind of pain we could inflict."

As if on cue, a bloodcurdling scream echoed from the cell next to them, and Micah stared at the adjoining wall, blood draining away from his face. When he glanced back to her, Arix only glared, her eyes smoldering.

"Your friends are already being questioned. And my friends are going to do anything in their power to make it a difficult experience for them." Arix leaned forward, the knife hovering dangerously at his throat. "Just tell me what I want to know."

A vein stood out in his temple, and Micah clenched his jaw, grinding his mouth closed.

Arix let out a frustrated huff. Time for a new strategy.

She stepped back from him, sheathing her blade and opened her palm. Tracing a sigil on her hand she blew across it, toward Micah. He blinked, eyes shifting in the dim light. Then his whole body relaxed, slumping into his chair as he smiled at her. Casual.

"Hello."

"Hello, Micah."

He glanced down, as if seeing his restraints for the first time, a puzzled expression coming over his face.

"I'm tied up."

"It's for your own safety."

It seemed to satisfy him, and he relaxed, a contented look on his face. "Did you have a question for me?"

Arix sat slowly and relaxed in her chair.

"How many rebels are there?" She said, speaking slowly and deliberately.

"Oh, a lot. I'm not really sure of the exact number."

"Micah, I need a number. Make a guess."

"A little over ten thousand."

Arix eyes widened slightly. More than they had expected. "Where is your camp?"

"I don't know. Maeve keeps us hidden and moves us around a lot."

"Is Maeve the name of your incantor?"

A goofy grin spread across Micah's face. "She's pretty."

Arix could feel a headache pressing at the base of her neck. Enough to make her want to crack it, but she pushed the mild annoyance down and leaned forward like she was talking to a child.

She forced her words to slow, though her mind was racing, telling her to hurry.

"Does pretty Maeve use magick?"

Micah nodded.

"Are there more incantors? More magick users like Maeve in the Carn?"

He shrugged. "I don't think so."

"Who leads you? Is it Maeve?"

Micah shook his head, scrunching up his nose. "Lazh. He picks where we go next."

"So Lazh is your leader? What's his full name?"

"Lahz Mandair. He doesn't like it when we talk to Maeve."

"Why is that?" In her mind, Arix could already see a cocky Celeste, leaving her victim flayed, the room splattered with blood, but victorious. She was running out of time.

"Maeve is Lazh's niece. The most beautiful brown hair, like chocolate-"

Arix held up a hand as he started to continue. "His niece?" Her mind raced, already thinking through what this information may offer in defeating the rebels. "How old is she?"

Micah shrugged. "Fifteen, I think?"

The mask slipped then, just for a moment, but Arix felt her face twist into one of disgust and shock. Micah noticed. His eyebrows went up, worry lines streaking across his brow.

"Who taught her? Where did she learn the craft?" The words were coming faster now, more demanding.

Micah just stared, focused on the wall behind her.

"Micah!" Arix clapped, trying to focus his attention. She felt her desperation rising; rising like a great surging wave, knocking her heartbeat off rhythm. He started, shaking his head as if to clear it.

"Why am I here?" His face was slipping into confusion and fear. "I don't want to be here."

Arix could feel the cant dropping, draining away. She'd lost control for the briefest moment, and now the connection was disappearing. Her anger rose.

"Who taught her magick? Where did she learn it?"

Micah's eyes were wide, glancing about him, becoming frenzied as he pulled at the restraints, the magickal mask Arix had put over him slipping away to reveal the truth.

She was on her feet, hands on his shoulders, shaking him.

She was out of time. Out of time. She would lose.

And die.

"What the hell did you do to me?" Micah was yelling, twisting and pulling his body, trying to tear himself out of her grasp, out of the confines of the chair.

With a shove, Arix pushed his chair backwards, and he teetered for a moment, in that space between balance and falling, his irises as pinpricks. Then with a crash he was on his back, his head bouncing against the stone upon contact. She drew her knife, straddling his chest, holding the dagger along the base of his collarbone.

"Tell me what I want to know." She growled. Her head was pounding, the ache having crept up to dig in behind her eyes. "I swear to the Goddess that I will slice you into the smallest pieces possible if you don't talk."

Micah breathed hard beneath her, and she could feel the rise and fall of his chest between her legs. Spittle mixed with air passed between his lips, anger and terror carved into his features, into his eyes.

With a sneer, Arix switched her grip on the blade and drove the point deep into his shoulder. Micah cried out, as the blood quickly pooled, coating Arix's fist in sticky red. She leaned in close, resting her weight on the blade, and Micah whimpered.

She felt a flash of satisfaction at the sound.

"You are dead. You and all the rest, are dead. You will be wiped from history, wiped from the earth and forgotten. And I shall remain. I will stomp out your rebellion until nothing is left. Until your bodies are ash and have blown away in the wind." Her voice was harsh, raspy. Filled and overflowing with anger.

She yanked out the blade, and hovered over the wound.

"Tell me everything."

He spat at her, the spittle hitting her check and sliding down in a streak of pink. She didn't pause to wipe it away, nor the spattering of blood that followed as she drove her knife into his shoulder again, an inch to the left each time, close and closer to his heart. His lungs were filling with blood and he coughed and spat as the dagger went through his flesh, was yanked out, and then dug in again. Over and over again until Arix lost count.

And she felt nothing. No remorse for this man struggling to breathe beneath her. Nothing but pure unbridled anger. And satisfaction at the pain she caused. It struck deep in her, and yet, she reveled in it.

At last she stopped. When he had ceased moving, when he was still beneath her, blood pooling from his mouth. His eyes wide and frozen in terror.

She rose, pushing herself up from his chest. She backed away from him slowly, a voice in her mind telling her to hurry, hurry, hurry. But she stopped. Stared at the man on the floor.

Micah.

Her gaze traveled down across the floor down to her boots. Traveling up her legs, to the small spattering on her thighs, larger drops across her shirt. Her fingers touched her throat, smearing the blood there, and her face, blood flecked like freckles across her skin.

Only then did she realize she was shaking.

Her palms were coated scarlet, and she glanced around the room for something to wipe them on. She avoided looking at Micah's dead form, and instead snatched up the burlap hood he had worn, trying her best to clean away the blood with it.

The voice in her mind was screaming, telling her she was wasting time, wasting precious seconds, but she slowed, tossing the burlap on her chair before turning to the door. The latch stuck to her bloody palm, and Arix yanked it open, pulling her hand away as quickly as she could.

Her eyes trailed across the floor, forcing her to glance at the doors beside her.

To the right, the door was open, the bloodied form of a man left in a heap in the center of the room. All his fingers had been cut off, and there was a dagger stuck in each knee. But underneath all the blood, there was a staggered slow rise and fall of his chest. Beside the door, Celeste leaned against the wall, clean of gore, her knife dug under her nails to clean them, and a sneer on her face. Arix swallowed, and turned, glancing to the left. Her stomach dropped at the sight of Michael's door, firmly shut, soft voices coming from inside.

He had lost.

THIRTY-NINE

The air had been sucked right out of the room. Gone in an instant. Arix lungs burned as she forced breath into them, forcing herself to draw breath against the crushing realization of what was about to happen.

The council waited, standing in a small huddle on the far side of the room, watching her. Waiting for her.

Arix pushed her chin forward, and strode to the center of the room, fist over her heart. From the dimness, Lord Heseth's voice spoke.

"What have you learned about the incantor?"

"Her name is Maeve. She's young, only fifteen. The leader of the rebellion, Lahz Mandair, is her uncle. This could be used to our advantage in a coming fight."

Her information was met with a cold stare. "And how did she learn magick?"

"Unclear. I don't believe he knew that information. There's a good chance she learned from her uncle or another blood relative who trained in magick. There is also a good possibility that there are other incantors in the rebel forces. Learning from Maeve, training under her.”

“Unclear? Good chance? Possibly? Those are a lot of vari-ables, Miss Sable.”

Arix heard the pop of her spine as she straightened. “Micah didn’t know much.”

“Micah?”

“The prisoner.”

“Or perhaps you didn’t question him thoroughly enough.”

“Or perhaps he didn’t know as much as you thought he did.” She was bristling under the council’s cold collected stare. “I also learned that Maeve keeps the rebel forces hidden under a cloaking cant, moving them constantly. My guess is a small weather or sand manipulation cant. Something that wouldn’t drain a lot from her, while still hiding their forces in the heat of the desert.”

“Did you learn how many of them there are?”

“Around ten thousand strong.” Arix replied.

Lord Heseth glanced over and Arix turned to see Celeste give a small nod.

“That appears to be the consensus. Anything else?”

“It appears that Lahz Mandair tries to keep a close guard on his niece. Keep her away from the rest of the rebels, as she seems to be a favorite among them. The prisoner spoke fondly of her.”

“Good.” Lord Heseth mused. He suddenly straightened, a tight lipped smile on his face. “It appears congratulations are in order. You and Miss Ayala have passed the test.”

There was a hope, small and glimmering, but a hope. Arix clung to it with all her might, digging in her fingers and daring it to be true.

“What about Michael?”

“Mr. Woodhale has failed. He will not be continuing on.”

“Yes, but…” Arix struggled to form the words, and they came

out soft and hesitant. "...will he die?"

The air hung around them, empty and hollow, and Arix's heart caved within her, deeping down deep inside, a black hole, crushing the life from her from the inside out.

"You already know the answer to that question, Miss Sable."

And there it was. Crushing. Lifeless. All hope washed away, flushed into a cavern so deep and so dark, she wondered if there was a bottom to it.

"You are both dismissed. We look forward to the final test. We expect great things from you both." The look from Lord Heseth was pointed, and with a jolt, Arix realized he was smiling at Celeste. He had already decided who would be the Black Hand. He already thought he knew who would rise to victory.

Celeste nodded, calm and collected, then strode back up the stairs they had come down earlier. Chatting casually, as if two men had not just been tortured for information, members of the council filtered up after her. Arix's feet were frozen to the ground. She couldn't just walk away and leave him. She couldn't.

Orion's presence before her took up all the space in her vision, the edges blurred.

She glanced up, eyes wide, like a deer surrounded by archers. It took all her strength to force her legs to move forward, the final member of the council standing in the shadows, steel blue eyes glowing dimly.

Arix swallowed. "What will happen to him?"

He was grim; hard lines encasing his mouth "Don't do this to yourself, Arix."

"I need to know."

Orion let out a long sigh. "His family will be informed that he died a hero, in service of the crown. That will be the end."

A sob was tearing at the back of her throat but she shoved it down.

"When?"

"Now."

Part of the sob she was working so hard to contain slipped out, crackled and desperate.

"What am I going to do?" Arix hugged her arms, the drying blood flaking off as she rubbed her suddenly cold arms. Goose-bumps flaked red.

Orion reached out to touch her but she jerked away.

"You are going to be the Black Hand."

A sharp intake of breath was her only response.

"Arix, listen to me. Look at me. You were made for this. You were made to bring this kingdom forward into a new era. And doing that isn't going to be easy. It's going to take pain and death to get there. There will be sacrifices, and there will be loss. But you will do it anyway, because you are strong. You know what is at stake. And you will succeed."

What he said reminded her a little of what Celeste had uttered all those weeks ago. That being the Black Hand took hard decisions and death. That being the Black Hand wasn't a game. And it wasn't easy.

Slowly, she allowed herself to be pulled into his embrace. It felt wrong. All of it. The fabric of his vest was rough, and Arix tried pulling away.

"I'm covered in blood."

"I don't care. You did what you had to." He held her softly, his fingers brushing back strands of her hair. "You're stronger than the rest of them, even if you can't see it."

They stood there in the darkness of the moment, grief hanging about her head like fog, the closed door still looming at the edge of Arix's vision.

"He still hasn't come out." She whispered.

"And he won't. He knows what will happen next. He made a choice, Arix. And so should you."

Still she did not move. A part of her was whispering, chanting over and over. A mantra that she didn't want to ignore.

If I never go in, he'll never have to die.

"You should be with him."

No no no no. If I never go in, He'll never have to die.

"I can't."

"You should be the last thing he sees, Arix." He paused, a sad smile coming over him. "He loves you. If it were me, if I were the one about to die, having known my fate, I would want my best friend to be with me in the final chapter."

He cupped her cheek with his palm, thumb tracing over her lips. "I would want to see you one last time. To say goodbye."

Arix turned, staring at the closed door. Slowly, step after deadening step, she forced her feet forward and took hold of the latch.

Michael sat in the center of the room, facing away from her, his forearms resting on his knees. Opposite him, sitting in the chair was another rebel, his hands unbound and his hood lying beside him on the floor. His eyes flashed at her as she opened the door, and he sneered.

"Get up, Ozrak." Orion's voice echoed over her shoulder into the stone room. "You're being taken back to your cell."

The rebel stood, and sauntered past Michael without offering him a glance. Arix stepped to the side, letting him pass. She felt Orion's hand squeeze her shoulder, then felt his presence disappear.

Arix watched the slow rise and fall of Michael's back, the curves of his muscles showing beneath his shirt. Slowly, she closed the door behind her, the soft click of the latch sounding louder than it should have. Her lungs were constricting, spasming on themselves as she forced air into them. Forced herself into calm, even breaths.

"Michael."

He turned, surprised, to look at her. Then slowly, as they stared at each other, the surprise slipped into one of silent relief. He smiled.

"Arix."

She stepped forward, around him until she knelt on the ground, clasping his hands within her own.

"I guess this means I've lost?"

He was breaking her heart with that question, asking as if he didn't already know the answer. As if he hadn't planned for it all along.

"Yes." She whispered, the sound coming out in slow, hollow truth.

He nodded slowly.

"I've come to say goodbye." She knew she should cry, knew she wanted to cry, but no tears came. Instead only emptiness. Vast, jagged emptiness.

"I couldn't do it, Arix." He said, gaze at the floor between them. "I can't do the things they want me to do."

"I know. I should have known you wouldn't. You aren't that type of person."

He smiled at her, eyes locking into hers. "You were always going to be the one, Arix. I don't know why any of us tried at all. Even at the beginning, when we first became friends, I knew. And all I wanted was to be close to you, to watch you succeed. Maybe that's why I lasted this long. You really are going to make an amazing Black Hand."

Tears streamed down her cheeks, trailing clean lines through the dried blood. Arix swallowed the lump that was forming in her throat, the bricks in her stomach pulling her into the earth.

Michael reached out and wiped the tears from her chin, squeezing her hands in with his other. "It's nice to know someone will cry for me. It's more than I expected."

Arix's choked sob ripped from her throat. "How can you even say that? I love you!"

He stood, forcing her up with him. He fiddled with his finger, finally sliding off a golden ring, gleaming with a dark green stone in the center. Opening her palm, he laid the ring into it, and they both stared down at the glistening stone. Silent. Then Michael slowly curled her fingers around it, encasing the ring from sight.

"I want you to have this. I know cores bond with their masters, so I don't know if it will help you, but if you can, use it to defeat Celeste. She's a heartless bitch. She doesn't deserve to win. But you?" He cupped her face, his eyes filling with tears. "You, Arix Sable, you will change everything."

Her throat was cotton, tight and so pressing, she couldn't breathe.

He pulled her into him, crushing his body to hers, and held her so tightly that for a moment, the world went quiet. Everything that they had been through swarmed in her mind, calming her fear, chasing away what she knew was inevitable.

Arix nestled her head into the crook of his neck, feeling the warmth of his skin on her cheek, and tears drenching his collar.

"I love you, Arix." He whispered into her hair, kissing the top of her head.

"I love you too."

Arix felt the warmth of the blood, pooling against her stomach as Michael sagged in her arms, and she glanced down between them, seeing his knife. The front of his shirt soaked red, his breathing ragged and hitched.

The cry tore like an animal from her mouth as she fought to hold him to her, sliding to the ground under his weight. A great wail wrenched from her as she realized what he had done.

"No, no, no! Michael!"

Goddess, there was so much blood.

"Don't leave me! Please don't leave me." Her tears blurred her view of him, and she wiped them against his hair as she cradled him to her chest.

"I'm sorry, Arix." His words were broken, jarring.

It didn't sound like him. His voice was cracking and singed and it made Arix weep harder. This was not how it should end. This couldn't be how it ended. Her breathing was coming so hard and fast, and in her arms, his was slipping away into nothing.

"No, don't talk. Please, Michael."

"I'm sorry…" He coughed, blood in his mouth painting his lips scarlet. "I wanted to die on my own terms. I wanted to die like this. In your arms."

"No, please…"

"Don't cry, Arix."

"Please don't leave me. Please, please don't go. I can't do this without you."

But Michael was already still.

A great wail tore from her, her mouth open and her body drowning as she cradled his head to her breast, willing his heart to beat again. Willing for him to breathe. For one last word. For one last second.

Just for a moment. Just for a moment.

FORTY

She stayed with him, cradled him to her body until the torches went out. Held him to her even after he had turned cold and stiff in her arms, she didn't let go. And when Orion came late in the night, she sat, eyes empty, void of tears, for she could cry no more. The soldiers gently lifted Michael's body away from her, and she let them, following them down to a cold and quiet room and watching as they wrapped up his body and nailed it into its wooden box.

Arix had gone numb sometime in the night, and watched it all in a dream-like daze. There was nothing, nothing, she could do now. What was done was done.

Orion was leading her; her feet moving to keep her upright, her body like a sheep, following after him. They went up the stairs and back into the cold gray light of early dawning morning that filtered in through grand painted windows. And then she was at her door, hand on the clasp as Orion spoke.

"You should sleep. They'll announce the last test in a couple days."

Arix only nodded vaguely as he pushed up the door and she

stepped inside. Orion caught her wrist as she went in and she slowly turned to look at him. He was worried, Arix could tell, but she said nothing.

"Do you want me to stay with you?"

The words came out on their own, as if someone else had said them. "No. I'm fine."

Pain sat behind his eyes as he said quietly, "I'll send someone up."

She blinked, then turned away, closing the door behind her.

Arix wanted to sleep. She wanted to rest her head down into her pillow and forget. Her hands were shaking as she stood in the center of the cold room, staring down at her fingers. She knew she should strip out of these clothes, wash the blood off her. But she couldn't. It wasn't just anyone's blood, it was Michael's. The last little bit of him left.

It was Miss Charlotte who came to bustle her into the bathtub, to pass her a tea that would calm her nerves and send her into a dreamless slumber. Neither woman spoke, but once Arix had sunk into the water, her empty teacup set aside, Charlotte washed her hair, fingers trailing through and untangling the mess. Arix had thought she had no more tears to shed, yet the soft touch made her eyes fill, and they streamed down her face and mingled with the bath water.

After she'd been tucked into bed, she burrowed under her blankets to block out the morning light and let sleep take her away. Away somewhere dark and deep. Her body floated down into the yawning cavern, her mind leaking out and leaving her thoughts void.

~

Arix slept through the day and the following night, and awoke to the gray mist of dawn. Part of her wanted to curl back up and turn towards sleep, but she pushed that part of her aside and shoved herself away from the bed, ignoring the cold stones beneath her feet. She dressed quickly and left the room, slipping mittens on over her fingers.

There was one way to fill the emptiness. Only one way that she knew of to ever be alright again.

She would train. She would work hard and practice, and do everything within her power to win. She would do it for Michael and Revena as much as she would do it for herself. All these thoughts crackled through her mind as she descended the stairs, eyes glued to the floor in front of her. Abbas and Ulfur remained at her side, stoic and silent, following her downstairs and outside into the morning mist.

Tobias was not waiting for her at the barn, so she went running alone. She focused sucking in the freezing air into her lungs, relishing the burn in her throat.

She'd hoped to dream about Michael. Even to dream of rivers of blood. But her dreams had been empty. Much like the mist she ran through, her head had emptied itself out, leaving behind a yawning nothing.

"Arix?"

She hadn't realized she'd stopped on the path, but Ulfur's voice brought her back to herself. A blur of color caught her eye and she stepped off the path to follow. The speck of motion twitched and moved further in, out of her line of sight.

"Stay here." she said, and stepped off the path into the trees.

The hard shell of ice crunched under her shoes as she walked, ducking under limbs and pressing further after the blue motion. He stayed just out of reach, flitting away until finally he stopped in a small clearing. A large boulder stood at the far side, and the small winged creature perched on the top of it. He cocked his head to look at her as she made her way into the clearing, pausing to see if he might fly away again.

Bright indigo with a thrush of caramel on his belly, the bird watched her. Stared at her. As if he had things to say. Important things.

There was a cant to talk to animals, easy to perform and quick. But Arix simply stood in silence. Some things were better without magick.

Ulfur and Abbas were waiting when she stepped back onto the path.

They took off again, running along the path that led back toward the barn. Tobias was waiting with a rack of weapons when they approached, and when he glanced up, Arix saw pity in his eyes.

It made her insides burn.

"What do you want to work on today?" Tobias's voice was gentle. "Or if you want to take a break-"

"Knives" She cut him off. "I need to practice my precision."

Tobias nodded with a small smile. "Anything else?"

Arix stretched, reaching for her toes in a semi-squat.

"How much do you know about Celeste's training?"

Tobias's face hardened. "I can't share that kind of information with you, Arix."

"We're too close to the end, Tobias. I need to know."

"Then find out for yourself. I won't be a spy for you."

There was something there in his words. Deep and angry.

"I didn't ask you to spy for me, Tobias. If you don't want to tell me, you don't have to."

His features relaxed slightly and he let out a long sigh. "I know. Sorry. I don't have much to tell you to be honest. I know her trainer, Arnav, only from reputation. She brought him with her from Nero and they keep to themselves. I know she trains with the soldiers at the wall sometimes."

Arix straightened, and the two began walking back to the barn.

"Do they ever request anything for training? Anything unusual?"

"You mean like weaponry?" Tobias shook his head. "Not that I've noticed. They train in the morning, like us." He hesitated, as if he realized he was already sharing more than he had intended.

"I promise I'll do my own spying, I just need to know their schedule."

"They meet, train on mount first, then sometimes spar or work on specific skills like swordsmanship or archery. Their schedule is pretty similar to ours. Arnav usually has her in with the healers once every two weeks, and she's scheduled for massages twice a week."

"Why a healer?"

Tobias shrugged, a cheeky grin sliding across his face. "Probably for the same reason I tried to send you to a healer. Salves for muscle pain, cold wraps for the bruises, and ointments for the cracked knuckles."

"Yeah, but that was in the beginning, when I was sore and stupid and didn't know better." She grinned, pulling off her gloves and tucking them under her arm. She held her hands out to examine the knuckles. Scarred and calloused, but they hadn't been split and bleeding for months.

"Maybe to strengthen her break after your battle with the dragon? She healed up pretty quickly, and the only way that could have happened was with magick. Look, Celeste is a pompous brat. She's a noble who's used to nice things. Maybe she just likes being pampered."

Arix laughed aloud, and its hollow sound echoed through the trees. "Now *that* I believe!"

~

Arix stuffed her gloves in her pocket and shook her hair free, running her fingers through the tangles and trying to form it into a simple braid. Pausing at the dining room door, she saw the large table was laid out with a few small items for lunch, and sitting at the far end of it was Celeste, a book in one hand, a spoon in the other. She twirled the utensil over her bowl mindlessly, studying the pages. She looked serene. At peace. Just a simple woman enjoying her lunch. Arix took a breath and stepped through the doors, taking a seat further down the table from her opponent. Celeste didn't bother to glance up.

The stew was good, hot, filling her whole body with warmth. Yet even with the food and the warmth of the room, Arix felt cold as she watched Celeste dip into her food again, chewing thoughtfully.

She always looked composed. Never a hair out of place, never a mannerism left unchecked. Everything she did was deliberate. Calculated. In another life, Arix would have longed to be like her, settled and calm. More and more Celeste had turned into a viper in the weeds, lying in wait. So still; so deadly.

"You should eat before your food gets cold." Celeste said, her tone crystal clear in the silence of the room. Her eyes slid up from her book and a small smile graced that perfect mouth. "Good training this morning?"

"Yes, thank you." Arix replied, forcing herself to smile back. Inside her stomach roiled and tightened. "I trust you also had a productive morning?"

"I did. And slept so very well last night. I do rather miss a full castle though, don't you?"

Everything inside Arix clenched. Squeezed together until her lungs were screaming. Her grip on her knees tightened under the table, sure they would leave bruises.

"I suppose things will get quite busy again soon." Celeste went on, ignoring Arix's silence, a casual smile still gracing her face. "There will be an appointment ceremony and a large banquet. Diplomats from all over the country will come to the capital. And the city will be bustling and trade will be better than ever. So much new liveliness in the air."

"And I suppose all of it will be for you? To celebrate your rise to the Black Hand? All hail Celeste Ayala, the savior of Rökkur!"

Celeste said nothing, but her smile grew more and more malicious as Arix continued. She couldn't stop now, no matter how hard she wanted to hold her tongue. She was falling apart at the edges and Celeste knew it. Knew what kind of madness was taking over inside of her.

"Should I congratulate you now? In advance? Since I won't be there in the end to watch your rise in station."

"You could, although I don't want your praise. When we last sparred I hoped that would be the end for you. Perhaps a merciful death in the desert. Michael would have been an interesting opponent, if he hadn't been such a coward."

"Don't say his name." Arix growled, white hot anger shooting down her spine. Her nails were digging so hard into her palms she was sure she was drawing blood.

"What are you going to do about it?"

Finger by finger, Arix forced her fists to relax, prying them away from her palm. She stood, her whole body shaking under the strain of keeping herself from lunging across the table and killing Celeste right there and then. Every movement was pain but she did it anyway, turning away from the table, her chair legs scraping across the stone floor. Putting one foot in front of the other and walking out. Everything screamed in her to turn back; to fight. To win.

I will win. But not today.

Arix let her feet take her away, wandering where they led her. She found herself climbing the stairs back to her room, locking herself in and falling into bed. She was exhausted. Sweaty.

She would start with a bath, and the rest would fall into place after.

"What does it do?"

Her gaze shifted across the room, glancing at the ring that sat on her desk. Michael's ring. The water was heating in the bath and she yearned to dip into it and let the heat chew at her bones for a bit. But instead she moved to the other side of the room and lifted the ring, cradling it like a dead bird.

The triangular gem was a deep green, like the leaves of a tomato plant, encased into a viney gold setting. It was heavier in her palm than she had expected, heavier than before.

She took it with her into the bath, holding the ring in one hand, and her own amulet in the other.

"It doesn't glow quite as brightly."

Arix sighed. It was true. The gem in her amulet had a sparkle, a spark. Michael's was dull. Void. Empty. Like her.

The jewelry clutched in her fists floated beside her as she slid further into the tub, only her face hovered above the water line.

Michael had a strong earth-based affinity. He was a nurturer of plants and hearts, healing all he touched. Like the Goddess Arduinna, he cherished those around him. He had sparked life.

It would make sense that his ring would only further bolster that same care.

But how would it help her? It had bonded to Michael, and there was a possibility that it would never react to her commands at all.

"Breathe. Give it a chance to show you what it can do."

Arix focused, shifting her mind to the cant, shaping it in her mind's eye, forming the words and whispering them into existence. She felt the water shift around her, swirling into a small, steaming vortex. Her aches dissipated, the soreness in her heart lessening with each breath, healing and mending. With each breath he was with her, even now, living on past death's clutches. If nothing else, it was a comfort having a piece of him so close to her.

FORTY-ONE

Arix had to ask around to find Orion's office. She'd never had the need to find it before, but now, she needed a moment to talk business. In private.

Rapping her knuckles against the wood, she waited for Orion's deep voice before slowly opening the door. It was as she had expected. Larger in design than Desirae's office, the wall-lined shelves overflowed with books and scrolls. Instead of a giant map, Orion had hung a small painting of a woman in her mid-fifties that was surrounded on all sides with framed letters and accomplishments. Two desks, parallel to each other, took up the center of the room, one covered in maps, the other covered in papers. And behind the second desk, Orion stood, his hands braced on the surface in front of him.

Upon seeing her his eyebrows shot up and a smile overtook his features.

"What a pleasant surprise!"

There were no smiles in return as Arix took a stance in front of his desk. "I need a favor."

Orion motioned to an empty chair with mock seriousness,

trying to match her tone. "And how may a member of the council provide you with assistance, Miss Sable?"

"I need to know about the next test."

Immediately the smile was gone.

"I can't give you that information, Arix. You know that."

"Maybe, but I also know that you don't always play by the rules. You're the reason I wasn't eliminated when Tanis poisoned me all those months ago. I know I should have lost. Should have been removed from the running, but I wasn't. That was your doing."

Arix paused, waiting to see if he would deny his involvement. He did not.

"And with Michael..." She swallowed past the lump that formed in her throat at the name. "You let me be with him. In the end. I don't know what would have happened if I hadn't been there, if I hadn't-" The words turned thick in her throat. "I just mean that you let me say goodbye."

A pained look crossed his face, yet still, he said nothing.

"And you've had a hand in this in other ways too. You've encouraged me when I wanted to quit. When I thought I wasn't good enough. You've stood behind me. And you did it because..."

She faltered, hesitating to say what had been on her mind for a long time.

"Because maybe your investment in me is more than just having a horse in the race. Maybe it means more."

"Arix-"

She held up a hand. "No. Please let me finish."

Orion's mouth closed.

"Regardless of whether your actions are purely selfish, or perhaps spurred on from a more emotional place," His eyes were soft at that, looking past her rough exterior, and meeting somewhere far more intimate. "I need your help. I need to know what to expect. If I have some upper hand in this, maybe I can win against Celeste."

Her heart was slamming into her rib cage, slamming so hard against her bones that she had to glance down to make sure its outline wasn't visible against her skin.

Orion rounded the desk slowly, moving to the door. He opened it, and peered down the hallway in either direction, then closed it again. He leaned against the door, his arms crossed over his chest. The lines between his eyes were furrowed, and when he spoke, his voice was deep. Serious.

"Asking that kind of favor could get you eliminated. Removed completely from this test. You should know better than to ask me for something like that."

The hairs on the back of Arix's neck prickled, and her spine involuntarily straightened.

"I know what's at stake." Arix replied coldly. "Don't talk to me like a child."

"Then I'll treat you like an adult." Annoyance peppered Orion's voice, rising slightly in volume. "You're smart enough to know what's waiting for you."

Arix raised her chin. "A fight. One-on-one against Celeste. That I know. I'll probably have to use everything I've got to go up against her. The only thing I don't know is where it will be."

Orion gave no response, but Arix noted that a muscle in his jaw tightened.

"I want it to be in the glen."

Orion stared at her. "Which glen?"

"Here." Arix's mind was racing. "In the woods, where I train, there's a clearing. Let that be where the final battle takes place. I'm familiar with it. At least I better be after running through it for the past seven months."

His arms stayed crossed, but his features were relaxing slightly.

"What makes you think I can convince them where to have it?"

Arix huffed, flicking a stray piece of hair from her face. "You're capable."

"Steward Morrison owns a vineyard just outside the city. I'm positive he's going to suggest having the fight there."

"You can convince him otherwise." Arix spoke slowly, trying to convince him, as if she were trying to convince the council herself. "It might be bad. Bloody. Wouldn't people from the city want to watch? The council would end up with a whole city of spectators. Convince them it should be within the walls. Discrete, away from prying eyes. That way if things go badly, the Council will be able to control the narrative."

The corner of Orion's mouth twitched into a small smile. "They do rather like to have their thumbs in all the pies, don't they?"

Arix grasped his wrists, pulling them up together between their bodies. "For me, Orion." Her eyes were pleading.

"I can't promise anything."

"It's enough."

~

It was a week and a half later when the cream colored envelope arrived. The date of the final test had been announced for the following afternoon. Each contestant was asked to appear ready with their weapons of choice before the council. From there, they would be given further instruction.

Arix took her time selecting her outfit. Selecting her weapons.

She wore grays and browns to blend into the forest, and wore thick animal skin slippers instead of her boots. She packed her satchel with materials for harder hitting cants. Cants that Celeste favored. The last time they had fought, Arix had been vastly unprepared. And she'd paid the price for being so behind, for letting her sorrow drag her away from what mattered. Survival.

As she stepped out the door of her room, Arix paused. She took a deep breath. Ulfur and Abbas remained on either side of her, flanking and ready for her signal.

"Thank you." She looked first at Ulfur, then Abbas. "Thank you for being here. For watching over me."

Ulfur would not meet her eye, and when she leaned in and kissed his cheek, it was wet with tears. Abbas did not take her outstretched hand, but instead bowed, his fist firmly pressed over his heart. When he returned to his full height, Arix found that his eyes were also soft and damp.

"It has been our honor." Abbas' gravel filled voice echoed in the stone hallway. "May the Goddess bring you victory."

"And give that little shite a lashin' she won't soon forget." Ulfur chimed in.

With a curt nod and a smile, Arix turned and headed for the stairs.

She met Celeste at the doors to the councilroom, and side-by-side they entered and knelt. Celeste had her throwing knives strapped to her thighs, and instead of a satchel like Arix, she wore her pouches of ingredients directly on her belt. She too wore her hair back in braids, though hers were expertly crafted, twisted back in a design worthy of a noble. Even in a fight she looked fiercer than Arix did.

"We shall see."

Lakai and Lord Bardon stood in the center of the room, waiting, as the rest of the council sat behind them, facing the door. The two incantors stood at attention in silent anticipation. Lord Bardon spoke first.

"Welcome. This, your final test, is about to begin. A duel. A chance to prove your worth and your talents to me and to this council. The winner of this test will become the next Black Hand of Rökkur."

Arix's insides bubbled, her excitement mixed with dread, feeling like an anchor inside her.

"Use all you have learned. Everything you have gleaned from your months of training here. Victory is within your clutches." He turned to them, his gaze shifting between the two women, eyes staring through their souls.

"Are you ready?"

"We are." They spoke in unison.

Lakai stretched out his hands, and each took one. Then with a snap, they were gone.

FORTY-TWO

The woods around them were silent.

Every woodland creature, every bird; even the wind was still. Expectant. The earth waited. Ready to soak up the blood that would be spilled on it today.

The room of the council was gone, replaced by the glen.

Orion had succeeded.

The air gripped tightly to the snap of cold, and it burned in Arix's chest as she drew it in slowly through her nose.

Celeste stood on the opposite side of the clearing, squatting on the ground, sifting her fingers through the dirt.

To a bystander it may have looked as if the two were gathering their bearings, noting their surroundings, but to a trained eye, the fight had already begun. The two incantors were setting shields in place, and preparing cants, ready for an attack. Waiting to see what their opponent may throw at them.

Arix had hoped that Celeste might show some surprise at their location, but the girl had barely batted an eye upon their arrival. It only confirmed what Arix had guessed. Celeste was getting insider knowledge from the council. For how long, Arix didn't know. Had the fight been rigged in Celeste's favor from the start?

The first thing Arix had cast, before she could even blink against the harsh winter light of day, was Graezon's Deception. The aura would keep any cants from finding her weaknesses, and block any trying to read her thoughts. It was something she'd found, a note scribbled in the margins of one of Revena's books.

"When you're finished, find your way back to the castle." Lakai spoke softly. "We will be watching from there. May the Goddess guide you, may luck guide you forward. May the one who falls find rest in a battle well fought; may the one who will rise be worthy of their victory."

Lakai bowed to them, and then with a crack of air, he was gone. Arix moved, slowly backing away from Celeste, making sure to put a good distance between them. As she rotated around the glen, Celeste matched her, the two staying an equal distance from each other.

Just a few more feet to the left…

Focused on Celeste's footing, Arix almost missed a slight shimmer in the air, caught briefly in the gray light. It was so quick that she almost thought it was a trick of the light. But it wasn't. Celeste was already mounting her defenses.

Quickly, Arix cuffed back her sleeves, sliding her fingers across her wrist, her mind opening up as the thoughts of the beings around her came into focus. But she knew Celeste would be fast, and she was right. Not even a full second had passed, and suddenly the thoughts halted abruptly. Celeste had countered her.

"Was that your plan?" Celeste called across the space. "To just read my mind and win that way?"

Arix stayed silent, watching Celeste's fingers for movement. The girl was waiting, just as she was. On the defensive. But Celeste's posture was relaxed. Calm. As if she already knew the outcome of the fight.

"I've whipped you before and I'll do it again."

Fingers flashed and a bolt streaked across the space, centered on Celeste's chest. The girl stepped back as the bolt connected with her shield, sparks spraying out around her from the hit. For a moment her face had shifted to surprise, but now she was grinning, a wide wicked grin that split her face in two.

"Look at you! Using grown-up cants! About time."

The ground was already shifting beneath her feet as Arix jumped sideways, ducking to roll away from the thorny vines that were springing up from where she had been standing only moments before. She landed in a crouch, hands hovering off the surface of the earth, watching as Celeste finally stepped over a small rock. The ground around her shook as a large boom broke through the air, like a cannon had been shot to the left of them in the clearing. A great wave of air shot from the point, knocking Celeste to one knee, her arms braced in front of her. The cant she had been speaking stuttered, broken, and Arix grinned.

She'd added a couple traps in the glen in the week prior, and thank the Goddess they were coming in handy.

She drew an arrow from her quiver, side stepping until she stood on the edge of the clearing, cast her cant and fired.

The arrow flew, amplified by her incantation and caught Celeste in the left thigh, just above her knee. The girl screamed, dropping to the ground in pain. She glared across the space and snapped the arrow in two, drawing it out the back of her leg with a whimper. When she glanced back up, the clearing was empty.

Arix moved silently through the underbrush, careful to step on the rocks that protruded from the snow and ice, hiding the sound of her steps. She could already feel the amulet around her neck tingling across her skin as the few cants she'd cast were pulling power.

Celeste was already on her feet, her hand pressed to the wound that was already stitching itself back together.

"Tired already?" She yelled into the woods, scanning the tree line. Her fingers were pressing together, but she was too far away for Arix to see what cants she was casting.

Arix moved forward slightly, trying to catch a better look when suddenly her view of Celeste was gone. Replaced by a great wall of fire. She stumbled back, tripping on the ice, and her head slammed into the ground. Stars laced across her vision, but worse was the heat. The sudden heat of the flames that had formed a ring around her. They roared in her ears, and she could feel the skin on her face reddening. Images of Revena, of the dragon, flashed into her mind's eye and Arix froze.

"Move!" Screamed the voice in her head.

The walls were moving in closer, but she was already shaking herself out of the trance. She calmed her mind, calling forth a stream of water that moved over the ground, quickly dousing the flames and clearing a path for her to dash further into the woods.

There was no time to pick through the ice now. Celeste was behind her running through the underbrush, right on her heels. Luckily, she knew these woods better than Celeste did. She'd spent more time than usual in the glen, had learned where trees had fallen, where rocks offered coverage. It might not be much, but it would be something. And any leg up against Celeste would be worthwhile.

Dodging suddenly, Arix swerved around a fallen tree, zig zagging across the ground. Something clattered against the tree behind her but she didn't turn to see what it was. She already knew. And she knew another would be soon after it.

She felt, rather than saw the next dagger, sail past her head and embed itself in a tree as she skirted around it, dodging again, pushing herself faster. She had not gotten up at the peak of dawn every morning for these past months to train, only to be beaten by this entitled bitch. She knew she was faster than the other woman. But was she faster than Celeste's throwing knives?

Arix turned again, swinging herself around the trunk of a tree to double back on her trail, her own dagger now in her hand. Celeste was only steps behind her, and the two collided.

Arix jabbed with her weapon, aiming for the other girl's ribs. She felt the blade sink in as a shooting pain spider-webbed across her back and she dropped to the ground. Arix tried to roll away, but Celeste's knife was stuck in her back. She wheezed against the pain, the bone crackling as she reached her hand back to withdraw the knife. But no matter how she twisted to reach, her fingers only glanced at the hilt.

The blonde girl was up now, knocking Arix's dagger to the ground, where only the tip had pieced her side. Arix cursed under her breath, pulling herself backwards across the icy ground as Celeste advanced. They were both out of breath, fighting the pain their opponent had dealt.

Arix tripped over roots and rocks, scrambling to put space between them. If she could just have a moment to pull out the dagger, she'd be able to breathe again. But her lungs felt like they were drowning, and Arix found herself choking on nothing. Her mind dashed from one cant to another, scrambling at her defenses. She swung her arm in an upward arc as she huffed the words of an energy beam. It glanced off of Celeste's shield, spinning wildly off into the woods. Somewhere in the distance, a tree exploded into bark and limbs.

Her heart was racing, her mind careening. She was going to die. She was going to die.

Celeste was laughing, heartless.

"Is this the best you've got? A couple heavy hitters and a bad knife throw? I expected more! Goddess, how did you avoid capture for so long?" She flicked her wrist and a crackling beam of ice caught Arix full in the face, snapping her head back as she tried desperately to scramble backwards.

Her shield had cracked. She had nothing protecting her.

Her nose was bleeding, her left eye already swelling from the hit. The whole left side of her face felt numb. Arix pushed herself back until she felt her shoulder hit the trunk of a tree. A shock of pain snaked down her side and up the back of her neck. Sharp, insistent. She pulled herself up to a standing position, but her legs gave out and she sagged against the bark.

Celeste was over her now, her arm outstretched, sigils traced up her arm in ink. The tips of her fingers were glowing orange. The girl grinned.

"Any words for the world to remember you by?"

No. Not yet. She couldn't have come this far and end like this. She *would not* end like this.

"Fight her!"

A mangled cry tore from Arix's throat as she shoved off the tree, tearing at anything she could reach. Her fingernails clawed at Celeste's face, and the girl screamed, dropping as Arix landed on top of her. The two rolled, fighting for the upper hand. Fighting for victory. Tears streaked down Arix's face, mixing with blood and dirt as they rolled, the throwing knife digging deeper and deeper into her shoulder. With every movement, she could feel the blade scraping against the bone. It was all she could do to just hold on. Hold on and keep Celeste from using her hands to cast.

She rolled, pinning one of Celeste's arms underneath her, and the girl screamed again as Arix pushed to dislocate the shoulder.

"Stop!" Celeste commanded, and Arix could hear the magick laced in the words, but it wasn't enough to impact her. Celeste was panicked, and her focus was slipping.

Suddenly the pain in her back doubled and Arix arched against it, squirming to get away as Celeste tried twisting the knife in her back. She kicked backwards, her heel connecting with Celeste's partially healed leg. The girl screamed again, shoving at Arix, trying to roll her over and pin her again.

The two panted with the effort, fighting for dominance. Fighting for the upper hand. Arix might have been faster in a flat out run, but Celeste was stronger, even just by a little. It was enough. Enough to make Arix feel small. Make her feel helpless.

Arix felt another throwing knife embed itself in her thigh and she let out a roar, fighting to pull it out. Then she cried out again as Celeste planted another in her shoulder. Every movement was pain; every reaction agony. Celeste was winning.

She felt like an animal, being poked and prodded in a cage. She was pinned again; thrown on her back, each arm pinned to the ground beside her head. Celeste's whole weight was on her, bearing down, her knee digging into Arix's thigh.

There was no distinction now between the tears, sweat, and blood that poured from her face. Her one good eye rolled in its socket, searching for an opening. Searching for a way out. Yet only Celeste's grin filled her vision. Sickly sweet and vile. Satisfied.

She had tried so hard to be what they wanted her to be. She had tried so hard to fit the mold. To be like Celeste. It made sense that this was what they wanted. Celeste was the golden one, bred from the beginning for a place of power. Her whole life had led to this moment, and she looked ready for it. Though they had grappled in the mud together, Celeste still looked pristine. The white winter light behind her made it look as though she were haloed in silver.

She was what everyone wanted. Ordained. Clean. Unblemished by the problems of life. Celeste had never had to steal and beg for her dinner. She'd never fought for her dignity, fought for her life. And Arix would never be like her. Never. No amount of beautiful dresses and fancy titles would give that to her.

But Arix had not grown up with servants and private tutors. She had taught herself to shoot, to pick pockets, to survive. Sleeping beneath floorboards and in snowy, mountain passes. If she was going to win, she needed to use what she'd trained her whole life to do. She needed to survive.

Arix turned her head to the side, biting down with every iota of strength she had; digging her teeth into Celeste's arm. The taste of blood spurred her on, and she locked her jaw as Celeste screamed.

A punch.

A slap.

Nails raking her good eye, but Arix held on. One arm now free, she wrapped an arm around Celeste's shoulders and pulled her closer. Drew her into an embrace, all the while tearing at the soft flesh of Celeste's arm with her teeth.

Nonsensical venom poured from Celeste's mouth as she dug at Arix's face to release her hold. Arix drove her knee up, connecting with Celeste's stomach, and the girl doubled over. There was a soft give, and tearing. A fountain of blood, as Arix tore a chunk from the girl's arm. With a kick, Arix sent Celeste backwards, landing hard on her back. The girl clutched her ruined arm to her chest, eyes wide with horror, pain, and disgust.

"You bit me, you fucking whore!"

Arix was already moving, forcing herself up to her feet. Everything ached. Everything burned. She could barely see, but she turned, her cracked and bloody mouth forming the words, as she slipped into mist and disappeared into the woods.

"You rancid cunt! I'm going to pull every one of those rotting teeth from your skull when I find you! You'll burn just like Revena did!"

But Arix was already gone. Disappearing into an invisible wisp of smoke, Celeste's words echoing through the empty forest.

FORTY-THREE

The knife in her shoulder came out first. One good yank and it came out slicked in blood. Arix threw it aside in the snow, pressing her palm to the wound, the cant coming out rushed and mixed with spittle. The blade in her thigh came next. The wound fizzed and she winced against the itch so bad she bit the collar of her shirt to keep from yelping. It was shoddy healing work, but then again she had never been good at healing cants. As long as she wasn't pouring blood from her body, she would live.

The blade in her back was a little more of a problem. She couldn't reach it with her left arm, and her right was dislocated. Bracing her hand between the clutch of her boots, she pulled, the pain so blinding that it took her a moment before she could work up the courage to do it again. And again, and again, until on the fifth try, she felt the shoulder snap back into place. The relief was instant as she slumped over, gasping in great lungfuls of air. The knife in her back soon joined the pile on the ground, bloody and abandoned in the dirty snow.

She cast another healing cant, feeling over her body for more small injuries. Her ribs, or at least one, was cracked. Her nose was broken and the swelling around her eye was so bad she couldn't use it at all.

"Michael's ring."

Arix lifted it from its breast pocket, the green gem glinting in her palm. The pad of her thumb traced the edges of the stone, each crevice of her fingerprint caked in cold mud. She slid it onto her middle finger, chanting as she ran the fingers of her other hand across her ribs, up her collarbone and across her nose and face. She wasn't strong enough in healing magick to return them to brand new, but the pain eased. Her swollen eye remained closed, though the swelling went down substantially.

Sighing, she leaned back against a rock. What now?

She'd already proved that she couldn't hit Celeste head on. But she'd also shown that she shouldn't be overlooked. Should be underestimated.

She'd sought to be like Celeste, sought to be what Lord Bardon and Lakai and everyone else had wanted her to be. They'd wanted her to be elegant. Noble blooded, high class. A diplomat. But she wasn't any of those things. She never had been.

She was a thief. A rogue. Ready to claw and bite and cheat and chew her way to victory if she had to. She would do anything it took to win. Because she wasn't winning for herself. She would win for every Croak, every Wren, every Lace in Rökkur. She would win because she would do what it took to keep this country safe. Safe from people like Celeste. From the dignitaries and diplomats who only cared about lining their own pockets.

And she would win by playing by her own rules rather than playing by theirs.

Slowly, Arix straightened, her mind clear with what she needed to do. She'd set up four booby traps in the woods, and there were two more in the glen. She counted her arrows, once, twice, and then once again to be sure. She double checked her satchel of ingredients, frowning when she realized some of the vials had smashed during the scuffle. Carefully laying out the unbroken jars, she took note of what she had to work with. A few throwing knives, covered in blood, a few ingredients, most of them crushed or damaged during the fight, and her quiver of arrows and bow. Her dagger had been dropped and somewhere she'd lost her shortsword.

A wave of disappointment flared in her, but Arix forced it down. She'd done more with less before. But would it be enough?

When had she done her best against Celeste? She'd taken the girl by surprise when she used the heavier cants, the ones that hit hard and did good damage. But once the surprise had worn off, Celeste had beaten her down again. In hand to hand combat, Celeste had proven, once again, to be stronger. Those were her strengths. But what of her weaknesses? When had she seen Celeste truly scared?

A plan was forming. Slowly, inking in like water through a small crack. There were flaws in her plan, and every time she thought she had it, she'd find a key ingredient crushed or broken. But the idea continued to grow and she persisted. Arix's mouth twitched with the hint of a smile. If head on attacks didn't work against Celeste, she would try something different. She would try something better.

~

Celeste was burning down the forest. Burning it down hunting for her. But Arix stayed hidden, moving just ahead of the fire. As she moved, she trailed a stick with her, dragging it across the snow and ice and mud. It wouldn't be long now before Celeste grew tired of blasting the trees into cinders and began using tracking cants. Arix was planning on this. Though she had hoped Celeste would turn to casting Predator's Mark a tad earlier, things would turn that direction soon enough.

They had made their way around the clearing once already, and Arix could tell the girl was frustrated. Angry that an hour had passed and, still, victory had not been handed to her. She'd already set off one of the booby traps, her spewed profanities echoing through the trees as she'd slipped into the enchanted tar pit. Even if she did win, she'd never get that smell out of her hair. Arix slinked low to the ground, staying far enough ahead that she blended in with the foliage. She'd dropped the invisibility cant long ago, guessing correctly that Celeste would use a true sight sigil, on the lookout for telltale orange shimmer of the invisibility cant. Mud smeared across her face and covered her clothes, spare twigs and leaves tangled into her hair.

Every couple of minutes, Celeste would call out, taunting Arix, her unwounded hand held out in front of her, ready to consume her target in fire. Her other arm was wrapped tightly in a strip of bandage. Apparently, Arix noted with a grin, Celeste was as bad at healing cants as she was. Thank the Goddess for Michael's ring.

"It's time."

Celeste was moving back to the clearing, angrily pacing the outer edge, keeping just outside the treeline. Arix ducked low and silent, discarding the stick she had been carrying beside her on the ground as the two ends of her shallow trench connected. She watched as Celeste passed not twenty paces from her, peering over her head and into the charred woods behind her. She waited until the girl passed, then slowly let out her breath.

"Dvostruk." She whispered, breathing the words across the sigil she'd already traced on the back of her hand. She blew, and for a moment the glen was silent. Then, stepping out of the trees, staggered a copy of herself. The copy was covered in mud like she was, but it doubled over, clutching it's shoulder, an arm raised in submission.

The motion caught Celeste's eye and she turned, stiffening. She watched as the Arix copy moved forward then dropped to the ground, seemingly collapsed. Celeste stayed frozen for a moment, eyes on the form before she suddenly relaxed and turned in a circle to face the surrounding woods.

"Mirror Image? Pathetic! Come out and face me, Arix! You skulk around just out of reach like a scared little rabbit. You're a fucking coward, Bellarix Sable!"

Arix stayed low, watching. The words were meant to make her angry. To draw her out with their magick, but it was weak casting work. Celeste was already brimming with vicious hatred and it was hurting her focus more than she knew.

"You're a coward and a cheat. You knew we'd fight here and set up all these traps. You rigged this whole fucking thing by sleeping with Orion! You have no honor!" With every word, Celeste's eyes grew wider and wider, her voice rising in pitch until she was practically squealing.

If she hadn't been one of the deadliest incantors Arix had ever faced, it might have been funny. But underneath that tantrum, a raging flame burned, hotter than any dragon fire. And if Arix wasn't precise and careful, she would burn.

"I swear on my life even after you're dead and rotting I'll hunt down every last bit of family you have and impale them all on sticks outside the castle wall! Your name will rot into nothing!"

"Enough of that." Arix muttered under her breath, tracing lines and whorls into the dirt in front of her and drawing her fingers up and across the design.

Out in the clearing, tips of mists filtered in from the charred trees, wrapping slowly across the earth like thousands of gray snakes.

Celeste let out a huff of frustration, flippantly throwing her hand up as if she were physically pushing against the fog. A sweeping wind rushed across Arix's face and she shivered against the cold. The fog withdrew, pushed by the wind back into the woods.

"Come out and fight me!"

It was a command this time, more magick laced into the words. It felt as if someone was nudging at her, like an insistent mother to a shy child. She wanted to go, to move into the clearing. The magick was getting stronger. Celeste was calming down, adding more intention to her cants.

"Tishina i magla."

There was a chance it wouldn't work. There was a chance it would fail miserably.

Arix held her breath as the fog began to gather again, slowly refilling the outer edges of the glen. Slowly building until it became a thick carpet along the ground, wisping up until she could barely see Celeste's outline.

Arix waited, her breath caught in her throat, pausing to see if the cant would work. Celeste was moving her arms, trying to cast another wind wall, but nothing happened. Within the circle of fog, all was silent.

"Please hold. Please." Arix whispered to herself, drawing a circle and a line around the sigils that were traced in front of her. Slowly she stood, turning up the sleeve on her arm, revealing the soft blank skin that remained.

Ahead of her Celeste was running through the fog, trying to find her way out, but it was too dense from the inside. She was lost.

"Uzash."

Deep within the fog, Arix watched as Celeste froze. While most of her body was obscured by the fog, Arix could still see the girl's shoulders stiffen, her whole body becoming as still as a statue. Then slowly the girl inched backward. Inched backward until she tripped, stumbling. Then she was off, blindly running through the mist, tearing through the fog cloud. When she neared the edge of the clearing she veered again, running back in the opposite direction.

Celeste had said she had no honor. Had called her a coward.

And maybe she was. Using magickal fear and monsters made of mist to torture her opponent; it was low. Unsportsmanlike. But to Arix, it wasn't a sport. It wasn't a game. It was life and death. And the real world didn't play fair.

And here she was now, a stone's throw away from Arix, eyes wide and rolling. Her braid undone, dancing through the air like a broken marionette as she ran. It had been her own fault really. Chasing Arix around the circumference of the clearing, and giving her time to draw out the largest casting circle she'd ever made and drawing Celeste right into the center of it.

Who was the scared rabbit now?

The monsters she had conjured in the mist, monsters that only Celeste could see, were things that Arix had read about in Desirea's textbooks. Paramours and dragons and things she had forgotten the names of. And all the while, the true magick of the mist worked, easing into Celeste's heart and whispering the lies that every person believes about themself.

You'll never be enough.

You are nothing.

You are worthless.

You were never loved by anyone or anything.

At last, Celeste stopped. Stopped dead in the center of the clearing. She was trembling, head jerking as she stared at invisible things around her. Each rise and fall of her chest outlined through the mist.

"You underestimated me." Arix said, loud enough for her voice to carry.

Her words flitted across the fog like a butterfly, and Celeste snapped to look at where the sound was coming from. Her mouth opened and closed, a fish drowning on air.

"Are you afraid, Celeste?" Arix paced along the edge of the clearing, careful to stay out of reach of the fog. "Do you even know the meaning of the word?"

She knew she should end it. It was within her grasp. Within her power to bring it to a close, here and now. But something in her was screaming for vengeance. Screaming for justice. Screaming for all the wrongs to be made right.

"Have you ever known what it feels like to wonder where your next meal is coming from? To worry about the safety of your family? Have you ever given up everything you possess for a scrap of bread?"

Celeste fell, her arms wrapped around her knees, rocking back and forth as she huddled on the cold frozen ground.

"You said this was all rigged. And you're right. Everything about this country has been rigged from the start. And it's people like you and your family that have been reaping the benefits."

She neared the hunched girl, and could count the ridges of her curved spine.

"Yes, the game is rigged. But I'm done letting you win."

Her grip tightened on the hilt of the throwing dagger she'd pulled from her back. Celeste raised her head for a moment, turning to face some sound amongst the magickal fog.

"Now it's my turn."

Arix wrapped her arm around the girl in an embrace, clutching the back of her perfect blonde braid and drew back. Blood sprayed the ground before them. Celeste slumped, her throat slit from ear to ear, her blood warming the frozen earth.

It was finally over.

FORTY-FOUR

They stared at her as she entered, watching like a wake of vultures. She was shaking, almost violently, though she couldn't tell if it was because of the cold or because of what she'd done.

She did not bow or clap her fist over her heart, but instead stood just inside the door of the councilroom. She stared them down, eyes flitting from one to another at the table. There was a mix of emotions in the room. Most were shocked. They had since steeled away their features into ones of tedious apathy. There were a few smiles, expected, from Bishop Forir, and some unexpected, from Warden Sviengard and Warden Los Ke.

At his seat near the end of the table, Orion's gaze was fire and heat and sizzling energy. The look between them one was of promises. Promises and victorious pride.

The council continued to watch her, as she stepped forward into the center of the large room, throwing her arms wide.

"Celeste is dead. I have come to claim my title. To claim title of the Black Hand."

A second passed. Then another.

Arix felt her heartbeat pick up, erratically leaping around her chest cavity.

Then Lord Bardon slowly stood. His eyes slid down the table briefly then came back to rest on Arix.

"Bellarix Sable. It is not in the power of this council to grant you the title of Black Hand. That power belongs only to the king."

The whole room stilled. True and utter silence. Even Arix's heart ceased its frantic chase to stop and listen. She had heard the words, knew that they would have been spoken eventually, and of course they made sense…

She would be meeting the king.

Lord Bardon made his way around the table and came to stand before her.

"But you can't meet His Majesty looking like this. Go, bathe. Someone will be by to fetch you and then you will be presented to his Royal Highness."

She was in a daze. Lord Bardon's words drifted through her mind, and her body moved in response. Bowing, then turning to leave the room. But her mind was gliding on turbulent winds, her imagination rising and rising until she thought it would never stop.

Miss Charlotte was waiting for her, the bath filled to the brim, the good soaps and creams laid out. A simple black and red dress was laid out on the bed with black slippers and a black ribbon choker with the crest of the king: a four headed dragon. Black, silver, and red; colors of the crown.

Every bit of mud was washed away, every twig and leaf removed until she was sparkling. Her cuts were bandaged with ointments and cloth wraps, and her bruises were powdered. Her eye was still swollen shut, and there was little to be done about it, so Charlotte sent Wren to find Lakai.

Arix sat silently in front of the vanity as Wren brushed out her hair and Lakai worked on her face. Her maid was shaking almost as much as she was, and after the third try at Arix's tendrils, Miss Charlotte took over, shooing the other girl from the room.

Before she left, Arix caught Wren's glance in the mirror and the two shared small smiles.

"There." Lakai said, leaning back to admire his work. "Good as new."

The puffiness was gone, but the bruise remained, which Miss Charlotte powdered away into nothingness. The bruises on her shoulders were also gone, and all that remained of the stab wound in her shoulder and back were thin white lines, which were also covered in salves and powders until her skin was one tone of gleaming cream. Even her freckles had vanished from her face, leaving her looking less like herself than ever before.

Arix pressed her fingertips around her eye sockets, gingerly feeling the skin before Charlotte smacked her hand away.

"You'll ruin all this work I've done."

Arix obliged, dropping her hands into her lap. Lakai was watching her, and when their eyes met in the mirrored reflection, he offered her a small smile. "This is it, Arix. Everything is about to change."

"Yes. Yes it will."

A knock at the door. The three turned toward the sound, frozen. Then all was bustling again as Lakai was shooed away and Arix was fitted into the dress, the choker placed in the hollow of her throat.

Outside, Lord Bardon was accompanied by six heavily armed guards, wearing their finest. Arix glanced among them for Abass and Ulfur were not there. These guards were stiff, standing at attention, and ushered Arix to a wing of the castle she had never gone to before. And for good reason. The north wing, reserved especially for the king's chambers.

Their journey was quiet, unsettlingly so. It felt as if the whole looming building was watching. Waiting. The very stones under her feet held their breath as they approached the bottom of a long staircase. Guards were posted, and they nodded to Lord Bardon and bowed, leaving their posts and going back down the hallway where Arix had come. The six soldiers replaced them, guarding the bottom of the staircase as Lord Bardon led her up, the steps curving around themselves as they entered the tower.

Her heart beat so loudly it was a wonder it didn't echo in the cavernous space, and Arix willed her breathing to calm. Willed her lungs to expand with breath and exhale it back out slowly.

As they rounded the last corner, a shadow stepped out of an embrasure and into the light. Orion smiled.

"Ready to meet the king?" He asked.

Arix swallowed the stone in her throat, knowing that any attempt of a smile would fail her. "Not really."

Orion turned to Lord Bardon and they clasped arms. "The dawn of change."

"The advancement of a kingdom." Lord Bardon responded, his gaze flickered a moment to Arix. "Are you truly sure?"

His voice was strained.

Orion placed a hand on Lord Bardon's shoulder, drawing the man's gaze back to himself.

"The time has come."

Lord Bardon nodded, satisfied with the answer and turned, making his way back down the steps, leaving Orion and Arix alone in the torchlight.

"What's about to happen?" Arix asked while she watched Lord Bardon descend, and hated how small her voice sounded, echoing around them.

Orion pulled her forward, turning her gaze back to him, and

gripped her shoulders tightly. "Everything you've done. Everything you've accomplished has led to this moment, Arix; has led to the next few minutes. Everything you've fought for and all the things you believe in, they have set you on a path towards your destiny. You and I will do amazing things. There's so much we can accomplish if we work together."

He kissed her forehead then and stepped back away from her towards the great wooden door that loomed behind them.

"Are you willing to do what is right for the realm?"

Arix's gaze shifted, staring at the door behind him. His words reminded her of something Bishop Forir had said only a couple weeks ago.

"What's behind that door?"

Orion smiled grimly. "Your destiny."

Something was pulling at the corners of her mind. Pulling at her; an itch of apprehension. She faltered.

"I'll ask you again, Arix." Orion said, holding out his hand to her. Eyes hard. "Are you willing to do what is right?"

"Do you really know what is right anymore?"

Arix's gaze narrowed and she took Orion's hand. "I'll do what I *have* to."

Orion's face melted into a small smile. "That is all I can ask of you."

Leading her, Orion reached for the handle of the door and pushed it open. It was dark inside, the vast room lit by only one small pinprick of light. Arix blinked, her eyes adjusting to the darkness. On the opposite side of the room a large chair faced away from them, dimly wreathed in shadow from the single candlestick that sat on the floor beside the chair. It was nearing the end of its wick, and stuttered against the draft from the open door.

Orion stepped through, closing the door behind them as Arix slowly stepped across the space. The chair was positioned in front of a window, the sky having shifted from red and orange to inky black an hour ago.

Stepping around the chair, Orion came to stand in front of the form, his features steeled into a blank stare. He beckoned to Arix then and she rounded the chair, coming face to face with a man. He was slumped, clutching some papers to his chest, and stared past them out the dark window. His hair was unkempt; clean, but hanging around his face in gray streaked wisps. He wore nothing but his nightshirt and socks, carefully pulled up to his knobby knees.

"Your Majesty?" Arix breathed, taking in the signet ring loosely hanging off the boney middle finger. He was gaunt. His skins stretched over his bones; the only thing holding the man together.

He made no motion that he had heard her, but only blinked, continuing to stare as though she were not there at all.

Arix turned to look at Orion, her eyes wide with questions.

"He does not know us." Orion spoke quietly, voice flat. "His mind abandoned him years ago. What you see is only a shell of what remains of our great king."

Arix knelt down in front of him, trying to draw his attention to her, but the king's gaze went through her, lost in a foreign land. Her hand reached out to touch his knee, but even then there was no response.

"How long has he been like this?"

"About a year. He's been failing for decades now, but only recently did he vanish altogether."

Her mind was reeling, sifting back through what she knew. "So…" she started, fitting the pieces together. "It wasn't the king who called for a Black Hand. It was the council."

Orion said nothing, his silence answer enough.

"What did they think would happen?"

"The realm needs a leader. Someone to rally behind against the coming threat."

"But only a king…" Her words faded out into silence.

"Only a king can appoint a Black Hand." Orion finished for her.

Arix stared, a knot forming in her stomach.

Orion knelt down beside her and stroked the cheek of the king. "I had hoped he would recognize me. Maybe here, now, at the end."

His brow was furrowed in sadness as he stared at the old man.

"But I suppose, it's just the final wish of a son to his father."

FORTY-FIVE

The final piece clicked together in Arix's mind. The final thread that tied it together. One giant tapestry to tell the story.

Her insides felt like jelly and stone all at once.

"You're his son."

"Bastard son." Orion clarified, his thumb sweeping across the sunken cheekbone. "My mother was nothing to him. Nothing but a distraction after his wife died. It's only because of his guilt that I grew up the way I did. After I was born, he refused to acknowledge me as his heir, but gave her a small piece of land and an unimportant title. It was only much later that I learned the truth."

Arix stared at him, jaw locked. All this time…

She could see it now. They had the same nose, the same steely eyes. It was obvious to anyone who opened their eyes and looked.

"Did your mother tell you?"

"No. She carried that secret to her grave. It was Bardon who came to me with the truth, when the king was beginning to deteriorate more rapidly. The council wanted someone they could manipulate should the time come."

"The time to…"

"To replace the king."

Arix watched Orion's hand stop, frozen in midair. Trying so desperately to reach through the madness toward his father. To say goodbye.

"What are we doing here, Orion?"

Slowly he stood, his hands limp at his sides. Shoulders hard as stone.

"What must be done."

Fury burned in her. Hot and desperate. Her throat closed around the emotion that welled in her.

She saw the sadness in him. Heard the pain in his words, heavy with loss and regret. As if the pain and loss of the whole country had been packed into those words, and they pulled him down, out of his own body and into the earth.

"You knew it would come to this. This whole time?"

At the tone of her voice, Orion turned his face up at her, eyebrows knitting together.

"Yes."

"And the council, do they know?"

"Yes. You noticed the extra guards posted downstairs?"

Blood rushed through her ears loud enough that she wondered if Orion knew the tangled up anger that coursed through her.

"A coup of sorts. Though not many here will object."

She took a shaking breath. "What will you tell your people?"

He stood slowly, his momentary sadness gone. Replaced by determination. Duty.

"That he died in his sleep."

Her scoff came out louder than she had intended. But she didn't care if he knew how disgusted she felt. How used.

"Was this your plan all along? Pick the one girl who might do your dirty work for you?"

His face flickered to one of surprise.

She took a step back, away from him, away from the king. "I won't do it."

Sadness. Sadness and fatigue on his face. And a hint of something else. Something hard.

"Arduinna…"

"Don't call me that."

He let out a frustrated sigh, stepping forward to grab her arms.

She punched him in the mouth.

He reeled back, almost knocking into the king, grasping his reddening jaw.

"You used me. Used *us* to become king." Her voice caught in her throat.

"I swear, Arix. I didn't."

"And if Celeste had won? Then what? She'd be standing in the exact same spot as me, ready to cut you down for even suggesting—"

"If Celeste had won, she would never have even been part of this conversation."

"Why? Because her family is rich? Because the Ayala family might have a greater say to the throne than you?"

Orion had righted himself, and was slowly moving across the space again, his tone hushed like he was speaking to a wounded animal caught in a trap.

"That's exactly what we are."

"In part, yes."

All Arix could manage to do was stare at him.

"But in part because I never trusted Celeste. Not for a second. And because I trust you."

The familiar ache of tears squeezed her throat, slowly beginning to cool her anger.

"Arix, I love you."

"Don't say that to me. Not here…when you're about to ask me to–" Her gaze slid to the king.

He hadn't moved during their fight, hadn't even flinched when she'd hit Orion.

"Just don't say that."

Her anger was ebbing out, leaving her exhausted. All the aches and pains she'd experienced in the glen only hours before were returning, weighing her down and chipping away at her inhibitions.

Orion took another step forward, and this time she let him touch her. It was a light grasp of her arm, but she didn't flinch away.

"I want you with me, Arix. I want you as my Black Hand."

The Black Hand. She'd forgotten the title was hers now.

"Almost."

"This decision has not been taken lightly, Arix. The king is gone. He won't come back and be what we want him to be. And he won't ever see the world around him like you and I do. Every day the threats against us rise. And every day we go on without a leader. Without a king."

He turned, motioning to the old main slumped in his armchair, withered hands resting in his lap like broken bird wings. The papers he clutched so tightly were blank; void and empty like his mind.

"This is happening. It's already done. The decision has been made, the change in the guard has already been put in motion. Downstairs people are being awoken from their beds and being told the king is dead."

She stared at the withered face, gray eyes blank.

"I would not have wanted you to be here if I didn't already

trust you with my life."

Slowly she turned back to Orion. She didn't know if she believed him. Didn't know if she trusted him now, like she had learned to trust him during the past few months.

"And if I say no?"

Orion's expression did not change. He didn't have to say it for her to know the answer. Someone would die tonight. It would either be the king or his bastard usurper son.

In the hall, he had asked her if she would do what was *right* for the kingdom. Was this *right*?

She thought of Revena and Michael; what they might do if they were in her shoes. What would Celeste have done?

"They are not here, Arix."

Would they have called for the guards? Held Orion at knifepoint? Branded him a traitor?

"They are not here, Arix."

If she did, who would she serve? Who would appoint her as Black Hand? What would become of her then?

"You will survive."

She'd always found a way out of sticky situations. She'd always squeezed through cracks in walls, slithered up chimneys, jumped from rooftop to rooftop, always one step ahead of the dogs that snapped at her heels. She'd done things in her life, but nothing compared to what she'd done here. Nothing compared to what she'd suffered in these castle walls. And after everything, it all came down to this?

"This is your final test, Arix."

She turned her gaze up at him, wondering who she was. She wasn't the Arix who had come here almost a year ago. She was something different. Something dark.

What bothered her more? Killing a half dead old man? Or

knowing Orion was the one asking her to do it?

"And if I do this…it will never really end. You'll be king. And you'll just keep asking me to kill more and more." She searched his eyes, looking for something, but not sure what.

He cupped her face gently, leaning forward until their foreheads touched. "Being king means making hard decisions."

"And being the Black Hand means I'll carry them out."

A moment of silence yawned between them, and time seemed to slide through the ether around them at a slow, tar-filled pace. Then Orion slowly pulled away and took a step back. Knowing that Arix had made her decision.

He turned and took one of the king's hands withing his own, kissing the knobby knuckles.

"Osiris guide you."

Then he turned towards the door, closing it with a soft click as he disappeared into the hall.

Arix stood in the silence, the pinprick of candlelight guttering as the wax melted and slumped. The light would flicker out soon.

She moved towards the bed near the wall and lifted one of the crisp white pillows from its place. Stepping back to the king, she watched him, searching for a response. A flinch, a look of worry, anything that might indicate that he knew what was coming.

Nothing.

"Goddess forgive me."

She pressed the pillow to his face and pushed. Held it there and waited.

The king did not fight. He did not resist. He went into the darkness without a sound.

As she stepped into the hallway where Orion waited, she turned one last look back into the king's room. The candle had flickered out in a puff of gray smoke.

The only sound on the stairs were the echoes of their shoes and the staccato tap of Arix's heels, which somehow felt irreverent. But wasn't that how it always went? Death brought life. It always had.

"And it always will."

FORTY-SIX

By the time they had descended the stairs, any resistance to the change had already come and gone. There were more guards in the hallway now, at least four at every major entrance. No signs of struggle or conflict. No signs of blood or dead followers of the king. Simply echoing hallways, hushed and waiting.

Arix followed in step behind Orion as they made their way to the throne room. Gathered near the front were the members of the council, grim faced and somber. The rest of the room was taken up by those who remained at court. The lords and ladies pulled from their beds. It was strange to see them here. Though they had all resided in the castle over the last months, Arix had felt alone. As if she and the other competitors were the only residents of Castle Zma'ai.

Scattered along the outer edge and waiting in the halls were the maids and servants, valets and stewards, craning their necks to get a better view. They parted as Arix and Orion made their way through, the tittering of voices dying down.

The same happened as they entered the hall, the sea of nobility parting, the sound in the room dying down into nothing. Arix pushed her chin forward, and kept her shoulders straight. All eyes were on her.

Orion approached Lord Bardon, nodding discreetly and stepping into line with the other council members. Arix joined their ranks, turning to watch as Lord Bardon held up his hands to the already silent room.

"The king is dead. Passed in his sleep this very night."

Scattered whispers and gasps met his statement, and he raised his arms to silence them again.

"The king is dead. Long live the king." Lord Bardon turned and knelt, his head bending.

There was visible confusion in the crowd. No one knew who he meant. But one by one, they dropped as well, peeking through their bed-head and lashes to see who would remain. And one by one, over the sea of bowed heads, one stayed standing.

When Orion made no motion to follow with the rest of them, the whispers became a sea of voices. Arix caught bits and pieces of it, incredulous disbelief, indignant protest, and then slowly, starting as one comment and growing in size until it was all anyone dared to breathe aloud:

"See how much he looks like King Taurus?"

And as realization swept them, heads turned to the massive painting that hung on the wall of their king. The whispers faded away. There were none who pretended to keep their eyes to the ground, and all watched as Orion stepped forward, up the dias to stand below the throne.

Lord Bardon rose, and everyone followed with him. He raised one arm, and clapped a fist over his heart.

"Long live the king!"

The echo was timid. Unsure.

"Long live the king!" Lord Bardon repeated, his fist hammering his sternum.

This time the echo was louder.

"Long live the KING!"

The response was fervent. Loud. And it reverberated through the castle's very stones.

Orion's face was grim. He held out his hands and the crowd was silent. They were leaning in, waiting for what he had to say. What explanation he might give. Arix could feel their trepidation like a dense smoke that filled the room. But she could also feel a relief; their king was dead, but it meant something new could grow. A tornado had passed through the kingdom, sweeping away with it the royal house of King Taurus. Such devastation held weight, held pain. But after the storm had come and gone, what was left but the lumber with which to build something new? The promise of something great.

Orion was that promise. Someone they were unfamiliar with, someone that might be unpredictable. But they were moving away from the old way. Away from a powerful realm under a mad king. And into the dawn of something else entirely.

"This very night, King Taurus passed from this world into the arms of Osiris. We mourn his death, and mourn the world that was created under his rule. But his blood runs in my veins. I take the mantle of king with honor, respect, and the highest hope for Rökkur's future. I will lead us into a new age. A new advanced age of magick and mystery. And as my first act as king, I hereby appoint Bellarix Sable as my Black Hand."

Someone nudged her forward, and then Arix was moving. Floating up the steps to kneel before Orion.

"I ask you, Bellarix Sable, do you promise to rule beside me, to love my people, to smite my enemies, and to bring us ever forward into the most powerful kingdom in the world?"

"I do." They did not sound like her words said with her voice. They sounded deep. It sounded like the voice of a soldier. Someone who had seen battle and lived.

"Then drink from this chalice. By doing so, you follow in the footsteps of all Black Hands who have walked before you. Take and drink, and be made new." His eyes were sparkling as he stared down at her.

This was everything she'd been waiting for. What she had worked towards and fought for with tooth and nail. What she had sacrificed so much for.

Arix grasped the cup in both hands and drank deep of the sweet liquid.

She drank in the power, and with the power, a promise. A promise to the dead and to the living. To Revena and Michael. To Celeste and the Carn. To all the past kings and Black Hands, and to all that might come under her watch.

"I promise to survive."

Continue Reading For
Bonus Content

LORE & BEGINNINGS

LORE & BEGINNINGS

Before time, Kaoss sat in the ether, patiently waiting as she molded forth her four children. Her firstborn was Arduinna, given the power of the earth and its vegetation. The second was Zephyrus, with control of the air, wind, and atmosphere. The third, Vulcan, who was given domination of heat and flame.. The final child, Nereus, authority over the waters and their depths. Kaoss loved her four children, and taught them the ways of creation. As the god-children grew, they played together, creating a world for themselves to learn and grow and experiment. Arduinna was the first to create life, growing land and earth and dotting the landscape with grass to roll in and trees to climb. Zephyrus followed, creating great gusts of wind that they could fly away on, looking down over their land beneath. Vulcan created the sun, so that they may bake under its warmth and never feel the cold of the cosmos. Nereus created great oceans and lakes and the children swam through them, giddy with the power they held.

As they grew, so did the world.

Arduinna, the Goddess of the earth, created worms and beetles to nurture the ground, helping it to grow and feed itself. As she grew, she created larger animals, mice and moles, possums and armadillos, wolves and bears. She worked together with her brother, Zephyrus, and together they created flying creatures that would live in the air but eat from the earth like bees and chirping chickadees and eagles.

Volcan fell in love and married Nyx, the Goddess of night, and together they shared the sky and created beautiful sunrises and sunsets, painting the sky in new colors. Arduinna, happy for the pair, created the moon as a gift for her new sister, and the sun and the moon danced around the world together, symbols of the love between Volcan and Nyx.

Nereus, the Goddess of water, not to be outdone by her older sister, created the fish of the seas. Great singing whales and tiny minnows. A rainbow of scales that shimmered beneath the depths. She sculpted reefs and underwater caves, and spent much time in solitude, discovering them and herself alone.

Millenia passed, each of Kaoss' children happy in the world they had created for themselves. But as time passed, each child grew more restless, the itch to create growing stronger and stronger. Together they came to their mother for wisdom. She took them into her arms and embraced them, and asked if each would be willing to give up some of their hold on the world they had created and make something entirely new. They agreed, and unified, they molded together mankind. From the earth he was born, emerging from the dirt, as air filled his lungs. He drank deeply of the water and the sun warmed his body. Kaoss, took hold of man and breathed into him spirit; the gift of inventiveness and creation, the gift of choice. Kaoss sat back into the ether then and smiled, saying "The greatest gift a mother can give her children is the opportunity to forge their own paths." And so man was born. He grew, doing both good and evil in the world, taking the gifts the gods had given him and choosing to live as he would.

But as with any family, there were troubles and secrets between Gods and Goddesses, and secrets that even Kaoss had kept from her children. Since the very beginning, when Arduinna and Zephyrus had created birds together, Zephyrus had harbored a deep love for his sister, and seeing the happiness of his brother Volcan and Nyx, desired Arduinna for himself as a wife. Knowing she was his sister, he kept his desire for her hidden deep within him, his lust for her consuming him from the inside. One day Osiris, the god of death saw Arduinna bathing in a fresh spring, and he fell in love with her beauty, creativity, and fertility. He courted her, speaking of her beautiful snow peaked mountains and her lush fertile valleys. Zephyrus was furious at the passionate love Osiris had for his sister, thinking that it was only her chastity that Osiris wished to have of her. And so, in the dead of night, under Nyx's watchful moon, he crept up upon Arduinna's sleeping form and forced himself upon her, the seed of air entangling with the roots of earth.

Arduinna, ashamed, hid herself away from her brother and from Osiris, her spirit dying inside her from the evil of her own brother. She blamed herself for his advances and cursed the birds and flying things they had made together. All over the world, the trees and grass began to die, their greenery turning yellow and brown and falling to the ground as the very earth mourned her disappearance. Zephyrus searched for her, but in vain, for she had hidden herself away from all. Vulcan, guessing what had happened between them, turned his warmth away from the world as Zephyrus became more and more crazed at her disappearance. The world grew white with snow, and the wind howled sullen and bitter as one by one, the other gods turned their back on their fallen brother. The world had grown harsh with winter and the days dreary, all while Arduinna hid herself away, Zephyrus's child growing in her womb.

Osiris also searched for his love, angry at Zephyrus, but lonely for her. After three full moons, he found her hiding deep in the earth, cowering so far that the winds could not find her no matter how hard they whistled and cried. Seeing that she was with child, Osiris pulled her to him and whispered his love for her despite what had been done to her honor. Arduinna, overcome by his love despite her ruined virtue, emerged from the earth, bringing with it the birth of all things new. And with it, bore a son whom she named Typhon, father of monsters. Thus dragons were born into the world, a perversion of the birds that Arduinna had made with her brother.

Zephyrus, fearing the wrath of his brother and his sister's mate now that the truth of his shame had been revealed, ran to his sister Nereus for protection. She sheltered him from Vulcan and Osiris's wrath, making him promise to stay far from Arduinna and to forget his lust for her. Zephyrus could not make such a promise, his feelings for her too great. He fled, and continues to race about the world, always moving, and never to be found by his brother's rage.

While Zephyrus ran, deep within the cosmos a god watched the four children and their world. He came before Kaoss demanding she explain the debauchery of their four children. Kaoss refused, saying she owed him nothing after he had left her alone in the cosmos to raise their children alone. If any blame was to be distributed, it would all be on his head, as the father who abandoned his children. Aion, the god of time and father to earth, air, fire, and water, was furious at the rebuke, and called down a terrible curse upon his children. He bound them in a wheel of time, doomed to ever loop in on itself, and binding them to their pain. Locked into the seasonal cycle, every summer the siblings re-lived their happy days of youth in the sun before the rape of Arduinna began the circle anew, the earth slowly dying in autumn, and the wind howling over the cold winter earth until Arduinna rose again and delivered new life to the world in spring. Thus the seasons were born, and with it, trapping the gods and Goddesses into a wheel of time.

Kaoss, seeing the limits that had been placed on them, decided to bestow a final gift on the world. She took her very life essence and created something that would bring magick to the world of men. A well, a stream, flowing out upon the world, and carrying with it the essence of all magick: earth, air, fire, water, and spirit. She bestowed it upon the creatures she had made with her children in the hopes of bringing the promise of power and victory back to the world locked in time.

ACKNOWLEDGMENTS

Thank you. Thank you, friends and family that have encouraged me on this journey and given me all the support I could have asked for. This has been a journey 10+ years in the making, starting so long ago with a bad fantasy movie and ended where we are today. This entire process has been so surreal, and I keep wondering if I'll wake up one day and it'll just have been a lovely (yet extremely anxiety inducing) dream.

To Allan, my husband, my partner, I so love that we can share writing and storytelling with each other. That we can bubble over plot twists and character arcs and get so wrapped up in the story of books and shows and *life*.

To my parents, who always encouraged the creative streak in me, who listened to all of my "Hey mom, let me read you this" and "Hey dad, how does this sound?" moments and let me ramble on about characters and plots and worlds they knew nothing about. I know fantasy (especially the dark fantasy I love to write) isn't your favorite genre, but I so appreciate all the encouragement you've shown me and my stories. I will never forget the day I finished the first draft of this book, how you video called me in the middle of the night to hoot and holler in your pjs and congratulate me for finally coming to the end. That meant more to me than you'll ever know.

To my dear friend Camille, who was the first to remind me that I write for a younger Hannah, a younger me. That the stories I create are for her to escape away into and to ride on the backs of the wind away from the darkness in her mind and her soul.

To the gang: Kayla, Michael, Nik, Christa, Jacob, Taylor, and Kat; thank you for listening to me talk incessantly about this book, for letting me read the first chapter to you, for beta reading, for being storytellers with me in our D&D campaigns, for dressing up and coming with me to Ren Faires, and for just being with me in life. I couldn't have gotten this far without having you all as such deep friends.

To Nik Ellison and Nevena Jevitc, who worked on the map and cover art for this book. Thank you so much for turning the images in my head into visuals on the page. You have connected this world to readers in a way I never could have without you.

To Lindsey, my best friend, who played so much make-believe with me, from Tarzan and Jane to Prince and Princess. Thank you for always being a creative sidekick, to giggle and whisper and share worlds with.

To Lizzie and Jenna, my first writing partners. You were the first to write stories with me and to jump with me headlong into the worlds we created. You were there during such a formative time for me as a writer, and you both got me so excited to scribble in journals, on buses, traveling back and forth between our towns, writing absolutely scandalous things for a 16 year old. You two made me realize that books are almost always better shared with friends.

To the book club of 2019, for encouraging me to write, to be proud of the things I put down on a page, and for keeping me humble while reading all of the amazing stories we created while together. And to the book club of 2021, for reading through my first draft (as awful as it was) and loving it anyways.

To the amazing BookTok community, who watched me open up my book for the first time, who cried with me, who laughed with me, who *demanded* to read The Black Hand, and who started this whole journey of self-publishing in the first place. I've become friends with so many of you, and been encouraged by your journeys in writing and publishing. Your advice and your confidence in me has been immeasurable. Thank you.

H. M. REINHARD

Hannah is a self-proclaimed nerd who enjoys playing
Dungeons and Dragons, sewing costumes, voice acting, and
has always loved immersing herself into other worlds through
reading. She has always considered herself a storyteller, no
matter the medium. Hannah lives in South Carolina with her
husband and their three cats.